"*Siren Song* is packed with fast and fun fights that had adrenaline slamming through my system."
—*All Things Urban Fantasy*

"This series just keeps getting better, maintaining a delicate balance between urban fantasy and paranormal romance. The emotional components are just as strong as the action sequences, set against an increasingly interesting world."
—*Publishers Weekly* on *Demon Song*

"Entertainment ignited!"
—*RT Book Reviews* (4½ stars, Top Pick!) on *Siren Song*

"*Blood Song* is a terrific story with a unique and well-drawn heroine. Combines a unique story, terrific characters, and enough action for any fantasy fan."
—*Fresh Fiction* on *Blood Song*

"Adams does an outstanding job of telling a tale about a very strong woman put into an impossible situation. This story grips you by the throat and doesn't let up until the very last page."
—*ParaNormalRomance* on *Blood Song*

"Adams manages to not only keep the pages turning in an action-packed story that never lets up, but she also creates characters that you care about. Urban fantasy seems to be all about strong kick-butt women standing alone against a mighty foe. But Celia isn't alone. She's got friends, family, and coworkers who are her support network and they all have strengths, weaknesses, and problems that we, the readers, can relate to." —*SFRevu* on *Demon Song*

Tor Paranormal Romance Books by
C. T. Adams and Cathy Clamp

THE SAZI

Hunter's Moon
Moon's Web
Captive Moon
Howling Moon
Moon's Fury
Timeless Moon
Cold Moon Rising
Serpent Moon

THE THRALL

Touch of Evil
Touch of Madness
Touch of Darkness

WRITING AS CAT ADAMS

Magic's Design
Blood Song
Siren Dong
Demon Song
The Isis Collar
The Eldritch Conspiracy

CAT ADAMS

THE ISIS COLLAR

A Tom Doherty Associates Book New York

This is a work of fiction. All of the characters, organizations, and events portrayed in this novel are either products of the author's imagination or are used fictitiously.

THE ISIS COLLAR

Copyright © 2012 by C. T. Adams and Cathy Clamp

All rights reserved.

A Tor Book
Published by Tom Doherty Associates, LLC
175 Fifth Avenue
New York, NY 10010

www.tor-forge.com

Tor® is a registered trademark of Tom Doherty Associates, LLC.

ISBN 978-0-7653-6715-0

Tor books may be purchased for educational, business, or promotional use. For information on bulk purchases, please contact Macmillan Corporate and Premium Sales Department at 1-800-221-7945 extension 5442 or write specialmarkets@macmillan.com.

First Edition: March 2012
First Mass Market Edition: March 2013

Printed in the United States of America

0 9 8 7 6 5 4 3 2 1

DEDICATION AND ACKNOWLEDGMENTS

As always, without the support of Don Clamp and James Adams, these books wouldn't happen. Nor would they without the assistance and faith of our terrific editor, Melissa Singer, and our agents, Merrilee Heifetz and Lucienne Diver. I'd especially like to thank Dr. Christopher Johnson, author and friend, for his assistance in coming up with a terrifically horrifying disease that could occur in the world if only magic existed. It's great to know a doctor who helps us injure characters in a way to fit our timelines.

We needed to set our medical thriller in a hospital. We chose the name St. Anthony's for a reason. In the winter of 2011, James Adams had a severe bout of pneumonia with complications. It was touch and go for several days. Thanks to the excellent care he received at St. Anthony Central Hospital, in Denver, he recovered fully. Cie can't thank them enough, but wanted to make a gesture to acknowledge them.

AUTHOR'S NOTE

Always keep in mind that this is a work of fiction, in an alternate reality. Obviously.

When it became apparent that we needed a witch doctor and that we would probably have to put in specifics, we had a decision to make. We could use an existing religion, and risk offending readers who believed we "got it wrong" or were insensitive to their beliefs in some way. Or, we could make it up and do whatever we wanted. We made it up. To the best of our knowledge and belief there is no "Orvah" whether similar to Voodoo or anything else. Any similarities to any existing religion should be disregarded.

The same is true of the portrayal of the Egyptian deity Isis. We do not in any way wish to insult the beliefs of anyone, living or dead, and would remind you that the Isis in this book is not meant to be the Isis in anyone's religious pantheon in this reality.

THE ISIS COLLAR

but someone determined to do harm can keep their intentions hidden. Otherwise there wouldn't be any attacks . . . anywhere. There was no reason to mention the police weren't the sole answer, since yet another terrorist attack had been front-page news today.

The dapper Latina let out a frustrated sound and stood, laying her palms flat on the polished wood surface of her desk. "I'm asking politely, Ms. Graves. Please leave. Class is about to let out and I don't want the children traumatized by your presence here."

My eyes narrowed and I likewise stood. The kids had nothing to do with it. If she just didn't want anyone to see me, why not stay right here in the principal's office, where grade-schoolers only venture when forced? No, she was afraid of me, and aggressively so. I knew I should be calm and pretend I was her friend, but I was stressed and it was making it hard to keep my anger in check. My fangs probably showed when I spoke, but to hell with it. "There's no reason to be insulting just because you don't believe me. Traumatized? Please. They'd never even know. I would remind you that *you* weren't aware I'm part vampire until I told you." I've spent a good deal of time in front of the mirror just to make sure the elongated canines don't show very often. I was dressed nicely and not a soul had screamed or even flinched when I'd first arrived at the school and asked to meet with the principal.

At least she had the good grace to blush. "I didn't mean it that way. I meant your *weapons*. I'm sure you're armed because you believed you were going to face some unknown threat the *clairvoyant* warned you of. However, there are very young children in this school who could be frightened by seeing you." She glanced at the clock high on the wall behind me.

"Thank you for your interest, but I need to get back to work."

Right. Pfft. Jeez! She made it sound like I was interviewing for a job at the elementary school, not trying to save everyone from unknown disaster. Like she could even see my weapons. Maybe I should go get Isaac, my tailor, and have her say that to *him*. My clothes are tailored specifically so nobody knows I'm carrying. Even cops haven't noticed in the past. Admittedly, she was right about the source of the information. Dottie Simmons was a very powerful but unknown clairvoyant. She was probably a level eight but had kept that a very careful secret her whole life—tricky to do in today's hyperregulatory atmosphere. Her age is probably the reason she's gotten away with it. The State of California didn't start testing grade-school kids until the fifties—long after she was in school.

But the fact Dottie isn't registered as a certified clairvoyant doesn't mean she isn't fully capable of predicting events. Without another word, I turned and walked out of the principal's office. I had to tense my muscles to keep from slamming the door behind me. The length of frosted glass might withstand the slam an annoyed child could give it, but the supernatural strength of a half-vampire Abomination would shatter it.

My cell phone was out of my pocket before I'd gotten ten feet down the hallway lined with lockers that only reached my neck. A quick speed dial put me through to the one person with the local police I thought might actually listen to me. Maybe. I hoped. I fidgeted nervously as I waited for Alex to pick up the line.

Heather Alexander had been my best friend Vicki's lover. We were friendly, but not close. I'd hoped we might get closer after Vicki's death. After all, we both loved her, both missed her. But if anything, our busy schedules and the pain of our loss had pushed us even further apart. Still, I knew Alex would take this seriously, and she'd help if she could.

A harried but pleasant alto came onto the line: "Alexander. Go ahead."

"It's Celia, Alex. I've got a problem."

The silence on the line told me I had her attention. Since in the recent past our mutual experiences have included greater demons, magical assassins, and international drug lords she knew to take me seriously. "What's the problem?"

I lowered my voice and squeezed into an alcove that held a pair of knee-high water fountains. I was glad I'd left my purse locked in my car. It and I both wouldn't have fit in the space. "I got an anonymous tip this morning from a clairvoyant I know. Something bad is going to happen at an elementary school today. But nobody will listen to me—which is ticking me off. I know a kid here, Alex. A little girl with siren blood. Her sister will be the first Atlantic siren since the Magna Carta was signed."

"The sister of the one who helped you seal the rift last Christmas?"

I nodded, even though she couldn't see me. "Yeah. I owe her. Hell, the whole world owes her." Saving the world from the same demonic threat that had destroyed Atlantis had been a horrible thing to put on the shoulders of a twelve-year-old. "I want her eight-year-old sister not to have to go through anything else." It was the truth, but that wasn't the only reason. My own sister had died when I was twelve . . . and she was eight. There was something about the Murphy family that had gotten under my skin. They'd purchased my gran's house, and somehow I'd made it my mission to ensure that Julie Murphy made it to ten. It was a magical number in my head, for no reason I could think of.

"So what do you need from me?" Alex sounded willing to help, which was exactly what I needed.

"I need to clear out this place. Call the principal and tell her to evacuate the school."

A second long silence followed and then she burst out laughing. "No . . . really. What do you need?"

Laughing was just what I didn't want her to do. "That's what I need. My source is a level-*eight* clairvoyant. The same person your former coworker Karl used to get my memories back. When I got here, the magic shield was completely down and nobody realized it. Something's going down. I don't know *what* exactly yet, but . . . just get these kids out of here before bad things happen. I'm serious." I looked out the window at the empty swings and wanted to be sure they didn't stay that way. My gaze moved down to the brightly patterned floor tiles as my frustration grew.

"I'm serious, too, Celia. Do you have any idea how many laws I would break by trying to evacuate a school with no orders from higher up? It would be my badge, at least. And possibly time in a *Federal* pen."

Crap. I let out a deep sigh and shook my head.

"Miss Graves!" The angry hiss of words came from my left and made me look up suddenly. Principal Sanchez and the heavyset security guard with a name badge that read: *R. Jamisyn* were standing in front of me, arms crossed over equally broad chests. "I thought I'd made myself completely clear."

I held my hand over the cell phone's speaker and looked her in the eye. "You said you needed evidence. I'm trying to get it."

Her eyes narrowed. "No. I said it was time for you to leave." She backed up a pace and waved her hand, motioning me out of my cubbyhole. Her eyes were pointed at the door and I had no doubt she wanted me on the other side of it. "Officer Jamisyn and I are going to escort you off school grounds. Then I'll be speaking to the police about keeping you away in the future. I'm sorry it's come to that, but the bell is going to ring any moment."

Crap, crap, *crap*! Now what? But the security guard had his hand on the Taser on his belt and if I drew on him, anywhere close to school grounds, I'd not only be going straight to jail, don't pass go, don't collect $200, but probably would lose my concealed-carry permit. Or worse. I put the cell back up to my ear. "Do what you can, Alex. The nice officer is going to escort me away before I scare the kiddies."

She sighed in my ear as Sanchez glared at me and pointed to the door. "Sorry, Celia. I'll see if I can get a squad car to drive by, but I don't think there's anything else I can do. I hope you're wrong."

"Oh, yeah. Me, too. You have no idea." I ended the call with a sigh as I trudged down the hallway ahead of Sanchez and Jamisyn. But as far as I stretched my vampire senses, I couldn't feel any threat. So . . . maybe Dottie was wrong. Clairvoyants weren't infallible. Even my former best friend, Vicki, who had been a level nine, couldn't always read the exact when and where. If she could have, her murderer couldn't have snuck up on her.

As I reached the door, Jamisyn reached past me and opened it. I had no illusions he was being polite. He had his eyes on my every movement and I made sure not to give him reason to become aggressive.

The trees around the school were full of seagulls, perched in the branches like some weird interpretation of Hitchcock's movie. Yeah, I said *gulls*. They hang around me like lovesick puppies, ever since my siren blood woke up. At least they don't poop on my car anymore. "Go on, shoo. Go eat some fish at the dock." The birds obediently lifted their wings at my wave and flew away.

The bell rang as I stepped over the threshold, and I expected to hear doors opening and kids swarming the halls between classes. But it was absolutely silent when the bell stopped . . . eerily so.

That's when I felt the press of magic against me. A muffled explosion vibrated under the soles of my feet. I looked around down the hallway, but other than the nearly silent bang, you could have heard a pin drop. What I was feeling wasn't the typical barrier against evil that so many businesses and houses have. This was a spell. "I think we have a problem," I said, turning back to Jamisyn and Sanchez.

The principal's face was frozen in position, mouth open. But no, not precisely *frozen*. I experienced what a thousand hummingbirds probably see every day. Everyone in the school was running in slow motion. Principal Sanchez and Officer Jamisyn were moving. In fact, I would bet they believed themselves to be moving at normal speed. But watching them was similar to the "hyperfocus" I get when the vampire inside me wants to come out and hunt at sunset. Their movements were a crawl.

Except this time, it wasn't me. It was broad daylight— the fact made more evident by the bright sun that was beating down on my sunscreen-slathered skin and making it sting.

I slid back into the school. I needed to confirm my suspicions. There was a window set into the door of the first classroom, and I stopped and peered in. Sure enough, the kids inside were half out of their seats, ready to pick up their pencils and notebooks.

This was not good.

Jamisyn opening the door must have triggered the spell. Or maybe it was me, stepping over the threshold. I raced from room to room in the first hall, my heels echoing in the silence. Every class was the same.

At first I thought that time had slowed, but a glance out the window showed cars moving at normal speed and pedestrians briskly walking down the shaded sidewalks. It was just the people in the school who were moving slowly. The reason for the spell came to me in a flash that made bile rise to my throat.

Maximum damage.

If nobody could get away from a bomb or a killer, everyone would die. It would be, sadly, child's play. I wasn't exactly sure why I wasn't affected. It could be the vampire blood, that I was outside when the spell started, or maybe the protection charm disks I had in my jacket. Either way, I knew now why Dottie had insisted that I went to the school when I'd wanted to stay under the covers and pull the pillow over my head.

The flash of red on the wall caught my eye and I chuckled at the irony of it. Most every kid who has gone to a public school has wanted to do it. Heck, most every *adult* has, too, including me. I made a fist and smashed the thin glass on the front of the fire alarm, then pulled the lever down.

Bells shattered the silence and echoed down the halls so loud it made my head throb. Out on the street, one or two people paused, but when nobody ran out of the school, they moved on, probably figuring it was a fire drill. In the distance, I could hear a phone ringing, only because it was a counterpoint in pitch.

That was good, because without a call from the office, or anyone answering when the dispatcher called, they would send an engine. Now I just needed to get the attention of the general public.

Principal Sanchez had been right. Because I didn't know what sort of danger I was getting into, I'd put on every weapon I could easily find on short notice. One of those wasn't precisely a weapon. It was a distraction, a defense. I raced down to open the windows facing the street, pulled two "smoker" charm disks from my inside pocket, and threw them hard against the nearest locker. The smoke is black and thick, a screen to disappear behind with a client in tow. But the smoke doesn't clog the lungs or sting the eyes, which is the nice thing about magic. It billowed out of the windows with me waving my arms to help it along. Now there was something to match the bells and people would come.

I raced back to the door and carried Principal Sanchez out, hoping that once I got her past the threshold, she would be out of the spell's influence.

It worked. "Each of us . . . what?" She blinked repeatedly as she realized where she was—on the sidewalk, probably a dozen steps from the front door. The fire bells were ringing loud. Smoke was billowing out of the windows and people were running toward us. "Oh, my lord! Fire!"

I grabbed her by the shoulders and forced her to meet my eyes. "Listen to me. There's a spell on everyone in the school. Probably tripped when we opened the door. There's been an explosion in the basement. I can't sense any fire, but I've got the fire department coming to get the kids out. We need to find out whether you can get back in the school without being affected by the spell again."

Some spells are like that. If you can break away from the influence, often it won't reaffect you. Without another word, she pulled away from me and raced back up the steps. I followed her in case she needed to be brought out again. But she didn't slow down, so I'd been right about the spell. She looked in door windows, as I did, finally realizing I wasn't lying. "I'm sorry!" She yelled it at me to be heard over the bells.

Everybody says that after the fact and I find it more than mildly annoying. I had to struggle not to frown or growl, because this was not the time for recriminations. "Don't worry about it. We've got to get the kids out!"

She propped open the first classroom door and started to untangle the first child from her chair. I shook my head no and pointed toward the teacher. "If we get the teachers first, we'll have more hands!" I was already tired of shouting, tired of the noise that was making my head pound. Sanchez nodded and headed toward the front of the class, where a slim, older woman was staring at the clock and pointing, with a piece of chalk, at the door.

Like a lot of schools in the district, Abraham Lincoln was built on a single story and every classroom had a fire door that opened directly onto the playground. As principal, Sanchez had a key. The first thing she did was unlock the door and prop it open. It was the smart thing to do. She must have been a firefighter in a previous career, too, because she picked up the teacher like she was a cardboard cutout and tossed her over one shoulder before heading out the door. I did the same to an older brunette girl sitting in a chair in the corner. I was guessing she was a student teacher or a college intern.

More people had arrived because of the smoke and were being directed by Jamisyn, who either had gotten away himself or must have been pulled out by a passerby. Sirens in the distance were getting louder. I set the girl down and shook her lightly to clear her head. While I was explaining what had happened to her, I spotted movement near the end of the building.

I had turned, taking a couple of steps in that direction, when someone tapped me on the shoulder. I turned my head and was surprised to see Terrance Harris, one of the Santa Maria de Luna cops. He was a recently arrived Haitian immigrant, a level-six mage. He'd been brought in to be part of the magical enforcement squad. I'd met him once before, at a Christmas party. He nodded toward the school, but I noticed that he was looking at a point near the rooftop of the building, on a ledge. I followed his gaze. I didn't see anything. "I knew when I saw you over here that this wasn't just a building fire. You set off smoke bombs because of the curse, didn't you?"

The distinctive accent didn't distract me. Instead, the words made me look at the unobtrusive middle-aged man suspiciously. "What do you know about it?" He looked like he was off-duty, because he was wearing a T-shirt and jeans, but it seemed awfully convenient to see a powerful mage at a place where an equally powerful spell had been cast. That "they always return to the scene of the crime" thing is mostly true.

He pointed at the ledge. "I can feel it. The source of the spell is up there. It's a powerful one. I'm thinking it was done last night and set with a trigger or timer. It's too complicated and too public for someone to have done this just now."

Could I trust him? Would either of the mages I knew be able to tell me all that about a spell just by encountering it on the sidewalk?

Actually, yeah, they would. Bruno could for sure, and probably Creede, too. Bruno was a level nine. Creede an eight plus. So maybe I shouldn't shortchange Harris. I turned to ask him if he could tell anything specific about the curse but was distracted when I spotted more movement in the place that had caught my attention a moment before.

A basement window was being opened . . . from the *inside*. Okay, that just screamed sneaky. There were plenty of exit doors; why crawl out of a window unless you were up to something?

I gestured silently toward the dark-skinned man emerging from the open window. He was trying hard to use his camo clothing to blend in with the shadows. Terrance followed my gesture and started heading that way, pulling what looked like an actual carved wand from a holster on his belt. I don't know a lot of witches or mages who use wands, although I've seen them for sale in weapons stores.

Harris shouted, "Police! You in the window. Freeze. Don't move!"

Crap. I'd been hoping for a little more . . . subtlety. I know there are laws that say they have to give that warning. It just seems like it gives the bad guys an edge when you can't sneak up on them. The man in the window pulled down on his cap and it became a face mask, just in time to keep me from getting a good look at him. As I expected, instead of not moving, he started moving faster, kicking to get out of the window before we could get to him.

Go figure.

Terrance raised his wand and twirled it in a fast circle before throwing power at the masked man. *"Glacia!"*

I knew that spell, which was, literally, "freeze." It should have stopped the guy cold in his tracks. Except that I was right about him being a spellcaster. He threw his hands sideways and deflected the magic. Toward me. Then he took off running down the street.

A wave of ice cold hit me and made my muscles tense. But there's a reason I spend serious money on protection charms. It only took a second for the medallion around my neck to heat and push away the cold. I didn't wait to have something more serious hit me. The best defense is a good offense. I put a hand inside my blazer, extracted a charm disk as I ran, and brushed my fingertips over the raised lettering to be sure I'd drawn the one I wanted. Pouring on the speed, I hit the guy from behind with a flying tackle. We tumbled to the ground in a tangle of limbs and dirt. Before he could utter the next curse, I stuffed the charm in his mouth and slammed his jaw shut. The *Speak No Evil* charm is specially made for spellcasters. For the next hour, he wouldn't be able to say anything that could be harmful.

He gagged and coughed as the liquid in the charm slid down his throat. "You folking titch!" He spat out the words and then realized what I must have done. He tried to curse me, but it came out as *"Beneficent Harmony!"*

Terrance, breathing hard from the run, pulled hand-cuffs from a holster on his belt. His skin was at least two shades darker than that of the man under me as he slapped the first cuff against the caster's wrist. "Good thing you did that. You don't want to even know what that curse would have done."

He was probably right. I kept my weight on the guy until the cuffs were on and then got to my feet. "Stay with him until the other cops get here. I need to find out what he did inside the building. I heard a small explosion coming from the basement a few minutes ago."

"Don't be an idiot, Graves. Let us take care of it. I'll call for reinforcements; they'll be here—"

"Too late," I completed. "They don't even know they *need* to be here yet. Call it in, but I have to keep getting those kids out. That's the important thing. I'll see what caused the explosion."

He let out an exasperated sigh as he pulled the other mage to his feet. "Then let me go. If it's another spell, you can't disarm it. If it's a bomb . . . well, you don't have authority to do that, either. There could be chemicals or toxins, and I've trained with them. Stay with the prisoner; I'll go."

I shook my head and finished picking up the charms I'd dropped when we tumbled. "I also don't have authority to keep a prisoner in custody. Remember that most of the cops around here don't like me. They'd love an excuse to lock me behind bars for the rest of my life." It was a painful truth to admit. There were cops—people I'd gone drinking with, shared stories with—who now wanted me dead or locked up because a master vampire tried to turn me. They considered me evil, despite the fact I could stand in a church, wear holy items, and walk in the daylight. And since the "Zoo," otherwise known as the California State Facility for Criminally Magical Beings, had been reduced to a wide piece of glass in the desert by a massive explosion, they'd have to find somewhere else to put me—probably somewhere far worse. No, thanks. I'd rather take my chances with whatever I found inside the school. "As for chemicals, I'll stand a better chance than you. Vampires heal faster."

Harris winced at my crack about his fellow officers, but he didn't bother trying to deny it and I didn't give him the chance to argue. I just sprinted back toward the building. He could either leave the prisoner and follow me, or stay where he was.

I really wanted to know what was going on in that basement, and call me crazy, but I figured the quickest route to find the trouble was to backtrack the crook. So I slipped into the building using the basement window that he'd left so conveniently open and took a look around.

I'd expected to find myself in a furnace room, maybe a closet. Instead, I was standing in a music storage room. A beat-up old upright piano was tucked into a corner and a host of noisemaking implements like triangles, kazoos, and tiny brass cymbals were stored in stacked and labeled clear plastic totes. A battered metal file cabinet had drawers marked with the names of various instruments.

I stopped, stilling my breathing, extending all of my senses to the max. I've developed quite the sensitivity to magic with my other predator senses. There are some less happy vamp side effects as well, but I didn't have time to think about those right now. I wanted to find whatever it was the bad guy had been up to.

Nothing. At least not in this room. Crap. I moved toward the still-open door, listening as hard as I could.

The alarm was a distant rumble below the thick concrete slab above that all the older buildings in town have. The school on top had been scraped and rebuilt when I was a kid, but the foundation and main-floor slab are probably a century old. Either the lower rooms didn't have bells or they'd been disabled. That's how I was able to hear the distinct sounds of someone fiddling with something. The noise was similar to when I'm having the oil changed in my car. Fabric rustling, the *tink* of different metals meeting, the squeak/scrape of screws or bolts turning under force. Subtle but noticeable.

I took off my heels and crept down the hall in nylon-clad feet, staying on my toes so there was little sound and varying my steps so it was hard to determine the source. A hiss of air behind me made me turn. My Colt 1911 was in my hand and pointed at the hiss before I even remembered moving.

Harris was there, gun likewise drawn, but his was carefully pointed at the floor as he stared down my barrel. I opened my mouth to ask him what the hell he was doing there, but he responded by raising one finger to his lips, so I mouthed the words, *Where's the prisoner?*

A quirky smile pulled at one side of Harris's mouth. He motioned his hands together in front, wrists touching like handcuffs, and then showed a long, straight vertical line and mouthed, *Flagpole.*

I grinned. Good move. I knew the guys on the hex squad were assigned magical handcuffs and they had some way of knowing whose cuffs they were when another officer came upon a cuffed prisoner. I don't know the science or metaphysics of it. I should probably ask some of the cops I know someday.

I let Harris slip ahead of me to take point. I had no way of knowing whether he was lying. I didn't think so, but having him in front of me meant I could keep an eye on him. Never a bad thing.

We walked down the hallway, checking the storage rooms for potential danger. I was sure we'd checked them all. Except . . . we *hadn't*. We got to the end of the hall and I realized that while my eyes saw four doors on either side, my internal count said we'd only checked seven rooms. I frowned and that made Harris frown, too. He shrugged and motioned to my worried face with a *What's up?* expression.

I didn't know if he'd understand, but I mouthed the words *one* through *eight* as I pointed to each door. He nodded. Then I pointed to both of us, made walking motions with my fingers, and extended five fingers and then two so I didn't have to lower the Colt.

His brow furrowed and he thought for a moment. Then he had the same realization as me and he mouthed, *We missed one.*

I nodded while realizing I didn't know *which* one. *Spell?* I mouthed again.

Now his jaw set and I realized he was angry. He nodded and closed his eyes briefly. I could feel his magic swell out in a wave that crawled along my body like bugs. I wanted to flinch or scratch but didn't dare take my attention off the hallway.

For a long moment, I did move my eyes to watch Harris's face while he searched. Alex once told me that for every expression we see a person make, there are a dozen or more micro-expressions we don't. It's one of the first things an interrogator is trained to look for, because they're nearly impossible to fake. A twitch of the lip, a wrinkle over the bridge of the nose, even an eye flick away from the questioner—they're all indications of guilt or innocence.

Admittedly, I'm not well trained in such things, but from all indications, Harris was frustrated and annoyed. Whether with himself, me, or the person we were searching for I didn't know. Harris leaned toward me until his lips were right next to my left ear. My peripheral vision revealed he was carefully keeping his 9mm pointed low and away from me. "I'm going to walk back and touch every door. See which one I miss." His words were so low and soft that without the vamp senses I would have missed them entirely.

I nodded and he moved away from me, crouching low enough that he couldn't be seen through the reinforced windows in the doors. I mouthed the words *one* through *seven* as he touched, but my mind said *eight*—the exact reverse of earlier. At the end of the hall, he looked at me with a question on his face. I just frowned, shook my head, and raised five and two again.

My skin itched furiously from the high levels of magic around me. There was definitely a spell going on . . . some sort of powerful distraction or aversion charm. It didn't buzz against my skin the way wards usually do, but I could definitely feel it. Probably a good thing, too. If I hadn't I might never have even noticed the extra door.

Wait . . . doors. What if it was *just* about the doors?

I had an idea. I motioned for Harris to stay put. Crouching down, I moved slowly toward him, but instead of looking at the doors, I kept my eyes on the floor and counted the *tiles*. There should be eight oversized tiles between the doorways and six across the hall. At the point where the first doorway should be, I could see out my peripheral vision two doorjambs. I counted another eight squares and again, two jambs.

But eight more tiles and . . . I could only see *one* jamb. On my left. Without looking up to see Harris, I pointed to my right. I crouched down on the third tile, closed my eyes, and felt along the floor, sliding fingers along the edges of the tiles. Sure enough, when I reached the edge of the third tile, there was a gap between the floor and the bottom of an invisible door.

The problem I saw was that if the caster had spent the time and energy to do the slow-mo spell and the aversion spell, why not booby-trap the door as a final fail-safe? I would. And I always try to credit the bad guys with being at least as smart as I am.

I could still hear that shuffling and tinkering sound behind the door and would bet even money there was a person behind the door I couldn't see.

Harris joined me on the tile facing what appeared to be a blank wall. He mouthed, *You're sure?*

I nodded and raised my gun, aiming for a spot at about knee level. I moved over until I had my back against the wall. Harris followed and grabbed my gun arm and tried to yank my Colt away. He stank of sudden panic. But he was just plain human as far as physical power and . . . I'm not anymore. My arms didn't move.

Harris is a cop. Cops don't get to fire into blind doorways. Actually, bodyguards shouldn't, either. But I was aiming low enough that it wouldn't be a kill shot, and I knew what ammo I'd brought. When I go into an unknown situation, I take the time to balance my bullets. One copper-jacketed safety round, one snake-shot round filled with salt and iron beads, and one soft lead filled with holy water. Then the same over again. Various supernatural beasties react to different things, so usually one of the three will have an effect. Spells often don't account for mechanical threats. They're geared toward the human brain but not the tools it can use.

Before Harris had time to react and do anything more aggressive, I fired three quick shots. The gunfire echoed through the hallway and a sudden scream followed.

I dropped into a crouch, spun, and kicked with all the strength I could muster from that position. A part of the wall flew inward on oiled hinges I couldn't see. It hit the drywall with a sharp bang and did not bounce back. I guessed that the force of my blow had embedded the knob in the wall.

A burly, tattooed man was rolling on the floor, shouting four-letter curses that had nothing to do with magic, his hands pressed tight over a bleeding wound in his calf. The air filled with the scent of burning flesh. Either the iron or holy water had done the trick.

Harris gave me a hard look, but moved swiftly through the door. Raising his wand, he threw a wordless spell at the man on the floor. He was instantly silent, though his lips kept moving. Hate-filled eyes glared at the two of us.

"Holy Crap, Graves!" Harris shouted. There was no need to keep our voices down anymore, but the sound seemed to echo off the walls and blast into my ears with the force of an air horn. "What the hell were you thinking?!" The caster raised a hand and started to make movements in the air, but Harris grabbed him and threw him facedown, wrestling with him until he could get a pair of flexible cable ties out of his pocket and around the guy's wrists. This time he didn't need my help, so I didn't offer. "You could have blown us both up!"

I didn't bother to respond. I was busy looking around the room. I saw the charred remains of a side of the ductwork. It was a small hole, not really big enough to do more than blow a hole the size of my head. The edges were wet but not with water. I just couldn't tell what it was over the scent of charred metal.

But that's not what worried me. There was a . . . contraption in the center of the room. It was black metal and round, about twice the size of an ancient cannonball, and had what looked like valves coming out of the metal at odd angles. I've seen a variety of bombs before in training videos and this didn't look like one. Frankly, it looked like something that should be attached to an old furnace. It glowed with powerful magic that pressed against my chest hard enough to hurt, and had a digital display with a countdown timer, so a bomb definitely came to mind. Two of the three bullets I'd fired were floating in midair right in front of me. Marks on the floor showed that they'd bounced off the tiles before becoming trapped in whatever spell was around the object. Apparently, it was sheer luck I hit the other caster with the snake shot, which hadn't ricocheted like the larger rounds. He must have some fae in his background to have the iron shot slip through his personal magic.

Harris had been right that I wasn't qualified to do anything about the . . . whatever it was in front of me. But I remember from college that any spell that required a physical casing to keep the caster safe was a nasty piece of work, so in my mind it *was* a bomb. The best thing I could do now was to call this in to the bomb squad and get the rest of the people out of the building.

I turned my attention to Harris, who had not only gotten the caster into the ties, but had also dialed for the bomb squad on his cell phone and was explaining about the masking spell. I waited for him to hang up the line and asked, "Do you need me to stay here, or should I go back and help the others?" I really, really hoped he'd say no. Yeah, I had come down to investigate, and I'd stay and help if I had to. But I have my limits. I'll fight me some monsters, face bad guys with guns. I'll even face demons. But *bombs*?

The prisoner was now sitting sullenly against the wall, ankles and wrists both bound tight. It would make it impossible for him to walk, let alone run or fight. I put my Colt back in its holster.

Harris smiled while the other man glowered. "Nah. Nathan and I are old friends, aren't we? He won't try to escape and embarrass himself. Besides," Harris assured me, "the ties are spelled higher than he'll ever get out of. He's not going to get away. Let me get him in a fireman's carry and I'll go up with you. He nodded at the machine. "We'll leave this to the experts."

Fine by me. More than fine. Really. I turned to go through the door, as he bent to grab the prisoner, but the moment I reached the threshold, things . . . changed.

A subtle whisper of will pushed at me. It was magic all right, but not the brute force of the two men we'd encountered thus far. This was something entirely different. It eased through the protection of my charms like water seeping through microscopic cracks in rock.

Touch it . . .

What the . . . ? I could swear I heard a woman's voice, a warm alto that beckoned to me. I grabbed the doorjamb to steady myself. "Harris? Something's wrong."

His voice was breathy and panicked when he responded. "I know. I hear her too. We need to get out of here. Now!"

Nathan was smiling slightly, apparently listening to the voice. But he wasn't able to respond and I knew that I certainly had no plan to do what she was telling me.

And yet I found my head turning, until I felt like an owl, with my face pointed so I could nearly look down at my backside. The muscles in my neck and shoulders began to protest; a throbbing rose in my left temple. But these minor pains were no distraction from the words that hounded me.

Touch it. . . .

My fingers started moving without conscious thought, trying to reach for the glowing aura that raked along my skin.

"Don't do it, Graves!" Harris was apparently fighting his own battle against the voice, because my glance revealed he'd moved as far away from the machine as the room would allow and was now sitting on his own hands.

"I don't want to. Do something, Harris. You're the mage. Haven't you got anything in your bag of tricks to make us both deaf or something?"

He let out a laugh that was part sarcasm and part fear. "I wish it was that easy. It's in our heads, not our ears. I could knock us both unconscious, but then nobody will find the bomb before it blows, and they'll have more people in the building searching for us."

He was right. Bomb teams usually have a mage, a straight human, and a psychic. If the psychic foresees that the bomb will go off before it can be disarmed the squad simply evacuates everyone and puts a containment field on the area but doesn't go in. Standard practice, which is why the psychic is usually the team leader.

Touch it. . . .

The cracks in my protection were widening. I could feel the muscles in my arm tingling. My hand was beginning to disobey my command to grip the jamb. I tightened my grasp with what felt like my last ounce of free will. The wood splintered under my fingers as my knuckles grew white and the tendons of my hand locked into position.

But I had two hands . . . and while I'd put all my energy into keeping my left hand still, my right had developed a mind of its own. When my right arm began to rise and reach backward, I started to panic. It wouldn't be easy for me to touch the shield with that hand, but if the voice could make my body contort or dislocate, it would be possible. The pain in my head had grown from an ache to blinding agony. Muscles aren't intended to be stretched to their limit and kept there—even vampire muscles that heal constantly. "Harris, you've got to do something! This is magic . . . you're magic; do something. Freeze me in place if you have to, or knock me out or make me start screaming so people can find us." Because now I was part of the problem. I just knew that if the voice wanted me to touch the shield, that touch would either set off the bomb or cause other things to happen that I wouldn't like. I could feel it in my bones.

I heard voices outside now, but they seemed too far away, given the size of the building. Maybe that's how we were able to sneak up on Nathan in the first place—sound dampening on the room kept him focused on his task.

I was beginning to think he wasn't the bomb's creator. He was likely just a hired hand brought in to make sure nobody got to it before it blew. Maybe he was the intended trigger—the one the voice we were hearing was meant to control.

Another sharp pain stabbed through me. My right arm was struggling to touch the glowing sphere, even as I fought to keep a grip on the doorjamb and keep my feet planted firmly on the floor. I was not going to take even a piece of a step back toward that *thing*. If my body was going to betray me, it was damned well going to have to work at it.

So why not make the problem part of the solution? "Harris? Can you cast at all?"

His voice was breathy when he started to reply but strengthened as he talked. "Little bit. Nothing too complicated."

Thankfully, what I hoped for wasn't complicated at all. But it was only going to work if Nathan *wasn't* in here with us or just outside. By now, I didn't think that either of the mages Harris had caught was the creator of our little problem. This magic felt . . . feminine somehow. And I was the only woman here to my knowledge.

"I need you to make a trip wire. Cast a spell so that if the voice *does* make me touch the bomb, the second spell will go off."

"And what's the second spell?" Harris sounded skeptical, probably because he realized I was admitting we might fail here. I was going to fail pretty soon. He was right.

"Set the bomb to implode. We contain the blast in this room and force the bomb in on itself."

His voice was flat now and sounded hollow. "That would kill us."

I forced my eyes to the right as far as they would go so I could at least meet his wide brown eyes. "But the kids won't die, and the building won't be turned into little pieces that will punch through the neighbors' roofs." I paused long enough to pull on my shrinking reserves, keeping my body from obeying the powerful force that was turning me into a puppet.

I stated the reality for the first time, and I hated saying it. "Face it. We're probably going to die today, Harris. Let's make it have some meaning, huh?"

He was silent long enough that I wasn't sure if he'd heard me. But then his voice came, sturdy and resolute. "Okay. For my little girl upstairs, I'll do it."

2

Crap, he was a father of a kid in this school? No wonder he was nearby. "Jeez, Harris. I didn't know."

He shook his head as I yanked my hand back once more. "That's why I was here instead of at work. I was supposed to take her for testing." He shook his head, as if to clear it. "We don't know what this thing is going to do. If we don't keep it in this room, there's no telling what'll happen. Willow might have to go through life with only one parent, but she'll be alive. If it has to be a choice, I choose her."

I did my best to blink back the tears that formed in my eyes. "Willow's a pretty name. What grade?"

"First," he said, sounding distracted. "She wants to be a ballerina when she grows up. Now shut up. I have to concentrate if I'm going to pull this off. You just keep your hands to yourself and away from that freaking bomb."

Touch it . . . now!

My whole body jerked with the command and I had to struggle with everything I had left not to obey. I didn't know if the caster of this particular spell was listening and realizing what we were doing or if it was just a timed command for whoever was in the room to count down to the event. But either way, the new order was more urgent and my skin was twitching in earnest now, my fingers stretching while my arm shook with the strain of keeping from reaching those last few inches. I still had command of my feet, and as long as I kept them pointed toward the door, anatomical limits would keep me in check.

Relax . . . let your mind drift.

Oh, crap. While the caster might not be in the room, this new command made me realize she knew Harris and I were here. She was reacting to my plan. Oh, crap. I felt tension seep out of my body, the same way the magic had crept in. If my leg muscles relaxed, I'd fall right over onto the bomb. My heart was beating like a jackhammer even as my eyelids were drooping, like I was trying to stay awake when I'd been driving too long. "You need to speed it up, Harris. The voice is trying to make me go to sleep, so I fall over and set off the bomb."

"I'm hurrying. I'm hurrying. Just hang on for a few more seconds and I'll wrap the spell all the way around you."

I yawned, then shook my head, wanting nothing more than to curl up and rest, like a cat in a sunbeam.

Wait. A *sunbeam*. That's exactly what I needed. Moments before, a tree's shadow had lain across the basement window, casting the room into darkness. Now the sun had moved on and bright sunlight streamed into the room. The sunbeams flowed through the spell with only a slight change of color before hitting the wall right next to me.

Sunlight was no longer my friend. But the enemy of my enemy was acceptable today.

I leaned sideways as far as I could, letting my relaxed muscles work in my favor. I kept my hand on the doorknob to limit the swing of my body, but soon my face was square in the warm sun.

Imagine being in a tanning bed set on high or standing in front of a blast furnace with your eyes wide open. The heat was intense and immediate and made me hiss in pain. That was good because it awakened the vampire inside. Normally, the supernatural part of me isn't an issue except near sunset. But I wanted that part of me to feel the burn right now. The witch was playing games, trying to beat down a weak, human foe. But I'm not human, and she wasn't going to win against me.

I hissed again and then roared from the pain. Reflexes snapped my neck around, taking me out of the sun. I turned toward Harris, seeing him with the most extreme version of vampire hypervision—that registered people only as colored auras that smelled of . . . food. Thankfully, I'd had a nutrition shake before coming to the school, so I wasn't particularly hungry. But I had no doubt that I was glowing lightly, and my eyes were probably red, because Nathan, the hired wand, straightened abruptly and started to kick away from me. His eyes were wide and the pulse in his exposed neck was racing, the thundering of his pulse making me aware of his fear.

Relax . . . touch it.

I turned and snarled at the bomb, "Go to hell, bitch."

Harris didn't seem worried, but mostly I think that was because he wasn't really looking at me. He was concentrating on the runes he was drawing on the tile with his wand. They shone gold as he wrote, as if the wand was a glow-in-the-dark marker. "Keep your head together, Graves. Think about the kids."

While I needed the predator's strength of purpose, I also needed my humanity and compassion. That balance was something I worked on daily; I always want to know that I could bring myself back from the brink in a crisis. "I'm okay. Just keep working." My voice was low and snarls lurked at the edges of my words. They made Harris look at me for the first time.

"Aah!" He jerked back and half-crawled away from me, smudging one of the runes in the process. "Jeez, Graves. They weren't kidding about you down at the station house."

I'd opened my mouth for a scathing reply when the colors surrounding the bomb began to flicker. I didn't know what it meant, but I was betting it wasn't good. "Can you see that?"

He nodded. "I'm on it. I just need to mark down this last rune." He held the wand like an artist's brush and stared at the circle of glowing symbols, preparing to write the final rune. The weird thing was that even though I didn't recognize more than three of the sigils, the ones I did know didn't have any business being in the same spell. Harris was either doing something really creative or making things worse . . . intentionally.

Wasn't he sitting on his hands earlier? What changed?

A specialized charm slid into my right hand almost without thought and I used that hand to motion to the floor. "Seems like shaping the blast to channel *up* is sort of counterproductive to keeping it in the room, don't you think?"

Harris froze, his wand hovering over the tiles. "What?" His voice was a throaty whisper that sounded more *alto* than baritone. It was just what I was afraid of. It had gotten too easy to move in the past few seconds. The witch's attention was somewhere else, and now I knew where. She'd gotten inside Harris's head and was about to make him do her dirty work. If he survived, he'd at least lose his job for failure to shield and might go to jail as an accessory.

I threw the charm in my hand hard against the floor. The "boomer" is all light and sound, without the energy that might set off the bomb. Still, it packs a wallop to the senses. I was expecting it, so I closed my eyes and accepted going immediately deaf. Harris and Nathan took the effect full on and were stunned into unconsciousness. I only had a few moments if the flashing of the magic shield around the bomb was any indication. As fast as I could I hauled Nathan up in a fireman's carry and yanked Harris to his feet by hauling up on his wand arm. I swiped my foot across his runes as I passed, just to make sure whatever he'd written wouldn't make things worse.

It wasn't a solution, but it was the best I could do. I was out of the room like a shot, running smack into a band of six officers. Five were in riot gear, two of them with the words *BOMB SQUAD* in big white block letters on their chests. The sixth didn't need the lettering. He was in full protective gear, and the runes and sigils that had been drawn on his suit glowed like magnesium in the dim light of the basement hallway.

I startled them, which was bad enough. Far worse, I was a scary vampire-looking creature dragging a mage officer and carrying another "victim." It was quite possibly the worst first impression I could make and all guns turned my way and pointed at my chest in a flash.

My best defense was a good offense. "I'm Celia Graves; I'm a professional bodyguard." I dropped Nathan to the floor and raised my hands. "The bomb's in there and it's about to blow! We need to get the hell out of here!" With the door open, everyone could see the fast-flickering magic and it certainly looked like Harris wasn't able to walk without help.

All heads turned to the two officers with *BOMB SQUAD* printed on their flak jackets. The man on my left nodded, one sharp movement of his head. Or, actually, *her* head, because the voice was female. Grabbing the transmission button on her radio, she called, "All personnel, clear the area. *Now!*"

I heard the thunder of footfalls overhead, and muted shouting in various languages. The cops grabbed Harris and Nathan away from me and hurried toward the stairs at the end of the hall.

I followed but wound up in the lead going upstairs. They were burdened; I wasn't. Logically I should have carried the others, but I wasn't about to protest.

I called over my shoulder as I reached the landing. "Are all the kids out?"

The nearest cop cocked his head and stared at me for a long second. Then he nodded and responded in a light tenor, "We think so. The firefighters unlocked the emergency doors in all the classrooms, so it's going faster."

Thank God. Seriously. I'm not particularly religious, not a true believer like my gran, but at moments like this? Oh yeah. I pounded up the last of the stairs, into the main hallway. It was illuminated by sunlight. The power had been cut, but every door in the place was open. I started to sprint for the main exit when I saw a flash of movement, a bit of color coming out of a door-way on my right.

A kid. Small and dark skinned, with ribboned pig-tails and huge dark eyes. What in the *hell* was she still doing here?

I'd done enough running this morning that the bot-toms of my hose were trashed, but I still skidded a little when I slowed to scoop her up. I didn't even think about being in full vamp mode.

She totally freaked out.

"Vampire!" she shrieked, kicking and hitting at me. She was tiny, but she was fierce, fighting me for all she was worth. It made it hard to hold on to her with-out hurting her. I swore as sharp little teeth dug into my forearm. "Let me go! What have you done to my daddy?"

"Willow?" Harris's voice behind me sounded stunned, a little groggy, but at least he was talking. The cops dragged him, arm extended backward as if to touch his daughter, past the room at a run, expecting that I would follow.

"Daddy!"

"It's all right, baby. I'm here."

It would've been touching if I wasn't bleeding and in pain. Oh, and terrified. Let's not forget that. Because the bomb was about to blow. I could feel it. The magic had built to a climax, power crawling across my skin in burning waves that literally stole my breath.

Like all magic, the blast was taking the shortest route to air, straight up. The edges of the floor in front of me began to glow, power misting around the edges of each tile until they began dissolving in front of me. I was going to plummet into the basement carrying a child who wouldn't survive the fall.

I ran into the nearest room to escape the collapse, but the tiles were giving out here, too. No doors close enough. There was only one way out and it was going to hurt.

It's hard to describe the feeling of jumping feetfirst through a closed, reinforced-glass window. The shock to the spine is first as the metal wires try to slow down your momentum. But I'd put a lot of force into my flying kick, the magical explosion gave us an extra push, and the window gave way. It wasn't a clean break by any means. I wrapped my jacket around Willow's face and head as best I could as slivers of wire and glass tore at my legs and arms. My body did fit through the window opening, but the metal wasn't kind to my shoulder as the blast pushed me through. I landed hard on my back on the asphalt and my shirt rode up as we skidded for a solid thirty or forty feet. Road rash isn't a fun thing as it's happening, but I couldn't turn over or move my arms for fear of hurting Willow.

So I endured it, knowing I'd be picking pieces of gravel and glass from my back and scalp for hours a week or more. At least it would only be hours rather than a year, with the accelerated healing.

A pair of officers rushed forward to help, taking Willow from my arms and pulling me bodily toward the perimeter that had been set up across the street. I saw Harris and the other cops near the ambulances.

Every muscle in my body ached and itched and I couldn't seem to focus my eyes, which I worried about. Then I saw a friendly face. Julie Murphy came racing toward me as I cleared the yellow tape, her blonde pigtails flying behind her. She wrapped me in a hug. "Celia! They said you'd never make it out in time."

I let out a pained chuckle. "Never count me out,

kiddo. I'm tough to keep down." She pulled away from me and smiled. Then she noticed her arms, which were covered with smears of red. She started screaming for help. I guess I was bleeding and didn't realize it. Oh, yeah. I should have realized I was bleeding from the pain in my back. Duh. That was when my body started to protest and pain rushed through me in a wave fast enough to make my stomach roil. The paramedics raced my way with bags in tow. One of them smiled at me and I recognized him.

But then he frowned at just about the time the ground raced up to meet me. I don't remember whose arms caught me as my nose connected with the curb.

3

You look terrible!"

The glare I shot Dawna was probably less than effective, what with the dark glasses and all, but I glared at her nonetheless. I had already been in a foul mood. Having her criticize my appearance didn't help. Of course she looked perfect. She was wearing a hot pink tailored business suit that showed off both her coloring and her figure. She's half Vietnamese and exotic looking. She also has the best fashion sense of anyone I know. I swear she missed her calling as a stylist to the stars. Instead, she works as a receptionist in my office building. She seems to like it most days. God alone knows why.

"I didn't mean it like that! You know I didn't." She shot me a stricken look. "It's just you're pale, even for you. And you're limping. And what's with wearing sunglasses indoors?"

"Headache." I stuck with a one-word answer because I really didn't want to talk about it. Not even to Dawna, who is one of my best friends in the world.

"Still? Shouldn't all of this have healed by now? I mean, I'm just a plain old human, and I've never had a headache last for more than a day—let alone two weeks."

I grabbed my messages and started for the stairs. Maybe if I kept moving we wouldn't have to continue this conversation. Because if it went on much longer, I wasn't sure I could remain civil. I know she's just worried about me. But that didn't make me any less frustrated. I didn't want to take my mood out on her and wind up saying something I was going to regret.

"I have another doctor's appointment tomorrow evening."

"Evening? Do doctors even *do* evening appointments?"

"This one does."

"But . . . ," she started to argue when the phone rang. Since she's the receptionist, she had to answer. I pretended not to see her signal for me to wait and hustled up to my third-floor office.

It had been two full weeks since the "incident" at the grade school. Normally the vampire side of me kicks in, healing injuries in minutes, days at the most. But it hadn't. Oh, the road rash was gone. But the bite mark was still swollen and sore, with nasty bruising, and there was this huge, black bruise on my thigh that was seriously ugly and simply would not go away. And then there was the headache. It was hideous: blinding pain, light sensitivity, nausea. I'd been to the clinic on campus, a chiropractor, and four specialists so far and nobody seemed to have a clue. It was frustrating as hell. *Almost* as frustrating as dealing with the insurance company.

I opened my office door. As usual, I had to push my way through a buzz of energy that prickled my skin. I have some serious wards on my office because of the weapons safe that holds all the tools of my trade, some of which are seriously valuable and would qualify as major magical artifacts. I'd hate to lose them. So I keep them protected.

I closed the door in a none-too-subtle hint that I didn't want to be disturbed. Dawna would probably be annoyed, but she'd respect my privacy. Dottie . . . well, I'd learned early on that Dottie does pretty much whatever she pleases. Still, she doesn't undertake the steep flights of stairs without good cause. In a week or so the construction folks were supposed to show up to install an elevator. We'd had to wait until we could get one that wouldn't lose the building its "historic" status.

God, how I hoped my head would be better by then. I didn't even want to think about how painful the noise would be otherwise.

"Don't think about it," I told myself sternly. "I could be fine by then." To distract myself, I flopped down behind the desk to go through messages and the mail.

The top five messages were all from the same man. Alan Tuttle, Security Chief of MagnaChem, a local pharmaceutical manufacturer. God, but the man wouldn't give up! He wanted an escort for the new owner and some of his staff to his plant in Mexico where the drug gangs had all but taken over the town.

The most recent message was marked *URGENT* and had a note attached to it because the message had been too long for the slip.

Fifth call – I did what you asked and told him that you weren't feeling well, and wouldn't be taking any out-of-town jobs for the next few weeks. I suggested Miller & Creede to him. He said the owner of the company has a "personal issue" with

Creede and won't use them. He said that they were willing to double your usual fee if you would clear your calendar and leave for their offices in Mexico immediately.

Well, hell. *Double?* I charge a fairly high fee to begin with. It was a real shame that I was too sick to go anywhere. But, no. I couldn't work. Not like this. Too bad about Creede, though.

The only other interesting message was from Bruno. He was back from the East Coast! For the moment he was staying in the Graduate Student Apartments, but they were kind of a dump. He said he'd be moving out as soon as he found a house he liked.

I grinned. He was back. Bruno and I have our issues. I trust him with my life, just not with my heart. He's broken it twice. I'm not sure I'll ever get past that. But he's more than my former fiancé. He's my friend. He's also a world-class mage and a great guy to have around when things get hairy. Which, sadly, happens a lot in my life. Too, he makes me laugh and that means a lot.

The first two letters in the stack of mail wiped my smile right off my face. All of the doctors I'd been visiting insisted on getting insurance information to file claims even though I was willing to pay cash.

I have my insurance through the university—part of a special alumni package that gives full benefits provided I pay and pass at least one class per semester. Letter one was from the health insurance division. It ever-so-politely denied any and all of my health insurance claims incurred since the vampire bite that turned me because, as an Abomination, I was part vampire, and therefore *dead* and the policy clearly states they do not pay claims postdeath. They offered their sincerest condolences and indicated that the appropriate paperwork had been forwarded to the life insurance division to pay out my death benefits to my beneficiary.

The second letter, from the life insurance division, regretfully denied said benefits on the basis that as I was an Abomination; I was part human and therefore *not* dead.

Typical. Throwing the letters onto the desk in disgust, I returned to the stack of phone messages. After all, I'd made a lot of calls the past couple of weeks. Surely Alex, or the principal from the school, or Harris . . .

I flipped through the little pink slips of paper a second time to be sure.

Nada.

Now that was just weird. Almost as weird as how fast the incident had disappeared from the news cycle. Just a couple of days reporting on a "failed attack" on a local school, with the culprits apprehended on scene. Congrats to the police and fire departments on a job well done, yadda da yadda da. But no word about repairs or moving students to different schools or anything I'd expected to see.

Still, it might not be any sort of cover-up. After all, news moves on. And the hottest Hollywood power couple's filing for divorce and the assassination of the British prime minister had taken over the headlines.

The last specialist I'd spoken to had very specifically asked me to find out if anyone else at the scene of the "incident" was having similar symptoms. But how could I find out if no one would answer my calls and the news wasn't covering it anymore?

Of course it's easy to ignore a phone message. It's not nearly so easy to ignore someone standing on your doorstep or, in this case, in your waiting room. Perhaps it was time to make an in-person visit. Not to the police station. They'd stonewall me, or throw me out on my ear. Better to go back to the grade school. Principal Sanchez owed me one. I wasn't above playing the guilt card to get information, not if it would help me get rid of this damned headache.

The magical barrier around Abraham Lincoln Elementary had not only been reinstalled, it had also been amped up considerably if the pain I felt crossing it was any indication. It *hurt*, the pain almost driving me to my knees. It did cause me to stumble, which made my already-pounding headache that much worse.

Striding up the walk to the main entrance felt . . . surreal. It looked so *normal*. There was the flagpole Harris had cuffed the first caster to. The classroom window I'd crashed through with Willow had been replaced. I could see children sitting at their desks, studying.

Walking through the entrance, I suppressed a shudder. The floor was fine. Solid as a rock. What I'd seen inside the school—the dissolving tiles—had it been some sort of illusion? I felt strange walking on it. My pulse sped up, and I found myself stretching my abilities to the limit trying to find any trace of magic.

Nothing. Everything was just as it should be. Which was just freaking weird.

I hurried toward the principal's office, the click of my high heels echoing oddly in wide corridors lined with metal lockers. I made it all of the way into the office without spotting the school security guard, or anyone else in authority. It bugged me. It shouldn't be that easy just to stroll in like this. Of course putting in more security would be like locking the door after the thieves: too little, too late. But still, I didn't like it.

I didn't run into a single adult until I reached the office door. Once I was there, though, there was quite a fuss. The school secretary jumped up from her desk. Short, stocky, and middle-aged, she threw her chubby arms around me in a huge hug that made my injured arm throb. "I'm Marjorie Jacobs. I can't thank you enough! None of us can." Her thanks were so loud, and profuse, that closed office doors were opened, revealing the school counselor, the assistant principal, and, finally, the security officer Jamisyn. The one person who didn't show up was the person I'd come to see.

"Principal Sanchez will be so disappointed she missed you." The secretary shook her head sadly. "She's so grateful. We all are! If that bomb hadn't been a dud, we could've all been killed."

"They've decided it was a dud?" I was surprised to hear it. It sure hadn't felt like a dud. And the bomb squad psychic had definitely said we needed to clear the building. And what about the illusion of the dissolving floor? That had to have taken a fair amount of magic. How could the authorities not have found anything? That made no sense at all.

"Had to have been." This from a man standing beside an office sign reading: Vice Principal Colin Parker. "They did a thorough investigation. Complete sweeps of the building. Nobody could find evidence that the bomb in the basement went off. And these were top mages brought in just for this project. We did a complete cleansing—just in case. But there's no sign anything was wrong. Which is why we felt no need to let the press start a panic. After all, no harm done." His smile was a little slick for my taste, his words just a bit rushed. It was obvious that he was more than willing to sweep the whole mess under the rug. Something about him bugged me. It took me almost a full minute to figure out what it was. He reminded me of Ron, the attorney who rents space in my office building. He's a pompous ass with delusions of adequacy. This Parker was just like him.

"Did they even find residue of the spell that kept everyone frozen in place?"

"You know, they didn't," the secretary admitted. "Which is just odd. But no harm seems to have been done. And they're still investigating. I'm sure the authorities will figure it out sooner or later."

"And in the meantime," Parker said, giving a pointed look at the clock, "we need to get back to work. If you'll excuse us?" He phrased it as a question, but it was an order and the secretary scurried back behind her desk. "I'll be sure to let Principal Sanchez know you stopped by."

I wrote my cell phone number on the back of one of my business cards and passed it across the desk to Marjorie. "Have the principal call me. Please?"

"Absolutely."

I could feel Parker's eyes boring into my back as I walked through the door Jamisyn held open for me. I hadn't come here to be treated like a hero. But I hadn't expected a three-minute brush-off, either! Jerk.

"Parker's an ass," Jamisyn said as he followed me into the hallway. "Don't pay any attention to him. None of the rest of us do."

I found myself smiling. "I guess that's why he's the *assistant* principal."

"Oh, yeah. And believe me it chapped his hide when they brought in Ms. Sanchez above him. He was so sure he had a lock on it. But half the staff would've quit on the spot if they'd given him the job."

We'd reached the outdoors. This was my last chance to make this trip more than just wasted time. It was so frustrating. Damn it anyway. I really *needed* some information. Something was off about this whole thing; something tied to my not being able to heal. But I wasn't getting anywhere, and I wouldn't if I couldn't get someone to tell me what I needed to know. "So, Jamisyn, do *you* think it was a dud?"

He looked uncomfortable, his eyes shifting from the glass doors behind us to the gulls that had begun circling overhead, and out to the street. "I think there's more going on than they're telling." He forced a smile, but he wouldn't meet my eyes. "But what would I know? Nobody tells me anything."

"I wish I could've talked to Ms. Sanchez." I didn't bother to hide my frustration.

"Yeah, well, she had a meeting with the principals from the other schools." His eyes widened for a second, almost in panic.

"Other schools?"

"Oh, um, you know . . . in the district. Other grade schools."

He was lying. But before I could follow up on it, Parker tapped on the glass door behind us, making Jamisyn and me both jump in surprise.

"I gotta get back to work. Good luck," he called over his shoulder as he bolted.

The way things were going, I'd need it.

4

Since I'm a glutton for punishment I went straight from the school to the police station. I mean, really, why not make a day of it? I pulled into the covered parking garage attached to the Santa Maria de Luna PD, cruising around and around until I found the spot I was looking for right across from the little white Toyota belonging to none other than Detective Alexander. If Jamisyn's good-luck wish worked, she should be getting off-shift soon. If not, well, I was in a dark, cool, quiet place that was ever so much better for my headache.

I only had to wait an hour.

"Oh, shit. It's you."

"Gee, Heather. You'd think you weren't happy to see me or something." I was mostly being sarcastic. Still, a little part of me was hurt that she had been ducking my calls and was obviously unhappy to see me. We might not be close, but we'd always been friendly.

"What do you want?" she snapped. She tried to walk around me, but I stepped back in her way.

"Were there bombs in more than just the one school?"

"Damn it, Graves!"

Wow, not even "Celia" anymore. This was serious. "What?"

She ran fingers through her hair and let out a frustrated breath. "You keep doing this. You keep putting me in the hot seat, asking me to do things I *can't*, wanting me to tell you things you're not supposed to know. Do you have any idea how much trouble you get me into? You want information? Why come to me? Why not ask Rizzoli?"

I took a step back, my hands coming up in a defensive gesture. Alex was practically snarling at me. This was way more attitude than usual. More than the situation deserved. I was about to say so, to ask what had her so hot under the collar, when she winked at me, her eyes flickering in the direction of a camera I'd seen posted in a nearby corner.

Aha. Okay, so she wasn't really pissed off. Which was good. But she also couldn't talk. Still, she'd managed to pass on one important kernel of information. Rizzoli is Special Agent Dominic Rizzoli, FBI. Who wouldn't be involved if this were just a local matter. Which meant that somehow, somewhere . . . this had crossed state lines. Holy crap.

"Heather . . ."

"Don't you 'Heather' me," she snarled. "You were Vicki's friend, not mine. Vicki's dead. Don't think you can use her memory to make me forget my duty. 'Cause that's not going to happen."

The words stung. Even if I'd read the wink right, that we were putting on a show for the cameras, it still hurt. Mainly because I still missed Vicki. Maybe just as much as Alex did.

"Fine. I won't bother you at work again."

"Good. Don't."

5

I wasn't able to reach Rizzoli either that day or the next. Frustrating, but not unexpected. I might have a handy-dandy consultant's badge, but there are limits to how much good it does me. Rizzoli would get hold of me when he was ready, and not until. I, meanwhile, had other things on my mind.

Dusk was falling as I entered the Pacific Health Complex. It wasn't so much a hospital as a clustered group of private-practice specialist physicians. If this doctor couldn't figure out what was wrong with me, I was afraid I was going to have to give up. Of course this one had been recommended by Gwen Talbert, my therapist and a very highly respected physician, so maybe he'd have better luck. Or more skill. Either one was fine with me.

I looked at the building directory when I walked in. Most of the offices were closed for the day, but this particular doctor offered evening hours. And why wouldn't he? He was an Orvah practitioner. It was an art distantly related to Voodoo whose doctors sort of depended on darkness for a lot of their healing. He was the only certified specialist in this area of the state.

The amber-skinned receptionist with a name tag that read *Simone* smiled as I reached her desk. "Can I help you?"

"Yes," I replied, "I'm Celia Graves. I have a seven o'clock appointment with Dr. Jean-Baptiste."

She checked a list and then nodded before rising from her chair. "Of course. Right this way, Ms. Graves. I'll need you to fill out some insurance forms."

I almost laughed and decided not to mention that said *forms* probably wouldn't yield any actual payment from my insurance. I couldn't remember whether I'd brought my checkbook.

"The doctor is running a little behind, so we have some time."

Naturally. What doctor *isn't* running behind? "Could we at least draw the blood? You asked that I not eat, but I have a . . . medical condition. I really need to get something in me so bad things don't happen." That was putting it mildly. I was trying really hard not to stare too long at Simone's lovely, slender neck. Pretty, silken skin that was alive with color. One of the things I wanted to see the doctor for was how my inner vamp was wanting to come out and play more often since the bomb and it was getting harder to fight it. I clutched my purse tighter, feeling the outline of one of the nutrition shake bottles inside. It wasn't what my stomach wanted this close to sundown, but it would satisfy the hunger.

"Oh! Of course. We can certainly do the lab work first. I'm sorry. I remember you mentioning your . . . condition when you set the appointment close to night. But the doctor did insist on an evening appointment. And I'm sure he has his reasons."

Well, they'd better be damned good reasons, because everybody I'd run into for the past hour had looked pretty much like a Happy Meal. It was all I could do to keep myself in check.

"We'll get you taken care of." And she did. I was whisked into a brightly lit, modern lab where obviously well-trained techs found a vein on the first try. I felt the pinch in my arm and had to shut my eyes. Smelling the blood was bad enough. I wasn't sure what would happen if I actually saw it—thick and red in the glass tube.

The second the blonde in blue pressed a cotton ball to the crook of my arm, my other hand was in my bag. I slugged down one bottle like it was the first taste of water I'd had in a week. The second one I sipped more leisurely and I felt the twitching under my skin ease. I wasn't sure if removing the symptoms was good or bad, but the vampire thing wasn't something the doctor was going to fix, so I figured I'd take my chances.

I was sitting in the hallway finishing the last of the chocolaty goodness when Simone reappeared.

"I'm very sorry, Ms. Graves, but I'm afraid I need to get identification and credit card information from you." Her face flushed, whether from embarrassment or anger I wasn't sure. "I just spoke with your insurance carrier. It seems they're denying your coverage. They claim you're, well, *dead*."

So much for not mentioning it. I figured at least it would have to go through the processing period or not get noticed until working hours tomorrow. I sighed and began rummaging in my purse. This was just getting ridiculous. The minute I got back to the office I was scanning those letters and sending them to my attorney. Let him deal with the idiots at the insurance company.

Simone glanced from my driver's license to my face and back again until I felt compelled to explain. "It's the Abomination thing. They're claiming I'm dead so that they won't have to pay any of my claims."

"I see." She handed back my license, but took my credit card with her. She'd barely gone when a nurse in Snoopy scrubs weighed me and lead me into the exam room.

When I followed the nurse through the doorway at the end of the hall all impressions of the shining white and stainless-steel office disappeared. The room was dim, lit with burning torches set into pockets in the walls. I could barely hear the low whir of fans that pulled the smoke upward and away from the room. Mostly the sound in the room was from an artificial waterfall in the corner that filled the air with a cool mist. The moist air was filled with such a strong mix of scents that I nearly started sneezing. Everything from peppermint to catnip, licorice, and bitterroot. Oh, and let's not forget the animals. I didn't think it was legal to have live animals in a medical building. Yet here they were—goats and chickens and lizards and snails in glass tanks.

Um.

There were small groups of people in various areas of the large room, dressed in colorful outfits that made my red shirt look positively pastel. Men and women in lab coats were talking in low tones and one was standing in the middle of a circle, shaking a headless chicken.

Um again.

I was still gathering my senses around me when a tall, handsome black man walked in through the opposite door. He was wearing a standard white lab coat and had a stethoscope around his neck. He reached out his hand toward me and locked piercing, intelligent eyes with mine. His accent was minimal and there was an interesting edge to his *a*'s that made me think of England. "Ms. Graves? Sorry to keep you waiting." He passed me back the credit card I'd given Simone. "I'm Dr. Jean-Baptiste. Let's get started, shall we?" He waved me toward a padded leather chair that looked surprisingly comfortable. I sat down, and when I looked up again, I got my second surprise.

He'd donned a headdress of leather with beads, feathers, and what I feared was chicken claws. In his hand was a carved wooden stick—too long for a wand but too short for a cane. There were more feathers attached in long streams.

It was as though putting on his tools of the trade transported him in time and space. It might have said *M.D.* on his shiny brass name tag, but the *witch* shone in glowing eyes filled with power enough to make my skin crawl.

"There is something wrong with your blood. Have you fed on anyone sick lately?"

It was such a matter-of-fact question that I reared back in surprise. "I haven't fed on anyone. Ever."

His expression showed his disbelief, like an ob-gyn reacting to a pregnant woman telling him she was a virgin. He raised the carved staff and brought it down toward my forehead. I raised a hand before I thought and stopped it cold a foot away from me. It ticked me off for no apparent reason. His brows rose and then he dipped his head. "That angered you. My apologies. It is part of the examination. You have no experience with Orvah magic?"

I shook my head. "Not since college, and it was just a chapter in my practical magic course. I'm only here because Gwen Talbert recommended you."

He let go of the staff abruptly, leaving me holding it in the air. He sat down on a rolling padded stool and put a small white laptop on his . . . well, *lap* while I tried to figure out what to do with the stick. "Tell me," he commanded. "Why *are* you here?"

Torches, goats rumbling in the background, and . . . fingers racing across a keyboard. Frankly, it was a little hard to focus. I put the stick on the floor next to my chair and started slow, trying to figure out exactly what to say. At this point, I'd said it so many times that I nearly had the symptoms memorized. "I've had a blinding headache since a bomb exploded in the local grade school, and most mornings I can barely stand for the pain in my leg. A bite wound from a small child simply won't heal for no reason anyone can find. I've also been having really weird dreams—where I'm stalking people, hissing at them. But I wake up in bed. I'm afraid to even fall asleep some nights. I swear it's about the bomb. You heard about that, right?"

He nodded. "Hard not to. It was all over the paper for days. But all the reports said it was a failed attempt, that nobody was seriously injured."

"I know. And that's what's weird. Because I'd *swear* two bombs went off. The first explosion happened when everybody was frozen in place and the second one was down in the boiler room." I hadn't talked this freely about the incident with the previous doctors. But maybe that was why they hadn't been able to help me. Gwen trusted this guy. I trusted Gwen. I decided to put my faith in doctor-patient confidentiality and tell him everything.

"I got some road rash, and the bite from a child I was carrying out of the building. But while the scrapes and bruises went away almost immediately, the bite site is still really tender and bruised and then there's this spot on my calf that hurts like fire. It's weird. The vampire part of me heals really quick. Why are these injuries still lingering?"

"Ah . . ."

I perked up at the tone of his voice. It said something had occurred to him. "Yes?"

He stopped typing and raised an index finger to point at me. "So it's not so much *that* you hurt, but that you *still* hurt. Before this event, had you ever had a headache? Ever thrown out your knee?"

Thinking back, I had to shrug and shake my head. "Other than one Sunday morning in college when I vowed never again to drink tequila, no headaches at all." He smiled ruefully, like he'd made a similar vow in his youth. But I had to add, "Unless you count concussions. I've had a few of those. Hard to avoid in my field. But my legs have always been good. All the doctors say there's nothing wrong. MRIs, CT scans, X-rays, and full blood workups. Nothing. I've been to a traditional witch doctor already, but nothing. I'm hoping you've got something new up your sleeve."

There was a long pause while he thought. His pen tapped against the white lab coat, printing tiny dots of blue that he probably wouldn't discover until he put it in the laundry. The chicken feet bounced in time with the pen. "My specialty is blood illnesses and I sense sickness in you." He motioned to the stick at my feet. "Could you pick that up, please?"

I picked it up and handed it out to him. He didn't take it. "Tell me a lie, Ms. Graves."

My eyebrows touched my lashes. "Excuse me?"

"Please," he asked politely, with a sweeping, courtly gesture. "Humor me. Lie to me about something while holding that."

I shrugged and tried to think of something that was such an obvious lie that it would tell him whatever he needed to know. "Um . . . my mother and I have a close and loving relationship." I had to school my face to stay blank after that whopper. Fortunately, I'm very good at blank.

The stick in my hand felt suddenly warm and the eyes of the carved monkey started to glow blue. "Is glowing good or bad?"

He just smiled. "Now, once again . . . have you recently ingested sick blood?"

God, were we back to *that*? "No. I've never tasted human blood and I only have animal broth. No blood at all." The stick didn't glow. I didn't expect it to.

Dr. Jean-Batiste let out a slow breath that seemed . . . weary and worried. "We will do some testing, of course. But I had you come here now, when the vampire part of you is at its strongest, so that I could test a theory. You see, what I fear might be happening if none of the other doctors are finding anything, is that your pain might be related to *not* drinking blood."

A buzzing formed in my ears and I felt my pulse speed up. A vampire I knew had once said the same thing and I wanted to hit him. Just like now. "Why would you say that?"

He shrugged. "You're part vampire. Vampires subsist on blood. If you're only feeding the human part of you, I have no way of knowing whether you're endangering the vampire part of you—or what result that might have." He tipped his head back and forth. "Still, there's little in the blood that can't be replenished by a healthy diet. If we could determine what's missing that is causing the pain, we might be able to create a supplement for you. But we will also check for bad mojo or curses. Do you have anyone who wishes you harm?"

I let out a small, sad chuckle. "Lately, it seems like nearly everyone. From the death curse to a greater demonic possession and a variety of magical stalkers. I'm sort of in the crosshairs of most of the underworld."

His lips pursed and he took back his stick cautiously. "So I am quite likely to find bad mojo about you in the spirit world. We will be cautious, then. I'll finish with the few other patients and we will begin. Let me show you to a waiting room where you'll be more comfortable."

And where I couldn't influence his other patients with my *bad mojo*, I'd bet.

He stood and we started to walk back out to the reception room. As he held the door for me, he touched my arm, causing me to stop. "I normally wouldn't reveal this, but it could be important and I want you to think about it. I have examined two others who were at the scene of the incident at the grade school. One adult and one child."

I knew he couldn't tell me the identities of the patients, but I was curious. Could it be Harris and Willow? Orvah was practiced in various parts of the world, but had particularly strong roots in parts of Haiti.

The doctor continued. "The child is having similar complaints of non-specific pain in her legs and head. The adult is having serious memory problems. In fact, he has no memory of the day in question at all. It is a blank slate. I want you to think very carefully about that day and try to tell me as much as you can about what happened during the incident. I'll give you a clipboard and some paper."

By the time he came to get me, the back room was quiet except for the contented clucking of roosting hens. I'd written up a list of every detail I remembered. Dr. Jean-Baptiste read over the list quickly once and then more slowly while I stared at him from the comfort of the leather chair. He tapped the middle of the second page. "You don't mention the man in the scary suit with the magic marks on it."

Scary suit? I frowned and tried to think. I couldn't remember. "Sorry. I don't remember anything like that at all. Could she have made it up?"

He scratched his temple where the feathers were probably itching and began to shake his head, tiny movements that barely moved the chicken feet. "I don't think so. She was pretty descriptive about that. She believed he was hurting her father. What I'm wondering is whether you share symptoms with both the child and the adult. I think something's affecting your memory. And I am wondering if perhaps the memory problem and the headaches are related."

I motioned around to the racks of spice bottles, the distinctive musk of goat, heavy in the air. "So do you think you can figure out what it is?"

He smiled brilliantly. "Have you not noticed anything different about the room since you came back?"

I flicked my eyes around the room again. "It's . . . um, *quieter*?"

His chuckle was genuinely amused, but the intensity of his profession was still underneath. "Yes, that. But you've also been sitting in the middle of an active casting circle for the past ten minutes. You truly didn't feel it when you walked in?"

No. I hadn't, and I should have. What the hell?

Apparently, my shocked look was enough. "Well, that is certainly interesting." He typed a few notes onto the laptop. "I can tell you this: You have been affected by powerful magic. It's interfering with your memory and it seems to be both long- and short-term. I don't know if it has anything to do with your leg pain. But when you walked back in the room, you had to struggle to get through the circle. That you don't remember it is very interesting indeed. Unfortunately, I haven't determined how to unravel the spell yet. I'm going to take the details to some experts I know and see what they can come up with. For the moment, I'd suggest caution, rest, good nutrition, and some memory enhancement and protection charms. Then, with some time . . ."

Eww. I wasn't liking the sound of that. "You don't sound particularly hopeful."

He shrugged. "It is difficult. There are not many practitioners with the level of power to create such a spell. I should be able to determine a signature. But I cannot. Somehow the caster has tangled their magical signature with those of many, many others. This is not a spell that can be worked by a group, but if I did not know better, I would swear it had been. Too, there aren't many spells I don't at least recognize the base of. It's like figuring out a word from the Latin root. I haven't found a base I know yet. That's the best I can tell you right now. And I won't lie to you. I can't tell you when . . . or if . . . I will."

Great. Just great.

6

Two nights later I woke because my skin was burning and freezing water was lapping at my body. The sun was coming up. It was freaking cold, but the sunlight was burning every inch of exposed skin that wasn't soaking wet. I was lying on the beach outside my house, in my pajamas with gulls calling a raucous good morning as they dipped and dived through the air above me.

What the hell?

The last thing I remembered was going to bed at 10:00 P.M. I rose, hurrying across the beach to the house and into the bathroom.

How did I get outside? When had I left my bed? What had I done?

I didn't know.

Worse, the dreams I'd had were so incredibly clear. I could remember those. The light scent of floral perfume, the sight of that couple hurrying from the opera house to the safety of their car. The sweet, coppery taste of blood laced with fear that filled my mouth and made me shiver. Desperate and terrified, I checked every inch of my clothing for bloodstains. Nothing. No hint on my teeth or gums. Knees weak with relief, I sank onto the toilet and cried until I was gulping huge mouthfuls of air and the floor was covered with soggy yellow tissues. My head hurt worse than ever, but I was afraid to take yet another aspirin because I couldn't remember what I'd done last night.

What was happening to me? What was I going to do? I'd been following Jean-Baptiste's advice. It wasn't working. Nothing was working.

I might have stayed in the bathroom feeling sorry for myself, but the doorbell rang. It's not a loud bell, but the sound sent a flash of searing pain through my skull. I winced and began limping my way to the door.

The bell rang again—and my temples pounded—again, so I grumbled out loud, "Hold your horses. Jeez, I'm coming."

I opened my front door and there was Rizzoli. If he noticed my swollen red eyes, he didn't mention it. Instead, he smiled at me and shook his head as though supremely amused. "You need to cut back on the sauce, Graves. You look like hell. And why are you limping?"

"Been this way since the bomb blast at the school."

Disbelief was plain on his face. "Shouldn't you be healed by now? I mean, vampire blood *and* siren blood notwithstanding, even a vanilla human shouldn't be limping this much time after a failed attempt."

I snuffled back what I couldn't blow out. No tissues next to the couch. I'd have to fix that later. "It didn't fail. There were two bombs. Neither of them was a dud." I lowered myself carefully into my favorite recliner and rested my head back into the poofy pillow. He took a seat on the couch, which, while not terribly comfortable, was a pretty white print that matched the wallpaper. "I left you a message about that."

"I know. I got your calls. And I'm sorry I haven't come by sooner. The brass . . ." He paused, trying to come up with a polite way to end the sentence. Apparently there wasn't one, so he changed tacks. "Why did you ask about other bombs in other places?"

I tried to remember. There'd been a reason. An important reason. Crap. "What day did I call?"

He sighed. "You don't remember?"

"Just give me some background, okay? Sometimes if you give me some clues the memory resurfaces."

"Your message said you'd been back to the school, and that you'd gone to see Heather Alexander. She told you she couldn't talk to you."

I sat up straight, and it made my head pound. "The guard. The guard at the school said something."

"What? What did he say?"

I tried to remember, but it was useless. I barely remembered going to the school, let alone specifics of a conversation. I wouldn't have been able to come up with as much as I had if Rizzoli hadn't prompted me.

His dark eyes looked me over carefully from head to foot. "You really are in bad shape, aren't you? What do the doctors say?"

I threw up my hands in frustration. "Nothing. They say nothing. Because they haven't got a freaking clue."

He winced. "That sucks."

"Yeah. It does. But that's not why you're here, is it?"

His expression grew weary and I realized I wasn't the only one who looked bad. Rizzoli's normally a good-looking man if you're into dark Italian-American types. Every time I'd seen him his suits were well cut, fit him perfectly, and no wrinkle dared appear. Not today. The charcoal suit was still good quality and well tailored, but it looked as though he'd been wearing it for a couple of days straight, only bothering to change into a fresh shirt.

"We've found evidence of devices having gone off at six different schools. I found out about the one near Denver, Colorado, by sheer accident. It was in the same school district where the high-school shootings happened a few years back, so when the *furnace malfunction* was discovered in the basement, it made the local six o'clock news and got splashed onto the Internet."

"And you put two and two together."

He rested his booted feet on the coffee table and I instinctively motioned for him to put them back on the floor. He did. "Well, actually, all I put together was one and one. But it did make me search the Internet for other weird news and I started calling around to ask whether any other similar reports of post-furnace-malfunction illnesses had come in at the local level. That's when we found Chicago, Daytona Beach, and Dallas. Boston only got reported this morning, which is why we think there might be more out there." He yawned wide. "I'm hoping you have coffee, because I'm going to need it for the trip."

I stood up and started to limp toward the kitchen, saying over my shoulder, "I have coffee, but where are you off to? One of the schools?"

"Not me," he replied. "Us. I need you to come down to our field office to help me with something."

That stopped me cold. "The last time you showed up, it didn't go so well." That was an understatement, and he knew it. The last time he'd knocked on my door, I'd been living in a different house. He'd appeared in the middle of my Christmas Day party, claiming my going with him was a matter of life and death . . . not to mention national security.

It had been. I'd barely survived.

He waved his hand at me like I was overreacting, but there was a tension next to his eyes that revealed his words as a lie. "This is a piece of cake—nothing like that last time. But it is important. The assistant director dropped by my office this morning and specifically requested you for this job."

I raised my brows and then sighed because I now understood that Rizzoli was being pushed. In the FBI hierarchy, the assistant director rarely *dropped by* the office of a field agent. While Rizzoli had gotten a temporary promotion during a crisis, it apparently hadn't stuck . . . or he'd refused it. So I was being "fetched" and he was the delivery boy. The thing was, I needed him available to me when I asked. He was really handy for putting pressure on people I couldn't because I didn't have a badge in my pocket. I had a nifty laminated card, but what does that mean?

Because who listens to a bodyguard? Nobody.

Really. A crossing guard has more credibility.

"So," I said after a long pause. "Two coffees to go then. But while I get cleaned up you'd better heat me up some of the broth I've got stored in the freezer. And we need to keep it short because this headache is really hammering me. Maybe I should just cut it off altogether."

He didn't comment on that. "Go get dressed. I'll start the coffeemaker."

It took a few minutes. I had to dig around to find clothes warm enough for the weather and then we were out the door. Just yesterday, it had been sunny and warm, a typical spring day. But today, winter had returned with a vengeance. "I will *never* get used to this." The words came out in a mist of steam that matched the snow covering the ground. No, there shouldn't be snow in Southern California, especially in March. Blame it on the rift. According to the weatherman, the world's brush with the demonic dimension messed with the climate. The jet stream was presently somewhere over Brazil and wasn't expected back anytime soon. On the plus side, glaciers in the Arctic Circle were back to the levels of a hundred years ago and they predicted there wouldn't be any wildfires this year. I could stand a little snow for those benefits. But relearning how to drive has been a challenge for many people.

Rizzoli had parked his crappy government-issued sedan right next to my sporty convertible Miata in one of three marked places. Though technically, you could probably park fifty cars in front of my beach house if you didn't mind digging your vehicle out of the sand on a regular basis.

I'd nearly reached his car when he held out an arm to stop me, catching me across the chest. The impact made me cough and stopping short almost dumped me on my fanny in the slush thanks to my bad leg. Rizzoli didn't say anything or look at me, just pointed what looked like a high-end remote control toward the black sedan. A chirp sounded from the remote, and then another. He kept holding down the button until five tones had sounded and the whole device glowed green. "Okay. It's safe. We'll talk once we're on the road."

Safe? From what? I eyed the car suspiciously. "Should I be worried about getting in?"

He shrugged. "Probably not. But careful keeps me alive. This remote checks for both traditional bombs and anything magical or demonic that might affect the car or anyone in it. If I hadn't already adjusted it, you wouldn't have been able to get inside with those fangs."

Sweet! I needed one of those. "Ooh . . . where'd you get it?"

His dark eyes twinkled despite looking bloodshot and tired. He gave me a small smile over the roof of the car that told me the remote wasn't a consumer model. "I could tell you, but then I'd have to kill you."

Of course. The government got all the good toys. Still, I was betting I had some he'd never seen before.

The engine purred quietly after he put in the key and pressed the start button, but the thrumming under my feet told me there was more under the hood than I'd find in similar cars on the showroom floor. I waited impatiently while he steered out onto the open road. "Okay. So what's up?"

"We detained a foreign national last night. I need you to get some information out of him before bad things happen."

Um . . . excuse me? I turned my throbbing head to see if what he was suggesting even bothered him. "Just so we're clear . . . *how* were you planning I'd do that?"

He flicked his eyes away from the road long enough for me to see that he knew exactly what he was asking. "You're a siren. Do I really need to say it out loud?"

I glared at him. "No."

When I didn't say any more, he was forced to ask, "No, I don't need to say it, or no, you won't help?"

"Both." No way in hell was I going any further in this plan, regardless of whether it would get him in trouble. Because I was controlling myself, my voice didn't come close to the outrage I was feeling. "I can't believe you'd even ask! I nearly wound up in *prison* for mental manipulation, Rizzoli, and that was before I even realized what my psychic abilities could do to a person. So, no. There's nothing you can do to convince me to help you. Just take me back to my house. Find someone else to help you."

He sighed and tapped his fingers on the steering wheel. I could see it out of the corner of my vision. I stared out at the scenery, refusing to look at him, admiring the ice crystals dripping off waving palm trees. His voice was serious as death when he spoke next. "It's important, Graves. I wouldn't ask if it wasn't."

I felt my eyebrows rise high on my forehead. "Yeah? I'm pretty sure it's not more important than my spending the rest of my life in a cage too small to sit up straight in. In fact, if I remember right, magical torture is banned by the Geneva Convention. Me using my innate abilities to force someone to talk is torture. It just is. Is this more important than winding up in front of the judges in The Hague? Turn around, Rizzoli. My answer is no."

Another exit whizzed by on the interstate and the car didn't slow. Rizzoli reached down and pulled something from his pocket. Okay, that time I looked. He pressed a button on the cell phone and held it up to his ear.

"Report. Have you secured the siren?"

I suppose it would have been sporting to tell Rizzoli about my enhanced hearing. But . . . nah.

It was a little surprising to hear the annoyance in my driver's voice. I got the impression it wasn't because of having to call in but because the speaker referred to me as *the siren*. Interesting. "Her *name* is Celia Graves.

Yes, she's with me in the car. But we have a problem. I need to explain the situation. Fully."

"That's need to know, Agent. And she doesn't."

"Sir, if you want her cooperation, I'm going to have to tell her at least some of what's going on."

There was a long, charged silence.

"We need her. But understand that I'm holding you fully responsible for her behavior. Understood?"

"Understood." Rizzoli ended the call without another word. Maybe the other guy had hung up on him, but I didn't think so. It made me wonder if he was going to get in hot water because of me. I hoped not. But he was right about one thing. If they had any hope of getting my cooperation they were going to have to tell me what in the hell was going on.

"All right, listen up. I told you that there were bombs in other locations. They were always in pairs. The first one hooked to the air ducts would go off first, freezing people in place and disbursing . . . well, we don't know what just yet. The second wipes all evidence and memory of the first.

"The guidance counselor at the school in downtown L.A. happened to be a level-seven mage with a black arts defense background. Sheer fluke that, just like you, he felt a pair of bombs go off. He recognized the first one as something very dark and forbidden— something even the big boys in the sorcery circles don't play with. We've had our best people working forensics on the magic and they keep saying it's a mess, that the results they're getting just aren't possible."

He took another deep breath before continuing at the same breakneck speed. "In the meantime we've been monitoring the teachers, kids, everyone involved, trying to figure out what the first bombs do. So far we can't find anything wrong with the kids. But the *adults* in the schools . . . that's a different story. They're dying at an alarming rate, but none of the deaths seem to be magical. They're just showing up at the hospital with what seem like mild symptoms, say they're in extreme pain, and then . . . they never check out. Nobody in the press has put it together yet, thank heavens. And in one case . . . something happened. I can't tell you about it. But if it gets out, all hell's going to break loose. Even as it is now, people are eventually going to start to notice. In a few days the story is going to be impossible to contain."

Crap. I believe in disclosure. I believe the public has a right to know. But I also know how much damage mass panic can do. I wouldn't want to be the one calling the shots on this case. Hell, I wouldn't even want to be in Rizzoli's shoes.

"So. Someone cast a spell, but nobody knows what it does. What does the guy you have in custody have to do with it?"

The nod said he expected the question. "We started watching the Internet, low-key stuff in the anti-American chat rooms, hoping for anyone who claimed responsibility or bragged about it. What we found was far more disturbing. The event was definitely organized. There were indications that this is a timed magical event. That there are more bombs, and that when they've all detonated the spell will be released full force."

"Do you have a date?"

"Not yet. That's one of the things we want to find out. If there's a deadline, we need to know what it is."

"What about the two guys the cops arrested at our school?"

"No good. They were hired wands. Didn't know a thing other than how to set up the device. But the guy we have now—we think he can tell us what the spell does. But we have to be careful; as soon as they figure out he's been captured, they'll pull the plug. They put a curse on him that will activate if we use physical force. But it can also be remotely detonated. Our agency witch confirmed the curse. It's one of the worst and could take out the building if it activates."

I wasn't even sure what to say. My mouth opened several times, but no words came out. Finally, I managed to sputter, "If you're trying to encourage me to help, you're failing miserably."

He let out a small sound that deepened the creases in his broad forehead with both worry and fear. It reminded me that he wasn't just a desk jockey for the FBI. He was a field operative. If this scared him, it was worth being scared about. His voice lowered to a deadly growl. "My boy was in the school in L.A., Graves. I spent half a night putting together Mikey's first two-wheeler so he could have the birthday he's been talking about all year. I want to know what that asshole and his friends did to him, or so help me God—" His eyes were flashing and his grip on the steering wheel was white-knuckled.

Whoa. I'd never seen Rizzoli like this. Not during a political crisis or even a demonic one. This was personal to him and it was going to make him call in every favor and push every button he had on me and everyone else until he had answers. "And you've already had your son checked out?"

"Doctors, witches, and even some psychics and priests. The witch found a spell on him all right but not one that could be removed. It's somehow melded to his skin, has become a part of him. They don't know what it does, who cast it, how to get rid of it, or even what culture the magic is from."

The doctor's words echoed through my mind: *I haven't found a base I know yet.* Well, fuck a duck. I already have a spell like that, too. A death curse was put on me when I was a child. So far it hasn't killed me, but I've been told removing it might. Even with the caster long dead it hasn't faded much. The last thing I needed was another one and I wouldn't wish it on anyone. "How long do you have before they know the guy you got is missing?"

"Could be anytime. He might already be dead. But if he's not, I want to know what he knows."

I understood but . . . "I won't force him to talk, Rizzoli. I don't have any control over that particular ability yet. He could wind up brain-dead." Let's not mention to the nice federal officer that I'd left several other people like that fairly recently. Admittedly, they were bad guys who were helping a demented siren turn me into a mental vegetable . . . but still.

He didn't turn to look at me, but the smile that curved his lips creeped me out. "No, I have something very special in mind for you, Graves. And I don't think you're going to mind doing it. In fact, you might really like it."

7

The road to ruin is the one that's smooth and paved, and the fastest cart to carry you is good intentions. Words of wisdom from Gran and they were oh so true today.

I'd sworn never to use my psychic abilities again to torture or coerce, but what Rizzoli was suggesting wasn't precisely either one.

I stared through the two-way mirror at the slender middle-aged man with the pockmarked face. He glowered at the bearded Asian agent in the room with him but didn't speak a word, no matter how hard the agent tried to convince him to do the right thing and not hurt innocent kids. The layered black clothing on the captive spoke of an extremist religious order, perhaps one of several that had arisen in eastern Europe lately. The heavy salt-and-pepper eyebrows and Roman nose made me think of Croatia or Bulgaria, but I could be wrong.

Rizzoli leaned close to my shoulder and whispered, "All you have to do is *suggest* he cooperate with us. It's not torture and doesn't change anything that's happened. But we'll know where the other bombs are and what they do." Then Rizzoli did the one thing I'd been praying he wouldn't do. He pulled out his wallet and flipped it open to a posed family portrait. His wife was blonde and a tad chubby but pretty in a pale blue silk dress. A little girl, still a toddler, sat on Rizzoli's lap while an older boy, obviously Mikey, stood at his father's side proudly, a hand on his shoulder. Damn it. The kid had his father's dark good looks. Rizzoli's hand tightened on my shoulder with something approaching panic. "Celia. Please don't let anything happen to my son."

He'd never called me Celia before and it made me let out a pained sound. What were my morals worth? What price, ethics? "What if he doesn't know anything? What if he's just an innocent dupe you picked up by accident?"

The voice in my ear must have been the same one that accompanied the apple in the Garden. So reasonable, logical. "If he doesn't know anything, he can't tell us anything and he's free to go."

Free to go. Even though he'd already admitted to being involved with people who put an exploding death curse on him. Not freaking likely. No, he knew *something* and I didn't figure that somehow the guy in black was going to be allowed to go back to his buddies. Maybe it wouldn't be the FBI proper who did the deed, but they'd find someone who would. Still, why was it little Mikey's fault? What did a kid who just wanted his first two-wheeler have to do with stupid, ugly politics?

I grabbed the wallet out of Rizzoli's hand and stared at the happy family, not the man in black or the distraught father standing next to me. Was it wrong for me to want a child I'd never met to be safe? Didn't I have the right to want him to grow up happy and healthy? Couldn't I want it . . . a *lot*? That wasn't coercion or torture. It was just me, wanting people to be happy in a way I'd never been lucky enough to have in my mess of a family.

Movement erupted from the corner of my eye, but I kept my gaze hard on the photograph. I could look at the photo and worry and fear for those sweet kids. More, I could *care* whether they lived, free from harm.

The longer I stared, the more the toddler resembled my little sister when she was a baby. I'd lost her early, at the hands of greedy, thoughtless assholes who thought kids were easy targets and could be used or abused at will. Maybe if her kidnappers had *cooperated* she'd still be alive.

Rizzoli's hand covered mine and eased away the wallet that I'd nearly crushed in a supernatural grip. "That's enough, Graves. He's cooperating." Rizzoli's voice was soft, sympathetic—the voice a person uses in the hospital or to bring a person down off the ledge. "That was even more than I'd hoped for."

Huh?

I shook my head and blinked back the tears I hadn't realized were rolling down my face. When I could see again through the film of salty water, the man in black was crying openly, his thin shoulders shaking, his face on his folded arms. The Asian agent was blowing his nose into a large cloth handkerchief.

Um.

"Did I do that?"

Rizzoli wouldn't look at me, but his voice was harsh and scratchy. "That's a hell of a talent, Graves. I thought maybe you'd worry a little and he'd feel remorse, but this is a lot better. They made me your handler because they said your siren abilities wouldn't affect me." He cleared his throat. "Maybe I don't think of you sexually after getting snipped, but I'm still getting a charm made. You might want to get tested to see if you're a projecting empath."

My *handler*? I wasn't a dog or a trained seal. But it would make sense to have him be my contact if he'd had a vasectomy. Infertile men weren't affected by a siren's psychic talents. I didn't really understand that. Logically, it should affect them, since they're perfectly capable of sex. But magic is weird sometimes.

What I didn't get was how he knew I'd get emotional. He apparently thought he had me pegged and damned if he didn't. At least this time.

A heavily accented voice began to speak through the tinny microphone. "They chose me because I can do the timed-release spell on the children. The adults, not so much. But they said it was the children that mattered. I told them I hate children. But I lied. I hid my little ones away, told my wife to keep them from their schooling so they would not rot and pass on the illness."

Rot? Illness? Just like that, my tears were gone and I turned my full attention on the room. Rizzoli nearly vibrated with contained energy beside me. His face was bathed in shadows, but the intensity in his body nearly glowed. It occurred to me that I didn't know what his talents were, if any. There were certainly plain humans in the FBI, but most of the agents at Rizzoli's level had some abilities.

The man cleared his throat again and snuffled, opening his mouth as though to speak. Now we were getting somewhere. I felt the tension dry up the rest of my tears.

Unfortunately, my change in mood also sobered the other two men. That wasn't good, because the man in black abruptly went stony faced again, realizing he'd already said too much. He wiped his eyes angrily, probably wondering how the agent had caused him to speak. But the agent was still looking confused. I'd imagine FBI agents don't often sob in front of prisoners.

"You've got to start crying again. It was working." Rizzoli's voice was an urgent hiss.

I couldn't help but let out a frustrated sound and throw up my hands a tiny bit before whispering, "I don't know how. The first time was a fluke. I swear."

He turned his head and gave me an incredulous look. "Oh, please. Your life has *sucked,* Graves. I'm amazed every day I find out you're not curled up in a fetal position in the corner with a gun to your head. If you don't have reason to cry, nobody does."

The sad part was, he was right. And yes, if I focused on all the bad crap that had happened during my life, I apparently could turn the men in the room into basket cases. "But do you really want him in a mood to hold a gun to his head? We don't know if he can activate the curse without help."

Rizzoli noticed I didn't deny the occasional desire to curl up in a corner with firearms and reached out to squeeze my shoulder gently.

But I didn't need sympathy. My life was my life and I owned it. My mouth opened to tell him just that when the temperature in the room suddenly dropped like a rock.

Um . . . that wasn't good.

The two-way mirror frosted so suddenly that the room beyond all but disappeared. I should have been more careful than to evoke the memory of my little sister. Ivy might have died young, but she hadn't moved on to a better place. She'd decided to remain here, on earth, hanging around her big sister. I didn't know why, but I had a good idea.

"What the hell is wrong with the air-conditioning?" The annoyed New Jersey Italian started to head toward the door when I held up a finger to stop him.

"It's not the building, Rizzoli. I think I accidentally invoked Ivy's spirit." The wind she raised in the room blew my hair until I had to pull strands from my mouth. "*Ivy!*" I hissed the word in frustration because she was out of control. Maybe it was because I'd been so emotional when I was staring at the picture, but she was in a full fury. The lights flickered wildly until they finally blew with a crack of frozen glass.

Rizzoli looked like he was totally out of his element and freaking out. His voice remained low, but it was gaining a frantic edge. "Do something, Graves. If she scares the prisoner, this whole place could become the new Ground Zero."

Um. I hadn't even considered that possibility, but he was right. Using the dead, ghosts, zombies, or vampires to scare prisoners into confessions was Torture 101.

I looked up into the dark, bitter wind that stung my cheeks. The only light was what was coming under the door and the faint glow from the next room. Yelling would only get Ivy more agitated, so I decided to go the opposite way. I forced my face into a smile that belied my worry and let out a little laugh. "You need to calm down, sweetie. See? I'm fine. Nothing wrong. I was just playing around. You don't have to be worried. It's all good."

But she would have none of it. One of the problems with spirits is that they know things that are . . . well, *beyond* what the rest of us poor humans do. Ivy might not be able to read minds, but she had a good idea of where the source of my worry was. The wind that was my younger sister began to spin through the room and then slammed through the glass so fast I couldn't stop her.

A rumble underfoot made Rizzoli grab my arm and yank me under a heavy metal table. "Get down! He's going to blow!"

The drop to the ground did nothing good to my throbbing leg, but I crouched and covered my head like people did in the films of old air-raid drills I'd seen in grade school. Damn. This wasn't how I'd planned to spend my last few minutes on earth.

8

What happened next was totally unexpected. Instead of fire and pain and a massive explosion, there was a warm, gentle breeze and silence and the trembling under my feet eased to a gentle sway. I slowly lowered my arms and looked at Rizzoli. He stared back at me, obviously baffled. Crawling out from under the steel table was a slow process because my calf muscles weren't cooperating and I was watching the ceiling for falling objects. "Was that a quake or an exploding prisoner?"

Rizzoli's brow was furrowed in confusion just before he frowned. "Neither. I've been inside this building during a quake. The floor reacts different. And he's still there." He stepped forward to the two-way mirror and used his jacketed elbow to wipe away some of the dripping fog on the glass.

The room was unchanged, except that both men were staring up at a spot near the ceiling that was swirling with multiple colors. I'd been thinking it had been Ivy in the room with us, because it's nearly always Ivy who comes when I'm upset. But unless she'd discovered some interesting new tricks, this wasn't her. Since my sister was only eight when she died, she didn't learn very well and as a ghost, she isn't very powerful.

This entity reminded me more of Vicki, who had been as powerful a ghost as she had been a clairvoyant. She not only retained her mind, she also could communicate by writing on glass with frost. But Vicki had well and truly gone to a better place. She'd sacrificed herself to close the demon dimension, and holy men from every faith had assured me it would send her straight to the greatest possible reward.

But they'd also said she couldn't have been that powerful to begin with, so what did they know? There was only one way to find out.

"Vicki? Is that you?"

If it was her, she'd recognize my voice. The swirling colors stopped, and if a ball of energy can turn, it did. A loud popping sound made me step back from the glass. Windows and mirrors had often made that sound when Vicki wrote on them, because of the ambient temperature difference between room heat and frost cold enough to write. But these pops actually made the *glass* crack. And then letters appeared. Just two.

No.

That made me frown and Rizzoli turned to stare at me, possibly confused at my question, or at my expression.

"Then, what *is* your name?"

No.

That nearly made me laugh, because it was so absurd. I couldn't tell if the spirit was being obstinate or if that was the only word it knew. It was powerful, to be sure, but maybe not so bright.

Think again, Celia, appeared in the glass, and with a sharp crack loud enough to make me cover my ears, the whole window erupted into a pattern of breaks that should have made it fall out of its frame. But the windowpane held and the words remained.

My jaw dropped, literally. Even Vicki couldn't read minds and couldn't do that to glass. What the hell was this thing?

"What does that mean?" Rizzoli had his head cocked, staring at the words like that dog in the old gramophone ads. "What are you supposed to think about?"

I didn't know, so all I could do was shake my head.

I could see a dozen tiny versions of the prisoner through the wall of cracks, all of them staring at the mirror. For him, the words I was reading must be backward, so I'm sure he was struggling with *aileC ,niaga knihT*. No doubt he thought it was some strange sort of code. Or heck, maybe it meant something in his language. I wasn't quite sure what alphabet he used.

I was still pretty sure that the prisoner couldn't see inside this room even though his attention was certainly focused on the mirror. But then he let out a yelp and jerked his hands off the table. The other FBI agent did, too. Rizzoli and I both moved closer to the window to see what was up.

The cheap metal table in the lower room was smoking and a growing circle of glowing red had appeared on the surface. Black letters seemed to rise from within the molten tabletop.

Tell them or you will learn pain.

The prisoner huddled in a corner, holding a burned hand to his chest. He was clutching an object on a chain and muttering furiously with wide eyes. His gaze was locked on the words that had risen from the table altogether and now hovered in the air for all to see. The man was obviously terrified. I mean, I certainly was. I could see his pulse increasing in his neck and knew that if I was in the same room as him, he would smell of fear. I couldn't figure out why he hadn't exploded yet.

I found myself whispering in totally serious tones. "I'm not doing this. If you're not doing this, are we going to be held responsible? Does the Geneva Convention even cover sentient non-corporeal beings?"

Rizzoli's voice was likewise serious. "I don't think Hell was a signatory."

A low chuckle caught me unaware because it both came through the speaker from the other room and seemed to echo from behind me. The agent in the room did what he was supposed to do. He turned toward the entity overhead and raised his gun, backing around the superheated table to protect the prisoner. The agent tossed down several charm disks and barriers rose in a semicircle that separated their corner from the rest of the room. His sidearm was probably loaded with a similar combination of bullets to mine. The FBI is where I'd gotten the idea. I was certain he could fire through the barrier. But I had no idea if the entity couldn't fire right through in return.

"Who are you?" I asked with bravado, like it would answer. It had already refused once. "What do you want?"

The voice that came was low and male and had a strength that a ghost simply shouldn't have. There are other . . . beings that can appear without form, but they tend to be either really good or really evil. "You want answers but are hampered by . . . morals. I'm not."

Well, okay then. The burning table sort of gave it away, but that certainly removed the last question. If it had a name, I didn't want to know it now. "I don't want the help of the demonic. I banished your kind because I want nothing to do with you and yours." I knew not every single demonic entity had been banished when the rift collapsed. A number of people had already been possessed by then and not all of them had been found. But if one was actually following me . . . well, that was a worry. A big one. "Please leave now."

Another laugh made the small hairs rise on the back of my neck. "I'm nowhere close to the demonic, Celia. But since you asked nicely . . . I'll leave. For now."

The demonic are well known to lie, so I just rolled my eyes and promised myself I'd be speaking with more than one expert in exorcism if I made it out of here today. I've already been exorcised twice, once to rid me of the taint from the vampire and the second to clear me of a link to a greater demon. But the death curse keeps the lines annoyingly open.

The sparkling ball of energy near the ceiling flickered and began to slide down the wall. When it reached about chest height, it floated toward the corner where the FBI agent stood behind the barrier, keeping his gun trained on the entity. The energy stopped outside the barrier, right where the prisoner was huddled. The captive held the object on the chain toward the sparkling ball as the barrier flared in response.

The agent fired once. His bullet went right through the entity and splattered against the wall. Clear liquid rolled down the cream-colored paint. If it was holy water it had no effect. That was confusing. More disturbing still was that the flickering and flaring of the magic barrier had finally ceased and words appeared—just like on the window and the table.

Only the truth can set you free.

Then the entity disappeared, leaving behind a smoking table, a ruined mirror, and two men huddled under a completely worthless magic barrier—because really, if a ghost . . . even a demonic one, could carve a message right onto the magic, it's useless.

Of course, that phrase wasn't something generally associated with imps and demons. Just the opposite, in fact. And add in the holy water pooling on the floor. Except there were the smoking table and flaming threats of pain to consider.

"Can we pretend you didn't come to my house and start this day over?"

Rizzoli seemed a little stunned by what had just happened and let out a slow breath. "I will if you will."

I nodded. "While we're pretending, can I just be an ordinary human again?"

He chuckled and started walking toward the door and the promise of light and fresh air, both of which sounded really good to me at this point. "Sorry, Graves. My imagination's not that good. I'm pretty sure you were never ordinary."

I gave a snort of laughter and followed him through a maze of corridors that led to the outer doors. We got as far as the front sidewalk when his phone rang. The prisoner had started to talk again and they needed him upstairs.

I followed, even though I was fully expecting he was going to tell me to find a cab and go home. But he didn't.

Apparently, the call had told him where to go, because he turned left when I turned right and I had to stop short to turn back. The new room was even smaller . . . just big enough for the two of us and the Asian agent who was now sitting at a recording studio control board.

"What do we have so far, Yao?" Okay, then. He was Chinese. I admit I'm not good at recognizing the facial differences in that area of the world. I need to work on that.

Yao didn't turn his head to look at Rizzoli. He kept watching the scene unfolding behind the two-way mirror while he spoke. "The sketch artist is still with him."

I looked through the window and it seemed like nothing was happening. The man in black was just staring at the petite white-haired woman. But both of her hands were moving fast across a pad on the table. I realized she was holding a pen in one hand and a pencil in the other. As I watched, an image began to appear on the page.

I must have looked confused, because Rizzoli leaned closer. "She's a telepath. We don't want to risk any more chances of blowing the guy up. All he has to do is think about his boss and Kristi will draw."

My smile was automatic. "But she's not just drawing, is she?" Unless the guy was unusually adept at shielding, I was betting the FBI telepath was gathering as much information about the man, his boss, and the plan as possible.

Rizzoli's grin was answer enough. "We'll know for sure soon."

Kristi's hands stopped moving and I expected that she was just going to stand up and walk out. I'd seen it before with telepaths. They're not as social as you'd imagine. They often *think* they're social, but none of it is verbal and they confuse the two inputs. But the Feds must train them better, because she tipped her head and stared at him with sympathy. "Do you want to tell me about it? You think she's playing with fire, don't you, Gavrail?"

My brow furrowed and it matched the other two men in the room. But the man in the room with Kristi simply sighed and shook his head. "She is . . . how you say in this country? Foolish prideful—she believes she is more than she is."

"Egotistical?"

That made Gavrail put his hands on the table and tap fingers against the metal surface. "Yes. And no. She has power, but it is false power. And she makes poor choices of the use of the magic. Hurting children is bad, against the Maker's will. They are innocents, but she considers them less than fleas. It is not womanly, not right."

Part of that perked Kristi's interest just like it did mine. "Why is it false power?"

Now Gavrail was less confident. "I don't know. It . . . *feels* false. I don't know, but I fear her. She does not have the caution born of training."

Interesting. I poked Rizzoli in the arm. "Does she have an earpiece in? Could she ask him what makes him think she doesn't have training? I'm wondering if it's the same caster I encountered."

Yao looked up and back. Rizzoli nodded. Yao asked and even though Kristi gave no indication, I could tell she heard. She tapped the picture significantly and asked a leading question. "Did you see her do something . . . foolish prideful that a witch shouldn't do? Something that made you not want to work for her?"

The disgust on his face was immediate. "She forced an old man to put petrol in her car. Mocked him while she moved his arms this way and that. He was stooped and crippled, yet she smiled as he cried out. I have known sorcerers who are cruel, but they are not vicious without cause, for they know magic returns evil greater than it was sent. They do not risk foolish pride. She—" He spat on the floor. "That one knows no better."

"I agree she is foolish about this spell. Can you tell me why you fear it so? What will it do to the children? Is it without a cure?"

Gavrail was so incensed about the old man that he started to speak. "It is a disease that—"

He stopped speaking suddenly and his eyes widened until they were bulging. Hands went to his throat as though trying to remove a rope that had tightened. I felt familiar magic slice through the very walls and Kristi was forced to put her hands to her temples with a sharp cry. For a long moment, nothing happened. But then Kristi stood up and walked toward Gavrail. Her hands raised and her nails turned inward. Gavrail didn't try to stop her. He just stared at her, fear plain on his face.

But what I couldn't understand was why Rizzoli and Yao were just sitting there. Were they waiting for something actionable? Personally, I like to *prevent* events, not wait for a crime to happen. That's what bodyguards do.

I bolted from the room because I fully understood what Kristi was going through. At least it eased some guilt in me. After all, if a trained telepath was open to this woman, false magic or not, I'd done pretty good to get out alive. I was about to kick down the door to the interview room when Rizzoli grabbed my arm and pulled me off-balance. I jerked away and pushed him backward against the wall. He hit with a loud thump and a picture rattled on its hook a dozen feet away. "Don't try to stop me, Rizzoli. She's going to kill him if we don't stop her. You don't know how powerful this witch is."

Rizzoli went very still and spoke softly enough that I had to stop moving just to hear him. "But we *want* to know. We won't let Gavrail die, but we have to know if Kristi can fight off the influence. This is our spell containment room. We have magical sensors all over, tracking the magic back to the source. We can shut down the room if we have to—shield it to where even a level nine couldn't get through. We won't let it go too far. Just walk away, Graves. Don't screw this up. I don't want to have to arrest you or, worse, shoot you."

I didn't like it. Not at all. I didn't doubt Rizzoli had a plan, or at least someone above him did. But I didn't want to be party to someone dying, even if he wasn't precisely innocent and I was only a party by being in the building. I crossed my arms over my chest and stared at the door. Technically, I didn't work for the Feds, which meant they could very well arrest me.

Or shoot me.

Damn it.

"If this goes badly, we're done. Understand?" I turned and glared daggers at Rizzoli. "Done. I will hate you forever."

His face went very still. "If this goes badly, I probably won't be around to hate."

I didn't want to think Rizzoli would go over the line. He's a good man. I really believe that. And I was exhausted. Diving under the table hadn't done either my head or my leg a bit of good. So despite my misgivings, I went.

9

I
t's really sad when you're completely exhausted
and it isn't even eleven o'clock in the morning. I
wanted nothing more than to curl up in a little ball
and go to sleep. No, scratch that, not sleep. Not when
I was liable to end up God knew where with no memory of how I got there. So instead of going home, I had
the cabbie drop me off at the office. I needed to make
a few calls, do some research into the entity, maybe ar-
range another exorcism. You know, the usual.

My office is on the third floor of the only big old
Victorian mansion downtown. It's a registered historic
landmark, perfectly tended, and is worth a not-so-
small fortune. I own it, a fact that simultaneously
thrills and scares the crap out of me every time I see
the place. I try not to worry about things like property
taxes and maintenance fees. But of course I do. Vicki's
mother, mega–movie star Cassandra Meadows, may
have decided to drop her suit contesting Vicki's will,
but I really did want to give all of the cash portion of
my inheritance to the special school being set up in my
sister's name. My accountant, on the other hand, wants

me to keep at least 10 percent for expenses and emergencies. I was still waffling on that.

I paid the cabbie, my mind going over who I should call first. Once upon a time it would have been an easy decision. When in doubt, call Warren Landingham. Warren, "El Jefe," is the head of Paranormal Studies at the university where I got my degree. He'd been a father figure to me, and a close friend. But both he and his son had betrayed me. Granted it was to save Warren's daughter, Emma. And yes, Emma is second only to Dawna as my best friend, but it was still a betrayal. And try as I might I couldn't just forgive and forget. I don't trust easily, but I'd trusted them both. Which made the pain that much worse.

I could call Dr. Sloan. Aaron Sloan is a grizzled old guy with wiry white hair and brows that bristle over the top of his Coke-bottle glasses. He's as brilliant in his own way as El Jefe. But while Warren is more of a generalist, and plays university politics, Aaron focuses almost exclusively on curses and the demonic. If he doesn't know the answer, he knows who does, or can find out.

He'd given me a textbook the last time I'd been to his office—*Man's Experience of the Divine*—and I never had taken the time to read it. Now might be the time to start. It would be embarrassing to call him and find out I had had the answer sitting on the shelf in my office.

"Morning, Celia. Are you okay?" Dawna's face had a thoughtful and worried expression. I noticed she didn't say I looked bad again. Smart girl. It's just one of the reasons I like her so well.

"Rizzoli dragged me to the FBI offices to help interrogate a witness. I'm feeling a little twitchy. What do we have for food here?" "Twitchy" was our private code for the vamp trying to get the best of me. At first after the attack I'd had to eat every four hours. Which was a real nuisance—particularly since I couldn't eat any solids at all. Thankfully, things have settled down a bit. If I make sure to take my liquid vitamins, and have lots of protein via au jus or broth I can eat three times a day. Unless I'm stressed. Today was shaping up to be very stressful.

She pursed perfect mauve-tinted lips. "Hmm . . . bad morning interrogations probably call for a big cup of meat broth and some chocolate Ensure. Or . . . ooh! Wait. I have some *phở*. We could strain it to keep the noodles and other stuff out. We could use the blender, but that's almost sacrilege."

My smile was automatic. No, it wasn't a traditional breakfast, but Grandma Long's *phở*, a Vietnamese noodle soup, was legendary.

"Thanks! Are you sure? I don't want to steal your lunch."

The phone started to beep and she reached for the handset. "You won't. You drink the broth. I'll eat the meat and noodles. It's all good."

It made perfect sense and I got to the small office kitchen in record time. We have a full-sized refrigerator because everyone in the building works really weird hours and needs to have food available around the clock. The moment I opened the door, the scent of the *phở* erupted into my nose from beneath the plastic cover on the bowl. My fingers were tapping on the counter as the microwave heated the soup, until it occurred to me that I needed to find a secondary container and some way to strain the noodles. Three plastic forks and a tumbler later and I was ready.

I was trying to manage the forks, hot bowl, and tumbler when the bowl started to slip. Dawna was there just in time to grab the pot holder and steady the bowl before the whole mess wound up down the drain. "Got it. Go ahead."

The third hand was just what I needed and I managed to get most of the broth from the bowl into the glass. It was worth the fuss. The beef broth and spices wowed my bland-stricken tongue. I could only hope it wouldn't be too much for my stomach. But it would still be worth it. I nodded to my friend as she speared a forkful of noodles and twirled. "Amazing, as always. My compliments to your grandma. Did I ever thank her for the batch she made me after the attack?"

"Yep. Although I have to admit, she was horrified that you ran it through the blender. That's why I mentioned sacrilege."

"It was the only way I could get it down."

"I know." She ate another bite of noodles. Apparently she'd decided to join me for brunch. Since the phones were quiet, and Dottie was due in soon, I didn't see any reason for her not to.

"Speaking of your granny, how goes the building situation? Has she moved in yet?"

When Vicki died, she gifted some real estate to me, Dawna, and our friend Emma. I got my house, which was actually the beach house of the estate where Vicki used to live, plus the office building. Dawna got the apartment building she lived in and was now struggling with an extended family who all expected to live there for free. She shook her head wearily. "I turned over the whole mess to my brother. I mean, I don't really care whether people live there, but I have to at least pay the taxes and insurance on the place. I told Tal if he would manage the place and figure out reasonable rents for everyone, then *he* could live there for free."

I took the last sip of broth that was free of stray noodles. "Isn't he the one who worked for that big building management company in L.A.?"

She nodded. "That's why I picked him. He knows people who do janitorial and repairs and such. It's too big a job for just one person, but he delegates really well." One last noodle got sucked through her lips and then she rinsed out the bowl in the sink. "So anyway. Enough about me. Why's your life sucking today? What sort of interrogation could you be able to do?"

So it hadn't gotten past her. She was just giving me time to think and eat. "It's a mess, and I'm not sure I'm even allowed to talk about it."

"Bummer."

Ever one to change the subject, I looked out the doorway toward the front of the building. "I'm surprised the phones aren't ringing."

She shrugged. "I put the lines on hold when I eat or when I need a bathroom break. But sure, we can go back that way. Are you just here to pick up messages or are you going to actually, you know, work?" Her voice was teasing, but there was an edge of concern underneath. After a truly hellish couple of months, I'd taken a short holiday. But the mess at the school had turned it into a long holiday. Which I couldn't help, but really couldn't afford, either.

"Actually, I was going to do a little bit of research. Unless *you* might have some free time." I looked at her hopefully. "I've got a textbook on divine entities. I ran into something today that was non-corporeal, but intelligent." I paused and made sure I had her attention. "*Vicki* intelligent. Or maybe more."

"That's . . ." She let out a breath and didn't finish her sentence until she was back at her desk, the phones were off hold, and the book's cover was open. "Not good. Not good at all. I loved Vicki like a sister, but she was a major aberration in the spirit world. So you're thinking a demonic shade? There are still a few left out there. Hopefully just lesser demons, but still—"

I leaned on the corner of her desk, both for emphasis and to keep my balance. Damned leg. I shook my head in frustration. "Didn't feel very *lesser*. But he said he was most definitely not demonic."

She put a finger on the page to mark her place and looked up with wide eyes. "*He . . . said?* It could *speak?* Like out loud?"

My nod was emphatic. "And not just in my head. Three other people heard him. He wouldn't say his name, but he knew my name and responded verbally to comments I made in my head. The only manifestation was a swirly ball of energy, but I got the feeling he could probably do more if he'd wanted to. I'd planned to do it myself, but the more I think about it, the more afraid I am to open the book. What if there's something written there that . . . well, *attaches* to me?"

"Eww, that's ugly powerful. Okay, I'll start reading. What are you going to do?"

A small snort escaped me before I could stop it. "What do you think? Get some more protection charms. I think I need the industrial-strength variety. And I'm all out of boomers."

That perked Dawna up. "Are you going to Levy's? Could I go with?"

"To Levy's? Why would you want to go there?" I went there all the time because it was the best weapons shop in three counties. But Dawna? She didn't own much in the way of weapons.

"Isaac was tailoring something for me and called to say it's ready. So can I go?" She didn't expand on that, which was interesting.

Yeah, I'd love to have her along because we always have a great time together and we haven't been spending as much time around each other as we used to. It would also save me cab fare. "I was thinking about going right now. It's not officially your lunch hour. Ron will have a fit."

Dawna gave me a grin of pure delight. "Not a problem. Watch this." She picked up the handset and pressed two digits before turning on the speaker. "Ron?"

"Yes?" He sounded impatient and brusque—so pretty much normal.

"I need to go to lunch early and I'll probably be back late. I need to get some shopping done." Oh, man! That was just asking for a screaming match. Ron *hated* shopping. He felt it was a complete waste of time and had once harangued Dawna for being ten minutes late when she'd gone to pick up office supplies.

There was a long pause and I hovered over her desk, waiting to have to jump in and defend her. My jaw dropped when he responded: "That's fine. Just put a note on the door. I'll catch the phone until you get back."

Dawna looked far too self-satisfied when she answered. "Thanks, Ron. Be back soon." Oh, there was definitely a story there and I would know it before the end of the trip.

She made a quick stop in the bathroom to freshen up while I slathered sunscreen on every open piece of skin; then we hurried out to the lot and her trusty

Honda. I managed to wait until we were safely inside the car where nobody could hear me scream; I did. "Ahhh! What did you do with the real Ron? I don't want him suing me because you put some kind of spell on him."

She laughed long and loud until I finally joined her. God, it felt good to laugh, even if it was the nervous kind. She put the car in gear and let me stew for a minute while she pulled into traffic. "It's okay. I earned a little reward. I've been here since two."

"Two? A.M.? You're kidding me! Why in the world did you come in so early?"

She stifled a yawn as she pulled to a careful stop at the traffic light on the corner. She rolled down the window, savoring a breeze that was fresh, if cold. "He needed a notary. One of his clients had to fly to Europe and that tropical storm over Bermuda was worrying him. He wanted to sign his will before he boarded the plane. I told Ron he owed me . . . several." She lowered her sunglasses to the tip of her nose. "This is the first."

Hard to argue with that logic. I relaxed and rode, not even caring about the gulls circling above like tiny white vultures, until we pulled up to Levy's Custom Apparel. Isaac Levy is a good man and a good friend—we've known each other for years. His specialty is suit jackets tailored and spelled in such a way that you can carry an arsenal without any of it showing, but still having everything available at hand for a quick draw. His clothes are expensive as hell, but worth every penny.

Someone pulled out of a space just as we got there and Dawna managed to slip into the spot a hair's breadth quicker than a blonde in a Mercedes.

Thankfully, I had to take only a few wobbling steps to cross from the glare of the morning sun that made me squint and caused a sudden throbbing in my head into the relative darkness of the shop. The sudden shift from light to dark made my head pound even harder, although that didn't make any sense. Even before I blinked the tears from my eyes I knew Isaac Levy was in the shop, thanks to the scent of his signature cologne and the uneven footfalls caused by a bum knee.

Isaac Levy is one of those people you can't really forget once you meet them. The ring of wiry salt-and-pepper hair, the bushy eyebrows over piercing brown eyes, the bulbous nose—he's not really attractive, but he's intelligent, funny, and utterly unique. He's also an amazing magical technician. Besides the jackets he does artifact work. Charms, weapons, he's the best of the best. He's been married to the love of his life for umpteen years, having won her away from Morris Goldstein, a wealthy jeweler. Isaac promised her that if she'd give him a chance, he'd give her twice as much jewelry as Morris would. He's done his best to keep that promise. The woman practically clanks when she walks. Even the most overdecorated rapper would be jealous.

"Celia, Dawna. How are you lovely ladies?" Isaac reached and took my hand, bestowing a breath of kiss on the skin. Aww . . . how can you not love the guy? "Darlings, it's so good to see you." He gave us each a huge hug, then took a step back, looking me critically up and down.

"You need to eat more. And you're pale. Even for you." It was friendly scolding, but there was real concern beneath it.

"Actually, this is normal now," I said sadly. "The vampire thing."

He let out a small growl. "I'd hoped it would . . . well, get better."

"No. It's sort of permanent," I assured him. "But I'm okay. Just . . . pale." I turned to Dawna, who was looking around with wide eyes. I didn't really blame her. The place was like the TARDIS, bigger inside than out, and filled with the coolest things. But even I was impressed this time. There was another whole new section of the store with shelf upon shelf of gadgets and magical equipment, like crystals, crystal balls, and other magical foci.

But that wasn't where Dawna was staring. No, her eyes had locked on a set of glass cases dead in the center of the store. It was a brightly lit display of holy item jewelry for every religion I'd ever heard of, and a few more that I hadn't.

"Wow. You've made even more changes." I walked around the room with Isaac following at my heels, taking in every reaction to what I saw. I finally stopped back where I started, next to the wall-mounted display of charm disks.

He gave me a brilliant smile. "Do you like it? Ira Sachs decided to retire and made me an offer on the building. And this way Gilda and I can work together without stepping on each other's toes."

I nodded. The place looked great and I saw a lot of things I'd been lusting after online but hadn't had the chance to handle. I'm a tactile person. I need to see a charm or weapon, see if I can draw it or use it instinctively. I could see myself writing a big check today.

I looked around for Dawna. As I'd expected, she was busy looking at the jewelry counter. I still had my back to the door when I heard a voice behind me. "I thought I saw your car outside. You haven't been returning my calls, young lady." The light baritone was amused and was accompanied by a wave of powerful magic that made my skin tingle. I tried not to react but failed.

I answered without turning around and could feel him stepping closer as his magic slid across my bare skin as though I didn't have a stitch on. "What are you doing here, Creede?"

"Back to last names so soon?" The whisper of fine silk caressed my ear as he leaned against the wall next to me. He knew exactly what he did to me when he was close. "I thought we went to first names on our last date." I inhaled the scent of expensive cologne on clean skin and knew I was going to regret turning around, though I knew I had to.

"And who is this?" Isaac examined John closely, and I knew he could tell me more about the man from what he was and wasn't wearing and how he held himself than most detectives could after a full week of research.

I sighed and turned. "Isaac Levy, John Creede, owner and one of the founders of Miller and Creede. John, this is Isaac. He's a dear friend of mine, does all of my jackets, and most of my holsters and weaponry orders. He's the best in the business."

Isaac smiled even more broadly at the compliment, extending a chubby, ring-bedecked hand. After all, who in the business of security *hadn't* heard of M&C? They're the biggest and best in the business, and Creede's the primary reason for that.

Creede gave the proffered hand a firm shake. "I've always admired Celia's choice of equipment. I met your lovely wife on my last visit, but I've been wanting to meet you personally. You're a talented charm maker."

Isaac nodded in acknowledgment of the compliment.

Creede looked good, but then, he always did. His hair was a touch longer than last time I saw him. The golden curls made him look less severe. But the honey-colored eyes that were directly across from mine were still filled with amber fire that flickered and pulled at my stomach. It was intentional and he knew I knew. All I could do was either give in to the teasing or leave. Since I had shopping to do, I guessed I was in for some squirming.

I asked the obvious question, because in the circles Creede ran in, Levy's store was slumming. "And what brings you to this part of town?" Actually, he'd been in the store before, but Isaac hadn't been here. But as far as Isaac was concerned, nobody had been in until he spoke with them personally.

Creede dipped his head toward Isaac and raised the bag in his hand I hadn't seen until now. "I thought I might have some jackets tailored. I want to change where I carry some of my weapons without anyone noticing."

"Nobody does better work than Isaac."

"I know. That's why I'm here." He winked at me. "Well, part of why I'm here."

"Quality work takes time," Isaac warned.

"I don't mind. I've just noticed that the craftsmanship in Celia's equipment seems to be better than in mine. And I can't have that."

Isaac laughed.

"If you don't mind, I'll take a look around the place." John had wandered plenty last time he was here with me, but he was at least trying to be polite and give me some time alone with Isaac.

"Not at all. Make yourself at home. Celia and I have things to discuss." John wandered off happily. I, on the other hand, was left scrambling. Because, like his wife, what Isaac likes to discuss most are my marriage prospects, or lack thereof. Given a chance, and a gender switch, he'd be the world's biggest yenta. I needed a change of subject—fast.

"Isaac, do you have protection charms that will hold off demons?"

He leaned in and elbowed me lightly in the ribs, his eyes fixed squarely on Creede's nicely packaged backside. "Keep that one close and you won't have to worry about demons. He *glows* with magic."

"It's not like that, Isaac. It's just business." Actually it might be like that. Or not. I was never sure with Creede. When we both had time we would sometimes go out. But we almost never had time. He was, if anything, more of a workaholic than me; something I would never have believed possible.

And then there was Bruno.

He seemed to read my mind. "Let me guess. Bruno." The way he said the name held a world of disapproval.

Both Isaac and Gilda think Bruno did me wrong, and they're not inclined to forgive him for it. Still, Isaac is wise enough not to push . . . much.

"*Anyway*," I continued quickly, "I have a problem, and I'm hoping one of those boxes has the solution."

"Really?" He tilted his head to the side, in a gesture much like a curious bird. "Tell me about it."

I told him what had happened as simply as I could. During the explanation his expression grew serious, his eyes going nearly black and narrowing with suspicion. "Do you think it's part of that rift from last December?"

I shrugged. I frankly didn't know. "Could be. But this felt very different. I don't know if it's serious, but I want to be protected as best as possible."

"Anything that can slip in and out of Federal police barriers is serious, Celia. Let me look around. I have some new things in back that might work."

"Sure. I'll check out the jewelry."

His smile got a little wider and a *lot* more acquisitive. "Yes. You do that."

I joined Dawna at the counter. She was examining a delicate gold and garnet cross that I realized might be a nice present for Gran for her birthday.

Creede appeared at my side. "I have something I want you to see, over here." He put a firm, no-nonsense hand on my elbow and guided me away from Dawna. He wasn't normally that aggressive, so I went along without protest. It was likely he wanted to talk to me about something work related and didn't want to make a private issue public.

He led me to the medical magic section, one of my favorites. Spells could cure a host of ills, from simple cuts and scrapes to broken bones. I scanned the tiny identifying labels under each carefully packed box. "See anything here for demon possession?"

He pulled in a sharp breath. "Is that what's wrong with you?" A small growl followed the words and his voice lowered to a whisper. "Jesus, Celia, why didn't you *call* me and why are you just walking around the streets? C'mon, we need to get you to a priest."

His urgency startled me and I pulled back from his frantic grasp on my wrist. "Creede, slow down. I'm fine. I haven't been possessed—at least not in the past few months. Why are you so jumpy today?"

He let go of my arm and leaned back to stare at me quizzically like I'd grown a second head. His arms crossed over his chest and his chin lowered. "I got a call from Dr. Jean-Baptiste about a particular spell. I decided to check you out myself without you expecting me."

He got a call? So he was one of the "experts" the doctor mentioned? Jeez, I could have done that myself without dinging my credit card for a specialist.

Creede continued to talk. "The last time I saw you limp like that, you had a bleeding leg full of glass shards. You're squinting at the slightest hint of bright light. Your magical aura is all wrong. Something is definitely wrong with you. Talk to me, Celia, or you might find yourself trying out that body-binding charm I made for you while I take you to a hospital."

Okay, that was several levels above disturbing. "My magical . . . *what*? I don't have an aura."

He sighed. "Yes, you do. You're supernatural. Vampires have auras and so do sirens. You have a very distinct pattern that's not like anyone else's, and it's not the same today as it was the last time we had dinner together. There's something chewing at it. The colors around your head are scrambled and weird looking. Demonic possession would definitely do that."

Could a demonic *entity* have been housed inside the bomb casing? That would certainly have been dangerous enough to warrant a metal case. Crap. "That honestly never occurred to me. But I've had a headache I can't shake since the problem at the school. And my leg hurts every time I put weight on it."

That made his frown deepen and he looked around the room before pulling me to an ornate chair outside the dressing rooms in the back of the store—the store's grudging acknowledgment that not everybody likes to shop. "You've had the problem that long? He didn't give me your name for confidentiality reasons, or details other than asking about a spell affecting your memory." He snorted in amusement. "But seriously . . . how many half-vampire women with siren blood are there in town?" He stared at me for a long moment. "Sit."

I did. He straddled my legs so that he could look down on the top of my head. He began to whisper a spell that was too soft to make out and I felt power flow from his fingers, his very skin. It was like lowering myself into a heated pool. The sensation of pulsing magic made me warm and drowsy and very relaxed.

That is, until his hands hovered over my hair. The gesture was gentle, so soft it bordered on tickling. But my skin instantly began to tingle and the pleasurable shivers that ran down my spine were so hard that I had to curl my toes to stop myself from shuddering visibly.

But Creede wasn't trying to tease me. He was utterly serious as he traced his fingers over my hair without moving a single strand. A golden glow filled my vision until the room disappeared from view. My brain felt fuzzy and I couldn't seem to concentrate on anything other than the buzz of white noise in my ears. My insides were liquid with feelings I shouldn't be having in the middle of a weapons store. When he reached my shoulders he stopped and I flicked my gaze up to see his furrowed brow. The flames in his eyes grew until they were the eyes of a cat caught by a flashlight after dark. "There's a spell at work here. No question. It's not demonic, but it's amazingly complex. I understand why Dr. Jean-Baptiste couldn't unwind it." †

Crap. "What kind of spell?" I could hear the sudden fear in my voice and my heartbeat sped up to match my quickened breath.

Creede knelt in front of me, his hands still on my shoulders. His gaze locked with mine and the compassion in his eyes made me believe the words he spoke next. "I don't know. But I'm going to find out. I promise." His fingers squeezed just a bit. "All right?"

A promise from him could be put in the bank. "Okay. Thanks. What should I do until then?"

The corner of his mouth turned up a fraction and his hands moved until they were on either side of my face. "Quit trying to be superwoman. Ask for help when you're hurt. Remember that if *you're* hurt, it's serious."

It sounded so logical when he said it. But . . . "That's not so easy for me."

The quirk of a smile became an amused flash of teeth. "Tell me about it." Without any warning, he leaned forward and eased his lips against mine. I found myself being pulled into the kiss before I realized what was happening. His hand slid around my head, fingers twining in my hair, and my eyes closed automatically. I leaned into him before I realized I was doing it. My breath froze in my lungs and I couldn't seem to think past the dual sensations of magic and gentle pressure as he slowly moved his soft, full lips against mine. Warm breath on my cheek, magic sweet as candy, and the caress of his tongue made my knees weak and my stomach do flip-flops. His hand, lightly stroking my hair, sent electric shocks to my scalp. It was a good thing I was sitting down. My heart began pounding hard and my fingers buried themselves in the fabric of the armrests to keep from wrapping around him and pulling him into my lap. I wanted to ... a lot. The strength of the desire terrified me.

The kiss was probably over in seconds, though it felt like it lasted a week. He drew back slowly and I wound up suspended, eyes closed, enjoying the remaining pull of the magic that tugged at my stomach. A quick, nearly chaste kiss in the back of a store shouldn't really be that big a deal.

Right.

The fuzzy tingles ended as quickly as they'd begun, when he yanked several hairs right out of the top of my head, causing my startled, "Ow! Damn it, John! What was that for?" My hand went to the source of the pain and I rubbed while he held up his prize to the fluorescent lights overhead and inspected the strands.

"I need to do some testing in a proper casting circle to figure out the source of that spell, and since the major disturbance was around your head, I'll stand the best chance with hair."

His infectious smile made me glare at him and let out a small growl. "You could have just asked instead of grabbing it while you were kissing me. And you didn't have to do *that* to begin with."

I knew I was being petulant and couldn't seem to help it. He sighed. "I wasn't still kissing you, just for the record. I'd never hurt you like that. But I did have to. I like you calling me John."

There was something in his eyes that surprised me. I suddenly realized I'd hurt his feelings when I called him Creede. That was new. I was also startled to discover it bothered me. "I've called you Creede since we met. Last names are part of the business. It's nothing personal. You know that."

He nodded, but the intensity in his eyes didn't match the acknowledgment. "And it was fine while we *were* business. We're not anymore, Celia. This is personal. You know it just like I do."

We stared at each other for a long moment. I blinked first and lowered my gaze to stare at my feet. I didn't want to think about it, couldn't really deal with the reality of what he was saying. I wasn't lying to Isaac. I expect that Bruno and I will get back together.

Eventually.

But I also can't deny that John and I—yes, in my head, I did think of him as John—had an intense chemistry. I have to struggle not to throw myself at him whenever we're together. And he's impressed me, both as a mage and as a bodyguard. I trust him with my back, which I couldn't say about many people. He's intelligent, powerful, and magnetic. Trust and attraction—a heady combination.

Was it more than business? Yes. How much more? Thus far I hadn't been willing to find out. Relationships are complicated and I'm not very good at them. Why get involved just to discover it won't work?

"Can we keep it business for a little longer if I promise to call you John? I need to find out what's wrong with me before I think about anything serious."

He stared at me for a long moment and then dipped his head once. "I told you once that winning you would be a marathon, not a sprint. Today just proves that. Deal. You stock up on any charm you can find to stave off the demonic and I'll find out what this spell is. Tell Isaac I'll have to do the fitting another time. I've got a few minutes before a meeting this afternoon, and then I have to go out of town for a day or so. But I'll get back to you on this tomorrow at the latest. You find anything on the wall to stave off the demonic and *use* them."

That made me frown. "You just said it *wasn't* demonic."

"That's true. But the spell could have opened you to a random event. I'd recommend as many aura protection items you can afford and maybe a *Clear Mind* charm or two."

Oh. Yeah, that made sense. And hey, if I was lucky they might stave off the sleepwalking. Maybe. But it made me nervous, too. I don't like being vulnerable and he'd just told me I was. "You think you can figure out how to fix the spell, right? So it shouldn't be a big deal."

His face became the poster child for intensity. "I *will* fix the spell. I'll go to my workshop and start a casting to break down the elements of the spell. That can work by itself even while I'm out of town. I'll have to move around a few appointments, but I can manage it. Expect a counterspell done by dinnertime. Keep your cell handy. You might have to come to me for the working when I figure it out."

He sounded suddenly so much like Bruno it made me smile. They were very competitive and talented enough that they felt that nothing should be beyond fixing. And they'd never admit that they couldn't unwind any sort of casting.

I stood up, put a hand on his arm, and met his flame-kissed eyes. "Thank you, John. Really. I don't want you to worry about me. Still, I think it's sweet. And I know this screws up your day. But you're making me feel a lot less scared about something I've been trying not to think about."

He let out a slow sigh and pulled back his hand just enough to interlace his fingers with mine. "I don't want to worry about you, either, Celia. But you live a life that makes it almost impossible not to. Now shoo. I'm going back to the office to clear my calendar and then to start to work on this. Get your charms and get somewhere safe until I call."

Sounded like a plan to me.

10

Safe **is** a relative term.

Dawna tossed me the keys on the way out to the car. "I know how much you hate being a passenger. Besides, I'm tired."

"Maybe you should take the rest of the day off."

"I would, but I have this important research project I need to work on." She gave me a tired smile as she climbed into the passenger seat. "I'll be fine. Really."

There was no point in arguing with her. Besides, I wasn't in the mood. The snow had all melted away, leaving behind rich green sprouts and flowers only a little the worse for wear. I had a bag full of new goodies in the backseat, including lots of protection charms and the pretty garnet cross for Gran. I even bought a shiny new agate pinkie ring that promised aura protection. I'd already broken one *Clear Mind* charm and felt my thinking sharpen. I felt ready for anything—for at least the next twelve to twenty-four hours, or so promised the packaging.

Dawna was wearing several new bracelets with delicately braided runes in pretty patterns, plus her jacket, specially adapted by Isaac to hold several wooden stakes and a few holy-water squirt guns. I convinced her to splurge on the One Shot brand because they're reliable in a crisis. There's no beating that, even though they're twice the cost of most of the alternatives.

I guess I hadn't realized how much she was still struggling with the fact that she'd been attacked by a vampire. Lilith had been an ancient bat, so powerful she qualified as a full-fledged demon. She wanted me and had used Dawna to get information.

I was amazed she was still sane.

It's significant and worrying that she's never talked to me directly about any of this. Her therapist talks to my therapist who talks to me. It's hard to get much information that way because it's constantly filtered under the guise of "the best interests of the patient." But I knew that Lilith had made Dawna a human servant and when the vampire died, she'd felt it to her very core. Maybe it was finally time to break the ice about that night.

"Gorgeous jacket. Isaac does good work." The cherry red blazer was one Dawna'd had for a year or so, a designer original we'd picked up at an outlet store for a song. It still looked the same to the casual eye. But my eye wasn't casual. "Just at a glance, I'd say he gave you some room under the arms for extra stakes or knives and flared the back so you could draw the guns. Anything else?"

She smiled and flipped up the collar to reveal a rosary attached to the fabric with Velcro. Cute. "Added backup in case there are two."

I nodded and watched the traffic while I tried to figure out how to ask my next question. "Have there been occasions lately that would call for added backup?"

There was silence in the seat next to me for so long that I finally looked over at her when I could spare a glance. Her lips were tight together and her eyes stared at nothing while tears rolled down her cheeks.

"Dawna?"

I could smell her pain, could hear it in her voice. "Last week I decided I wanted a grilled cheese sandwich for supper from that new little restaurant down the street. They use three different cheeses and you can pick your bread. You know the one?"

I did, so I nodded.

"It was dark by the time I left because I got caught up in a magazine article. I didn't think much about it. I've been doing better about being alone at night. I was almost back to my car when I heard a voice whisper from a doorway. It said, *You should have died with her.* It took a minute to sink in, y'know? But then I heard it again, from way up high when there was nothing high around to perch on. It scared me, Celia. It felt like I was being stalked. It . . . made me remember . . . and—" She couldn't go on. I couldn't pull over on the freeway to give her a hug. So I reached across the car and put a comforting hand on the back of her neck.

I took a deep breath and let it out slow. Stalking and scary. I knew all about both. "Will the blazer make you feel safe?"

She nodded. "It does already."

"So Isaac taught you how to use the stakes?" It was a loaded question and maybe it was evident in my voice. Because Isaac doesn't do classes.

She shrugged and sounded confused. "They're stakes. What's to learn?"

I winced internally but only let her see my nod. "Do me a favor. Hit my arm. Really punch it."

She frowned but obeyed. I barely felt the tap. I put on the blinker to turn into the office parking lot. "Again. Really put your shoulder into it."

Dawna shrugged and punched again. She hit me with what I think she believed was force, because she wound up grimacing and shaking her hand like it hurt. "Damn, girlfriend. Your bicep is like a *rock*. There isn't enough room in here to budge it."

I parked the car and turned in my seat so I could watch her face. "And that's just plain muscle. Not bone. Now imagine trying to push those two-inch-wide stakes under your arm through to the other side of my arm with a single blow, with the same amount of working space. Trust me. You would barely have made it through the skin."

What I was trying to tell her finally sank in and the fear returned in a wash that paled her skin. "But I thought—"

I touched her arm. "Everybody does. It's okay. Really. People buy the stakes but have no idea what to do with them. You might get lucky and wound a bat and make it run just from the smell of the wood, but if you really want to protect yourself, you have to learn how to actually use them." It was obvious this was really important to her. It might have been a suggestion from her therapist that she get some protection to ease her mind. "If you want to learn how, I'd be happy to teach you."

Her face brightened. "Would you? Really? That would be . . . well, *amazing*!"

She meant it, which sort of surprised me. It could mean that she really didn't have a grasp of what I was offering. Still, she was my best friend. I'd do everything in my power to make sure she felt confident to handle bats. If she was right and some vampire had targeted her because they thought she'd betrayed Lilith . . . well, that was a whole new ball game. "Come by my house tonight around eight and bring whatever you want to learn more about, including those charm disks. You need to see what they do in controlled circumstances."

"Tonight? Couldn't we do it now?"

It made me laugh as I was unbuckling my seat belt. "Well, *you* need to get back to the office and *I* need to get over to the college. I need to talk to Dr. Sloan about the entity at the FBI office. I'd hoped to sound like I'd at least read his book, but I'll just have to own up to not having done my 'homework.'" I gave a rueful grin. "But oh *hell,* it's Friday afternoon."

"No classes?"

"No classes. *And* I don't have my car. Crap."

Dawna looked at the building and it was obvious she didn't want to go back inside. She was probably noticing that there were more cars than usual in the lot. Someone had even parked in my reserved spot, so I'd had to take the last free space. I've never understood that tendency of people to ignore signs and bright yellow letters against black pavement. But they do, and then look surprised when you confront them. "Is it two o'clock?" Her voice sounded annoyed, bordering on bitter.

I glanced at my watch. "Quarter 'til."

Her nose wrinkled. "It's the French settlement conference. Big, angry family who are fighting over Mommy's million-dollar estate. That'll be a pleasant meeting, I'm sure. It sure won't be quiet. I didn't sign on to this job to be a combination nanny and bouncer."

I didn't bite on that bait, because in my mind, that's pretty much what a receptionist is. And I know Dawna knows that. She's said it herself more than once. "You're just cranky because you've been up too long."

"You're probably right." She climbed out of the car. I made a motion to toss back her keys, but she stopped me with a gesture. "I've got a date tonight anyway. I'd have canceled for the lessons, but I'd rather not. You're going to need it to get home. I can pick it up later."

"You sure?"

"Yeah. No problema." She pasted a smile on her face and started across the lot. I was right behind her for the first couple of steps, but then my cell rang. When she paused, as if to wait, I waved her on. It sounded like they really needed her in there.

I pressed the button, answering, "Graves."

"Take the job!" I couldn't put a name to the panicked voice on the other end of the line, but it sounded familiar. It wasn't someone I spoke to regularly, but I'd spoken to him before, and recently.

"You have to take the job," he pleaded. "You *have* to. Her psychic told her that she had to get you out of the way if this was going to work. She won't kill you if you just leave."

"Who is this? What job?" I asked, but I had a pretty good idea about the last part.

"It wasn't supposed to be like this. Sanchez is dead. Marjorie's in the hospital. I don't want anything bad to happen to you, too." He was sobbing, now. "Please. Just take the job." He hung up before I could say anything else.

I was cold, and it had nothing to do with the temperature outdoors. *Sanchez is dead. Marjorie is in the hospital.* The only Sanchez I'd run into lately was the principal at Abe Lincoln, and Marjorie was the name of the secretary I'd given the business card with my cell number to. The caller could have been Jamisyn. Or maybe the vice principal . . . what was his name anyway? But I was betting on Jamisyn. We'd talked, and he actually had seemed to like me.

I stepped up on the porch intending to hurry up to my office and do a little computer search. The only job I've refused lately was MagnaChem. But what would a grade-school security guard have to do with a drug manufacturer?

The voices inside the office became audible before I'd taken a dozen steps from the car, and the short hairs on the back of my neck began to rise. Because Dawna was right. This wasn't going to be a quiet meeting. One of the voices was newly familiar to me. I'd heard it a week earlier, when it was trying to convince me to set off a bomb.

"I really feel it will be best if you listen to me." I felt that voice course through my veins, felt my body react to it the way it had in the school basement. My hand automatically went for my Colt and I pulled it back with effort. There were too many people in the office; I didn't want to add a gun into the mix. Instead, I pulled a couple of very particular charms out of my jacket and palmed them as I walked in the building.

Dawna didn't seem to notice me. She was more concerned with the obvious issues, more talking to herself than me. "I'd better get on the phone to the cops. I'd bet good money there's going to be trouble."

Yeah. Me, too.

"Mom told me I'd get enough to have a house with a pool! I have bursitis, Jill!" A heavyset man with a scraggly beard was screaming into the face of a woman with blonde hair. "So just back off!"

"Oh, for God's sake, Remmy. What are you smoking? She said you *needed* a pool, not that she'd buy you one. I was there . . . remember?"

Dawna broke in with a bright smile. "Excuse me, everyone?" They all turned to her cheery but professional voice. "We're about ready to get started. Ron is just finishing up a call, but the conference room is available if everyone's here. Is anyone missing?"

They all looked around them and shrugged. "No, that's all of us." It made me frown, because I could swear I'd heard her voice.

Of course, Ron wasn't the only other tenant in the building. While Dawna was moving the people into the big conference room, I sprinted up to the third floor. Well, tried to sprint. My bum calf just about gave out halfway and I had to lean hard on the railing the rest of the way.

Damn it. I really hoped Creede . . . *John* or one of the doctors figured out something soon. It was getting worse, I could tell. And just the thought of that panicked voice on the line: *Sanchez is dead. Marjorie's in the hospital.* I shuddered. Rizzoli had said the adults were falling like flies.

I hadn't . . . yet. I just wanted to keep it that way.

I went across the hall to my own office, just to see if anyone had made it through the magical wards I keep around it for protection. Nothing. I put my palm on the biometric plate and pressed *57, which would tell me who the last person to access it was. After two flashes, it read: *Profile 1.* That was me.

Dawna was back at her desk when I came down the stairs. I was confused and put the charms back in my pocket while she cocked her head and stared at me. "You look odd. Everything okay?"

I started to say I was fine, but the truth was, I wasn't. I tried to speak casually. "Hey, when we got out of the car, weren't there two women talking in here?"

She was looking at her computer screen and didn't hear me at first. She mumbled an, "Uh-huh. Why?"

I didn't answer, just stared at her with raised brows until she finally looked at me, a quizzical look on her face. "Yeah, actually there *were*. So—"

I nodded, feeling suddenly pissed at myself. "So where'd the second one go? Was there anyone in Ron's office?"

She shook her head. "Oh, hey! What about the security log? Didn't Dottie tell us there was a log we could look at to see who's come and gone in the building?"

Yes, there was, and I remembered her telling us. "Call her. Ask her how to find it. Once you have it, print me out a copy. I'm going to go to the college and ask around about witches who can disable magical shields without anyone noticing. Because I would swear our shield was in place and no way should a person with evil intent have been able to get through."

She nodded and reached for the phone. I paid special attention to the shield around the office when I left. It felt absolutely normal, but unless the witch flew out a window either she slipped out past us during the screaming match or . . . she was still there. I began to make a careful check of the possible entrances, including the back door, off the kitchen. It was locked and can only be locked from the inside. Then I went around to the front, looking for any footprints in the soft dirt underneath the windows. We keep the dirt loose just for that reason. With attorneys, bail bondsmen, and bodyguards in the building, we nearly always have enemies.

Then I remembered something that might explain the mystery. Bruno had once cast an illusion spell on himself so strong that six people in a room had believed him to be a potted rubber tree. Another powerful mage in the room had ratted him out.

I'm not a witch and I knew I was dealing with a powerful one. So I wanted to be very certain of my facts before I simply left my friend . . . and Ron . . . to the witch. Even he deserved better than that. I hurried back inside.

"Dottie's line was busy. What are you—" Dawna stopped speaking when I put a finger to my lips. I made motions for a pen and paper. Dawna understands about being bugged, so she just nodded and handed me a yellow legal pad and pen.

Turn on the perimeter, I wrote, and held the pad so she could see. She raised her brows and leaned back in her chair, obviously worried. The perimeter was added to our security system after a mage hacked past our prior system to plant listening devices. The perimeter locks down the building and sends a signal to the police. A fine powder is then released through the venting system. Invisible to the eye and completely odorless and tasteless, it luminesces under black light so that anything in the building when the button is pushed gets marked. It will wash off eventually, but not before the cops arrive. Anyone who tries to leave without permission catches the second marker, which is magical. I don't really understand the metaphysics of it, but in addition to itching like poison ivy, I guess it "flavors" your next few spells, and it flashes like a neon sign to other mages.

You sure? Dawna wrote back, and I nodded. She pressed the button on the floor near her foot—each of the leaseholders has one in their office in case nobody's at the front desk. There was no outward indication that anything happened, and even though I was expecting it I couldn't feel or sense the dust or any sort of magic.

But we have a special black light we use on driver's licenses to be sure they're not fake and Dawna turned it on. Sure enough, the tops of her fingers had a pale orange tinge that couldn't be from anything else.

I was looking around the room to see if anything of sufficient mass to be a person was out of place or new. It was like looking at one of those "hidden object" computer games.

My cell phone rang, and when I picked it up to look at the screen, it was Rizzoli. Crap. I wanted to take the call, but I didn't want any unintended listeners eavesdropping on us. I ignored the ringing. I could call back once I had verified nobody was in the building and had gotten everyone out. After four rings, it went to voice mail.

Then it rang again. Rizzoli, a second time. That wasn't like him. I'd have to take it. "Hello?" I spoke low and fast, hoping he'd get the hint I couldn't talk.

"What's happening, Graves? Do you need backup?"

That made me frown because how would he know? "Why do you ask?"

"The request got moved up the chain, owing to the new necklace I gave you. What do you need?"

Whoa. The FBI consultant badge Rizzoli gave me meant it wasn't the police who would respond to a perimeter alert anymore? It would be the FBI? I was pretty sure my jaw dropped, because Dawna looked at me oddly. But how could I tell him what the problem was without saying it out loud? "I'll text you."

"We . . . um, prefer voice for situations like this. Too easy for fakes."

Well, wasn't that a bitch? I let out a deep sigh and tried to figure out what to do.

Dawna wrote on the pad: *What's up?*

That's when it occurred to me. "I'll send you a JPEG. Stay tuned." I hung up on Rizzoli and started to write on the pad with my head down and my hand shielding the paper like a fifth grader trying to hide a note from the teacher.

Security breach at my office. Believed to be the witch who set off the bomb. Bring illusion specialists. I think she's still here. I'll do my best to keep her inside.

I took a flash photo of the page with my phone while it was still shielded, made sure it was legible, and sent it to Rizzoli with a few quick clicks. Then I folded the paper before even Dawna could see it. I mouthed the word *Rizzoli*, and her eyes widened. Then she nodded.

Then I said out loud, as casual as I could, "Pull up those decorator photos, will you? I'm thinking the stripes in the reception area are starting to fade where the sun hits. Maybe we need to try a different pattern."

By her expression, I'd asked for pictures of Bigfoot. But she did it. One of the reasons she's my best friend. We'd taken photos for the decorator so she could figure out, from miles away, what sort of wallpaper would work in the building and keep within the historical landmark guidelines that went with the plaque near the entrance. The other reason we took the photos was so that everything we took out of the building during the renovation could go back into the right rooms and their usual places.

A question was poised on Dawna's lips, but she didn't know whether to ask. I finally handed her the message I'd sent to Rizzoli. She put it on her lap, likewise hiding it from the room. After reading it her eyes went wide and she started looking around.

My cell phone binged to tell me I had a text message. I glanced at the screen. *Done.* I showed the screen to Dawna and she breathed a sigh of relief.

The voices in the conference room were getting louder and Ron was having to raise his voice to be heard over the din.

I wanted to start the search of the building while they were still busy. I still had two of the total bodybinding charms Cree . . . *John* had given me, along with a couple of confusion charms in case I had to fight. But with a witch powerful enough to duplicate Bruno's stunt, my only real hope was the ones John had done. Even Bruno had been impressed by them because he'd never been able to get one to work right.

I picked up my cell phone and texted a quick message. But I didn't send it. Instead, I turned it so Dawna could read it.

If something's different from pic, I'll point @ pic and u thumb up or down if OK. K?

She closed her fist with her thumb up in the air and smiled. Good enough. She wasn't leaping up to join me in walking around, which didn't bode well for vampire fighting. Still, this was a witch and a powerful one. Frankly, I didn't want to search, either.

I limped into the reception area, my right shoe making a heavier click on the hardwood floor that was barely audible over the shouting match in the next room.

The first thing I spotted different from the picture was a Ficus tree. Visions of the rubber plant came back to my mind and I kicked all my senses into high gear. Sometimes the nose or ears will take over when the eyes are being deceived. I stared hard at anything *but* the tree, sensing the feel of the room. I inhaled deep and slow and for the first time caught the barest whiff of women's perfume—a delicate floral that was meant to be remembered only after close contact.

After a moment, I caught Dawna's intensely wide pupils and motioned toward it with my eyes alone. She gave a thumbs-up. Hmm. I guess I'd just never noticed it before.

That's when fate intervened. After a cop I knew died, I'd been given a cat named Minnie the Mouser. Since I'm seldom home and the office is open most of the day and night, it made sense for her to live here. Even Ron has gotten attached to the little orange and white ball of fluff with the big attitude and tiny voice. He keeps a host of toys in the corner of his office, along with a padded bed for Her Majesty's comfort. We all do.

Entering the room, Minnie sniffed the air before focusing her stare on the chairs. There were only two in the photo, opposite the couch, but there were more scattered all over the building. While they're bulky to move around, we had done so more than once before when extra clients came in who would be waiting awhile. The chairs were insanely comfortable despite their stuffy Victorian appearance, and sitting makes people less annoyed than standing. I passed the seating group like nothing was wrong but turned a quizzical face to my friend.

She slipped off her shoes and came out from behind her desk in nyloned feet. In a flash she was out of view, likely racing to the vacant office down the hall where we kept two others in the set. The rest were on the second floor and I doubted that Ron would bring one down from there on the narrow staircase, no matter how important the client.

I pretended to ignore the chairs while keeping my peripheral vision firmly fixed on them and the cat. I examined the wallpaper, comparing it to the photo in my hand.

When Dawna returned, a shake of her head and a thumbs-down with a frown made my pulse abruptly pound. My headache suddenly made itself known again. It had dulled from whatever magic John had used, but now it was back in blinding glory. The intensity of the pain made me suck in my breath hard and fight to focus.

That was when Minnie hissed at the chairs and arched her back before racing out of the room. The pain faded under the rush of adrenaline, when I felt familiar magic brewing in the room. I didn't hear even a whisper over the yelling in the conference room, but I knew I didn't have time to wait for Rizzoli and crew. The witch knew I knew and she would target me first. The fastest way to incapacitate the witch was to throw one of the charms at the chair she'd become. But if I picked the wrong chair and hit a cushion, the charm could easily bounce back and bind both me and Dawna.

There was another option. I was loathe to use it if I didn't have to, but it would certainly solve my current problem. I have knives that are so magically powerful they're considered artifacts. It took Bruno five years to make them for me, bleeding himself every day to bind the magic. One of those knives had killed Lilith. Her evil had turned the metal permanently black. No witch, no matter how tough, could withstand it.

The problem was, I didn't know which chair she was. I hated to waste the charms, but a combination strike might be my only option. I faked a pair of sneezes, which made my head throb again, and then snuffled. I reached into my pocket like I was going for a tissue and drew out the charms. I practice really hard so when I throw charms, they land where I expect them to.

I threw one charm with each hand, as fast as I could. They hit the floor in front of the left- and right-hand chairs. Before I could think much about what I was doing, I pulled one of my knives from its sheath and tossed it; the blade flipped through the air before burying itself nearly to the hilt just above the ornately carved rosewood leg of the corner chair.

A scream of pain and anger filled the room. A flaming blast of magic hit me in the chest with frightening intensity and threw me backward. I landed in a heap at the bottom of the stairs. I only saw the woman's platinum blonde hair as she shifted back to human form and plucked the glowing, white-hot knife from her arm. Then she dropped it like it burned. It probably did. She was holding something in her other hand. It was thick and square, but that's all I could make out.

With a fast movement despite the pain, she jumped through the nearest window feetfirst, just like I had when I was saving Willow. The sound of shattering glass was like another scream. Then she was gone.

Well, so much for keeping her here. I had a feeling Rizzoli wasn't going to be pleased with me.

I thought about chasing her, but frankly, I wouldn't be able to keep up with her, thanks to my worsening limp. I was abruptly tired beyond measure. I had about as much energy as I'd had the last time I'd had the flu. I just wanted to curl up under a blanket with a bowl of chicken noodle soup. Sans noodles and chicken, of course. John was right. Something was really wrong with me.

The door to the conference room flew open and Ron marched out, looking angry. "What the hell is going on out here?" The tension in his voice was apparent. "We're *trying* to have a meeting in here before people have to catch flights out."

I opened my mouth to explain when it hit me. "Um, well, see . . . there could be a problem with your clients catching flights anytime soon."

"Ooh," Dawna replied with a wince because she realized it, too. "Yeah, that's probably true."

Ron is tall and lanky and has a face that's all sharp angles. I'm sure he's effective in court because he can be intimidating, but he's also able to turn on fake charm like the best used-car salesman. He looked around the room and spotted the tattered blinds and glass littering the floor. He closed his eyes and put one hand on his hip, pushing aside his thousand-dollar suit jacket, while the other went up to rub his forehead. "Is that *blood* on the Oriental rug? What the hell, Celia? I'm getting really tired of the drama in your life."

Him and me both.

A text message binged on arrival. Rizzoli: *Lower the barrier. We're here.*

They were? I checked the time. It had only been eight minutes since I'd sent my photo message. It's at least a thirty-minute drive from his office. Even if he was already en route when he called . . . this was too fast. Was I being followed? I'd definitely have to talk to Rizzoli about that, because my business depends on keeping things private. A federal shadow would not be good at all. But first things first. I sighed. "You might want to alert your clients that the FBI is here. Hopefully none of them have anything to hide, because I just chased a suspected terrorist out of the building. I don't know how long she was here, but she was using illusion magic to look like a chair in the reception area. It could be coincidental, or one of them could have brought her."

His eyes went wide and his jaw dropped. While he's a pain in the butt, he's smart. The wheels started turning behind his intense green eyes and he turned in a flash and nearly sprinted back to the conference room, muttering curses that would make a sailor's ears burn.

"Well, that went well," Dawna said in a fake cheery voice. "Now what do we do?"

I sighed and mentally threw any hope of getting to the university today out of my mind. "We lower the drawbridge and wait for the cavalry we called to trample us."

11

t wasn't quite as bad as I'd expected. But close. Rizzoli and three other agents arrived first and then more showed up as the minutes went by. I drank a couple of shakes and used the bathroom while they were with Dawna.

I was right, though; Rizzoli wasn't at all happy that the witch wasn't here anymore. "So let me get this straight. She was right there, as a chair, doing nothing aggressive? All you had to do was pretend to ignore her and wait for us, Graves, and we'd have had her in custody."

True enough. I could have done that. Hell, I probably should have. "There were lots of people in the building, Rizzoli, and we had no way of knowing what she was planning. All I could tell was that she was doing some sort of casting. She could have been casting a curse, or worse. I have no idea why she was here to begin with, and I wasn't happy about leaving her alone to do her own thing until you got here."

"She's right, sir," said a woman in a gray suit—Rizzoli had introduced her as a forensic witch—who was kneeling on the carpeting near where the fake chair had been. She spoke with authority. "Ms. Graves probably did the best thing possible by putting her on the defensive and forcing her hand. There was something being worked in this room. If it was a booby trap, it would have taken out our team, or maybe the whole building when we walked through the door. I'm in the process of unwinding the spell to verify that. Plus, now we have her blood. It won't be hard to analyze it and search for it in the database of magical beings. I can set up a tracking spell once I get back to my casting circle."

I was *right*? Sweet. That's a nice change. I didn't like that a spell was being cast, though.

Rizzoli nodded appreciatively. "Okay, then. Good job, Celia. So let's concentrate on how she got in to begin with and why she was here. You say you were outside when you heard her voice. Tell me about that. Where had you been and how long had you been gone?"

I sighed. I'd told the story three times already and it wasn't getting any more interesting with repetition. The only thing I left out was the kiss because . . . well, it was none of their business and I didn't need it on the record. "What I'm more concerned with is what she took with her."

That made both Rizzoli and the witch stare at me. "You didn't mention the first time that she took something," Rizzoli said. "Any idea what?"

I shook my head. "I just remembered and I haven't a clue. It was square, and about this big." I measured with my hands an object about the size of one of the throw pillows on the couch. "But my office hasn't been tampered with and there's nothing really of value—at least *magical* value—down here on the first floor."

Rizzoli pulled on a pair of plastic gloves. "Then I guess we'd better find out what else might have been of interest."

He led Dawna and I through each of the rooms, staring at us as we looked through cabinets, closets, and desks. But we couldn't find a thing she might have taken, unless it was in Ron's room, and he was the only one who'd know that.

I was about to open my mouth to suggest Rizzoli talk to Ron when Dawna let out a little yelp. "I know what it is! There *is* something missing, Celia!"

I hurried to her desk, where she dropped to her knees. She checked under the desk and between the desk and half wall. "What?"

"The book. That special book you'd asked me to look at from Dr. Sloan. It was right here on my desk when we went to Levy's and now it's not."

Holy hell. She was right. It wasn't something I'd even thought about but had been dead center on her desk. I looked over at Rizzoli and he snapped his fingers. Two men appeared as if by magic.

"Dust this whole area for fingerprints and do a magic trace." He wrote down Dr. Sloan's name in a paper notebook from his hip pocket. "Let's get out of their way and back to see what they've found in the other room."

I looked again at the broken window. "I can't imagine why she'd want to steal a book about the divine that's probably available on Amazon.com. I'm a lot more freaked out she was able to get in here in the first place. That says that she knows who I am and can walk right into a building that's spelled to keep her out."

The witch drawing runes on the rug looked up. "You have a spell on this building specific to *her*? Why?"

Rizzoli raised his brows and give me a questioning look.

"Well, no. The spell's not that specific. But it *is* a strong magical barrier that's intended to bar entry to those with evil intent."

The woman went back to drawing symbols in chalk. I'd seen that kind of thing before; done right, it would lift the blood spots and any skin samples into the air where they could be collected in test tubes . . . and leave our rug nice and clean. Nifty spell, that. Rizzoli's witch shook her head. "That sort of thing is completely useless against someone of this caliber. She could walk through it the way you walk through morning mist. I'm frankly surprised I don't recognize the magic signature in her blood. I know most of the upper echelon of magic."

"You can read someone's magic signature just by encountering it?"

She nodded. "Absolutely. Like, John Creede made the binding spell in this charm ball . . . and it's a nice piece of work. Pity you missed the suspect. It probably would have held her. What did work was the knife Bruno DeLuca made. Damn, is it impressive. Best item I've encountered outside of religious artifacts at the Vatican." She paused for a moment and stared at the silver knife in my wrist sheath. "I have to admit I'm surprised you have items made by both of them. They're not known to run in the same circles and they don't hand out their craft like penny candy. But they were definitely gifts, offered by hand, not taken by force. So, they're yours and I don't have to ask ugly questions about how they came into your possession."

Wow. All that and I didn't remember her even touching the knife. She'd done a casting circle on it, but I'd placed it inside and took it out again. I'd been watching closely, to make certain the blade wouldn't disappear with Rizzoli's team when they left. I needed it handy since the witch was still at large. "So if you cast a spell here, they'd know you, too? What's your name? John said he didn't recognize this caster."

She rocked back to sit on her heels and her fingers stopped fluttering over the chalk symbols. Her eyes, blazing with blue fire, were focused on me. "He said that? How did he come in contact with this magic before we arrived?" I noticed she didn't answer my question about her name.

"Okay, my bad. He hasn't touched this particular magic, but he did touch the magic affecting me from the bomb. I guess I'm assuming the witch who was just here was the same person who set off the bomb at the school. It felt like the same magic, here and at your office and the school."

She pursed her lips and tapped one slender finger on her pant leg. "And John Creede actually said he didn't recognize the caster? Because he knows a *lot* of people."

Had he? I felt my brows furrowing as I thought back. "No, I guess not. I didn't ask about the caster. I asked if he knew what the spell on me was. He said he didn't know the spell, but it was really complex. He took several of my hairs to check it out further."

She stood up in a single movement that was fluid and limber. I was betting she was either a martial artist or a yoga instructor. "Chief, I think I need samples of Ms. Graves's hair as well. We might be able to match any residual magic in her hair with the first series of events."

He nodded briefly, but I held up a hand to stop her. "Slow down. I really don't like having bits of me floating around out there. I'm already locking my hairbrush and comb in a warded safe to keep them away from people who want to use my hair to make anti-siren charms and vampire death curses. I don't mind John having them because I trust him. But I don't know *you* from Adam. Not even your name."

Rizzoli gave another small nod and made a motion at the witch. She pulled out a card and passed it to me as he spoke. "Abigail Wendy Jones. Goes by Gail. Graduate of Harvard College of Magic, cum laude, when she was sixteen. Been with the Bureau for five years now after teaching at the Academy for two. Level nine-plus talent. We only bring her in from Quantico for special cases that require a high level of expertise." He raised his brows to make sure he had my attention. "I think you know her father."

Gail *Jones*. I'd been suitably impressed until that last bit and then my jaw dropped. "And you want me to trust her after telling me who her father is?" Because I did know her father. John Jones is a talented mage. He's also a member of an organization of mercenaries who kill supernatural beings who had committed crimes and couldn't be successfully imprisoned. In short, he's a magical hit man. He'd coerced me into working with him more than once.

Gail Jones's jaw set and she looked uncomfortable. "Dad and I don't see eye to eye on a lot of things—including his lack of respect for the law. We're not a close family."

That twinged my conscience because I had the same feelings about my mother . . . and I am a firm believer that a person shouldn't be judged by their family tree. Heaven knows I wouldn't want to be.

Still—I bent my head toward Rizzoli. "*You* take them and if you want to give them to her, I'll hold you responsible for any problems."

If my lack of trust bothered her, Gail didn't let on. She didn't flinch. Maybe she'd gotten used to it, like I had. She just pulled a pair of delicate tweezers from her kit and handed them to Rizzoli. "We'll need three—and make sure you get the root. That's the important part."

She grabbed a plastic evidence bag and wrote my name on it with a squeaky marker before holding it open expectantly. Rizzoli stared at the top of my head for a long moment, tweezers poised. I wasn't sure what was going through his mind. Then he reached forward and I felt pain too large for the act explode through my head. Stars twinkled in my vision and I sucked in a breath to keep from screaming. What the heck? It hadn't hurt hardly at all when John had plucked some out . . . despite my kvetching at him.

And now my headache was back. Damn it. Every time I forgot about it for a moment it would reappear. It was getting annoying. I needed to get on with my day . . . what was left of it. I was going to call Bruno, and Creede, see what they knew about Ms. Jones. The Bureau trusted her. But I'd reserve judgment until I checked my own sources. I'm naturally a little paranoid, but this situation was pushing me over the top.

"Is there anything else you need me for, Rizzoli?"

"Why?"

"I've got a couple of calls to make."

"Call away." He waved in the general direction of the stairs. "Just don't go anywhere without letting me know."

I sighed. Unless I wanted all the nice agents listening in, I'd need to make the call in my office. On the third freaking floor. I so did not want to go up those stairs. I was tired. And hungry. Of course, I'd never gotten the chance to eat since the *phở* earlier. Now that the headache was back I was nauseous. The reception area might have the blood removed but there was glass embedded in everything, including the walls—which didn't seem logical since the glass should have exploded *outward*. That meant I was going to have to deal with yet another insurance company.

Suckfreakintastik.

My first call was to Creede. No answer. Then again, he'd said he'd be out of touch. But he'd also said he'd leave a message. Hmpf. He was a big bad mage; he could definitely take care of himself. But still, it wasn't like him not to call when he promised.

My second call was Bruno. He picked up on the first ring.

"Hey." A simple greeting, but it held a world of warmth.

"Hey yourself." I couldn't quite manage to make my voice sound normal.

"Uh-oh. What's wrong?"

"Bad day. Really, really, bad day."

He sighed, but forced a hint of humor into his voice. "Where does it rank on the epic scale of Celia Graves disasters?"

I laughed. Which was exactly what he'd intended. "Let's see, if the rift was a ten . . ."

"Oh yeah, the rift was definitely a ten."

I thought about it for a second. "Probably a six. Six point five."

He sighed. "Do you need me to come? I'm meeting with Dr. Sloan, but we can reschedule."

I thought about it for all of about ten seconds. "Actually, I kind of need to talk to him, too. I just figured he wouldn't be in on a Friday afternoon."

"He wanted us to have plenty of uninterrupted time for our first meeting about my dissertation."

Time that I was now interrupting. Oops.

I could hear Dr. Sloan's voice in the background. "Have her come on down."

"You hear that?" Bruno asked.

"I heard. Tell him thanks. I'll be there as quick as I can." I grabbed my purse and started downstairs. I'd made it all the way to the reception desk before I remembered I didn't have my car.

Rizzoli straightened up from something Jones was showing him. "Going somewhere?"

I nodded. "Actually, yeah. I need to meet with an expert about the incident this morning. He's also been investigating the death curse on me and I want to ask whether that has anything to do with my reaction to the school event. Actually, it's Dr. Sloan—the book that's missing is his."

Gail perked up. "You mean Aaron Sloan? Brilliant man. He guest lectured a few times when I was at Harvard. Frankly, I might have to call him myself if this spell turns out to be what I think it is."

That made both me and Rizzoli look at her sharply, but she just looked back at her runes, then closed her eyes. Her fingers moved, casting. But Rizzoli asked the obvious. "Should I send you with Celia to talk to him?"

She shook her head, her voice now slightly singsong. "No. I need to concentrate on this and still have to sample the people in the conference room for any coercion or memory reduction spells. Someone should have noticed a woman in the room before Ms. Graves arrived." Well, yeah. That was a good point. Then she opened her eyes and looked at me. "But it would help if you could pave the way with him. Tell him it's an E14 spell so far and might contain traces of D71 workings. That'll get his interest up and he'll probably call *me*."

Rizzoli nodded sagely, but I got the impression he didn't understand a word she'd just said. "E14 and D71. Got it. Let's go, Celia. I'll take you over." I raised my brows in a silent question. Why did I need company? "Consider it protective custody until we know more about why you're being targeted."

He gave a gentlemanly bow and waved me toward the door. I sighed and preceded him out the door with only a minor limp. Dawna was chatting with a cute gray-suit near the door and I got the impression from her sultry smile that their conversation had nothing to do with the investigation. "Going to the college now. Be good." I grabbed my purse from where it was hiding out of sight behind the computer monitor.

She smirked and winked. "I always am. Except when I'm . . . bad."

That made the agent smirk, too, and Rizzoli let out a small growl. "Go assist Special Agent Jones, Davies. She'll need someone to gather the evidence once she raises it from the floor, and you seem to have nothing better to do."

Agent Davies's gaze moved to the floor and he fidgeted nervously while Dawna blushed and scurried to her desk.

Ron noticed me and tried to catch my attention with eyes blazing, but I so didn't want to talk to him right now. What was happening wasn't precisely my fault, but this probably wasn't helping his settlement conference any. I pretended not to see him and scurried out the front door. I only made it past the agent guarding the entrance because Rizzoli was right at my elbow. Ron wouldn't be that lucky, if he tried at all.

I started to ask Rizzoli a question, but he held up his hand and put his cell phone to his ear. "Nancy? . . . Dom. Hey, find some reason to get Davies off this case. Pull him back to base. . . . Okay, yeah. Thanks."

I waited until we were in the car before I commented. "A little harsh, don't you think? It was just innocent flirting."

"Not so innocent, Graves. What worried me wasn't that he was flirting. It was that he didn't notice *you*."

That made me frown because I didn't get what he was saying. "Try again. Maybe I'm just dense today, but I don't understand."

He looked almost amused. "You really don't, do you? Okay, short version: You're a siren. Every other male in the room except those who are shooting blanks like me or are not heterosexual noticed you. Couldn't take their eyes off you. Except Davies, who couldn't take his eyes off your friend. That level of interest in anyone could impact this investigation. I don't care if they date— hell, that's almost guaranteed from the way they were looking at each other. But not here and not now. Got it?"

"Oh. That's a lot to get from a quick glance. What exactly is your specialty at the Bureau? I mean, most agents have some sort of special talent. Not many plain humans there, I'll bet."

He turned on the frontage road toward the university back entrance. "More than you'd think, actually.

There are good and bad things about having people with specialized paranormal talents in the department. The good is you get people who can solve cases better. But only *certain* cases. They tend to rely on their strengths, and when you only have a hammer, you see every problem as a nail. I prefer people with full tool belts, and humans bring that to the table."

His answer made me smirk at him. "One of your talents seems to be misdirection. Because you didn't answer my question."

He smiled, his eyes crinkling at the corners with good humor. "You're right. It is." He let that sink in with a prolonged moment of silence.

Finally I shook my head with amused weariness. "You're not going to tell me, are you?"

"Intuition."

I turned my head to stare at him. His smile didn't fade. "Excuse me?"

"You asked my talent. That's it. I'm a level-eight Intuitive."

Intuition was a measurable talent? "Really? Is that a psychic or magical gift? What exactly does it mean?"

"It started out as a clairvoyant talent but was moved to the psychic talents when I was a kid. But now it's considered partly magical, too, as science has learned more about the brain and meta-mitochondrial DNA. So now it's its own subset, which bumped me up the chart by about four levels. I sucked on the clairvoyant and psychic scales. I wasn't much better than a plain human."

"So you've got really good intuition? That's it?"

His reply was a laugh that was genuinely amused and not at all insulted. "It's a lot more useful than you think. I'm always in the right place at the right time. I meet people I need to and ask the right questions exactly when I should. I pick the correct people to go with me on an assignment to get the results we need to solve a case. So far, I've got a ninety-three percent average of satisfactorily closing case files. That gets you noticed in my business."

"Then you happening to be the person who showed up at my office the first time we met wasn't coincidence?"

As his hand flipped the lever for the blinker he shook his head and turned in at the university's back gate. The main entrance doesn't have a security shack. But this one, close to the administration building, does. I dug my student ID out of my purse and held it up, but I think it was Rizzoli's official badge that did the trick because wow, did the guard leap back inside the booth fast to raise the bar across the drive. "I decided to go to your office. I didn't have any real idea why, but over the years, I've learned to go with my gut—more than most cops. Got in trouble more than once, too. The nice part is that once intuition became an official talent, about two years ago, my supervisors started taking off my bridle." We reached the administration building. Rizzoli kept talking. "The Bureau is actually pretty good at nurturing talents. So they're using me as a sort of guinea pig, to see whether intuition can be trained to respond on command. That gives me a lot of freedom." He pulled into a parking space and turned off the car. "Like when I gave credentials to an untrained newbie siren."

"And like playing chauffeur right now?"

He shrugged as he unbuckled his belt. "That decision was a combination of intuition and common sense. I've learned that you wander off if I don't keep an eye on you, and I need you handy in case my team turns up anything new at your office. But there's probably another reason I'm here and it'll come when it comes. I've heard vampires have terrific intuition, which is why it's so hard to catch and kill them. Maybe you have it, too. It's a talent that *can* be honed, you know. I'm a lot better at following my gut now that I've started to analyze the whys."

I wanted to be annoyed that he accused me of wandering off, but it was sort of true. And what he said about intuition was interesting. "I've always been told I've lived a charmed life, despite the things that have happened to me. I was kidnapped and survived. I had a death curse put on me and survived. A vampire bite . . . survived. I've been told it's my siren blood and good training and equipment."

"Possibly. But you also have a knack for stumbling into situations, and having the right person on hand at the right time to help you out. That's intuition."

He was making me really think about things from a different point of view. "I was tested for everything in school. Failed miserably. And the sirens told me why. Siren abilities don't coexist with other strong talents. So, I'm guessing no empathy, no intuition. Or at least not much."

We walked up the sidewalk to the science building, listening to the birds and catching the scent of rich, wet soil and sweet bedding flowers. "Hmpf. That's a shame. The government put together some tests when they split it out into its own category." Rizzoli held the door for me to enter ahead of him. "One test is pretty good because it's physical—open pits with mattresses at the bottom, things that will catch your ankles and trip you into padded walls, doorknobs that give a mild electric shock. Lots of stuff like that. It provides your brain with the concept of danger but without significant consequences. It really makes your talent kick in."

We walked down a dim hallway. Classes were over for the day. "I would've sworn you had the talent. I've thought for a while we had something in common—something that made me seek you out."

"Why does that worry me?" I said it with a smile, but I was serious. We turned a corner and he stayed right beside me. Interesting—he knew which way to turn. "Have you visited Dr. Sloan before?'

Rizzoli smiled. "Nope. I've never met him. Just thought that was the right way to turn." The smile seemed to peel several years and about a half a ton of worry off his face.

I was going to respond with something mildly sarcastic when I heard voices at the end of the hall. Aaron Sloan has a very distinctive voice, probably from years of speaking in lecture halls.

I could also smell a distinctive cologne that had scented my clothing for two years, feel the press of magic that reached for me all the way down the hall.

Bruno DeLuca.

Part of me was anxious to see him and I found myself quickening my steps. The other part of me was terrified to see him in person again—because seeing his smile, his amazing body, would remind me of the woman who'd nearly stolen him away. Eirene, a royal siren, had been Bruno's lover. She'd convinced him she was pregnant and . . . he chose her over me, without a second thought, without discussing it with me.

That doesn't make for a good long-term relationship. Despite what I'd thought in Levy's, and a few warm phone conversations, there was a big hurdle to get over before I could be happy with Bruno. With anyone, really.

Rizzoli matched me step for step until we neared the room. As I reached the doorway, the conversation inside the room stopped as if a switch had been thrown.

"Celia." Bruno's voice was warm and his eyes ... wow. Those big brown eyes said so many things with just a glance. *Hi. Miss you. Love you. Sorry.* He was always really good at conveying entire sentences with a single look, so much so that we could carry on whole conversations across a college classroom without the teacher knowing.

He looked good. Better than good, actually. He'd dropped a few pounds and in the right places. And if I didn't know better, I'd swear he'd had a face-lift. So much tension had vanished from his face that he looked like a new man. Of course, the last time we'd seen each other, we'd just closed the demonic rift and we were both exhausted. "Bruno."

Rizzoli shoved past me through the doorway just then, his hand out toward Bruno. "Bruno DeLuca. Good to finally meet you. Special Agent Dominic Rizzoli, FBI. I've heard a lot about you. Hey, could we talk?" Bruno had put out his hand automatically, as most men do when someone offers theirs, and found himself being propelled, with a second hand on his mid-back, through a second door before he could do much more than open his mouth.

I was speechless at Rizzoli's lack of tact. Even Dr. Sloan was surprised. He stared after the two men for a moment before turning his attention to me. I raised an embarrassed hand. "Um, well. Hi, Dr. Sloan. Sorry about all that."

The professor's confusion made him frown, but he recovered in a second and his expression turned to one of excitement. "May I see your palm again? Anything new?"

Dr. Sloan is fascinated by the manifestation of my curse. He's the one who first explained it to me. I sighed and held out my hand. He pulled his glasses down from his forehead and moved forward eagerly. Lifting my hand with near reverence, he peered at the mark. It was an angry red today, but there was no pain. He let out an appreciative, "Ooh! You've been a busy girl, Ms. Graves."

It was so weird he could know that by looking at my palm. "I know you said the curse reacts when I come close to death. But why is it still happening? The person who cursed me is dead. Shouldn't that have stopped it?"

His head cocked and he blinked repeatedly, as though processing the information. "Did the caster revoke or remove the spell?"

I shook my head.

"Did *you* kill the caster?"

Crap. I realized where he was going with this. "I was there when she died. But that doesn't count, does it?" Magic is like that sometimes. It takes a specific, narrow event to change things.

Sloan's face showed his uncertainty. "Yes. No. Maybe. The scar is still manifesting. Perhaps it'll stop at some point. But the curse has been part of your psyche since you were a child. We can't expect that it will suddenly just cease to be. You've incorporated it into your personality. You could no more *not* throw yourself in the way of danger as a bodyguard than you could not blink for the rest of your life. The threat of death may no longer have anything to do with the curse. Or it may." His shoulder went up and down again.

Fair enough. "Have you developed any idea why it gets darker after I've been in danger?"

He nodded but didn't look up. "I have a working theory on that, actually. I believe it's not so much your eminent death so much as the rush of near-death adrenaline that causes the scar to manifest."

I felt my brow furrow and I looked down at dark liver spots on his aging scalp through a drape of my tangled blonde hair. I really needed to find a mirror and a comb. Soon. "Is near-death adrenaline somehow different than . . . well, the *normal* kind?"

He looked up then, so suddenly he nearly smacked his head into my chin. "Oh my, yes! The adrenaline produced in a fight-or-flight situation is much more diluted than the concentrated sort produced when the subject has accepted the true possibility of death."

"The *possibility,* not certainty?"

He smiled now, a brilliant flash of teeth that told me I'd gotten it. "Exactly! Near-death adrenaline is how mothers lift cars off their children or people pull victims out of rubble before the rest of a building collapses. It makes muscles supernatural for a few split seconds." He looked at me for a moment with something approaching wonder, then smiled slightly and shook his index finger at me before leaning back against the counter with a knowing expression. "You see? You, Ms. Graves, grasp the non-obvious quickly. It's no wonder you were Warren's favorite student."

That comment sliced at my heart more than a little, but I tried not to flinch. Some "favorite student."

"You understand *perspective,* which is rare today . . . and especially in one so young."

"A little bit." I didn't feel particularly young, especially not today. But I suppose I was to someone his age. He'd already been teaching in the sixties and I think in the fifties, too. He'd seen a lot, and sometimes you can lose perspective when you have forgotten more than some have learned. "But maybe you can help *me* with some perspective today. This morning, I saw an entity while I was watching an interrogation in the FBI field office. I need to find out what kind. A doctor thinks some physical problems I'm having might be demonic. Did you hear about the bomb that went off at the elementary school a couple of weeks ago? I've been having weird pains since then. Could something be following me? Maybe it's why the scar is manifesting?"

He gave me that look every professor gives every student when they're fishing for what should be a simple answer in the cobwebs of a frustrated mind. "Come now, Ms. Graves. You have a degree in the science, and I presume it was earned. *Might be* demonic? Weird pains? Be more specific. What evidence did it give of what sort of demon it was?"

I shrugged and leaned against the counter to take the weight off my leg. It was really starting to hurt again. I was overworking it. "That's the thing, Doctor. I *can't* be more specific because it doesn't fit any of the parameters I've learned about. I can only tell you what we experienced and maybe you can come up with the specifics."

That got him curious. I could see it, bird bright in his eyes. He ushered me across the room to a pair of chairs in one corner. A soda and a bottle of iced tea sat on the table between the seats. The chair I sat in smelled of Bruno's cologne. Nice.

"So, tell me about this entity," Sloan asked as he sat down opposite me.

I did. After minutes of explaining the situation I added, "And it could speak. Audible sound that everyone heard."

He was listening with his whole body, soaking it in. One of his arms was bent at the elbow, the hand lightly resting against his lips. It was interesting to watch his lips doing push-ups on his thumb, making the whole hand move. "Are you certain it was audible? It could have been in all of your minds. Simultaneously. Are you positive there was sound?"

"She probably isn't, but I am." Rizzoli reentered the room with Bruno hot on his heels. "We always videotape interrogations. There's actual sound, Doctor."

Sloan's brows rose and I nodded. I knew I'd heard it with my ears. I've heard voices in my head before. Demons who tried to trick me, even seduce me. But this . . . this wasn't the same at all. "It called me by name, Doctor, and responded to thoughts I hadn't spoken out loud."

Rizzoli turned to me. "Is *that* what that meant? When the demon wrote: 'Think again, Celia' on the window in frost?"

"Yep," I said while Bruno looked at me with undisguised interest. "I had just thought that the demon wasn't very bright because all it could write was *No*."

"And you're calling this entity a demon because—?" Bruno asked.

"Metal table . . . on fire. With no flame source in the room," I offered.

Rizzoli added, "Letters in black that promised the prisoner pain if he didn't talk to us."

"Of course," Dr. Sloan interjected. "That's part of the confusion, isn't it? Threatening pain and destruction. But look at the secondary issues . . . pain *if* the prisoner didn't reveal secrets of a crime and offering a warning that only the *truth* would set him free. Couldn't it be angelic instead of demonic?"

Angelic? "You mean like . . . *angels*? They don't normally intervene in the affairs of man, do they?" I mean, yeah, they exist. But what would they be doing there, at the FBI office? "Melting tables isn't really their sort of thing, is it?"

The doctor shrugged. "Burning bush, Archangel Michael's flaming sword. Fire cleanses as well as punishes. It's old-school . . . or Old *Testament* to be sure, but maybe after the demonic rift, They are taking a greater interest in our city."

He said the word to imply a capital letter. *They.* Purity personified. Um. Wow. I don't know how I feel about the possibility I'd had a brush with the angelic. I think if I took any time to digest it, it would scare me worse than fighting the demonic. My gran always said I had a guardian angel watching over me, but it sort of freaks me out that it might actually be true. I'm not exactly a perfect person. "Is there any way to check to be sure?"

He nodded confidently. "You have the primary text on it in your possession. The book I gave you."

I felt my face get warm. "Oh. Well, see . . ."

Rizzoli broke in. "I'm afraid that a dangerous witch broke into Ms. Graves's office today and stole that book. Is there another one in the college library that we might look at to find out what the witch might have been looking for?"

Sloan's face looked stricken. "Oh dear. No, I'm afraid not. It's a very rare volume. The only other one I know of is in the Oxford University library."

I winced. "I'm so sorry, Dr. Sloan." And I was. I hate to lose gifts. "I didn't realize. I should have kept it locked in my safe."

He waved it off. "My fault entirely. I don't think I ever mentioned it was rare, so how could you know? I can request the volume be scanned at Oxford and e-mailed to me, of course. And until then, I could certainly test for traces of one or the other in the flame residue. I'd love to look at the tape and examine the table if that's possible."

I looked at Rizzoli and he brightened. "Sure. I could make that happen. Where do you want the table delivered?"

That sort of startled Dr. Sloan. "Um, it would be better in situ."

The agent raised his hands as though helpless. "Unfortunately, our Bureau clairvoyant told us we needed to get it off the premises or something bad was going to happen. It's in a truck right now. I could have it here in a half hour. I can e-mail you the video."

"Isn't that confidential?" It seemed a logical question for me to ask. I wondered about interviews, aka debriefings, I'd had with him before on other cases.

"We didn't learn anything from the suspect until after the entity left, so we can give up the rearview video that doesn't reveal the suspect's face but *does* show the entity." He shrugged, like it was completely normal everyday stuff.

Hey, maybe it was. For him.

Dr. Sloan was looking both excited and terrified. "Yes, yes. We can bring it here. Well . . . not *here*. No, that wouldn't do at all. Maybe the lab." He stood up and rushed to the door, then stopped. "No. There are classes there tomorrow. I need a large enough location to seal the table in a circle in case it's a connection portal. Bruno, I'll need your help of course to plan the casting." He pointed at my former fiancé with brows raised.

Bruno raised his hands, slightly confused. "Yes, certainly. Whatever you need."

"Mr. . . . Rizzoli, is it? Let's take a walk. I think there's an empty room in the pharmaceutical college that has a loading bay. We'll go call the dean. I'm sure we can work something out." Sloan grabbed Rizzoli by the elbow and he must have been stronger than he looked, because the FBI agent was nearly pulled off his feet as the tiny professor raced out of the room with him in tow.

It was abruptly silent in the room, and awkward. I looked at Bruno, who was staring at me. "So. Um, hi."

"Hi." His voice was low and sultry and made me shiver. "You look good."

I laughed because I couldn't help it. "I look like crap. I'm white as a ghost . . . well, a bat anyhow. And my hair is stringy." I self-consciously ran fingers through it and pulled apart tangles. "It needs to be cut." In short, I was in no fit condition to be seeing him when he was looking like he walked out of an issue of *GQ* magazine. "No, *you* look good. Great, in fact. I look like the walking dead."

He shrugged with one shoulder and crossed the room to where I was sitting. "So maybe I like the walking dead. At least one of them." He leaned down and brushed his lips against my cheek. It felt nice. Safe and comfortable—vastly different from John but no less desirable. Just to prove a point to myself, I turned my face slightly and pressed my lips against his. Flames of magic rolled across my skin, more powerful than John's but with a different . . . taste. I lingered there, remembering old times when a kiss was often the beginning of something much more intense. Bruno let me kiss him, not making it more than it was. I moved my jaw, opening his mouth, and touched his tongue with mine.

When I pulled back first, I noticed the surprised look in his eyes. Not upset, just surprised. I suppose it was natural for him to be confused, because I sure was. "I . . . I'm not sure why I did that."

"Old habits die hard?"

My breath came out in a frustrated rush. "No. It's not like that. It's just that—" I had nothing. I had no idea why I'd kissed him, while I was still feeling the hurt he'd inflicted.

He sat down across from me and stared at me for a long moment. "It's just that you kissed Creede earlier today and needed to prove to yourself, and maybe to me, that you're being fair?"

My jaw dropped. Literally. I could feel air on my tongue. My mouth started moving, but no words came out until, "It's . . . I mean . . . we—"

"Celia." His voice was calm. "It's okay. I'm not going to fly into some sort of jealous rage. I could taste his magic on you, could sense where he'd touched you." He lifted one shoulder. "I know he has his sights set on you. It's not like it's a surprise."

My stomach felt hollow, yet it threatened to heave up into my throat. "I'm not trying to hurt you." The words were a whisper and my gaze was fixed on his neck. "I'd never do that." Shades of John's promise to me. Crap.

"Celia." His voice was soft. He leaned forward until his elbows were resting on his knees. "I'm the one who hurt *you*. I know that and there aren't enough words in the language to describe how sorry I am. I'm not even sure how to make it up to you. I think I need to get my head back together to figure it out. So I'm in the field instead of in the office. I'm getting back in shape and getting my doctorate."

"And I'm so excited for you. You've talked about that since we graduated."

He smiled and his expression was filled with pride and hope. "The land the Murphys own in Arkansas and the fee-simple magic attached to it was a doctoral thesis topic if I ever saw one, and they've been kind enough to grant me permission to visit whenever I need to. So I signed up for a year right here at USC-Bayview and I'm getting to work."

"I still can't believe you're going to be in Santa Maria de Luna for the whole year." I was really happy for him. He was never more *him* than when he was studying and learning new things. "God, that's incredible. And you got accepted into the doctoral program already?"

He nodded. "I know it's quick. But Warren sponsored me and the Board of Trustees agreed, provided Dr. Sloan would be my advisor. I wasn't positive he'd do it because he's so close to retirement." He grinned and it looked good on him. "But he said yes."

The grin was infectious and I found myself smiling right back at him. "So I guess I'll be seeing you around town."

"Yes, yes, you will. Just so you know, I turned down Duke to come back to our alma mater. In fact, several colleges started calling me once they learned about the

Murphy tract and that I had exclusive permission. But I wanted to be *here*. Not New Jersey, not Arkansas or Maryland. Here."

His expression didn't change, but his eyes did. They deepened somehow and the flames I remembered so well flickered and flared. They moved from mage to *male* and made parts of my body tighten with memories of his touch.

"Um. That's—"

"DeLuca?!" Dr. Sloan's voice echoed down the hallway. "Aren't you coming? You didn't follow me."

Bruno chuckled when I did and sharing the laughter felt good. He stood, then reached out to help me to my feet, but I got up awkwardly and my right leg gave out. Bruno grabbed my arm and kept me standing.

"You okay?"

I shook my head. "My leg's been bothering me since the bomb in the school."

Crap. I shouldn't have said that. I could tell from his reaction that he didn't know what I was talking about. How could he? I doubt it had made the papers back east. His eyes went wide, then narrowed suspiciously. "Bomb? School? What the hell, Celia." He looked at my leg and sucked in a sharp breath. "What attacked you? That looks bad. Have you had a healer look at it?"

I looked down but only saw the denim of my jeans. "Only a dozen or so. I've been to doctors, specialists, and witch doctors. None of them can figure it out. What are you seeing that they haven't? The latest one thinks there's a spell on me, but I don't know if they're connected."

He knelt down next to my leg, moving one of the chairs out of the way in order to put both hands on my calf. Dr. Sloan walked in the door just then, followed by Rizzoli. His brows rose so high it looked like his bushy eyebrows were a toupee and I felt I had to explain. "It's not what it looks like."

Bruno didn't even look up. "This is bad, Celie. I mean like killing you bad. What is this?"

"That's a very good question, Mr. DeLuca," Rizzoli interjected. "What do *you* think it is? None of our Bureau people have a clue."

"Joh . . . Creede is working to unravel whatever's attacking my aura around my head. Is the problem with the leg the same thing?"

Bruno shook his head. "I don't know anything about auras. Not my specialty. But this is attacking your flesh. Medical magic is what I'm good at. It could well be the same. I'd have to compare notes with . . . *John.*"

"Hey, a witch with the Bureau, Gail Jones, said top mages like you can identify the caster. Any idea who to talk to about this mess?"

He looked at me, his eyes both surprised and suspicious. "This is a spell? Wow. I pegged it as some sort of magical virus. It doesn't feel like a spell at all."

"Magical virus?"

Dr. Sloan nodded. "Oh, yes. The Centers for Disease Control doesn't talk about it much, especially not in public, but there is a magical branch of the organization for viruses that mutate and bacteria that can be magically transmitted, changing from a magical event to something that can affect more than the original target."

"Wow. That's seriously scary. But one's physiology and the other is . . . well, magic."

Bruno let out an odd chuckle. "Magic is part of my physiology, Celie. If I caught something that backfired from a spell, it's possible I could pass it on to family members. Even human ones. After that . . . well, it could take off. Like this has." He motioned to my leg. "I think we need to call in the Centers for Magical Disease Control to take a look at you. In fact, I'd like to look at your skin myself."

I couldn't help but smirk. "I'll just bet you would."

He didn't smile in return and that made my stomach hurt. "I've got an ugly suspicion. But first I need to put you in a quarantine circle." He looked at Dr. Sloan. "Could we use the lab for this? We might need the restraints."

Suddenly I was less than excited about this idea. "What exactly do you think I'm going to do, Bruno?"

He paused and his face was set in stone to keep from showing me what he was really feeling. When he finally spoke it chilled my blood.

"Scream, Celia, if I'm right, I think you're going to scream."

12

I refused to scream. But I was turning the air blue with cursing and yelling. "Bruno! *Stop it!* I swear to God I'm going to rip your head off if you don't let me up!" My knuckles were white from straining against the titanium restraints. The metal was bending but not enough for me to get loose. Everything looked red. It was too close to sunset for this crap. I don't like being tied down and Bruno knew it. At that moment, I couldn't remember why I'd agreed to this at all, except that he had me really worried about my leg.

His voice was calm from across the room. From my position on the table I could just see him on his knees, drawing runes on the floor where a thousand other symbols had been drawn by countless undergrads. This room had been built for that very purpose, to allow students to examine dangerous creatures without much worry of reprisal. Rizzoli was watching from the corner of the room, but Dr. Sloan was nowhere to be seen. That surprised me a little. He's usually first on the scene to examine stuff. "Celie, if I let you up, you *will* rip my head off. The bat in you is talking right now. Your eyes are bright red and you're glowing so much that I don't need the overhead light. Those bindings are the only thing between me and my head. So, dream on. You're staying right where you are until I'm done with this casting."

Being held down was really starting to mess with my head. It was too close to the past, not just right after I'd been turned into an Abomination, but further back, to when I was twelve. I tried to keep the panic out of my voice without much success. "Bruno, you *really* need to let me up. I'm starting to flash back."

He stood up and looked at me, his eyes filled with sympathy. "I know and I wish I could make it better. But it's too close to sunset. This can't wait until morning. You could be dead by then. Would it help if we knocked you out with drugs?"

He looked like glowing bands of shiny color to my vampire sight. He smelled heavy with sweet, rich blood and my stomach growled audibly. He jerked back a few inches and I strained to follow. His words had sunk in but just barely. Panic was rising in a black wave that lapped at my sanity. "Yes. You need to do that. Because if you don't, I'll call you. I can feel it inside me. I'll call you to me like your brother was called by Lilith and everything will change. Give me the drugs, Bruno. Please. I don't want this thing inside me to get out, but the restraints are too much for me."

His heartbeat sped up and he began to smell of fear. I felt a needle pierce my arm and I felt my body react without my will. The blood flow to that arm slowed to nearly a stop. "It's not working. My body's stopping the drug from getting to my brain. You have to do something more drastic."

Bruno's colors turned more blue. He was sad and worried, which wasn't as exciting as fear. "I don't want to hurt you, Celie. Isn't there another way?"

Anger flared for no reason and I knew the vamp inside was taking control. The only thing I could think to do was let it take over. Maybe Bruno would see there was no other choice. He's so sweet and I knew he wouldn't want to hurt me, but I also knew he would react in self-defense if he had no choice. I snarled and bared my teeth, then raised my head abruptly to grab those colors. He reared back, fast and hard, and I couldn't follow because of the metal band around my chest. But the band did bend a little. "Whoa! Okay, I guess not. Just promise you won't hate me in the morning."

His glow increased until it was blinding. I shut my eyes to escape from the bright sunshine, but the light crashed through my eyelids and all I knew was pain. I screamed, long and loud. It kept getting brighter and more painful while I screamed as fast as I could draw breath.

Then came a burst that was like the rising sun. It hit me in an agonizing flash and everything went black.

It was dark and filthy. I had finally stopped flinching when bugs crawled on me. I had too many bites to count, but I couldn't scratch them because of the ropes that bound me spread-eagled on top of a wooden table. "You don't want us to hurt your sister again now, do you, Ivy?"

She was sobbing. I wanted to say something to her, but I couldn't. They'd used duct tape over my mouth.

"All you have to do is call the ghosts, get them to tell us where the money is hidden."

A second male broke in. And while the first man had at least tried to sound gentle, this one didn't bother. "C'mon, kid. Call up the ghost or I'll use the cigarette again."

"I can't! She won't talk to me." Another burst of tears from Ivy made me crazy. "She's a mean lady."

"Do it!" Pain! Oh God, the pain. My back arched off of the table, my shrieks stifled, but still audible through the tape. Burning, searing pain on the skin of my upper thigh. The scent of burning meat, my flesh. Tears streamed down my face as I struggled against the ropes, but all that did was make me bleed worse.

"We're going to find out from the ghosts where that buried treasure is or it's all over for you and your sister, kid. Do you want that? Huh? Do it or someone is going to die!" I pulled against the ropes that didn't feel like ropes anymore. They were heavier and stiffer, like metal, and it was hard to expand my chest.

The darkness was beginning to suck me down, the dirt and bugs covering me until I couldn't breathe. Maybe if I stopped struggling the dirt would cover my ears and I wouldn't hear the screaming anymore.

"Celia!"

"Celia. C'mon, Celie, wake up. You need to wake up or this isn't going to work." The voice was deeper now, a sound of strength and warmth, filled with pain and love and fear. Fear for me. The power of that voice pushed away the men and my sister's dying screams, back to where they usually lurked, waiting for me to try to fall asleep at night.

My eyes fluttered open and I could see Bruno through the golden glow of a quarantine circle. I became aware once again of the pain in my leg. It was worse now than when I'd agreed to lie down on the table. "What's happening? How long was I out? God, my leg hurts."

"Yeah. I'm sure it does. The muscle is necrotic, and with every step you take, you spread the damage further. Your flesh is dying, Celia, and it's going to keep dying unless we can stop this disease." Bruno's voice was harsh and angry, but I didn't think he was mad at me.

He was scared—and that frightened me. "But you can fix it, right? It's magic, so you can heal me?"

His eyes closed and I thought I saw a tear roll down his face. Surely that was just a trick of the light playing and his magic? Then he spoke and I knew better. His voice cracked as he said, "No, Celie. I can't, any more than I can heal the common cold. But the CMDC is sending over a specialist from the unit they're setting up at St. Anthony's."

That seemed odd, because St. Anthony's isn't one of the bigger hospitals in the region. It's a community hospital and I knew they had set up a program of rotating specialists from the major hospitals in L.A., but a permanent unit? "They're setting up a special unit here, instead of in L.A.? Why?"

"Yeah," Rizzoli answered grimly. "They are. For a good reason. The hospital here has a bigger morgue."

13

When the CMDC agent walked into the lab, he was wearing a hazardous-material white suit, complete with hood and air pack. That didn't really help my emotional state. I tried to ignore him, to take my mind to a calmer place. I fixed my gaze on one particular tile in the ceiling. Tiny rust-colored blossoms, probably from a leak in the roof, were sprayed across the white acoustic tile in a random pattern. I'm pretty good at meditation and I've done yoga for years. But right then, with the night beating on my brain, with the urge to feed growing, it was hard to find inner peace. The part of me that was still human and thinking needed to warn the new man. "If you're going to try to touch me, you need to feed me first. Get me some beef broth or at least a nutrition shake. And you'd better hurry because I can feel these restraints starting to give."

My voice sounded strangely calm, as if it was separate from my body, which was thrashing around on the table, testing the limits of the titanium. I worried that I was going to destroy myself trying to get loose. But I couldn't help it, couldn't stop my body's actions.

"Mage DeLuca had something delivered. Think you can drink or should I just pour it down your throat?"

My body stilled as I focused on the figure in white. I knew that voice. "Gaetano?" The medic, who'd shown up from time to time in the company of John Jones, couldn't possibly be a member of the CMDC.

The man hesitated, then spoke slowly and cautiously. "Yesss. Have we met?"

Now that I was listening closer, I could tell that the voice wasn't quite the same. "*Christopher* Gaetano?"

The muscles in his shoulders relaxed a bit. "No. I'm Thomas. Chris is my son. People say we sound alike."

I nodded. "Pour it down my throat." I leaned back and tried to relax. I trusted Chris Gaetano, and I was betting he learned his bedside manner from his dad. Chris had been the first person to ever take me to Disneyland. He had a joy of life that was infectious, and while we eventually decided that there was no romantic spark, I still considered him a friend. "Don't get too close to my hands. I'm not really in control of them." Thomas came forward, too fast. I felt my muscles tense, my fingers become claws that grabbed at his arm. The metal groaned from the sudden strain. "I'm serious, Doctor. I don't want your son to be picking up pieces of you." I raised my head and stared at him with glowing red eyes, letting him take a good look at my fangs. "Little tiny pieces."

He was close enough that I could see his face, dimly, through the hazmat suit's hood. He swallowed hard; the hand holding the tall Styrofoam cup trembled a bit. I couldn't smell him through the plasticized suit, but I could see his pulse beating hard against the thin skin of his neck through the face shield. "Okay, Ms. Graves, we're going to take this slow. If you start feeling the need to attack, raise your hand, or at least a finger, so I know to back up."

That made sense, provided I retained enough control to do it. "What's in the cup?"

"It's meat broth from some barbeque restaurant. Actually, it smells pretty good. I'll have to try that place."

I knew the broth would work. It had before. A little while back, Dawna had gotten the staff of the barbeque place to start saving the drippings from under the massive steel smoker. The juice came from a variety of meats and tasted amazing. More important, it satisfied my hunger splendidly. With any luck, Bruno had called the same place. "Okay. Let's do this. Can you pour through the quarantine circle?"

He shook his head. "No. That's why it's important to tell me if you're getting stressed. Mage DeLuca is suiting up now and is going to lower the shield and keep an eye on you while you . . . feed."

I shifted my gaze back to the ceiling, letting the scent of the meat fill me. If I concentrated on the meat broth, anticipating the taste, I wouldn't focus on anything else.

Like pulsing veins.

"Cheer up, Doctor. Your son worked on me a couple of times. And he didn't have titanium bands to hold me down."

He actually chuckled. "Yes, but my son's insanity is well known in our family."

That made me laugh—and it pushed the vampire back enough to let me control my mind. I motioned to the quart-sized container. "Just get the bottom close enough to me that I can bite it. It'll come out slow enough that I won't choke while drinking it."

He looked nervous and I knew why. Holding the

container near my mouth would put him within reach of my hands, and if I got hold of him, no way he was getting loose. "Mage DeLuca should be ready in just a second. We'll see what he suggests."

Bruno walked in just then, wearing a similar suit to Dr. Gaetano's. He'd left his gloves off. I raised my brows and looked at his bare fingers. He shrugged. Or at least I thought he did. Hard to tell under that all-white fabric. "Need my fingers to craft. So, are you going to be able to keep your hands to yourself, or do I need to cast a body binding on you?" He used a joking tone, but he was serious.

"I need to eat, Bruno. If I don't, it'll get ugly later. I don't know how much of my head will be left by morning. My leg's making me irritable and the restraints are making me crazy. Bad combination."

He reached over and took the container from Gaetano Sr.'s hands. "I'll do it, Doctor. I stand a better chance of getting it down her throat. You start cutting her pant leg off."

I looked at him with shock. "You're going to *cut* my pants? Bruno, I just bought these jeans. They're designer originals."

He shook his head in the typical guy way, having no clue how hard it was to find clothes that fit and look good at the same time. "I'm sure Dawna will be happy to go shopping with you for another pair. You'll never even notice." The hell I wouldn't! "You'll be too busy eating." He took the lid off the container and the thoughts about my jeans faded behind the hunger. The scent, thin but clearly perceptible to my vampire senses before, now burst into the air and my mouth immediately started to water. He put two fingers into the liquid and drew them out again. My gaze followed his every move, every drip of the juice back into the plastic tub. "It's warm, Celia. Right at body temperature." His hand moved over my face, and after several precise movements of his fingers, I felt the pressure from the quarantine magic release so abruptly it made me dizzy. A few drops of broth dripped onto my lips and slid into my mouth.

I heard a growl erupt from my throat, a sound I didn't realize I could make. Bruno lowered the container toward my face and I met him halfway, my teeth snapping so hard I was surprised my lips weren't sliced. He was startled, but not enough to drop the cup. He let me grab the edge of the container with my teeth and slash at it as much as I needed to. Because I did. I *needed* to.

I hated that.

But the moment the beef, pork, and chicken au jus hit my tongue, my self-consciousness disappeared.

Hunger. I needed.

I drank and let a shudder of pleasure overtake me. I wanted to grab the cup, but I couldn't. So I was forced to drink only as quickly as Bruno poured—slow, just a trickle, so most of it went down my throat instead of down the side of my face.

It took a long time, but that allowed me to savor it all the more. When I finished the last gulp, I closed my eyes and paused to catch my breath. That's when I realized that not only had Dr. Gaetano cut off my pant leg, he'd removed samples of my skin with a scalpel and used the room's portable X-ray machine to snap pictures of my calf. My mind had recorded the feelings and sounds even while it had been completely focused on what I had been eating.

He was done and putting petri dishes in a padded

case with dry ice frothing mist into the air before I managed to gather my senses enough to talk. But as my stomach settled, I started to be able to think clearly. With that came worry that I didn't want to show. But Bruno knew better; I could see it in his eyes through the faceplate of his hood. He looked at me steadily. "So what's the verdict? Any ideas?" I was surprised at how normal my voice sounded.

The doctor released several latches and lifted his hood over his head. The almost casual gesture made me feel a lot better. Now that I could see him clearly, I could tell that he really did look like an older version of Chris, heavily muscled and dark haired, with twinkling eyes bordered by laugh lines. His hazel eyes showed intelligence and strength of purpose, but also a healthy dose of humor. "Not only an idea, but a diagnosis and a cure."

Wow. "Um . . . that's *great*. So what's wrong with me? It's not serious, right?"

Apparently that caught him by surprise, because he sputtered and started coughing. His mouth worked for a few seconds without sound. "No, Ms. Graves. Pardon the expression, but *hell* no. Just because I know what it is and there's a cure doesn't mean you're not still in danger. If you were an ordinary human, we'd be discussing amputation right now. You have a serious illness and the only reason you're not dead is because you already are . . . at least partly. Your body has amazing healing properties. Even as damaged as the tissue was, it was trying to heal as I was shaving skin with the scalpel."

Bruno had also removed his hood and was watching my leg with worry. "So is it what I thought? *M. necrose?*"

Dr. Gaetano reached into his bag and pulled out a fat syringe filled with a clear, almost greenish fluid.

"On the money. I didn't believe it when you first called. It's so rare that there have only been a dozen reported cases in this country since buffalo roamed. But the symptoms you described were so accurate that I took the precaution of stopping by the pharmaceutical research lab they have here on campus to see if they had a few doses of the specific antibiotic in cold storage for teaching purposes. You're very lucky they did. If we're going to be dealing with other cases of M. necrose we may have a very serious problem."

It was hard to see my leg from my position, but I managed to shift around enough to get a look at what appeared to be a large bruise on my calf. It was spreading, visibly growing as I watched. The pain was growing as well.

Crap.

Gaetano was talking to Bruno, holding the tantalizing cure just out of reach. "You should really consider getting your M.D., Mage DeLuca. A lot of people wouldn't have thought of something so obscure as a possible cause. We could use someone with your skills at the center."

Bruno let out a nervous chuckle. "Please, call me Bruno. I had a hard enough time with my magic studies without adding medical training."

"Um, not to interrupt or anything, but is there any chance we could get that drug into me? It's getting worse. Really fast." The bruise that had been the diameter of a baseball moments earlier was now halfway around my leg.

Dr. Gaetano turned and his eyes got wide. "It's accelerating. That's not right. This is normally a very slow-moving illness."

"Could you maybe enlighten me while you're giving

me the injection? It feels like someone is stabbing me with knives all the way up to my thigh."

He tapped the side of the syringe and took off the protective cover over the needle. "*Mycobacterium necrose* is similar to the bacteria that causes leprosy, also called Hansen's disease. Instead of coating the cells in your body with a waxy cover, it coats them with magic that interrupts the nervous system and stops the flow of blood to your tissue." Like a nurse, Bruno ripped open a foil square and removed a pad that smelled strongly of alcohol. Dr. Gaetano used it to clean a spot on my arm, then dropped the used pad into the waste can next to the table, where the alcohol continued to assault my sensitive nose. Thankfully, the vampire inside me was snoozing, so the smell didn't make me nauseous. I was me for the moment and worried sick because the pain was getting worse with each second. I winced and that made Bruno frown, because I hardly ever react when something hurts.

"Which is how it kills the skin?"

Thomas Gaetano shook his head and lowered the needle. "It kills more than skin. It kills all tissue, including bone and marrow. The unique thing about *M. necrose*, though, is what happens afterward."

"Afterward?" That made me furrow my brows, because what could possibly happen after the body was dead?

He nodded. "What's unique about this contagion is that in a significant percentage of cases, even with the tissue dead, the body continues to function. Legs walk, arms move. The eyes, ears, and brain function—but the person is gone. The body has a new function— seeking to reproduce the bacteria. And, like all bacteria, it knows its own transmission vector. The best way to infect a new host is to introduce saliva into wounds. Usually, the victim becomes aggressive, biting and scratching. The teeth are always the last to die."

"So, zombies."

"Yes, and no." His eyes locked with mine, his expression grim. "Zombies can be controlled by someone with enough necromantic abilities. Nothing controls a bacteria colony, and the only way to destroy them permanently is with fire."

I swallowed bile. I'd seen what uncontrolled zombies do to anything capable of movement. I'd had the memories magically blunted to keep me sane, but they were still there. And the flashback on the table had brought them so much closer to the surface. Ivy had been a necromancer.

Gaetano opened another alcohol pad, this time rubbing it against my purple calf. "It's moving too fast. We need to strike closer to the source." His eyes flicked sideways to meet mine. "This is going to hurt. It's thick and doesn't go through a small-gauge needle well. Try to stay calm."

The bruise was spreading over my knee. Calm wasn't really an option, but I could stay still while he worked. I nodded with grim determination. "It would help to hear more about this disease. That will take my mind off the pain."

At first, he ignored the question. He looked up at Bruno. "I need to have these antibodies split faster than normal. Can you do that without a casting circle and while it's still in the syringe?"

Bruno frowned, which made me think that what the doctor was asking for was unconventional at best. Then Bruno looked down at me, asking with a glance for permission. Some things don't really require words when there's trust. I nodded. "Go ahead. Do what you think is right. What's happening to me isn't normal."

One look at my leg, where the bruise was creeping toward my sock, and Bruno let out a slow breath. He raised one hand and it started to glow amber. By the time he'd covered the doctor's hand—and the syringe—with his own, the magic had coalesced to a brilliant iridescent rainbow. The northern lights on a tiny scale. "*Haste.*" He whispered the word, a bare movement of lips and air, but the effect was startling.

The liquid in the syringe started to froth, like it was boiling. Dr. Gaetano held up his hand. "That's enough. Too much more and the syringe will explode." Without another word, he slid the needle into the purple skin and slowly injected the drug. Maybe the drug had actually been boiling, because that's sure what it felt like going in. The searing heat made me gasp for breath and Bruno grabbed my hand. I think I returned his squeeze too hard, because he tensed and his face changed. But he bore the pain and I appreciated it. I did try to ease my grasp, but it was hard to do so because the doctor had moved the needle to a new spot and stuck me again.

He injected the drug in four places in my calf and a final time into my arm. Finally, he spoke again. "We call it Living Dead because that's what the victims become. It's what all the cheesy zombie horror movies are based on, but it's very real. And much more horrifying. Thankfully, there's a cure and the disease has always been slow to develop and easy to spot by trained mage healers and witch doctors. The only time it gets out of control is in remote villages in third-world countries where the nearest witch doctor is miles away."

14

Dr. Gaetano was busy typing into a tiny netbook, pausing every few moments to look into a portable microscope. Rizzoli was in the corner, issuing orders by telephone until the results of his tests came back. He'd been exposed. No, I hadn't bitten him, but the doc wasn't taking any chances.

Gaetano kept speaking while he typed. "The primary transmission vector of *M. necrose,* according to field reports from other countries, is saliva introduction to the bloodstream. I haven't found any sign this strain is any different, which is why I removed the suit."

"But don't we need to check out the school, or find anyone I've interacted with from there? I mean, I haven't bitten anyone . . . that I know of. But those kids—" I didn't mention there have been times I haven't remembered things. I didn't want to think about that.

It was obvious he'd been called from home, from the jeans and polo shirt revealed from beneath the white Tyvek suit. "You're right, we do need to track down the source, plus anyone Celia might have infected. Exposure was probably two to six months ago, but I don't think the vampire bite is the cause. I need a list of your sexual encounters in the last six months—specifically anyone who had open sores or unexplained bruises."

The statement, uttered so matter-of-factly, was so unexpected that I let out a surprised squeak and then coughed. "Um . . . there aren't any."

He raised his eyebrows while lowering his chin, like he didn't believe me. "Ms. Graves, please. We're all adults here and this is extremely important. We need to find anyone else who might be infected."

I understood that. I did. "I'm telling the truth. A kiss here or there, maybe some snuggling, but really—embarrassing as it is to admit—I haven't had sex with anyone."

Bruno busied himself with picking up the used syringe with gloved hands and putting it in the sharps container on the wall. He stuffed the remains of the Styrofoam container in after it. But he wasn't quick enough for me not to notice he was pleased at my admission.

Dr. Gaetano was examining my leg again, blocking my view, and poking at the skin with what felt like calipers. "How about the scars on your chest? How long have you had those?" Wow. He was noticing a lot of things. I had to admit that my V-neck T-shirt did reveal the tops of a series of scars on my chest.

"They appeared after an exorcism."

Bruno added, "Took two priests, a bishop, and EMTs to bring her back after her heart stopped."

I had another thought. "I was choked by a demon last year and had claw punctures in my neck. What about that?"

Gaetano shook his head. "We've never been able to

tie this bacterium to the demonic. So we'll let that go for the moment unless we can't find anything else."

"Honestly, it only started acting up after the bomb at the school." I blinked. "Wait a sec; she bit me."

Everyone turned to me, riveted. "Who bit you?"

"Willow, the little girl. When I was carrying her out of the school."

"How long ago was this?"

I told him. He shook his head. "I can't imagine that's an issue, but I'll want to see the child."

"That should be easy enough." Rizzoli slid his cell phone into his pocket. "They have her at St. Anthony's."

I shifted, trying to get a better look at him. There was something ... odd ... about his voice. When I moved, several hairs got caught in the table and were yanked out of my head. Ow. It suddenly occurred to me that I was feeling pain in other parts of my body ... because the pain in my leg was less. It made me light-headed and giddy even though I couldn't see much difference yet. But the lack of pain in my leg made me realize there was pain in other parts of my body. My stomach and shoulder and the small of my back. Had it spread? My heart fluttered nervously. C'mon, antibiotic!

"Can I please sit up now? This table is killing my lower back. I don't think I'm a danger to anyone. My stomach's settled and I don't feel like biting." It wasn't a complete lie. I wasn't hungry, despite the pain. And it wasn't as sharp a pain as my leg had been.

"I don't see why we can't release the bonds," Dr. Gaetano said. Everyone in the room looked at him, heads spinning like some freaky mix of *Thriller* meets

The Exorcist. "But I still need to get the names of any-one you've . . . *kissed*, along with any clients you've guarded, in the past few months. I understand you're a bodyguard? As for an event just a few weeks ago, that's highly doubtful. As I said, the incubation is months long."

Normally, the question about my clients would be one I couldn't answer because of the confidentiality agreements I use. But luckily for me, I'd taken a vacation after the closing of the demonic rift and that holiday job from Rizzoli and had just chilled. Other than a jellyfish sting on my arm and a pinched toe from a hermit crab on the beach, it had been a really quiet three months . . . until the school. "Actually, I haven't been working much lately. My last job was sort of taxing." I looked at where Rizzoli had been standing, but he wasn't there. I wasn't sure if that was good or bad.

"Release her?" Bruno sputtered. "Shouldn't we be transporting her to a secure facility until the drug takes effect? At the very least, she'll need physical therapy for months."

Dr. Gaetano shrugged. "Oh, we'll be going to the hospital for more tests. No question about that. But I don't see a reason for restraints at this point. The leg looks remarkably better already. The drug has taken effect, and she probably won't need therapy. Take a look."

Everyone looked back at me. I managed to move my head and leg so I could see the pale, unblemished skin. My stomach lurched with a combination of happiness and worry even though my head was still aching. "Whoa. That was fast. Will my head feel better soon?"

Gaetano shrugged. "You don't follow the normal parameters at all. Whether it's your siren heritage or the vampire blood, you heal really fast. I'd imagine the pain in your head will eventually fade. Obviously, I'm pleased. I want to take another saliva sample and do more tests at the hospital, but I honestly think we've got this licked."

Bruno said, "But don't you think—"

I interrupted him. "You're right; the normal parameters don't apply." I tried to take a deep breath that came out as a series of shallow coughs. "Too fast. Everything is too fast. I'm really worried about the people at the school."

Rizzoli appeared again and I hadn't seen him enter. I didn't like that. I also didn't like that he gave Gaetano a warning look. They knew more than they were saying. I was going to find out what that was, one way or another.

Dr. Sloan walked in as Bruno was struggling to get the chest bands to release. He went to the wall, fumbling to get the heavy, oddly shaped metal key into the slot that controlled the restraints. My fingernails started tapping on the metal, trying to hurry him by sheer effort. Finally the key turned and I heard a click. I hadn't been kind to the metal in my struggles, but thankfully the bands all slid back into the tabletop and I finally took my first deep breath since I'd arrived in the room. I immediately got off the table and started stretching to see what was just stiff and sore versus . . . well, versus other things that made my chest tight. "That was a close one." Dr. Sloan spoke sort of under his breath and it made me respond.

"What was?"

He shook his head as I tugged on the chopped leg of my jeans. They'd cut it short—really short, probably in case they had to do more injections. But I had swimsuits that covered more. I felt unusually bare in a room full of men. I didn't catch any of them staring, but I was ready to change into something a little less revealing.

"I heard Dr. Lackley's voice in the building. He's been working a lot of nights and he's been on a rampage lately about unauthorized use of the facilities. I didn't want him to catch us in here like . . . like *this*. I really want to work with Bruno on his project. I'd hate to have an incident involving him after lab hours. So I intercepted him and asked him for a copy of a student evaluation I knew he'd have to get from his office. But we'll have to leave soon."

Bruno let out a noise that told me he remembered the college president all too well and was happy to avoid a confrontation. Of course, he and I aren't on the best of terms, either. I wouldn't say that Donald Lackley precisely *hates* me, but he hates what I represent. I'm one of those really stubborn people who take advantage of openings and then won't leave. "Yeah, he'd be happy to use this as an excuse to boot my butt out of here."

I was technically an enrolled student, so I could use the facilities during school hours. But Dr. Lackley was just waiting for me to screw up. I was one of the last holdouts of a failed promotion that the school had canceled once the administration had realized the potential long-term costs. I had no doubt he was pushing the professor to kick me out of the gardening class, but this would be even better as far as he was concerned. The Board would never question a clear rule violation to end my insurance. Of course, what good is insurance if it doesn't work? Maybe I should just let it end.

We snuck out the back door of the building, leaving Dr. Sloan to deal with Lackley then meet us outside.

The night air was cold and moist, feeling more of fall than spring. The overhead lights were hazy through the mist, but my vampire eyesight quickly took over and the world became sharply defined. Even in the darkest shadows, I could see the outline of every tree, every person walking across the quad toward the dorms or snuggling in pairs on blankets on the grass. In fact, I could see each individual blade of grass. It's amazing to me how much of the world I had missed seeing when I was human.

Dr. Sloan was waiting on the sidewalk near the front door and joined us silently. I wanted to ask a ton of questions, but now wasn't the time. We moved as a group toward the parking lot, keeping quiet until we were well outside the invisible barrier that surrounded the science building. It was only then that anyone felt comfortable enough to stop and speak.

As usual, Rizzoli took charge. "So what's next? Who's going with who? I brought Celia here, so someone is going to have to take her to the hospital."

The headlights of a tall truck, slowly winding through the narrow campus roadways, appeared. Dr. Sloan said, "Oh, look, that's probably the table from the FBI. Come, Bruno, Agent Rizzoli—help me flag it down." He moved off with speed that was astounding for a man his age. Rizzoli smiled and followed at a sprint.

The table. Crap. I'd forgotten all about it. Was it the memory problems again, or just too much happening in too small a space of time?

Bruno groaned. "I should have remembered how he is before I asked him to be my advisor. I'll be the equivalent of a slave for the next year." He pulled me into a hug. "Go get tested. Be okay and *call me* when you know something. Okay? I'll check on you in the morning." I was enjoying the sensation of his body against mine, warm and alive. He is the best damned hugger ever. The scent of his cologne and his skin muddied my mind, and apparently I didn't respond quickly enough, because Bruno pulled back. "*Okay?*"

"Hmm? Oh! Sure, okay. I'll do that." I'd had to blink repeatedly to focus on his question, and he smiled with possessive amusement.

I cleared my throat and felt a blush rise again. "But you try to get some sleep sometime. Dr. Sloan will probably work you until you drop tonight, getting the circle up around that table." I leaned forward to give him a quick kiss, but he pulled back, an alarmed expression widening his eyes.

"That would probably be a bad idea until we know more, don't you think? No kissing until you're cleared by Dr. Gaetano. And no . . . other things, either."

It was my turn to roll my eyes. "Like I said, *other things* haven't been an issue for a while." In fact, the last *other thing* I'd indulged in had been with Bruno, years ago. But that was nobody's business. While I'd never really thought about it, and my therapist, Gwen, had never asked, it was probably significant. The more I thought about that, the weirder it seemed. I could nearly hear Gwen's voice in my head, asking whether I was carrying a torch for Bruno that hadn't allowed me to get close to anyone.

Eek.

He took my expression of sudden panic the wrong way. "Good. You're taking this seriously. Now go." He trotted off toward the two men standing next to the now-parked, unmarked, Army-style canvas truck. I listened hard, trying to focus on their conversation, but they were whispering and all I got was mud.

That left me and Dr. Gaetano alone. I looked at him and shrugged. "Guess it's you and me."

"Let's get moving. We'll get you checked into the isolation ward and start the testing."

Whoa. The *isolation ward*? "Isn't that a little extreme? I thought you said it was pretty much gone."

He nodded as he started to walk toward one of the few cars left in the parking lot, a low-slung silver car that was nearly the color of the touch of gray nibbling at his temples. "On your leg, yes. But I have no way of knowing whether your internal organs have been compromised. Until we test to make sure you're clear of the infection, we have to treat you as infected and contagious."

Oh, what fun. I got to go from being tied down to locked up. What a terrific night this was turning out to be.

"Again? You just took samples twenty minutes ago. What's up with the lab tonight?" The technician with a nameplate reading *Brad* was the same guy who'd been in three times in the past two hours. The blue scrubs and blood-draw cart were becoming a regular sight, which wasn't a good thing. He gave me a dirty look and I gave him one right back. I'd been locked behind glass and silver-steel doors for hours now, dressed in one of those stupid floral print cotton gowns. At least I was still wearing my bra and panties and, oddly, I did feel more covered than wearing the jeans. They'd given me the option to leave on my street clothes, but at least in the gown I wasn't flashing everyone who walked by down the hallway. Thankfully, Dawna was on her way down with fresh clothes. I felt horrible calling her considering how early she'd gotten up. But I had tried Emma first, who wasn't home, and Gran didn't really drive much anymore.

"You think maybe it's not us but the fact you're half dead? It's throwing off every sample we put in."

Well, yeah. That could be it, too, I suppose. "So why do you keep drawing blood? I thought it was saliva that was infectious."

He shrugged as he reached for my arm with latex-covered fingers. "Mine is not to ask why. The doctor in charge ordered more blood. I just get it."

I sighed and tried not to look as he tied off my biceps and pressed for a vein. My eyes closed just before I flinched from the poke of the needle. "You going to leave me any for later? I don't know how well I replace my supply without help."

He'd already seen the teeth the first time he'd come in the room—after the nurse who had been first assigned refused to get close enough for me to grab. He wasn't impressed or afraid, which surprised me.

It was sort of nice. But also sort of weird.

Just as he was pulling out the needle there was a thump against the wall that made us both jump. It was the tenth time since I'd arrived and it was getting annoying. The tech missed with the cotton ball and a small spray of blood followed the needle out of my arm. "Oops. Sorry about that. What was that?"

I held the cotton ball against my arm while he opened yet another Band-Aid. I already had two others on the opposite arm. "Don't know. But it's driving me nuts. You'd think an isolation ward would have thick enough walls to not bother the other patients." When I said "patients" his face lost what little color it already had. I've known a lot of lab guys who don't get in the sun much. But his sudden look at the wall made me realize he might know very well what was on the other side. "What? Who's in the next room?"

He caught himself and turned a fake smile toward me. I knew it was fake because I'd worn one myself many times. "I need to get these samples back to the lab. The doctor will be in shortly."

Yeah, right. *Shortly.* That was hospital speak for "whenever the hell he gets here." I let Brad go without questioning him more, but I would be finding out what was in that next room before I left.

In fact, Dr. Gaetano showed up with another man in a white coat after another hour had gone by. I raised my brows and let out a frustrated sigh and said to neither, and both of them, "Y'know, it would probably be better for patient morale if you didn't put a clock on the wall to watch the hours tick by. At least a magazine would have helped."

His gaze flicked up the wall and he nodded before opening the metal chart in his hands. "Good point. We'll have it removed." Then he met my eyes and a glimmer of humor peeked out from inside the vivid green. "But luckily for you, the wait is over, so I won't have to bring you reading material."

Oh, thank the Lord! "The tests came back negative?"

He nodded once. "Dr. Swanson and I were just going over the results. We're very fortunate to have him on staff. He's actually seen cases of *M. necrose* in the field in the Sudan."

The short, stocky doctor had a swarthy edge that resembled classic Greek, despite his surname. "I've been admonishing Dr. Gaetano for not taking photographs of your calf while the infection was at its peak. It's hard to judge when the saliva, blood, and tissue appear normal. But I finally found the antibodies I was looking for in your blood in this last sample. It's just taken a little while for it to develop."

Oh. Photographs. Yeah, that would have been handy in case there were other victims. Oops. I flinched involuntarily when something hit the wall again. Both the doctors looked at the wall and then at each other. "Okay, so what is that? The tech earlier stared at the wall like it terrified him."

Dr. Swanson shrugged. "It probably did. Frankly, I'm appalled it's still here."

Gaetano let out a weary sigh. "This isn't Sudan, Panos. The situation's not that simple."

The other doctor merely shrugged like it was an argument he wasn't willing to revive. "Perhaps. But I think it would be useful to show Ms. Graves what she narrowly avoided and why it's important she's very open and honest about her recent interactions with people."

The way he said it made Dr. Gaetano frown and let out a slow breath. "It's not a freak show. It's a person's *life*, Doctor."

Swanson's eyes were both sad and fierce. "No. It's a person's *death*, Tom. She deserves her life to mean something."

"Um," I interrupted. "If I have a vote, I'd like to see. I'm not easily shocked. If that matters for anything."

Dr. Gaetano passed over my chart to Swanson with a slightly disgusted expression. "Show her if you must.

But I want no part of it. I have rounds to make." He stormed out the automatic doors with fists clenched. I risked a glance at Dr. Swanson, who just shrugged.

"He'll get over it. Tom is a clinical researcher. He hasn't seen the things I have in the field."

Ah. "In other words, he's not jaded yet." I understand that. Been there, done that, have the bloody T-shirt.

"He's not being realistic. But that's going to have to change. And soon. We only have six isolation wards. If this really is the beginning of a coming pandemic, he won't have any choice." He turned and crooked his finger for me to follow.

Um. So no, while still in my hospital gown. "Can you give me a second? If I'm being discharged, I'd like to wear real clothes out of here."

He really had been a doctor too long, because that was apparently the first moment he noticed the gown. "Oh! I'm sorry. Of course. I'll wait for you in the hall."

It didn't take me long to change, simply because I had no idea when the door might next open. I hated that I had to wear the butt-cheek-revealing jeans but hoped the only reason Dawna hadn't delivered the clothes was because of the isolation ward. I doubt they allow many visitors. It's not ICU. It's even a step above quarantine. When I walked out into the hallway, Dr. Swanson was reading my chart. I didn't know how much was in there, but I was betting there was a lot from the specialists I visited, since several of them were based out of the hospital. "Interesting reading?"

Rather than being startled or appearing embarrassed, he looked up and nodded eagerly. "Fascinating. You've had an interesting life. And death."

"And life again. I'm planning to stay on this side of that coin." That made him quirk a smile my way. "Shall we?" I motioned down the hall, but he closed the chart and pointed in the other direction.

He moved into the lead since obviously I had no idea where I was going in the maze of hallways. We reached a doorway after a series of turns that left me unsure where the hospital entrance was if I had to navigate back. "The patient you're going to see is in an advanced state of *M. necrose*—where you could have gone without Mage DeLuca's and Dr. Gaetano's quick intervention."

I was getting a little nervous about him opening the door, but instead of the door opening, the press of a button opened a window through it. Great. How many people had done that to me while I was sitting swinging my legs from the exam table?

That thought was swept from my mind as I caught sight of what was in the room. I say *what* instead of *who* because I had no doubt there was no *who* left inside the walking corpse behind the reinforced door. "My God." I unconsciously crossed myself even though I'm not Catholic. There are some things that sort of require appealing to a higher power. "She's not alive, is she?"

I could tell the zombie I was staring at was female simply because of the curves and tatters of the skirt covering the blackened lesions on a background of red and purple oozing skin. The eyes were white and unseeing as the zombie walked around the room, searching for . . . well, I don't know what. "What is she looking for?"

Dr. Swanson looked at me significantly. "A victim. Someone to bite or scratch to transmit the infection. She won't find one, of course, unless someone is foolish enough to go inside. We had to nearly restrain her adult daughter from opening the door."

I shuddered to think what I would do if it was my gran inside that room. Would I care about the obvious necrotic skin, or would I run to her to envelop her in a hug? Scary. "Why is she even here? What are you going to do with her?"

He let out a huff of frustration. "Good question. I haven't a clue. In Sudan, we would have lassoed her and dragged her into a fire to cleanse the infection. But since she was a patient here when she died, the hospital's hands are tied. She's still mobile, despite the fact there are no brain waves or heartbeat. They have to worry about the family suing if they make the wrong choice about what to do. In my opinion, she should be burned."

"But what if she can be healed, like me?" Was it just luck I was given the treatment? Would this doctor have denied me that?

"There was no saving her once she arrived. I would have moved heaven and earth for her if she'd had vital signs when she arrived. She didn't. But the staff here has no concept of this infection. They put her in the morgue until I happened to pick up her chart and read the symptoms. I ran downstairs and managed to get the body before it became animated again. The bacteria took over once she was in this room. Thankfully, the staff who came into contact have received the antibiotic." It was at that moment that the corpse ran into the window, making me jump back for no reason. Just creeped out, I guess.

"Who was she? I'm worried I might know her." I had a sickening feeling I'd seen that skirt set before.

15

Saturday was a strange day. I had nightmares all night, waking up screaming multiple times. I couldn't remember the dreams, but I remembered the voice. The witch was there, taunting me, whispering to go out and hunt people. But I wouldn't. I couldn't.

Maybe after everything that happened yesterday, that was a good thing. Dawna had been in the waiting room, pacing. I changed into the new pants in the bathroom and not even her joking about my cut-up jeans being a hot new fashion statement could pull me out of dark and scary thoughts.

Worse still was the morning news programs, which stated *M. necrose* had broken out in Denver and Daytona Beach, two of the first cities where the bombs had gone off. They didn't actually say the disease's name but requested that children and school workers with "suspicious bruises" please check with their local doctors.

Crap. Children were falling victim now. There were special news bulletins on the radio and television, and the small units the CMDC had originally set up to deal with the few adults who'd been dying mysteriously were suddenly overwhelmed by the sheer number of victims. Parents of children from other schools were screaming for information. The press were having a field day. The authorities were managing to keep it contained enough that it wasn't *quite* panic and pandemonium, but it was getting close.

Of course it was worse because it was kids.

Which was, no doubt, exactly why they'd been the target.

Rizzoli didn't come by. He did call. He was madder than hell, too. His intuition told him to go back and talk to the security guard, but Jamisyn was missing. And since there was no hard evidence tying him to the bombs, or the outbreaks, it was only Rizzoli's gut making him want to track Jamisyn down. Apparently, Rizzoli wasn't able to convince the higher-ups to let him chase down that particular lead.

It was enough to make me sick. If the headache hadn't already done it. I was incredibly grateful that the pain in my leg and arm was gone. But the headache stubbornly persisted. What I really wanted was a hot bath. Soak out the tension, wash the hair, and generally try to reverse my crappy mood. I took my phone with me so I could check e-mails and try to reach John. Although . . . calling John while I was naked and in bubbly water seemed to be inviting trouble. I might tell him and he might drive over and—

Oh, that could be fun. The kind of fun that made me shiver deliciously.

I gave myself a little mental slap. Okay, so I wouldn't call John. But I did need to call Bruno. He definitely needed to be updated on last night. I'd left him a message after I been released from the hospital, but it just went to voice mail. No doubt the spell had taken longer than planned. I hoped nothing had gone wrong.

Of course, thinking about Bruno put my mind right back where it had been, because he and I *had* taken long, hot baths together. Very, very hot ones.

But . . . had he taken baths with evil siren princess Eirene, too?

Crap.

Was Bruno addicted to sirens? Could I trust anything he said since he wasn't wearing the anti-influence charm I'd given him? I leaned back into the bubbles and decided that as much fun as it might be to invite one or the other over, it wasn't a good time. Not in my day, or really in my life.

I needed to focus. I opened a new e-mail. Then I started typing with both thumbs while the heat from the water soaked into my neck and back. I typed up my e-mail to Drs. Gaetano and Jean-Baptiste, doing exactly what they'd suggested. I'd already taken copious vitamins, continued to break open memory charms, and waited to hear from John.

I was just up to the events in Levy's shop—and had noted disturbing lapses of memory where I couldn't remember all the details of an event—when the temperature in the room abruptly dropped. A presence entered the room; it was small and quick and agitated, flitting around in a frenzy of movement. A ricochet rabbit of energy. The lights above me began to flicker and spark, causing me to leap out of the water with a splash and a burst of bubbles. Wouldn't that be an annoying way to die . . . electrocuted by a ghost? I looked up at the spirit while I moved to dry floor and wrapped a towel around myself. "Ivy? Is that you?"

The entity stopped moving but continued to flicker and quiver. The lights flicked off. Once, for *yes*. It must be her. She was using our old code, developed when we were children. It only worked with yes or no questions, but we could generally communicate. "Is something wrong?"

One blink.

"Do you need my help?"

One blink.

"Is it about Mom?"

One blink.

Crap. There was nothing I could do for our mother. Ivy had discovered she could "haunt" someone in the family other than me when Mom wound up in jail after her third DWI. Mom's a siren, too, and being in jail, away from the water, threatened to kill her. It had been a startling discovery. I'd appealed to Queen Lopaka and managed to get Mom relocated to the Isle of Serenity, where she could get treatment for her alcoholism and serve out her sentence near salt water.

I let out a sigh. "Ivy—" I paused. Okay, I'd give my little sister the benefit of the doubt. This was the first time she'd come to me since Mom had been transferred to the island. "Is she hurt?"

A pause and then two blinks. No.

"Sick?"

Apparently that was more complicated, because Ivy didn't know how to respond. The light flickered wildly for a moment but then went dark. "Is she scared? Worried?"

Now a single definitive blink.

That's what I was afraid of. I put the toilet lid down and sat. "Okay. Hon, listen to me. We both know

Mom is sick. When she doesn't drink, she hurts. The withdrawal hurts. You know that, right?"

A tentative single flick.

"That's why she's in a place where she can get help. Are they talking to her about her drinking?"

A single blink followed by a wild series of flickers.

"Ivy. Stop. Are they helping her, even if she's sick?"

A blink.

"There's nothing I can do, hon. I want to help her. I do. But even Gran can't help now. She has to go through this all by herself and that will be hard. She'll be angry and scared and will cry and rant before it's done and she's better. But you don't have to watch. That's too much to ask of you. Maybe you should not go back for a while. Would that be easier?"

It was hard to talk esoteric stuff with Ivy. Emotionally, she was stuck at eight years old, and her grasp of adult quandaries was limited. "Would you rather stay here with me for a few weeks until she's better? We can play that video game you like."

A long pause. Then the lights started flickering again, so fast it looked like Morse code on angel dust. The bulb finally gave out in a bright flash before going black. Then Ivy disappeared in a burst of ectoplasm. I'd never seen her do that before. It would disappear eventually, but the jellylike substance near the ceiling was a reminder that even a ghostly sister can stomp out of a room and slam the door.

I sighed and looked around for my phone, hoping to finish the e-mail before the battery died. I realized that my sudden exit from the water had knocked my phone *into* the water. Damn it. At least it was floating, screen side down, among the bubbles. Maybe the battery and memory card hadn't been damaged too badly. I carefully plucked it out of the water and immediately put it facedown on a towel to pull out what water I could. When I carefully turned it on its side to get a look at the front, water dripped out and the screen was dark.

I let out a sigh and took it with me to the bedroom after sopping up the spilled water on the floor with another towel. It would be just my luck today to go to put on my makeup, slip on the spill, and crack my head open.

I was hoping that once the unit dried out it would work again. Otherwise, I'd have to buy a new one and reinstall my whole phone book. I hate it when that happens—I have a big list of contacts. Plus, I hadn't pressed the send button on the e-mail I'd just typed. So that was probably gone.

And for the moment, I was down to my house and office phones until I either replaced the cell or it started working again. I'd heard you could put a waterlogged cell phone in a zipper bag with dry rice and the rice would absorb the water.

If only I had some rice. Sigh.

I knew Rizzoli would probably want me to stay nice and safe here at the estate. He hadn't put any officers on me after the break-in at the office. Since she'd apparently gotten what she wanted—the book about demons—they weren't worried. So there was no one to make me stay home. Besides, I knew that I'd lose my freaking mind from boredom if I just sat around waiting for the other boot to drop. And while it's never a good idea to piss off a Federal agent, I really didn't consider it my life's work to make Rizzoli happy. There were people I needed to talk to. When I'd used the landline to call in for messages left on my cell phone, I'd gotten an earful from practically everyone in our crowd. But hey—not having the phone was a good excuse for not having to listen to it.

The only messages I was sorry I'd missed were the ones from John. "Hi, Ceil. I've got something. Call me." I saved it and went to message two. This time his voice sounded more unsure. "I've tracked the caster, but it has to be a stalking horse. . . . We should talk. Call me ASAP." Another save and on to message three. Tension and worry threaded through his words. "Unless something's gone horribly wrong at your end, you really need to ca—" Then a mechanical female voice: "End of Message. If you'd like to listen to this message again, press five. To save—"

I pressed 5. I listened, then pressed 5 again. There was an odd sound on the recording, right at the end. I couldn't make it out, even after repeated attempts. I saved the message, just to be safe. Then I pressed the button to return the call. It rang four times and went to voice mail. "John, it's Celia. Sorry I didn't call back yesterday. I know you'll be shocked to hear that things went horribly wrong, but it's all okay now. Call me and we'll talk."

I started to hang up, but no, I needed to try to reach him. If he felt it was important, it probably was. I dialed his office number. I knew he often stayed there, in a bedroom next to his ritual room. Four rings later, I figured he wasn't there, and I was just about to press the end call button when I heard a voice on the other end. ". . . help you?" It wasn't Creede's voice, but it was kind of familiar.

"Hello? Is John there?"

The smoothly professional male voice responded, "I'm sorry, our office is closed today. I'll put you through to Mr. Creede's voice mail."

"No! Wait. This is Celia Graves. John left me a message and said it was urgent I call him back. I can't reach him on his cell. Have you heard from him today?"

The man's tone changed slightly, becoming more friendly, and I suddenly realized I was talking to John's assistant, whom I'd met at a party to launch a wine John had helped produce. "Oh, I'm sorry, Ms. Graves. This is Andrew. No, I haven't talked to John yet today. I sort of expected him to be here already. He has his first meeting in a half hour and he's normally early. I'll let him know you called, and if you reach him first, would you remind him about the appointment?"

An initial client meeting on a Saturday was pretty common in our business. Most people who require bodyguards work odd hours and expect us to as well. Well, at least I knew where he'd be later. Because Andrew was right. John was always early . . . for work, that is. For dates, though? He might show up hours late, if at all. I swear the man is as much of a workaholic as me. "Will do. Thanks, Andrew. Bye."

After the call, I tapped one fingernail on the edge of the screen. I'd thought of asking for John's home number, but I doubt Andrew would have given it to me. Decent assistants don't give out that sort of thing. Given what was going on between us, I probably should have John's home number, but I've never asked. It's probably just how I was raised, but I always thought it sounded sort of . . . needy to ask for a guy's home phone number, even though it's fine for a guy to ask the girl. There's no rational reason, but there you go.

But that was only part of the problem. And I knew it. I promised myself that I'd discuss it with Gwen at our next appointment. In the meantime, I had other things to discuss—with other people. And I knew just where I wanted to do it. La Cocina is a wonderful little Mexican restaurant in an iffy neighborhood near campus. It's been the traditional hangout for my friends and me since my first week of college. Rather than repeat myself over and over on the phone I sent a group e-mail on my laptop, asking a few key people to meet me there for lunch.

Unfortunately, a glance up at the clock showed me I was going to have to scramble to make it to La Cocina on time. Sighing, I stomped back into the bedroom to change.

I dressed all in black, which suited my mood, and added only the garnet earrings that had been one of Vicki's last gifts to me, along with a new necklace that I'd had made to match. The original one had disappeared when I was turned. Slathering on the sunscreen, I started out the door.

I hadn't made it more than two steps down the stairs when the phone inside rang, which caused me to scramble to get the door open again and reach the nearest phone. "Hello?"

"Is this Celia Graves?" I didn't recognize the softspoken woman's voice.

"Yes. Who's calling?"

She breathed a sigh of apparent relief. "Oh, thank goodness. This is Gillian Paige. Did John stay there last night?"

My jaw dropped and I stammered, "Ex . . . excuse me? Who is this again?" Her name didn't ring a bell at all.

Her voice was bright and friendly, except with an edge of worry. "Gillian."

Another long pause from me because I didn't know anyone with that name. The silence made her add, "John Creede's sister? I'm sorry. I know we haven't formally met, but I've heard so much about you. I wouldn't normally call, but I haven't been able to reach John and I'm hoping . . . well, maybe that he just forgot our breakfast. Except he's never forgotten before, and we've had breakfast together every Saturday for six years. So . . . um, oh Lord, now I feel awkward . . . but have you seen him?"

John's sister. I didn't even know he had a sister. Or that he had breakfast with her *every* Saturday. So that made me wonder if she really was his sister and if this was a digging expedition? "Um, no. Unfortunately, I haven't. I've been trying to reach him, too. I was supposed to get a call from him, but I . . . lost . . . my cell. Where else have you already tried?" If this really was his sister, she'd know who she should call first. Like I did.

She sighed, not in frustration for me asking but more that she'd already done everything she could think of. "The office and the winery were my first calls. Andrew said he talked to you and that John never showed up for his conference call. And I talked to Pam at the winery, but he hasn't been up there for more than a week. No surprise since the vines are barely starting to leaf out. I was just hoping . . . he normally keeps me in the loop and I know you two have gotten closer lately."

I didn't know what to say, so I didn't say anything.

She sounded really odd now. "Um. Well, sorry to bother you. But if you hear from him, could you have him call me? I've been worried ever since he had to go to the ER for the food poisoning last month. It just didn't feel right. You know what I mean? He's so careful about what he eats and he does have enemies."

Food poisoning significant enough to go to the hospital? John hadn't mentioned that. A fluttering started in my chest that made me take in a sharp breath. A powerful practitioner, capable of setting up a stalking horse, whom John was tracking. A talented witch, capable of blowing up a bomb inside a grade school, whom I was tracking. Damn. "Yes, he does. Hey, tell you what. Let me get your number. I'll look around and see if I can track him down. Then one of us will call you."

"Oh, could you? That would be wonderful. John was right, you are a doll. Thank you so much. I live far enough away that I can only make it up once a week. But I'll come if you think I need to."

"No problem. Happy to do what I can." I took down her number, because even if nothing came of this, I'd like to meet her. I knew all of Bruno's family. I'd met most of Dawna's extended family and had the lowdown on all of Emma's cousins. So why did I know next-to-nothing about John?

Because I hadn't let him get close enough.

Because I was scared?

That bugged me. A lot.

I made it down to the car with no further delays. I would be a few minutes late, but only a few, if I hurried.

"Going a little fast there, weren't you, ma'am?" I let out a sigh and kept my hands on the steering wheel as the khaki-uniformed officer approached my window.

"I thought I was going the speed limit. Isn't it thirty-five here?" Okay, I'd been going thirty-eight. But most cops won't bother you unless you're six or more over the limit. La Cocina was tantalizingly close—just a block away.

"It is. But you were going nearly fifty. Could I see your license and registration, please?"

"What?! *Fifty?* No way." I reached into my purse to retrieve my license and opened the glove box for my registration and insurance card. It wasn't until I had both of those items in my hand and was passing them out the window that I actually looked at the cop. Gran had taught me to be respectful, keep my eyes averted, and answer questions honestly.

When I looked up into the face of the officer, even though it was shielded by his cap's visor, I recognized him. The last time I'd seen him, he'd been lurking in an alley behind the PharMart store, hoping to either frame me for murder or simply stake me. "Officer . . . Danson. I'll need your badge number, please." My voice might have sounded cold. I know I certainly felt a flash of anger at having to run for my life as he sent bullets flying after me. Go figure.

That's supposed to be an automatic thing. If a citizen asks, they're supposed to provide the information. "That's not pertinent. You were speeding. In fact, I think I'll need to search your car. You're acting . . . sus-piciously."

I hadn't been kidding when I talked to Harris. Most of the local cops are still pissed off that I hadn't been sentenced to life in prison for mentally manipulating a couple of them to help me a few months back. I regret-ted doing it, but I would have felt worse had the de-mon I was fighting gotten loose and destroyed the city.

The judge had reluctantly sided with me, but some of the police had declared a vendetta. All I could do at this point was accept the ticket and make sure the dashboard camera in the car behind me picked up everything that happened. I raised my voice until it was a medium shout that should be able to be heard on the recording. "Officer Danson. Please give me your badge number. And the name of your supervisor. I believe you're harassing me."

A second cop got out of the passenger side of the patrol car, a concerned expression on his face. "Is there a problem, Bob?" Okay, Bob Danson—maybe Robert. Good to know.

I spoke again, just as loud, while keeping my hands on the wheel and staring straight ahead. I wasn't going to make any sudden moves. "I don't believe I was going fifty, Officers. I dispute that reading. There wouldn't have been time to reach that speed after the red light at Fourth and Aspen. Please give me your badge number and your supervisor's name."

The new cop was taken aback. I could see his confusion in the rearview mirror. "Fifty? Nah, Bob. We got her at thirty-seven. What's up?"

Danson spun to his left and hissed at his partner. "Shut up, Ryan. Just get back in the car and let me handle this." I couldn't believe it, but my peripheral vision told me he had his hand on the butt of his weapon. And he was looking at his *partner*.

Okay, I was in serious trouble.

I lowered my voice again so that only Danson would be able to hear me, but I didn't look at him. Face forward and hands on the wheel, I nearly whispered my threat. "Officer Danson, if your intention is to make my life a living hell until I break and do something aggressive that will justify you staking me, you're in for a long wait. Give me the ticket. I'll take it to court and make you justify your actions. I'll subpoena the film from every dash cam and street cam. I'll call your partner as a hostile witness. All by the book and allowable. Eventually, someone will find you out. You'll slip up and forget to erase a tape or mess up the radar and then you'll be out on your butt. I'm part siren and I inherited money. I'll live a very long time and can afford to keep up the pressure. How far do you want to push this?"

He let out a growl that was worthy of a werewolf on the full moon. "Wait here." He stalked away. His partner looked after him with a baffled expression on his face.

I wasn't going to let him—or any of the other cops—get to me. If I did, I'd start to actively hunt them. I can't help that they fear me. I can help to make sure they don't act on that fear.

It was the other cop who returned my items as Officer Danson climbed back into the patrol car. "We'll let you off with a verbal warning this time, Ms. Graves. Please watch your speed." He seemed honestly befuddled by his partner's actions, but it wasn't up to me to be the bearer of bad news. Danson was nuts. Either this young kid would be dragged down with his partner, or he'd figure out how to avoid the nuts. I just smiled sweetly with my lips closed and reached into the sunshine to take back my items.

"Thanks. I will."

I didn't start the car until both officers were in their seats. I didn't need this crap and knew it was going to get out of hand again fairly soon. But today I had other things to think about. Soon the scent of cumin and peppers and oniony meat claimed my attention and I didn't worry about it anymore. Except that I set my car alarm and sprinkled both door handles with a special residue that would capture fingerprints.

Not that there should be any. Right?

I walked up to La Cocina y Cantina and was reminded again why only locals eat here. It's sort of a dive. The adobe coating is falling off the walls in chunks that reveal the skeletal rebar underneath. The sign is from the sixties and the turquoise paint is so faded it's hard to read. But the owners weren't worried about the outside. They concentrated on the inside. I knew the kitchen had shiny new equipment and high-end refrigeration and all ingredients were Grade A, top-of-the-line. Stepping through the door, I reveled in the heavy dark wood punctuated by gleaming white tablecloths and red bowls of homemade corn chips. I headed straight for the partitioned room at the back, which holds a large, circular table where a group can sit and share family-style meals. One of the owners, Barbara, saw me. She gave a cheery wave with her free hand and then motioned for me to wait before I joined the others. I paused in my tracks while she put down the plates on the table she was serving, then trotted over and gave me a big hug. "Celia! It's been too long. You're too busy lately."

"Actually," I said, laughing, "I haven't been in because I've been too *lazy*. I took a couple months off and have just been hanging out at home. But I should have come by."

"It's okay. We've been busy again since you chased off those bad vampires. How about a Sunset Smoothie on the house? As a thank-you for your hard work."

I smiled. Barbara and Pablo had created a very tasty

drink for me, full of cheese and sauce and beef broth and lots of spices. "Well, I'll definitely take the smoothie. But I'll pay for it. It's *my* thank-you for sticking around for those of us who can't come in every day anymore."

She beamed, then turned to take the order to the kitchen. "I'll make sure it comes out with the other orders. Go. Sit. Talk to your friends. There's a pitcher of margaritas on the table."

I hoped everyone in the room *was* my friend. I took a deep breath and opened the door.

I smiled at the occupants and took the chair next to Bruno. On my other side was Dawna. Rizzoli was here, and Dr. Sloan. I wished John were here, but of course he wasn't. A year ago, there would have been one more chair—for Vicki—and we all would have been laughing and having a fine old time. Now, the mood was ... tense. They'd been talking before I walked in, but now all was silent.

"So ... what's up? Who has news, because I sure do." All eyes turned my way expectantly. But no. "You guys first. I need to know how my news fits into yours."

But nobody spoke up. Finally, Dawna let out an exasperated breath. "For heaven's sake. Just go alphabetically by first name. Dr. Sloan, why don't you start?"

Aaron Sloan nodded and pushed his glasses a notch farther up his nose. "Very well. As you know, Bruno assisted me in examining the table from Mr. Rizzoli's office. It was quite fascinating! Basically, we learned it contained neither demonic nor angelic residue, but only standard magical traces from a practitioner with impressive skill."

"But that entity at the ceiling ... how would that—?" I turned my head to look at Bruno. He looked tired, like he used to after long nights of studying. It looked strangely good on him, because he was happiest when he was mentally exhausted. "Could you do something like that? Did you see the tape?"

He nodded and I could see a certain level of frustration there. "Could I do it? No, probably not, at least consciously. I don't think this was a spell, per se. I think it was more an out-of-body experience by a living being. That's not something I know much about. I've always considered magic to be tied to physiology, starting at the cellular level. Even if a mage can ghost, the magic should stay with the body, not travel with the spirit. I can't explain what I saw on that tape. At least not yet."

"Can you identify the caster?"

He nodded. "With time. There's no spell here, no physical being to follow. All I have is residue. It's like searching for a head of hair somewhere in the world when you only have one hair to work with."

I nodded. "So, a needle in a haystack."

"Worse." His lips twisted in a wry smile. "It's looking for the haystack with only the *needle* as your guide."

Ouch. "Okay, so we have an unknown caster who might have unintentionally come to the FBI building, and for an unknown reason."

Rizzoli spoke up after taking a sip of iced tea. No midday alcohol for the Fed. "Actually, that's not quite true. We have several clues and I think it all comes down to *you*, Celia."

That forced me to look at him. "Huh?"

"The facts are quite clear." He raised one finger. "You were called in to aid in an interrogation." A second finger went up. "You were in emotional distress, which

Ms. Long informed me has always brought the spirit of your sister to you."

That was true and she would know it well. I'd told her about a class project involving Ivy when I was in college. We tried various stimuli to see if she would manifest. I'd told my sister about the experiment and asked her to *try* to stay away unless I specifically called her. Only when I was in actual mental distress did she come without being summoned. "Okay, I get where you're going. But *why*?"

Rizzoli shrugged. "You wanted answers. The entity offered to help." He held up his ring finger. "And he knew your *name*. There was conscious thought and playfulness. Toying with you by making you guess. So it's likely a mage you know, at least well enough to banter with."

"I know a *lot* of mages."

"Yes, but only casually. Name five that you can talk to any time you want . . . who have enough power to pull it off."

I shrugged, suddenly frustrated. "Okay, fine. Bruno. John Creede. Bubba—though he's not much of a mage." I thought again. "Um, wow. Who else? Terrance Harris, with the police. No, that's too casual. Iv . . . no, he's dead. But wait. Could it be a recently deceased mage? A powerful one? Could someone like that hold their magic together on the other side?"

Bruno and Dr. Sloan both looked at each other; then Bruno shrugged. "I would have said no until today. It's uncharted territory, I'm afraid, Celia. Who died?"

"His name was Ivan. He was the personal guard of King Dahlmar of Rusland. He was killed just before Christmas. He had the oomph to pull off an illusion like the rubber tree one you did in my office. Once, I truly thought he was a newspaper vending box, complete with papers inside."

Dr. Sloan thought about it seriously for a moment, then shook his bald head. "I'm going to say no. Perhaps if he'd died last week. But no, that's far too long. Let's concentrate on the living."

"I know who it could be." Dawna's voice surprised me, but she was very clever and knew a lot of things by osmosis of knowing most of my life history. "And you'd know, too, if you thought about it, Celia. You *amuse* him. He said so at the mall." Her lip turned up in a smile that reminded me immediately.

I sucked in a sharp breath. "Jones. John Jones."

Bruno looked confused, but Rizzoli swore under his breath. "Of course. He's just crazy enough to try it. Just for fun or to make a point. He gathers people, like a collector. He'll find your weaknesses and use them against you for his own purposes."

I let out a chuckle. "That's already happened. More than once." Jones had sort of blackmailed me into helping him get Kevin out of prison when Kevin had been illegally and secretly captured and held there. There was something in Rizzoli's eyes in that moment— something of some old relationship with the mage still hiding, waiting.

Dr. Sloan. "So, for the moment, we'll say we know the identity of the entity. I agree that Jones is a likely candidate. I've heard of him. He's a very powerful mage." He turned to face my side of the table. "Bruno, what happened at the hospital today? Were your tests clear?"

He shrugged. "I gave Dr. Gaetano a saliva sample this morning. But it'll be a few more hours before I know anything. Other than that, I've been working with you on the table. How about you, Celie?"

Wow. Where to begin? "Um, Rizzoli, how much can I tell them?"

He looked thoughtful. "There's not much they don't already know, with the exception of Ms. Long, and she knows all but a few details. Okay, you've all heard the news about the outbreaks?" Everyone nodded. "Well, we think they're connected to bombings at schools all over the country. Unfortunately, we don't have any suspects. We're looking for some people to bring in for questioning, but they've disappeared."

"Not just them. Creede's gone missing, too."

You could've heard a pin drop for about ten seconds; then all of them started talking at once. Dawna's comment came through clearest. "You're sure he hasn't just gone off to do his thing like he does sometimes?"

"Maybe." I thought about that last message cutting off. But I knew he had a special charm—one he could break to call in all his people in an emergency. Nobody at the company knew anything was wrong, so he hadn't broken it. Were his sister and I getting worked up over nothing? Yeah, he really had a sister and her name was Gillian. I'd done a Web check before I drove away from my house. He'd mentioned in an interview meeting Gillian every Saturday for breakfast and the area code of her call was the town where John had said she lived.

The door to the room opened just then and mind-blowing scents arrived moments ahead of trays full of steaming food. Barbara set my smoothie in front of me before any of the others were served and I took a happy sip through the straw. She watched me as she put down plates with a warning they were hot. I would have complimented her, but it was too good—my lips wouldn't release the plastic tube. So I gave her a thumbs-up and she smiled.

Talking stopped for the next ten or so minutes while everybody dug in. A waitress came and went, removing empty plates and replacing drinks. I got a refill of my "drink," for which my stomach was grateful. And I remembered that there was something else here I could eat. They had flavored honey sticks to use on the sopapillas. I loved letting those melt on my tongue. I ordered a sampler of them, but the waitress said they only came with the dessert. So I ordered a dessert. Someone would wind up eating it.

About halfway through my second smoothie, Bruno raised his finger. "I've been thinking about it. If Creede isn't using the ritual room in his office and isn't at his house, then he probably has a hidey-hole somewhere. Most of us have a safe place where nobody knows to look for us. If so, he's probably fine. Just intent on his spell."

Actually, John did have one of those. "His sister said she called there. They hadn't seen him." Although, realistically, he could have as many as he wanted.

Rizzoli spoke through a mouthful of enchilada. "He has the money and power to have a dozen hidey-holes all over the state. No help there."

We were interrupted by my ringtone, coming from inside the bag of rice in my handbag. The stop at the grocery was just before the police pulled me over. Thankfully, nobody saw me do anything but pull it from my purse. I didn't want to have to explain a bag of rice.

I pressed the button to take the call. "Celia Graves."

"Good afternoon, Celia."

My therapist, Gwen Talbert, sounded . . . odd. It made me frown. "Hey, Gwen. What's up?"

"It's nearly two o'clock. I have you down for an appointment today."

She *did*? Of course, I couldn't check my calendar, but if she had it down . . . oops. "I'm sorry, Gwen. I didn't have my PDA until just a minute ago. I'm sort of at the other end of town. Can I switch with someone?"

There was a long pause. "I don't do many Saturday appointments, Celia. But, yes. My three o'clock is here. He always arrives early. But please try to be on time in the future. People count on their appointments starting promptly. I'll see you at three."

I rang off and gave the group an embarrassed shrug. "Sorry. Forgot I have a doctor's appointment right now. I've gotta roll."

Dawna had started frowning again. "You've been forgetting an awful lot lately. You sure you're okay?"

"Honestly? No. Maybe when I find out what sort of spell is on me—" It's not something I wanted to think about. "But John's working on that. If I can just find him, he was sure he could find the answer."

Bruno let out a little growl at nearly the same time Rizzoli did. It was Rizzoli who spoke. "Did you start to write a journal like the doctor asked? Could it be you *know* where he is and forgot?"

I made a scared face without intending to. Oh, crap! I hoped not. "I wrote notes but couldn't e-mail them to Dr. Gaetano and Dr. Jean-Baptiste before my phone went dead. But I do know there are definitely some gaps in my memory."

At least two people opened their mouths to comment, but I stood up in a rush and picked up my purse. "I'm sorry. Can you all wait an hour or two to finish this discussion? Because I really need to keep this appointment."

When Gwen Talbert had gone back into private practice and become the director of Birchwoods, she'd agreed to treat me, but she'd made it very clear that she wasn't going to be at my beck and call. It was hard work to run a facility that size and her schedule was tight. But she's the only one I trust to deal with ... well, everything. And with the door open again on the night Ivy died, I was going to need Gwen more than ever. I was hoping I could convince her to make some of those memories disappear.

16

Absolutely not. I'm sorry, Celia. But no." Gwen's normal calm had been visibly shaken by my request.

I didn't understand why it bothered her. "But it worked so well last time. I know it's helped Dawna and isn't Emma considering it? Really, magical memory suppression isn't that big of a deal. It's even advertised on children's networks."

Her jaw set hard under flashing eyes. "And I'd outlaw that if I could. We're just now, after fifty years of using this technique, finding out the damage it can do to the memory centers of the brain."

That widened my eyes. "Damage? What kind of damage?"

She leaned back in her high-backed chair, frustrated. "Early-onset Alzheimer's, mysterious headaches, and even strokes. My research since your kidnapping has changed my mind about the use of the therapy. I'm only willing to use the technique now on very severe cases, and *only* on the moment of crisis."

Wow. Well, didn't that just suck moss-covered swamp rocks? My headaches were getting more frequent and worse. "Could it affect . . . *memory* itself?" I mean, there might be a spell, too, but who knew if they were related? I asked, almost afraid of hearing the answer.

She shook her head and I felt a wave of pressure lift off my chest. The relief was enough to make me light-headed. "No, there's been nothing in the research like that."

"Then it must be the spell. Rizzoli said the second bomb was supposed to erase all traces of the first one, even memories. And John did find traces of a spell he wanted to look into."

"That could well be it. Still, if you're having memory problems, maybe we need to explore that. Tell me about the last two days—with as much detail as you can. And please, tell me *everything*. It could be quite important."

While it wasn't a normal request from Gwen, I had to admit that I was flattered by her intense attention.

She listened with her whole body, taking notes as I recounted the days since the bomb at the school. While she'd only asked for two days, it was important to me that someone listen to everything that had happened to me since then and why I thought there was a problem. Writing things down had helped me focus my thoughts a lot, so some of it probably sounded sort of rehearsed.

Occasionally, she would interrupt with a logical question, but mostly she just listened. The hour timer rang, but she didn't miss a beat. She just shut it off and spun her hand in encouragement. "Please continue."

So I did. I let it *all* out—as much of the interrogation as I could that wouldn't be classified, the bomb, Ivy, Bruno, the cop who pulled me over, Dawna, John.

There was so much seething anger, fear, and pain roiling around inside me and I didn't even realize it until it all came out. "So," I said, snuffling after my fifth tissue in the past five minutes, "am I a complete loon?"

"Actually, you're not." It almost sounded like she was surprised. "Most people *would* be. You are very mature for your age, but . . ." There was always a *but* with Gwen. "You have to learn to give up some control. Much of your anxiety stems from taking everything onto yourself. You can alienate people just by your sheer dominance."

I shrugged, feeling my defenses leap back to full power. "I sort of have to. Nobody else steps up to the plate. If I alienate people who aren't doing their job . . . um, *so*? Do I care if they like me? No. I would *rather* they like me, but I would also rather they do the right thing so I don't have to get involved. Does that make sense?"

Like a spider leaping on a fly from above, the next words out of her mouth caught me by such surprise. I froze, barely breathing. "Like your mother?"

"Well . . . yes, I suppose. But I have stepped away from that. Like I told Ivy, she made her choices and she'll have to pay the price. Lord knows I have, plenty of times."

"So you wouldn't . . . for example, help her hide from the police?"

What a weird question. "Um, no. I never have before. In fact, I usually tipped off the cops where she was, especially when she was driving drunk."

"When's the last time you saw her?" I felt my hackles rise, and Gwen must have seen something in my face, because she said, calm as ever, "Celia, please don't get agitated. I'm only trying to help."

Agitated? Who was agitated? Just because I could feel my heart pounding and my fists were clenched? "Why are you asking me these questions, Gwen?" My voice was coming out in a growl. It was too early in the day for the vampire to need to come out and play. I'd even eaten, and I knew there was plenty of meat broth in the smoothie. I was in control. "I'm dealing with Mom. I am. She's in the best place for her right now. They can help her. I can't."

Gwen sighed. "I believe you, Celia. But I had to ask." She raised her voice. "You can come in, ladies."

Ladies? Huh? I turned and jumped to my feet as the door to the office opened. Two casually dressed women walked in. I vaguely recognized one of them but couldn't remember from where. It wasn't until her intense eyes met mine that I remembered. Her name was Baker. She was tall and buff, with hair cropped short in a buzz cut that should have been very masculine. I'd envied the weapons on her belt when I'd first met her and she'd added a few since then. She was a siren, the queen's own security.

Oh, crap.

The woman bowed her head in respect. "Princess. I'd hoped you knew something that you could share. But we didn't want to startle you, so we came first to your healer."

I felt a chill come over me as I remembered Ivy's frantic motions. "What's wrong with my mother? That's what you're here about, aren't you? Where is she?"

The second guard, with a name tag that read *Natura*, dipped her head politely. "I'm afraid we don't know. She was taking her daily walk along the beach path but never came back to the facility. Several boats went to the mainland that day, so . . ."

I tried to process what they'd just said. "Um, let me get this straight. You let a woman known for avoiding the law out of her cell . . . *alone*?" Holy Crap! "How long has she been gone?"

Baker let out a low, frustrated growl and wouldn't look at the woman with her. "Two days. While I wouldn't have made the same choices as my associate, Princess, please understand that, like you, your mother is royalty. That allowed for more privileges. And since one of her ailments was ocean withdrawal, walking near the water helped center her. For a time after she disappeared, we believed she was visiting with someone, but after searching the whole island, we're convinced she's left."

Great. Just fucking great. They've been treating my conniving mother like a freaking *celebrity*. She would eat that up and absolutely take advantage of it. I reached up to try to rub away the sudden headache that was making my forehead throb. Different headache for a different problem. No wonder Ivy was so panicked. Not only had she probably watched Mom slip onto a boat, she wouldn't be able to track her over water. Ghosts don't do well over running water, just like vampires. "Um, wow. I can't even describe the level of wrong that was. It had never occurred to me in my wildest nightmares that you might let her outside of a walled and spelled environment until she'd gotten massive therapy. But if you're asking if she's come to see me, the answer is an emphatic *no*. I am the last person on earth she would go to in a crisis. She'd be more likely to roll a junkie for money." I sighed and collapsed back into the chair where I'd been sitting. Well, gosh, hadn't this been an emotional roller coaster of a session? "Where else have you looked on the mainland?"

Baker's voice was now embarrassed. "We started with you, Princess."

I waved my hand in horrified resignation. "Please, don't call me Princess anymore. I'm just Celia. Part of the problem today is the royalty thing. Let's just pretend I'm *not*. Okay? Can I order you not to call me Princess anymore?" My eyes were shut and I realized I was beating my head backward against the pale blue padded headrest.

"Of course, Pr . . . I mean, *Celia*. You have that power."

Fuck a duck. That's not what I meant. "I don't want *any* power. Let's just go find my mother and get her back where she belongs. I'd rather not involve the mainland police if we can avoid it." I hated to admit that I was worried about her. She might not be in her right mind after not only being separated from the ocean but also going through alcohol withdrawal. I hoped she wouldn't do anything drastic or hurt anyone. She's not a violent person. But desperate people can do weird stuff. The siren guards were more likely to handle her gently. The local cops have encountered her before. She'd be locked up in a heartbeat and there wouldn't be any more chances. No more island paradises. Just cold, stone walls.

And she'd die.

I wasn't sure if I could live with that, even though she makes me angry enough to scream every time I talk to her.

I felt a hand on my shoulder and I tensed. It was gentle and I knew she meant well, but I couldn't help my reaction. Not today. Gwen's voice was warm and concerned. "Celia? Are you okay? Do you need to talk?"

The laugh that bubbled up and out had a hysterical edge. "Okay? Hmm, let's see. I got everything off my chest just in time to have an anvil fall on my head. No, Gwen. I'm not okay. I'll live, but this is very not cool. And no, talking more isn't going to help." I wasn't going so far as to say it was a breach of trust. She hadn't actually told them anything or let them listen in. She just asked a few questions and used her instincts to see if I was telling the truth. I wasn't as angry as I was tired and frustrated. It was another thing, another straw on my back, and I could only pray it wouldn't break me.

The problem was that the most likely person Mom would visit was Gran and Gran absolutely *would* help her hide from the police. I slapped a palm down on the armrest. "Y'know what? Let's just go find her. Mom is a creature of habit. She's only been gone two days. One of them was spent traveling. I know every one of her hangouts. She wouldn't go anywhere new." I stood up and showed my therapist my *told ya so* look. "Sorry, Gwen. Gotta go. One more thing I've got to get involved in that I don't want to."

"Pr . . . Celia. We can handle this. We are trained investigators and more than qualified to recapture a prisoner." Baker sounded confident, and yes, she might have reason to be. Let's find out.

"Maybe so. But tell me something, Baker. What was *your* first impression of my mother?" Those hazel eyes met mine for a long moment. "And don't feel compelled to spare my feelings."

She nodded once, short and solid. "I considered her passive-aggressive, manipulative, depressed, and angry.

A classic addictive personality. Frankly, I believed she was probably a flight risk. But . . . I am not the one who decides such things."

That pretty much described Lana Graves. "Good. If we can get her back, and I can get the queen to approve it, do you feel confident you could handle her security from now on?"

"I can make sure she completes her stay with us and doesn't injure herself. As for whether she can be treated—" She shrugged. "That depends entirely on whether she wants to heal."

I understood that. "Then it's time to start making some calls."

I wanted a little privacy, so I borrowed one of the conference rooms down the hall from Gwen's office. My call to Gran wasn't warm or fuzzy. She'd definitely seen Mom but wasn't talking. Sure, I could have sent Baker and Natura to question her, but to what end? Her silence when I asked specific questions told me everything I needed to know. Yes, Mom had stopped by Gran's assisted-living facility. She'd borrowed money and left.

"Okay," I said after writing down a dozen addresses from the phone directory. "Here's a list of the bars Mom used to hang out at. Some probably aren't open during the day, but I couldn't tell you which. How do you want to do this?"

Baker assessed me with that penetrating look that cops have—deciding whether I could be trusted. I stared back without flinching. I was fully on their side. I wanted Mom back on the island. If they could get her clean in that time, all the better. Finally, Baker took the piece of notebook paper from my hand and tore the list into thirds. She handed one piece to Natura and the third to me. "We'll split up and trade phone numbers. Whoever first finds the prisoner calls the others. Do *not* approach her until I arrive. We have procedures and I intend to make sure they're followed. Otherwise, we'll lose custody and she'll have to go back to prison on the mainland."

I sighed. I really didn't have the time or the energy for this. I was still worried about John. But he's a big boy, fully capable of taking care of himself. Maybe it's just like his sister thought and he was heavily infatuated with another woman and sleeping off a great date.

Did I just think *another* woman? And did it sting when I thought it? That implied things I didn't want to consider. Crap.

So yeah, maybe thinking about Mom was a better bet. At least it was a problem that was easily solved. It also kept me away from the house where everybody was likely to find me.

Baker and Natura followed me to the parking lot. I found Rizzoli standing next to my car. Okay, this was the second time he was just too close to where I was to be coincidence. "Are you *following* me, Rizzoli? Can't I even go to my shrink without being hounded?"

He didn't smile. In fact, the look on his face made Baker and Natura tense. Of course, that made *my* muscles go rigid. "No, I wasn't following you. I was following the person who *was* following you. Did you even notice you had a tail coming over here? I expect better from you."

I thought back. Crap, that was just inexcusable. I should've noticed, unless they were very good. But I'd been too busy thinking about what to say to Gwen—

how to even begin to explain where my head was at lately. I let out a small growl of annoyance. "No. That was stupid of me."

"Yeah. It was." He pulled out the device I'd seen earlier, the one with the blinking lights that checked for bad things. He pointed it at my car. Like before, a chirp sounded and then another and a third. But the fourth one . . . the one that should happen right before the remote turned green? It didn't chirp. The remote turned red. "Someone wired your car."

That widened my eyes. "Wired it to do what? Explode?"

He shrugged. "I just got here, so I'm not sure. I followed the other car until I lost them on the interstate and then came back. I got a plate number, but it was reported stolen." He shrugged once more. "Not that that means it actually was stolen. That happens, too. We'll check it out."

But if it wasn't the person who followed me— "This place is guarded hell for stout with wards up the wazoo. No way someone should have been able to *get* to my car to wire it." Of course, after all my care to be sure I dusted the door handles at the restaurant, had I checked it when I'd come out? Duh. No. Plus, Gerry the guard still worked here. He has made it clear to me that he wants me staked and beheaded. He's cofounder with Officer Danson of the "Celia Graves Must Die" Club. But if this was Gerry's doing, it was over. He was going to get arrested and could rot in jail for all I cared.

"It needs to be checked out." Rizzoli was stating the obvious, but apparently that's what I needed today.

"Look . . . Dom." His brows rose at my use of his first name. "On top of everything else going on in my life right now I have a family issue. I have to find my mother before she does something stupid. And if you know anything about my mom, she can take stupid to new heights."

He frowned and his eyes narrowed, meaning he *did* know about my mother. "I thought she was in jail."

I smiled, but it wasn't pretty. "She *was*. That's why I need to find her. These lovely ladies were sent to track her down."

His eyes closed and he let out an annoyed noise. He reached into his pocket. "Take my car. I'll stay with yours until the bomb squad gets here. I'll try to make sure they don't detonate the bomb, if that's what it is." He tossed me a set of car keys and put out his other hand, apparently expecting mine in return.

I caught the keys in the air and felt my stomach drop. I'd watched cop movies before and I knew what he meant. I looked at my beautiful convertible and winced. Yes, there are bombs that can't be defused, but please, oh, please, let this be one they *can*. I love my car. I saved up for years to buy it. "I've got a trunk safe with extra weapons. If you can get them out if . . . you have to, I'd appreciate it. But try not to have to." I pulled my key ring out of my purse, took the car key off, and handed it to him before turning and starting toward his boring sedan. Then I stopped and turned toward him. "Could I have that remote, too? I'd hate to lose your car, too."

He made a noise I couldn't decipher and tossed the box to me. "Push the red button on the bottom to link it to the car. Keep the remote with you. If anyone touches it, the remote will vibrate and sound a tone. I'll get another one from the bomb squad guys. And for God's sake, *be careful*, Celia."

The way he said my name was the same way I'd said his—an acknowledgment of a new level for us. An *I've got your back* level. "Thanks, Rizzoli. Really."

"Bring my car back. That's thanks enough. It would be miles of paperwork if it, or you, blew up." He didn't smile, but only just. I stepped past Baker, who was writing down the license plate number on her torn notebook page. "It's a common model. This will help to know it's you and can also help when you call. If I ask for *the code,* give me the last four characters on the plate."

Actually, that was a good idea. I wrote down *6B82* on my paper for good measure and saw Rizzoli look approvingly at us before he pulled out his cell phone and started making calls.

Rizzoli's car wasn't a bad ride, but it wasn't comfortable, either. When you're used to seats that fit perfectly and instruments in specific places, it takes time to get used to everything. Baker's eco-rental, with a GPS unit mounted on the windshield, turned left at the stop sign and I went right. Driving was like managing a boat down the road instead of the roller skate I was accustomed to. By the time I got to my first stop, downtown, I was glad the sign read *Closed,* because there was nowhere to park that this thing would fit. Another good reason for a small car in this town. But I did have to admit that the tinted windows were better for my skin. It was the first time, other than night, when my arm didn't hurt from being close to the window. Thank heavens I'd remembered to reapply my sunblock when I left the restaurant.

I was glad I'd written down the addresses in clusters by location. I wouldn't want to drive back and forth across town because I was sure I was going to clip someone with that honking big trunk. I'd already had several horns blown at me for coming too close to front bumpers when I passed, which was mortifying.

Harry's Bar & Grille was next on my list. It was a little hole-in-the-wall family bar with windows set high above concrete blocks and covered with neon beer signs. All the signs were lit, so it was a good bet it was open. I didn't recognize any of the cars, but that didn't mean Mom wasn't there. She could have caught a cab. I parked in the lot and went inside. No one there but two old guys sipping from frosted beer mugs in the darkness. I have a picture of Mom in my wallet and I took it out to show them. "Have you seen this woman yesterday or today?"

The two men shook their heads. The bartender, a narrow-faced man with some Middle Eastern in his heritage, looked at the picture while wiping down a glass. "Yeah. Lana, right? She was in last night for a few hours. Hadn't seen her for a couple of weeks before that. Everything okay?"

I pulled one of my business cards from my purse, not answering because no, everything was not okay. "If you see her again, could you call me?"

The bartender looked at the card and then tapped it with a fat finger when he noticed the name. "Oh. You're the daughter? Boy, was she hot about something you did. Ranted to some lady for close to an hour. I didn't listen other than to know she was mad."

All I could do was shake my head. I'd heard it before. I spent my whole damned life being told by one person or another about the wrongs I'd done my mom. She'd tell anyone who'd listen about how I'd abused her some way or the other. Yeah, it always hurt that she considered me an annoyance or, worse, a threat.

But that's how Mom was. I shrugged. "She's always mad about something. Could you call?"

He raised one shoulder. "If she comes in, but I doubt she will. Sounded like she and her new friend were taking off, heading up north."

Well, hell. That wasn't what I wanted to hear. "You actually heard them talk about leaving town? Any idea where they were headed?"

He paused, like he knew something but didn't want to reveal any confidences. "They was just talking. Nothing definite. Just ranting. A lot of them do that—talk a good game and then nothing comes of it. But I'll call you if I hear anything." He turned away then and walked down the bar length, taking the empty mugs with him on the way.

Uh-huh. I'd definitely come back to this place if I didn't turn up anything sooner.

The third bar was locked tight. The last place on my list was Sloan's Tavern. I'd heard Mom mention this place more than once as having a "great party." I could hear music inside, along with singing, which seemed a little unusual for not even four o'clock. I climbed up the two narrow, crumbling concrete steps from the sidewalk. Apparently this place hadn't heard of the Americans with Disabilities Act . . . and their insurance rates must be in the stratosphere. Drunks and stairs don't really mix.

I didn't even have to open the door to hear Mom's voice. She was apparently already messed up, because she was slurring. God, I didn't want to do this. But, as promised, I called Baker and Natura to tell them where I was. Now I just had to wait for them to show up . . . and keep Mom from leaving before they could collect her.

At least that was my plan. Before I got a call.

My phone burbled wetly to life and I pressed the green button. "Hello?"

"Celia, dear. You must talk to her. It's the only way."

I recognized the voice immediately, but it sounded odd, distant and mechanical. "Dottie? Talk to who?"

"Go inside and talk to her. That's why the girl comes and you can find out what's wrong." She paused and then concluded, "And you must hurry. Before the others arrive."

"What girl, Dottie? Can you tell me any more?" But the line went dead. The trouble with clairvoyants was that often they didn't even remember talking to you about their visions, so it wouldn't do any good to call her back. Dottie seems to talk her way through the event, where Emma visualizes it and tells you about it later. Vicki had been such a powerful seer that she feared even vocalizing events in case they'd come true just because they were spoken of.

I sighed and stared at the old wooden door with the barred window. If it was important to do this, I guess I would. But I didn't have to like it. And I knew Baker wouldn't.

Two steps and a squeaking door later and I was inside the dim interior. Although it wasn't **fair** to say it was dim. Only parts were. The rest was lit in vivid red and pink from neon stripes and hearts on the walls. It was like being trapped inside a box of Valentine's chocolates. The music assaulted my ears—a hideous disco version of "Sgt. Pepper's Lonely Hearts Club Band." Who would ruin a classic like that? The whole place smelled of alcohol and sweat, and as my eyes adjusted to the weird lighting, I saw five or six people sitting around a pod of tables in the corner. One woman with dark hair was facedown on her arm; the drink at her elbow had the same colors as a tequila sunrise, but smelled far different.

I saw my mother through the doorway to my left, playing pool with another woman. My mother's companion wore dark-rimmed glasses and a platinum blonde wig that was styled like Jackie O's when she was Jackie Kennedy. Don't see that very often. The face looked familiar, but only vaguely. I stared at my mother with something approaching disgust. She was so drunk she was swaying on her feet and was using the pool cue as a staff to keep herself upright. "Mom?"

She turned and squinted at me through glazed eyes. She actually looked better than I expected. When she'd left the prison here, she'd been gaunt and pale—near death. But now her cheeks were filled out a little and the leathery appearance of her skin was nearly gone. "Oh, man. Why are you bothering me again?"

I let out a sigh, determined not to let her get to me. "C'mon, Mom. It's time to go back to the island. You forgot to tell them you were going on this trip." I reached out to take her elbow, but she'd have none of it. She jerked away, nearly sending herself tumbling across the floor. "I want to make sure you get back safe."

"Just go away, Celia. I know you don't give a tinker's damn where I am or whether I'm safe. You haven't visited me *once*. Not . . . *once*!" Her eyes filled with tears, but it was a lie. She could turn those crocodile tears on and off at will.

"You're not allowed visitors, Mom. I can't come and see you. Not while you're still in treatment."

Her jaw set tight and the tears magically disappeared. "Treament. *Treament?* There's nothing to treat. I'm jusht fine the way I am. Everybody telling me how I'm *sick*. How I can get better. Well, guess what, Celie honey? I *like* myself this way. What'choo think about that? Huh?" She was in my face now, blowing hot, whiskey-filled breaths at me hard enough to make me cough.

"So *you're* Celia Graves." I looked at the platinum blonde on the other side of the green felt. Her voice had a malevolent eagerness that made me immediately tense. "I was told you'd be here, and here you are."

"Do I know you?"

"No, but I know *you*. You're the spoilsport." Her laugh gave me chills because I recognized it, and I reached immediately for my knives. I was face-to-face with the witch from the school. The one whose voice had haunted dreams for weeks after the bomb. She lowered her voice to a harsh whisper that I could hear despite the music. "You won't escape this time."

Her hand and mine moved at the same time, but before I could get the daggers out, she smashed a charm disk on the table. I saw a recent cut on her hand—like from a double-edged, silver blade. Magic flashed through me in a wave that stole my breath and singed the hairs in my nose. I pushed Mom against the wall, where she stumbled and dropped onto a convenient chair. I jumped onto the pool table and pounced at the witch. But she was gone after sending another blast of energy that slammed me against the wall. Then she sprinted out the door.

I'd started to get to my feet to follow when something hit me in the head hard enough to knock me sideways and make me see stars. Another missile hit me in the elbow. I let out a yell of pain and bounced against the pool table. I saw something else heading my way and caught it before it struck my leg. It was a billiard ball. The yellow-striped nine, to be specific.

I heard my mother cry out and watched her get knocked off the chair by a maroon seven to her temple. A trickle of blood started to roll down her cheek and she reached up to touch it.

"Why do you have to ruin *everything*?! You're a jinx! You always have been. Get out before you get me killed." She crawled out the door into the main bar.

I couldn't even think how to respond, because a barrage of pool balls began to rise up from the pockets of three tables and fling themselves at me. Then pool cues pulled away from their holders and hurled through the air, crashing into me. No matter how I tried to shield myself, I got pounded. My best bet was to leave. Taking a tip from my mother, I crawled into the main bar. The spell followed me. Bottles began to lift from the shelves and slam against the walls, ceiling, and floor around me, exploding hard enough to slice through my clothes and skin. Patrons scattered, except for the brunette passed out at the table.

Mom started screaming incoherently from under a table near the bathroom. "Get out! Leave me alone. You've taken it all away. My family. My baby girl. My *life*. Just get the hell out of here. You're a devil child. Evil, undead *creature*! *Begone, demon! GET OUT!*" she screamed, and covered her face as a glass smashed on the floor next to her leg.

A bottle hit me in the ribs and it hurt. But not as much as my mother's words. I wasn't a demon. I wasn't undead, and I hadn't taken her baby away. I'd done everything in my power to *save* my sister. I grabbed a pool stick and started to use the thick end to bat away the bottles, glasses, and mugs that were coming at me.

"*Cessess!*" I heard a woman's voice and looked up to see Natura and Baker standing in the entryway. Natura's hands were in the air and a wave of magic made everything clatter to the floor. The roar of sound, followed by the abrupt silence, made my head hurt. Well, actually, that was probably from the pool ball. If the purpling lump on my arm was any indication, those balls had been whizzing at me at near-hurricane speed.

Baker hurried over to where I was breathing hard and leaning on the pool cue. The other customers and the bartender huddled near the far end of the bar, staring at us with terror on their faces. Baker inspected the lump on my head and the cut above one eye that was starting to drip copper-scented blood into my eye. "I thought I made myself very clear, Celia. You were to wait outside."

Natura was pulling Mom from underneath the table and putting her arms behind her; one of my mother's wrists was already encircled in a spelled cuff. My mother's face was red, furious, and looked different than I'd ever seen. I wondered if the witch had done something to her or if this was just some new, evil aspect of her illness. "I *never* want to see you again. I *hate* you!"

Even Baker looked up at that, surprise clear on her face. But we both turned when the bar's door opened and a young blonde girl was silhouetted in the doorway. "Don't say that, Mom! Don't you *ever* say you hate my sister!"

17

recognized the voice. It had literally haunted me for more than a decade. I felt my legs collapse and it was only Baker's quick action that kept me from crashing to the floor in shock. The long braids were just as I remembered, and she was wearing a striped T-shirt and blue jeans. Just like the last time I saw her.

Mom dropped to both knees so fast that Natura couldn't catch her. "*Ivy?* Baby? Is that you?" She held out her free arm, her anger gone like a switch had been flicked. "Come to Mama, baby."

The girl raced forward, her braided hair bouncing on her shoulders, and threw herself against my mother's chest, arms wrapped around her neck. "Mom!"

It couldn't be. I looked down at my hands. I was still the same. I hadn't suddenly become twelve again. But I couldn't seem to talk. It was just too much, too soon.

Mom was sobbing now, her hand continually touching Ivy's hair, her back. Her face showed the incredulousness I felt. Natura had let her arm go so she could hold her child. I couldn't help but smile at the sheer joy of the scene.

Until the child turned her head.

I felt my heart skip a beat . . . for I recognized the girl's face. It wasn't my sister. "Julie?" I whispered it, but she looked up and met my eyes with a happy smile.

"I know. Isn't it fun?"

Fun? My mother held her at arm's length for a long moment and stared at Julie's face. But she was too drunk—all she could see was the daughter she'd lost so many years ago. "I love you so much, Ivy. I've missed you."

Julie/Ivy smiled and then kissed Mom's cheek before hugging her again. "Missed you, too, Mommy. But I'm back now and we'll be together."

My stomach lurched and my skin grew ice cold. Oh my dear God in heaven. My sister was possessing the body of Julie Murphy and she didn't want to give it up. I knew Julie was a spirit channeler. But her father, Mick, had told me she hadn't had an episode of contact since her grandmother had died when Julie was three or four. I didn't want to frighten her, but possession is a big deal. That's taking channeling to a new level. I'd seen Vicki do it—twice—but she was an adult. She knew the dangers and was careful not to take it too far. But I wasn't sure either the girl or the ghost would know how to sever the tie between them. "Ivy? I know it's wonderful to be able to talk to us, but you have to leave Julie now. Okay?"

I heard a bicycle slide to a stop on the gravel outside and then clatter to the cement as an older, dark-haired girl entered the room. "Julie! Why did you race away from me like that and why are you in a *bar*?" She stuttered to a stop when she saw her sister in the arms of a woman she didn't know. Spotting me, she turned a confused face my way. "Celia? What's happening?"

"Beverly, we need to talk. Let's go outside for a second." I got to my feet, dusted off my pants, and put an arm around her shoulders. She trusted me but turned back more than once to watch her sister hugging the drunk woman.

"Okay, but Mom will get mad if we aren't home soon. I don't know why Julie ran off like that. I nearly lost her in the traffic. She's never done anything like that before."

Traffic? I closed my eyes, feeling my heart drop. That was just what Ivy used to do and it used to drive me nuts. I guided Beverly out into the bright sunlight. When I stepped outside, the spell over the other patrons apparently broke and all but the bartender stampeded out of the bar and scattered. Beverly and I sat down on the stoop in what was left of the shade. "We've got a problem. If you were any other kid, I wouldn't tell you this, but I think you can handle it. There's a spirit possessing your sister right now. It's my dead sister, Ivy."

"Ivy? She's mentioned that name before. She told me just last week that she and Ivy made cookies with Mom, but later when I asked Mom about Julie's new friend, she didn't know what I was talking about."

I closed my eyes. If this wasn't the first time, that was even worse. Ivy used to love baking when Gran came over to the house. I had no idea Ivy had the ability to do something like that. "Have you ever heard of *overshadowing*?"

She nodded. "Sure. That's when a ghost takes control . . ." Her eyes went wide. "You don't mean that Ivy wants to *stay* inside my sister? Won't that erase Julie eventually?"

"It could. I think we need to talk to your parents about this."

"But what about Julie? We can't just leave her like that." She looked back inside the darkened bar fearfully. I shared the fear, but I didn't know what I could do about it at this precise moment.

"Beverly, this is the first time Ivy has hugged her real mother since she died."

Her face grew troubled and I saw something close to anger in her eyes. "So to make *your* sister happy, you're going to sacrifice *mine*? That's not . . . Celia, you can't do that."

"No," I said very strongly. "That's not what I mean. But if I go in there and *order* her to leave, she might get stubborn and stay just to spite me. And my mother has been distraught for so long I'm afraid she'd break out of jail again and come and steal her."

Now she went still. "Oh. That's . . . well, that's not so good."

I sighed. "And the guards aren't going to wait much longer. I'm going to have to think of something."

But the something came to me instead. From Ivy.

"Celia? Mommy? I think I . . . I think Julie needs . . . needs—"

I leapt to my feet and ran into the bar. Julie was sitting on the floor while my mother struggled against Natura, who now held her away from the child she believed was her daughter. "Ivy? Baby? What's wrong? Let me go, damn you! My baby needs me!"

I knelt beside her. "What's wrong, Julie? Or Ivy, or whoever you are."

"Celie, I think something's wrong with Julie. She hurts . . . here." She held up the sleeve of her T-shirt to reveal a dark purple bruise that I remembered well. "It hurts really bad."

Shit.

I looked at my mother and she looked at me with sudden panic. "Help her."

Trying to keep the fear from my voice, I looked into my sister's eyes. "Ivy, you have to leave now. Julie's going to have to go to the doctor to have that bruise fixed. You don't like the doctor, do you?"

She made a face. "No. But . . . I'm having fun. Can't I stay?"

I shook my head. "Afraid not, honey." I thought of something that might work. "Mom has to go back to the island. Isn't that what you came to tell me? That she'd left?"

Her head nodded. "Uh-huh. But you didn't understand. I couldn't tell you so I went to see Julie and she said she'd help."

I touched her shoulder but then moved my hand where I wasn't touching where the bruise was. It was spreading, as I watched. Oh, crap. She'd *kissed* Mom. Only on the cheek, but I'd need to talk to Baker before they left so they could all get vaccinated before they went back to the island. "And that's my fault. I'll be more careful to listen to you in the future. But now you have to go back with Mom and keep her safe. And Julie has to go to the doctor. Okay? So why don't you leave now and you can ride in the car with Mom."

Officer Natura gave me a *look* that said she didn't like that idea. But it wasn't her choice.

Ivy nodded sadly and then Julie gave a shudder and collapsed. I grabbed her before her head hit the floor and lightly tapped her cheek with my palm while I spoke softly. "Julie? Time to wake up, sweetie."

Her eyelids fluttered and she shook her head weakly. "What? Where?" She looked around, confused at her surroundings. I mean, who wouldn't be? She looked from my face to Beverly's. "Celia? Bev? What's happening?"

The simplest explanation was the truth. "You helped Ivy come give me a message. Thank you."

The entity that was Ivy hovered near the ceiling, torn between staying near Julie and near her . . . our . . . mother. I helped Julie to her feet and then went over to Baker while Beverly took Julie to sit on a chair near the doorway of the bar. I whispered fast, trying not to sound as frantic as I felt. "You need to get my mother to a hospital. Quickly. Do *not* take her to the island."

Baker looked at me with alarm and likewise spoke quietly. "We have medical facilities that are the equal of anything here."

I shook my head and hissed, "It's not that. Julie has a very serious illness. I just got over it myself. It's transmitted by saliva and she kissed my mom. Natura might have been exposed also." I took a pen and the list of bar addresses from my purse. I'd memorized Dr. Gaetano's number and scribbled it onto the back of the list. "Call Dr. Thomas Gaetano. Tell him I found another case of *M. necrose*. Have him meet you at whatever hospital you wind up at." I handed the note to her and put a hand firmly on her arm. "This is serious. You need to get the shot, too. Don't go back to the island until you do. I'll make it an order if I have to. You'll infect the entire island."

The two guards looked at each other and Natura went pale. She nearly let go of Mom, then shook herself and held her ground. Baker nodded. "What hospital? Should we follow you?"

Crap. That's right. They didn't even know the area, much less how to get to the emergency room. "Yeah. You keep my mom in your car and follow me. I'll take the kids. I've already had a dose of the antibiotic. Might as well limit the exposure."

Baker apparently agreed, because they pulled my mom toward their econobox. A regular cop would consider her digging in her heels to be resisting arrest. But Natura simply kept pulling and eventually they got her in the backseat.

I looked around, suddenly aware of just what a mess the bar was in. "You'll probably want a check to cover this, huh?" I sighed. It would be a big check.

The chuckle that rose from him was both sad and resigned. "Happens once a week at least. Besides, it was that blonde witch that started it. You just got caught in the middle. Don't worry about it. Take care of the kids."

There was one more thing I had to do before I dealt with the girls. Rizzoli needed to know that the witch hadn't left town. That, in fact, she'd been right here, just minutes ago. I dialed his number with trembling fingers, but didn't get him. I had to satisfy myself with leaving a voice mail.

I sat down with the girls, explaining that I wanted a doctor to look at Julie's arm. "How long has it been hurting?"

She touched the bruise and winced. "Not long. I noticed it a day or two ago, but it didn't start hurting until this morning. Now it feels like—"

"Someone's stabbing knives in it?"

"Yeah." She nodded. "Do you know what it is?"

It was my turn to nod. "Uh-huh. They'll have to give you a shot. Is that okay?"

Julie shrugged. "I used to get shots all the time. I had allergies when I was little."

"Okay, hop in the sedan in the alley. I'll call your mom to come pick you up." They moved to obey and then I suddenly remembered *why* I had Rizzoli's car. Man, I really was distracted. "Wait a second. Hang on."

I held my arm over the doorway so they couldn't leave the safety of the bar, then poked my head out the door and pointed the remote in my pocket at the car. Whew. Four green lights. "Okay, get in. Don't worry about your bikes, we'll take them with us." Finally, Rizzoli's monster sedan would come in handy. I was going to bet both bikes would fit right in the trunk.

Once the girls were belted in and I had both bikes loaded—and the trunk actually *shut*—I sat in Rizzoli's car and pulled out my phone to try Dom one more time. "Rizzoli. Go ahead."

"I found Mom but also found another problem."

"Talk to me."

I sighed and turned the key in the ignition to start the car to a quiet purr. "A girl from the school—you probably remember her as the younger sister of the girl who blew the horn with me at the rift—has a painful bruise on her arm." I paused. "She's eight, Rizzoli."

"Oh, hell." His voice sounded pained. "Take her in. I'll bring your car and meet you at the hospital."

"It's okay?" It brightened my mood immensely. I was surprised just how nervous I'd been.

"Yeah, it's been defused. There was a rather nasty little spell attached to your ignition. It would have made you really aggressive . . . the bomb squad actually went to blows like an NHL Stanley Cup game."

All the better to have me picked up and put away forever. Or worse, staked on the spot. I frowned and felt the bruise on my forehead twinge. It reminded me of my own Stanley Cup bout. "Oh, and before I forget . . . the witch was at the bar I just left, down on Eighteenth. Just now. I got a good look at her face and I recognize her, Rizzoli. I have no idea why she would be involved, but it's the new owner of MagnaChem. G. Linda Thompson. She's been trying to hire me as a bodyguard for over a week now. I've been refusing, but someone called me yesterday and told me to take the job, so I looked her up. She seriously put the hurt on me today with some powerful magic. I've got bruises from head to foot from flying pool balls, bottles, and cues."

"Bruises that . . . wait. Hell. I'll call you right back—" He hung up so abruptly I thought the connection had dropped.

I was halfway to the hospital when the phone rang again. It was Rizzoli and he sounded angry, horrified, and relieved. "I just got off the phone with my wife. Mikey told her about a bruise on his hip yesterday. She mentioned it in passing at dinner last night. Today it's bigger and it hurts. She's on her way to the ER with him right now. I gave her Dr. Gaetano's number." He paused. "Thank you. Without you telling me about that—" He paused again and didn't finish. After a deep breath he changed the subject. "It's probably too late, but I have a couple of people going down to the bar you just left to see if we can do a magical trace. I'm going to need to get tested. I've hugged and kissed the kid. So has my wife."

Oh. He heard the first part and panicked. Which was good. But . . . "Did you hear the second part of what I said?"

"The witch was there. Right. Got it."

"And the witch is G. Linda Thompson. Owner of MagnaChem? Did you catch that part?"

Now there was a long pause. "Thompson? You mean Jamisyn."

My brows furrowed. "No, Thompson. She bought stock in MagnaChem when her dad died and then took over controlling interest. I read an article in the *New York Post* online."

Rizzoli's voice was patient. "And Linda Thompson married one Richard Jamisyn last fall. Does that name ring a bell?"

R. Jamisyn. "So that's the connection! But why would the millionaire owner of a drug company marry a security guard?"

The deep male laugh on the phone startled me a little. "Normally, I'd say you're too cynical and anyone can fall in love with anyone. But in this case, I'm starting to think it was because he was the right person at the right location. The person with the 'in' at the schools. Officer Jamisyn had a side career as a security guard *trainer* during the summer. He had a very interesting list of cities on his itinerary this past year."

I'll bet they included Denver, Chicago, and L.A. Hell. Nice to have the resources of the FBI to search a person's past. "But why would a drug company want to blow up bombs in schools?"

The answer he gave chilled my blood. "They have the patent on the antibiotic. How many doses do you imagine will be ordered by the nation's school system once this comes to a head?"

Holy evil plot, Batman. "So now what? I still need to call Julie's folks and wait with her at the hospital. Well, Julie's mother, anyway." Mick Murphy was in Arkansas, wrapping up the old life that Vicki's millions had changed forever. A vision had compelled her to leave part of her fortune to a total stranger. But it wound up being for a good reason. Her foresight had managed to give us the tools to close the demonic rift. Molly had moved the girls into Gran's old house so Beverly could be close to the ocean and get training on the Isle of Serenity.

There was another pause. "Right now you sit tight and stay with the girl. We're about to try to turn the MagnaChem corporate jet around in midair before it reaches Brazilian sovereign airspace. We just found out she boarded the jet and took off without clearance."

I blew out a slow breath. I hoped he found her and brought her back. The scared little girl in the seat next to me deserved answers.

And justice.

18

I was still looking for a place to park when the radio announcer came on with a "special bulletin." They announced that there appeared to be an unconfirmed case of *M. necrose* right here in Santa Maria de Luna. Not only did they use the actual *name* of the condition, they even had a sound bite with the bartender.

Crap, crap, crap. Were they *trying* to start a panic?

I pulled into the nearest parking spot and sprinted for the emergency room. If the bartender gave the press names, and he would, they'd be descending on Molly right here in the ER, which was just exactly what she didn't need.

I found her in one of the smaller ER waiting areas, sitting on one of those hard, plastic chairs. The girls ran to their mother and Molly began rocking Julie in her lap. Her eyes were dry, but haunted, and I would swear she didn't see any of the people milling around her.

I went up to the reception desk and tried to explain my problem. She didn't swear . . . but she wanted to. "Come on. There's an empty room just outside the isolation area. She can wait in there. I'll have a tech take samples and let Dr. Gaetano know where to find her."

So while Molly and the girls hid in a quiet room with a single bed, I went to move the bikes from Rizzoli's car to Molly's. I came back upstairs and heard the nearly silent sobbing before I saw Molly Murphy's face. There was such warmth there, in the cold, quiet, sterile place. The remote for the television sat on one of those rolling tables that fit over the bed, but we didn't turn on the set. Neither of us wanted to see the news.

Brad of the blue scrubs came in moments later, looking grim. It was one thing to banter with a half-vampire woman who had seen weird stuff. It was another thing entirely to see the bruise on a little girl and know what it meant. He was very nice and kind and I appreciated it.

It took a while for the doctor to get back to us. Not long really, according to the clock. It felt like hours . . . even days. Julie dozed in her mother's lap while Beverly paced like a caged animal. I perched on a straight-backed chair covered in cold vinyl.

When the doctor finally did come in, it was Thomas Gaetano, wearing blue scrubs, his hair still damp from a recent shower. His professional demeanor didn't waver, but I could tell he was weary, and worried.

"We have a positive culture."

Molly's body reacted as if to a physical blow. But she was tough. Her voice was steady, her eyes dry, as she asked the inevitable. "How bad is it?"

"I don't know." He ran a hand through his hair in an unconscious gesture of frustration. "It shouldn't have grown enough to identify that fast. We'll start her on the antibiotic, and we'll need samples from you and your other daughter. In the meantime, we need more tests. I'll speed up the check-in process for her and she'll have a roommate from her same school."

My heart sank. "Who?"

Gaetano looked sad, and angry. "A little first grader named Willow. She's pretty and very sweet."

"Do whatever you have to do to make her well." Molly spoke softly. She petted Julie's hair and her lip quivered. Beverly watched her mother with growing concern even though she was old enough to know there was nothing she could do. She stood in the corner with thin arms wrapped around her body. I went to her and put an arm around her. She didn't hug me, but I think it helped.

Gaetano noticed the interaction between the four of us. "We'll do our best."

"I know you will."

There wasn't much else he could say to her, and she wasn't asking questions—probably didn't even know what questions to ask. I didn't want to alarm her. There was no way I was going to describe what had happened to Principal Sanchez. No doubt she'd met the woman recently. I followed Gaetano into the hallway.

"How bad is it?"

"I won't lie to you. It's bad. And she doesn't have vampire and siren healing abilities. Willow is worse still. I normally wouldn't put them together, but I'm afraid I'm going to run out of beds really quickly. The Atlanta office is trying to have the affected areas stay isolated, so other hospitals will refer suspected people here. It's going to get busy fast."

"Can you have someone do for her antibiotics what Bruno did for mine?"

He shook his head sadly. "We were only able to do that for you because of your special nature. Julie's not strong enough to survive it."

Damn. "So, what do we do?"

"I get to work. You wait. And pray."

Before he went back to work, though, he gave me a quick once-over. I was still fine. No pain, at the moment, not even the headache. Although it had been so busy I hadn't had a chance to think about it. He was pleased, but asked me to stay in touch with him for the next few days. In the meantime he'd be keeping my mom, Julie, Willow, and Rizzoli's son, Mikey, in the isolation ward until he was confident that the vaccine was working. Bruno was apparently on his way to spend the night in the same ward. As far as anyone could tell, I had been Bruno's only contact with the disease, so if he checked positive, it was a bad thing. Gaetano had left word for John, but thus far he hadn't gotten a call back.

Dr. Gaetano also scheduled a time for me to come to the hospital's lab on Wednesday to see if I'd be a good subject to pull antibodies from since they'd started to develop. I hadn't been really thrilled with that idea, what with the siren and vampire blood. But if it became an issue of life and death for a bunch of kids . . . well, we'd have to see. Plus, I had no doubt Dr. Sloan would be fascinated with my blood tests.

Talking to Dr. Gaetano had reawakened my worries about John. Where *was* he? I went outside, turned on the cell phone, and dialed for messages. There was only one. It was from Rizzoli.

It didn't take long for the team to figure out that one of the guards from Birchwoods had wired your car. Once we realized he's threatened you before, we got a warrant to check out his place. We found all the ingredients for the aggression spell and a suitcase filled with unmarked bills, so I think we've got our hit man. He's in custody and he's already confessed he was hired by a witch to get you out of the way. I can get him on a charge of attempted murder of a federal contractor. The threat of life in a federal pen should loosen his tongue even more. We'll talk tomorrow. Get some dinner and sleep. You're probably going to need it. —Dom

So, it really was Gerry. Damn. I'd hoped he could get past irrational hate. But I suppose not. As for rest, I couldn't disagree. But food first, because sunset was quickening my heart even more and making me want to pace . . . to hunt. The shield around the buildings radiated with magic I normally shouldn't be able to see. The people in the building, behind the magic, glowed and pulsed, revealing the energy in their veins I craved. Crap. Even my headache wasn't stopping my muscles from bunching up every time someone quickened their pace a little. The ER had affected me in ways I hadn't expected.

I needed to get something to eat pretty damned fast if I had any hope of getting any sleep tonight.

19

My eyes opened in the early dawn, heart pounding with leg muscles twitching like I'd been running. I couldn't remember being out of bed, but when I moved my legs under the covers, I felt sand on sheets I'd just changed that morning. It was frightening to have no memory of where I'd been or what I'd been doing. Once again I checked for blood. There was none, but I couldn't remember whether I ate dinner before bed. Either I'd cleaned up the dishes or I hadn't. But I felt full.

I shivered and huddled in a chair in the corner until it was light. Safety came with the sun.

It felt strange, planning normal things when so much of life was not normal. But I needed something to take my mind off of everything, and I've found that good old-fashioned exercise can help a lot. A jog was out of the question. I wasn't sure what I would find out in the sand. This was something we could do inside the beach house. And I really had promised Dawna.

I looked from Dawna to the woman pushing a laden two-wheel dolly into my living room. Alex was petite and pretty. Normally she dressed very professionally.

Today, in honor of our activity she was in worn sweats, her hair pulled back into a tight ponytail.

"Thanks for doing this, Alex. I was afraid after that scene in the parking garage . . ."

She snorted. "That was just for show. One of your 'buddies' got a promotion. He's my direct superior now. He's been making my life hell."

Ouch. "Sorry."

"Not your problem. He's an ass. But I wanted you to know it was a bad idea to come to the station, and you really did need to see Rizzoli."

"Yeah. I did."

"Hey, Dawna." Alex turned to the woman lounging on my couch. "Explain to me again why I'm doing this on my *one* day off for the past two weeks?"

"Boy," I said while moving the couch and carpet to the side to give her more room to unload her cargo. "Your schedule sucks worse than mine. You need a better union rep."

The dirty look she gave me said she was well aware of that. "You'll need to clear out a bigger space."

I raised my brows appreciatively and tugged at the couch to pull it farther away from the open space I'd cleared. I closed the drapes so I could take off the sunglasses. "You managed to get the deluxe dummy? Not just the piece of crap from the police storage basement?"

"Turns out I'm three hours short of required staking practice for this quarter. My lieutenant handed me the dolly personally. Hope you don't mind if I log in my own time on it while I'm here . . . seeing as this is a *big* favor." She untucked the padded mat from behind the dummy and rolled it out on my floor. "Nasty burn in the hardwood. Most people start campfires on the beach."

At first I thought she was serious, but then I saw a tiny grin. I smiled in response because I knew she remembered just where the burn came from. "Tell that to Bruno. 'Oh, it's just a little chalk circle. No big deal.' Sheesh. Mages and their spells."

I rolled my eyes and she chuckled before she spoke. "C'mon. Give me a hand with the ballistic gel. It's hard to get into the slots."

I joined her at the dolly and lifted up the hunk of amber ballistic gel while she steadied the red plastic mannequin. The squishy cylinder was wobbly like Jell-O, but thicker and more dense. It was developed to mimic flesh for testing weapons involved in crimes, but the cops figured out it worked well for practicing driving stakes into flesh. I whispered to Alex when Dawna went to the kitchen to grab a bottled water. "Dawna's really going to appreciate this. She needs to start feeling more confident when she's alone."

Alex braced herself against the dummy while I shoved the gel into the round slots and pushed until it was firmly against the solid back of the dummy. "So you said in your voice mail. Is there a bat problem in her neighborhood? Should I get a squad out there?"

I shook my head. "Don't know. It sounds like it might be specific against her—she survived when the master vampire who'd bitten her died. Apparently, some of the other bats seem to think it should have been the other way around. She thinks they might be targeting her."

Alex nodded. "Reason enough to at least have some basic training and I'll probably call it in just to be safe. Never hurts to be careful. Bats aren't very careful about making sure they get the right target the first time, so it's not just her in danger."

The staking dummy was loaded and braced, so all that was left was attaching the spelled computer chip. While Alex opened the padded box it was housed in, I tried to ask something casually. "So . . . about my voice mail. Anything on the other question?" I'd asked her when I called about the dummy if she could check to see if John had showed up on any police reports— good or bad.

She flicked her gaze up for a second. "Sort of. I found three people named John Creede in the Greater L.A. area. John Colton, John Henry, and Jonathan Thomas. Which one is missing?"

The problem was, I didn't know. "Um. Good question. It's the John who's half of Miller and Creede. I don't know his middle name."

She looked up at me. "*Really.* So, John Colton Creede, then. Hmph. Wouldn't have figured that."

That made me frown. "Wouldn't have figured *what*?"

A tiny snort that might have been a laugh, combined with an eye roll, was all she'd give me for a long moment. "*Please.* But there's nothing. I checked out hospitals, morgues, and radio chatter for all three names. There's no mention of anything involving him. What makes you think he's missing?"

"No. Explain first. *Please* what?"

She rose easily to her feet from a crossed-leg position and attached the computer sensor to where a face would be on the mannequin. "Must we really go there?"

I crossed my arms over my chest and tipped my head. "Yeah. I guess we must."

Alex sighed and stopped what she was doing to turn and mimic my stance. "Fine. John Colton Creede is the millionaire owner of a multinational company that provides protective services for everyone from movie stars to heads of state." I nodded and she continued. "He's a level-eight mage who personally protected a diplomatic envoy in the Middle East back in '08, holding out alone against more than a dozen terrorist mages and witches for better than two days." Okay, that was news to me, but it sounded like something he'd do. "He's known to hop in a plane for jaunts to Monte Carlo or to sail down to Mexico for a weekend." Wow. Didn't know that *at all*. "He's also well known for being late to meetings." Well, yeah. *"But—"* She raised a finger significantly. "When he misses two meetings and a phone call in one day, what happens? His staff, his P.A., and even his family don't call the police in Los Angeles, where he's known to live—I *checked*. No. You call me." She smiled and the calm intensity in her eyes sort of unnerved me. "Sort of odd, don't you think? Frankly, Celia, if I didn't know you better, I'd probably be casually searching this house right now while asking to use the restroom. More often than not, it's the murderer who contacts the police first to establish innocence. And reporting it in an odd location is even more fishy."

Well, hell.

I opened my mouth to respond, but she just turned back to the dummy and kept talking. "I just can't decide whether you're too different or too much alike."

Dawna snorted and I glared at her. "Alike. Definitely. But ohhh . . . yeah. You should *see* the way he looks at her when she's not watching. Yum. But definitely too much alike. Not . . . you know, *complementary*. Type A personalities. Both of them. It probably won't work."

It was my turn to snort. I leaned against the wall, feeling the weight of that comment. "Tell me about it. But I always seem to wind up with them." Alex moved her head in agreement but didn't speak because it's not like she hadn't had the same issue with Vicki. Both very Type A. "Maybe it's because they understand the stress. They feel it, too."

Alex looked at me and then at Dawna before she smiled. It had sad edges. "Or maybe we're just masochists."

That made me twitch a little. "Or that."

She let out a heaving sigh. "If his sister wants to make a report after forty-eight hours, I can open a case. Let her know. It's easier to process when the family makes the call. Right now, I've done all I can do." She reached into the sash she wore over her official navy blue police warm-ups and handed me a carved stake. "Except offer to help you work off some of the stress." I didn't take the piece of pointed wood right away, until she thrust it toward me. "You can't hide that look in your eyes, Celia. Not from me. That's why I'm taking you seriously, even if I'm teasing a little. Worry and fear will get you. They're not rational and you can't make them go away just by wishing it. Take the stake. Work it off. Trust me . . . exhaustion isn't perfect, but it works."

Worried? Afraid? For a man perfectly capable of taking care of himself? In some ways, he was better at it than *me*. Totally irrational.

I took the stake.

Dawna proudly pulled out one of her brand-new stakes. "I have my own! What do I do first?"

Alex turned to her, raised one eyebrow, and said, "Get out of that ridiculous outfit and put on something you don't care about."

I fought back a smile. Alex had done in one sentence what I'd been struggling to find a way to say. Dawna looked gorgeous, as always. A yellow scrunchie held her hair in a perfect ponytail. The apricot bodysuit was cut high on the hips and made her tawny skin glow, while simultaneously matching the bunched leg warmers. The striped tights brought the two colors together and even matched the piping on her sparkling white sneakers. Totally perfect for either a spinning class at the gym or a Jazzercise video. But for staking training? Um . . . not so much. "She's right, Dawna. No fashion plates at this party. Look at us. We both look like *crap.*"

I'd gone for black warm-ups because, like navy, they don't show blood. There would be blood—well, of a sort. There were packets of red, mint-scented slime inside the ballistics gel. Drive the stake in far enough and the mannequin bleeds. Hit it with enough force to kill a bat and it sprays you. Part of the exercise is to make sure you can keep going when the stake is slippery or you're wiping sticky liquid out of your eyes. Same theory as when police academies spray trainees with pepper spray and make them keep chasing a suspect. Life sucks when you're going up against the bad guys who *want* you to hurt.

Dawna's face fell. "But I bought the outfit just for this morning. It's *pretty.*"

Alex just shrugged. "No question. It's stunning. But it'll be ruined. Fake blood just doesn't come out of nylon. You'll have to throw it away after. Is that all you've got with you?"

She nodded and I moved away from the wall. "C'mon. You can wear my gray sweats. They've got a drawstring waist and I don't care if they get stained."

Her sad little pout went away when the computer on the dummy finally reset and a screen set where the nose would be displayed: *Ready for first opponent. Choose level.* Then all of a sudden she was dragging me to the bedroom. "C'mon! It's ready. I want to start learning this stuff."

"Ow! Okay, you know what? This just *sucks*! I don't like staking." Dawna dropped the stake and used her red-stained fingernails to pull another splinter from her palm.

Alex responded by handing Dawna one of the ash stakes from her sash. "And now you know why we pay to get our stakes turned and sanded. Raw wood has splinters. I can give you the name of the guy who does this for a lot of us on the force. He's a retired cabinetmaker and does it for cheap. Five bucks a stake and he'll fit the hilt to your hand."

I handed a pair of needle-nose tweezers over. I'd pulled the first three from her palms because I have better eyesight, but she needed to get used to doing it herself. "Alex is right. Don't play the hero today. Of course, if you have no other choice when you're in the field, use what you have. Splinters won't matter. But for now, use the good ones. A bad first experience will make you want to stop training."

She nodded. "Oh, it already has. This is *hard*. I can't even get the right angle to drive it in to hit the blinking light."

Alex put a hand on her shoulder in a sisterly, nonpatronizing way. "Look, why don't you sit down and I'll show you some of the tricks I've learned. We're about the same size and I'll explain as I go."

Again Dawna brightened and she nodded. "Okay. Maybe that will help."

I was closest to the mannequin and reached up to press the selector switch. *Ready for Opponent Two. Choose level.* "What do you want? Level six?"

She took a deep breath and let it out slow. "Rack it up to eight. I need to prove to my lieutenant it was a good workout."

Wow. I let out a low whistle. "Man. I'm not even sure I can pull off a level-eight workout. I'll be interested to watch." I was about to press the start button and step back when she raised a hand.

"Wait. I need to scan my badge to save the data." She reached for her purse that was still slung over the dolly and pulled out the black leather wallet with her badge. I didn't realize there was a bar code in the holder now. When she held it up in front of the screen, it displayed her name and badge number, then scrolled: *Welcome, Heather. Prepare to defend yourself.*

She tossed me the badge. Her hands dangled at her sides; her weight rested on the balls of her feet. I sat down next to Dawna and my friend asked, "Why does it say, 'defend yourself' on the screen? And why hasn't she pulled out a stake?"

"She's a cop," I whispered, encouraging Dawna to do the same so we didn't distract Alex. "Cops can only pull a weapon when there's no other choice *and* the opponent has demonstrated it's a vampire. The dummy will hiss and the screen will show a pair of fangs and only then is she allowed to attack." That wasn't all, of course, but I didn't have time to finish my explanation. The dummy abruptly sprang forward, dipping toward Alex, fast and hard. The thick, coiled spring that formed the lower part of the dummy stretched with a squeak and a male shout came from its speakers: "Get away from me!"

Alex leapt to the side, pushing the dummy back upright. She moved back until she almost reached the edge of the pad.

"Ahh! What the hell?" At the dummy's first move, Dawna had raised her feet onto the couch. Now she stared with wide eyes. "What's happening? It didn't do that to me."

I leaned closer to her, likewise curling my legs onto the couch to give Alex that little extra bit of room while the dummy tracked her movements, turning on its swivel to keep facing her. It slammed forward again, nearly touching the mat, trying to knock her off her feet. "You were only on level one," I said. "On levels one through three, the dummy just sits there quietly and lets you shove the stake into it. You get sound on level three. Levels four through six add movement. The dummy tries to get away from the stake, so you have to fight harder to get it into the heart. Levels seven through nine have the dummy attack *you*. Level ten is . . . well, actually, I've never seen level ten. I have no idea what happens."

Alex spun and kicked, hitting the looming dummy in the chest and knocking it backward on its spring. It moved with preternatural quickness back to upright, which is why the computer chip has to be bespelled. Strange as it seems, regular computer programs struggle with supernatural speed. Then she spoke. "Pause. Hold position. Teaching mode." The dummy stopped moving and the screen started blinking *pause*. Alex commented as she circled the dummy. "What you're seeing right now, Dawna, is a suspect I might come upon in the field. I don't know who or what it might be, except it's shown aggression. Not every suspect who shows aggression is necessarily guilty of something, so I have to proceed with caution." She pointed to spots on the dummy's body. "There are mini-cameras set into the dummy here and here, recording my actions for our weapons master to review. Then he can suggest changes to my strategy or my form.

"Now I'm going to go back to the training mode and I'll start to treat the dummy like a real person. I'll be talking to it, trying to get the suspect to voluntarily surrender, to allow me to approach. At up to level six, that can work if I'm persuasive enough. But on level eight, the suspect will continue to attack and eventually will show fangs. Then I'm allowed to stake it. Until that happens, it's going to try to beat the crap out of me and will probably get in a few good shots. Just stay on the couch unless I get knocked unconscious. Then you can yell, 'Uncle,' and it'll stop. If I'm bleeding or you can't wake me, call an ambulance. But so far I haven't been knocked out at this level." She looked over at us. I nodded, and glanced at Dawna. Her eyes were showing too much white and her mouth was open, her jaw slack. I could see the pulse in her neck fluttering frantically and smell her fear.

I patted her hand and she jumped. Maybe this wasn't such a good idea. I'd thought the dummy would bother her less than seeing a real person spar with one of us, but maybe this was too much, too soon. "Sweetie, if this is going to freak you out, we don't have to use this level."

She turned to me, eyes still wide, then blinked and shook her head. "No. It's okay. I just wasn't expecting the voice. Will it keep yelling at you?"

Alex and I shared a look. We both knew that on level eight yelling wasn't going to be the biggest issue.

Swearing, screams of pain, and piteously begging the cop not to kill it were also part of the program. Crap. Dawna just wasn't ready for that. Heck, the screams and begging had given me nightmares for a month the first time I trained with my friend Bob Johnson . . . on level *six*. "Can you mute it?"

Alex gave a small, sympathetic nod. "Sure. No problem. That's available for use in residential areas where the noise might bother the neighbors." She stared at the dummy's main camera again. "Detective Heather Alexander. Change program. Silent mode. Residential area." A small display in the upper left-hand corner of the screen dutifully appeared. *Confirmed for police training. Mute.*

Everybody has a weakness due to a particular sense. Some people are visual and can't stand to see the sight of blood. Some are really bothered by bad smells, to the point of nausea or vomiting. Touch is what gets me. I'm squicked out by things that squirm—maggots and things crawling on me. Apparently, Dawna reacted to sound.

At least, I hoped it was *only* sound. I planned to watch Dawna closely to see if she was getting traumatized. She didn't need any more therapy bills. Alex looked at the computer screen. "Resume training mode."

Fortunately, over the next half hour, I didn't see the sign of any heightened panic in Dawna. We watched, enthralled, as Alex pushed, kicked, and talked to the dummy. She would give me a good run for my money at hand-to-hand combat and was really good at the talking part. I had a feeling she could normally get the mannequin to surrender even at level six. But not at level eight. "If you don't surrender quietly, I'll be forced to draw my weapon. Now, get on the ground! Face-down, hands behind your head, legs spread apart. Do it!"

She was breathing hard and a sheen of sweat made her bangs droop and stick together. I caught a glimpse of the display as they circled around the mat. *F*ck you, b*tch.* I wondered what that sounded like because I knew the department dummies weren't programmed to say actual swear words. The dummy moved fast and Alex was put on the defensive again. This time, she missed her mark and wound up spin-kicking through open air. The dummy used that moment to swing backward and catch her supporting leg. She went down with an *oof* and Dawna and I winced when the dummy came down again and hit her in the stomach with the side of its head, hard enough to force a pained sound from her throat. The dummy's head always turned at the last second to protect the computer screen. The display now showed fangs and the words: *You're afraid. You'll taste sweet. Die, human!*

Alex had struggled to a half-sitting position by the time the dummy came down again. Ooh, that was going to *hurt*.

But I was wrong. As the dummy approached, Alex pulled a stake from her sash and used the dummy's own momentum to drive the sharpened wood into its heart. There was a beep and red fluid spilled over her in a wash that made Dawna gasp. The scent of mint filled the air, which was just as well. The spray of red had made me twitch uncomfortably for an instant, but mint held no appeal to my vampire nose.

Alex said, "Pause. Hold position. Teaching mode." She and the dummy froze as if they were on a movie screen, locked in a final death battle. Alex moved only her head, turning toward us with her hand still locked on the stake. "Do you see what I'm doing here? The reason you were struggling with the stake was your hand position. See how I've got the bottom of the stake against the heel of my palm? If you grip the stake like a golf club, you can't get enough force behind a strike. You have to use your body weight to *push* the stake in. Think of it like an extension of your arm. You have more strength when you punch straight forward than when your wrist is bent. Down is always best if you can get on top of the vampire. But when all else fails, sometimes you have to allow the bat to attack toward you. Drop and roll. Make it come to you and then push it in."

The screen was displaying *Ahhhh! [hisses. screams].* But Dawna's eyes were fixed on Alex. She was using every muscle, every nerve of her being, to take it all in. There was clarity and understanding in her eyes. Whew, this was actually working. I'd just have to figure out some way to get her past the sounds of death. Maybe I needed to talk to her psychologist about that.

"Resume program." The dummy returned to an upright position and the screen read *Congratulations, Heather. You have killed the vampire. Please replace cartridge.* We needed to put a new heart package into the center of the ballistic gel.

I rose and helped Alex to her feet. Dawna excused herself to the bathroom, pausing to ask Alex, "Unless you need to clean up before you start again?"

She shook her head, accidentally showering me with tiny droplets of minty red. "Naw. I don't get that luxury when I'm actually in the field. They seldom come at me in singles, so I need to be able to work when I'm messy." As Dawna left the room with an odd look on her face, Alex leaned closer to me and whispered, "Will it bother her if I stay bloody? Be honest. How's she doing?"

I shrugged lightly and kept my voice down. "Fine. As far as I can tell, there are no problems without the sound. Don't know what to do about that issue, though."

"We'll talk later. I have some ideas." She wiped away the trickles of sweat dripping down toward her eyes and we replaced the heart cartridge just as Dawna came back into the room.

An hour later, we were *all* sweating. I'd had a turn at level six on civilian mode, which didn't require me to talk to the dummy or wait to pull out my stake. It was easy. So easy it frightened me a little because I started to get really aggressive. I found out later that as I was fighting, Alex began to raise the levels with voice commands I didn't even hear. She upped the six to an eight and then to police mode. Then to ten.

I was moving and dodging, kicking and stabbing without even realizing it. When I finally shoved the stake into the gel chest, it went all the way through to stick out the dummy's back. I heard my own battle scream as I drove in the wood, and it was a freaky sound.

Panting with sweat and minty blood running down my face, I finally turned to my friends. They stared at me with an odd mix of awe and wariness. Neither said a word. They just stood up from the couch, replaced the cartridge in the dummy, and, while I wiped down my face, began their own practice again.

Dawna had used Alex's tips to good effect and had killed the vampire twice. Of course, Dawna had also died twice, but that was the nice thing about training. You got to get up again when you died and you didn't wind up with fangs.

I sat down while Alex did another session. I was still breathing hard, which said I hadn't been working out as often as I should. Dawna had barely raised a sweat and seemed a little disappointed that it wasn't her turn again. She was really getting into this and was flexible enough that once she'd mastered the whole "stake" thing, she would be pretty good at it. Except for those annoying sounds. If only we could push the mute button on real monsters.

My cell phone rang across the room. I skirted around the action on the mat and picked it up, walking into the kitchen so I wouldn't bother the others. The display showed a number I didn't recognize. "Celia Graves."

"Celia? It's Molly Murphy. I'm sorry to bother you. I just needed to hear a friendly voice." She sounded like crap. The little hiccupping sounds in her breathing told me she'd been crying.

"What's wrong, Molly? Is Julie . . . ?" No, I wouldn't say the word. But my brain kept thinking it, no matter how hard I tried to shove it away. *Dead dead dead. You've failed.*

"Not . . . *yet*. But she keeps getting worse, Celia. The medicine isn't working. The doctor doesn't know what to do. He told me I had to . . . prepare for the worst. How am I going to tell Mick, Celia? He'll be here from the airport any minute. How am I going to tell *Beverly*?"

I didn't have any answers and found a chill settling over me. "I don't know, Molly. But I'll come to the hospital." Maybe whatever guardian angel was watching over me would take pity on her.

I hung up the phone and walked back to the living room. Alex was working with Dawna, explaining how she should turn her body when attacked from behind. "Hey, guys. That was Molly Murphy on the phone. Julie's taken a turn for the worse and she's asked me to run over to the hospital."

Alex responded immediately, taking her hands off Dawna's arm. "Oh, man. I'm so sorry, Celia. Just give me a minute to pack up the dummy and we'll be out of here. We can pick this up another time."

I shook my head and grabbed my purse. "No, don't bother. You guys are welcome to stay here and keep working. Just lock up when you leave. I trust you both and who better to watch the house than a cop who's *looking* for a fight?" I smiled, fangs and all, and they both laughed.

It only took me a few minutes to get out of my sweats and change into something more presentable and put on enough makeup to not look three days dead. The trip to the hospital was slow because of traffic. All the hospital lots were full, and there were news vans parked on the street. Crap.

I had to park blocks away, far enough that even with the sunscreen I'd slathered on my skin was feeling the burn. Dark sunglasses cut down on the glare, but the combination of bright sunlight and the workout with the dummy had brought the headache back with a vengeance.

There were reporters at both the main and ER entrances. I'm not exactly a celebrity, but recent events had raised my profile enough that I didn't want them to notice me. So I slipped around to one of the unmarked entrances at the back of the building and worked my way through the maze of hallways until I was just outside the isolation ward.

The first person I spotted was Bruno, sitting in a chair in the main hall with a magazine open on his lap. I raised a hand to catch his attention, and something in my face must have told him something was wrong, because he stood up and opened his arms. I walked to him and let myself be enveloped with warmth and caring. "Hey, you okay?" His voice was concerned, warm.

I nodded against his chest, but it was a lie. "Julie's worse. Molly asked if I could come. Why are you here?"

"Follow-up saliva test. I'm just waiting for the lab to call me. They've been backed up. Did you get the message from Dr. Gaetano?" I shook my head and he gave an extra squeeze. "I overheard him leaving it. Your results came back clear. So you shouldn't have any other problems."

It was a relief and muscles I didn't know were clenched loosened a bit. But that didn't solve the bigger problem. "That's good. But how many others *aren't,* Bruno? How many kids are going to wind up here, just like Julie?"

He paused for long enough that I pulled my cheek away from his shoulder to look at him. His eyes were both sad and angry. "A half dozen people more showed up overnight, Celie. All students and teachers from Third Street. The quarantine and isolation wards are filling up fast. Nobody's said anything. Not a word. But I can feel the tension in the hallways. They're getting worried, and especially since Julie's not improving. Have you heard from Creede?"

I shook my head and didn't want to ask the next question because part of me didn't want to know. I wasn't sure I could deal with the combination of emotions that would result. "Any word on my mom?"

He shook his head, just a fraction, and put a hand on the back of my head to pull me against him again. "They haven't said anything except they're still waiting on tests. The first batch was inconclusive."

I knew I should go to visit her, but what would it really accomplish? She was angry and scared and I was angry and scared and we would just feed off each other's emotions like we always did. But I had to ask, to see if I was being unreasonable. "Should I visit her?"

Bruno let out the sound that he always made when confronted with a seemingly insurmountable problem, part growl and part thoughtful hum. "She's headed back to jail from here?" I nodded and closed my eyes before shaking my head slightly in frustration. He sighed and I felt his forehead rest against my temple. "It won't do anything but get you both upset. But it'll be a sore point if you don't, too."

That's what I was afraid of. I just needed to hear it out loud. "Then you think I should, huh?"

He pulled back slightly and touched me under my chin with his fingers. "Well, your gran is here. In fact, she's already pissed that you haven't been here doing vigil with her. So, while it won't do any good with your mom, you probably need to do it anyway."

Oh, crap. Gran. Here. I should've known. And she *would* be pissed. Damn it.

Bruno pulled me close again, letting me rest my head on his shoulder. "It'll be okay . . . eventually."

That made me laugh. It was a little hysterical, but it was better than crying. And it was exactly the reaction he'd planned. Nobody knows me better than Bruno. He "gets" me. We have the same sense of humor, share most of the same attitudes. When it works with us it's so very good. I took the moment of solace he offered and let my mind and body be whisked away to a better place.

Until the screaming started.

We both reacted as if cattle prods had been shoved into our spines. We sprang away from each other and turned, searching for the danger. It was interesting seeing which people ran toward the danger and which ran away. The doctors and nurses, by and large, went toward. The clerks and orderlies, away. I would have thought at least the orderlies would stay. They're usually stuck with the strong-arm stuff when it came to violent patients. But the looks on their faces as they passed by the waiting room said they wanted no part of whatever was down the hall.

There are laws about what you can bring into a hospital, so all I had were charm disks. I came on such short notice to comfort Molly that I didn't even think about bringing my knives. Well, I wasn't totally unarmed. I had a level-nine mage by my side.

And who needed more than that?

We rounded the corner and got our first look at the future of the city, and possibly the world, if we didn't stop this disease. The man was big, tall, and bulky like a construction worker or pro boxer. He filled the hallway, standing still but sensing around him, searching for something to attack. His skin was black—and I don't mean like an African-American's, but black like something from the back of the refrigerator, where you would rather throw away the bowl rather than risk taking off the plastic wrap. What remained of his clothing was stuck to the goo oozing out of the lesions that covered his skin. Doctors and nurses surrounded him, completely baffled about what to do.

Bruno skidded to a stop beside me. I wondered what our options were. "Jesus. Is that the endgame of *M. necrose*? I've never seen it."

"Yeah. But he's way worse than Principal Sanchez was. This guy's eyeballs are missing. That is, except for what's left dangling on his cheek. And for the record, *eww*. But he's tracking the people around him." One arm made a grab for a nearby nurse and managed to catch the fabric of her scrub top. She was quick, I'd give her that. She stripped out of that thing so fast you'd think it was burning. Her bra was snow-white, matching her widened eyes.

I could smell the death on him, but he sure was active for a corpse.

Bruno said, "I might not be able to pack the body-binding spell into a charm like Creede, but I sure can cast it directly." I felt the hairs all over my body rise in unison as he raised power without half-trying. He whispered the words and I felt the energy leave his outstretched hands and fly toward the zombie in the hallway. *"Corpus bidim."*

The spell should have frozen the man's muscles, causing him to fall straight over and hit his nose on the linoleum.

Note I say, *should*. Because that's not what happened. The power struck him all right, but, like a movie said when a nuclear bomb exploded uselessly against an alien ship, *the target remains*. Bruno got a shocked look on his face. One of the doctors looked at

266 • CAT ADAMS

him and said, "Whatever spell you tried to cast . . . do it again. He's still moving."

Bruno cast a second time and the power he used not only raised my hair but also brought on a sudden bout of my hypervision. I really should have had a nutrition shake before leaving home. While I enjoyed drinking fruit or vegetable juice, they didn't satisfy my hunger. I had to have either broth or a shake to keep the vampire down.

But the second spell likewise had no effect. I tapped his arm and he noticed my glowing skin and reddened eyes. Nobody else did because everyone was too busy watching the zombie, who was baring sharp-looking teeth and clawlike fingernails, all the better to spread the infection with.

"What the hell?" Bruno's voice held equal parts disbelief and anger. He'd probably never failed at casting before, but I knew why as I stared at the zombie with different sight.

I tapped Bruno's arm a second time. "I know what's wrong—why the spell isn't working."

A doctor looked at me and his eyes widened. He reached for the cross around his neck as Bruno said, "Why? What can you see that I can't?"

I pointed toward the zombie. "You're casting *one* spell, against a single individual. But *that* is a million billion individuals, working together. He's glowing with tiny dots of energy." It was bizarre, unlike anything I'd ever seen before. Each dot seemed to have the same bands of energy I'd see in a living person. "What else can you try?"

"Freeze, cut him apart . . . a thousand things. What do you think will work?"

I had an idea. It was on the theory of divide and conquer. "Crowd control during a riot. What works best?"

He shrugged. "Scatter, disorient the group. Make them . . ." A smile lit his face. "Make them disperse." He walked forward, toward the doctors and nurses. "Folks, I'm an A and C cardholder and I'm declaring this an emergency. You need to find somewhere else to be. My lady friend and I can take care of this, but you need to be out of our way."

Most of those present were happy to obey. Only two doctors remained behind. One of them, a middle-aged man with silvered temples, shook his head. "We can't leave this man if he's still treatable. Can you guarantee he's deceased?"

I nodded. "There's no blood flowing through his veins. His heart isn't pumping and I can't see any brain activity. There's no fear center reacting to me. Is that enough for you?" I let the doctor see my fangs and red eyes. "Trust me. If he was alive, I'd know it. Frankly, just the scent of his skin is making me nauseous."

Bruno raised his brows. "I'd believe the nice Abomination if I were you."

The doctors looked at each other and without a word, turned and walked away, leaving us with the colony of disease that wanted to make us just like it/them. The empty sockets turned our way. "Okay, then. Crowd control. We'll start with distraction." I pulled several charm disks from my pocket and threw them hard at the floor in front of the zombie. Light and sound exploded and I went abruptly deaf. I knew the sound probably wouldn't have any effect, but intense light is sometimes processed oddly by microbes. It could be good, or bad.

The zombie lurched away from the light and froze briefly, as though trying to figure out how to proceed. Bruno began a series of complex, targeted castings that I knew were intended to threaten each bacterium individually. The goal was to hopefully cause a threat response to our two attacks and force them to huddle together at the core of the body. I can't really explain how I knew what we were planning, but I knew.

Bruno threw a spell that looked like a starburst firework. A thousand tiny points of light raced through the hall to hit the body, killing small groups of microbes. If Bruno hadn't had a nearly unlimited amount of magic to work with, this wouldn't work at all. But our plan was working, slowly but surely. Unfortunately, I was running out of charm disks. If this guy had been my size and weight we'd already be done. But his sheer mass was making it take longer.

"I still have one of John's binding disks. Do you think it's weak enough yet for that to work?"

"I . . . don't think it matters anymore." I'd been watching Bruno, but now my attention snapped back to the zombie, which was apparently starting to feel desperate. He lumbered toward us, wildly flailing, with claws and teeth bared, making odd noises that weren't words. We backed away. The guy's arms opened wide enough to nearly touch each side of the hall. There wasn't much room to move in the narrow space.

"Bruno, when I count to three, dive into the nearest room. Let's see whether the little guys have pain centers." I didn't give him time to do anything more than open his mouth when I said, "One, two, three!"

He trusted me and reacted without question. He dived into an examination room and I bunched my leg muscles and pushed off from the floor. I sailed high, over the head of the creature, just barely missing smacking my head into the ceiling tiles. Arms reached up to grab my legs, but I tucked them under me and somersaulted over him to land behind his back. I kicked out and hit him hard in the back with every ounce of energy I had. There was a disturbing squish as my heel hit dissolving flesh. I heard a snap as his spine broke. He flew forward down the hall, skidding part of the way on one arm and his face. Bruno peeked his head out of the room and pursed his lips in appreciation. "Nice. Good hit."

The zombie was having a hard time getting up with a broken spine. Yeah, the bacteria colony could probably figure it out, given enough time. We didn't intend to give it any.

The body-binding charm was next to hit the floor, and Bruno lashed out with a similar spell. The combination was too much for the zombie and he froze in place like a really disturbing statue. "That's fine for the next ten minutes. But we need to get this locked up somewhere where it can't get loose."

Bruno shrugged. "I recommend a crematorium. That's the only real fix for this. Most hospitals have one on premises for vampire bite fatalities. But I have no idea where it is."

He offered to stay with the zombie and keep him disoriented while I went to find a doctor. My vision was back to normal, and other than the delicate fangs that I could usually cover, there was nothing about me to make anyone look at me twice. One of the older doctors was able to tell me that the crematorium was in the basement, next to the morgue. We probably needed to figure out who the dead guy was, but there was so little left of him to go by that it might take a missing-person report to connect the dots. But to do that . . . "Hey, before you torch him, make sure you take some pictures. Maybe someone could ID him by his clothes or jewelry. At least his family would want to know . . ." Well, not *details,* maybe. But still.

"What are we going to do if it happens again?" It was a logical question from the head physician while he helped push the gurney toward the makeshift incinerator. "I mean, I know Mage DeLuca is checking the rest of the building, but it seems like that took a lot out of you and it was only *one.*"

Unfortunately, I didn't have much of an answer. "I guess you'll need to call the police. Maybe their mages can set some sort of barrier spell that's targeted to the disease."

He gave me a *look.* "Perfect. A spell to keep the sick away from the hospital. I'm sure our accountants would be thrilled, but it's not much of an answer."

I shrugged. "I'm not a witch, but I'll bet there's something that'll work. It might take trial and error, but this is going to get worse before it gets better."

He let out a sound that might have been a tearful laugh. "That's what I'm afraid of. But we do appreciate your help today. At least he didn't make it up to the second floor, where the quarantine wards are. The last thing we need is a secondary vector. We'll have to disinfect the whole hallway as it is."

Oh, no doubt. It stank to high heaven in the whole area. I'd nearly coughed up my liquid cookies. I wanted to back off on visiting my mom, but when I mentioned that to Bruno, he frowned at me in a way that told me he didn't approve.

So I headed upstairs, leaving Bruno and the doctor to put the zombie into the furnace. Frankly, that's not something I really wanted to see. I went upstairs to the quarantine ward. Dr. Gaetano wasn't there, but the nurse told me, with a smile on her face, that my mother had been cleared and was being *released*. Huh?

The nurse probably didn't expect my frown before I bolted down the hallway.

I peeked through the window of her room, standing where it would be hard for her to see me. Sure enough, she was getting dressed and didn't seem to have any . . . jewelry that would prevent her from walking out the door.

Maybe I'm a horrible daughter. In fact, I have no doubt I am. But I didn't go into the room. Instead, I grabbed the nearest nurse and explained the situation. She agreed to call a security guard to keep everyone in the room.

Then I scrolled through my phone's address book until I got to Security Officer Baker. I didn't even give her a chance to do more than pick up when I whispered, "What the hell, Baker? Why isn't anyone here watching my mom? They're about to *release* her. Didn't you tell them she was a prisoner?"

"What?" Her outrage was immediate and I realized that it wasn't her at fault. "Natura was . . . Oh, *fire and water*, never mind! My apologies, Princess. I will be there in ten minutes. No more. Could you, and I hate to even ask, keep her there?"

Like I had a choice. But I sure as hell wasn't going to be in the room when the lady with the cuffs arrived. No, as much as I wanted to see Molly and Julie, it was better for everyone if I stayed away until my mother was back in custody. I sent a text message to Molly's phone to explain and told her I'd try to talk to her tomorrow. Yeah, I knew I wasn't being the best friend, but sometimes that's the best I can do.

Damn it.

I squatted, ready to sit down in front of the doors to keep them from opening until a guard arrived. That's when I heard the voice.

"What precisely do you think you're doing?" The words were cold, crisp, with edges like razor blades. I'd heard my gran use that tone before, but never with me.

"Gran . . ." I turned to talk to her and the words froze in my mouth. My grandmother is tiny, and seems to grow more frail every time I see her. But she has a will of iron, and nothing in this world will shake her belief in God, and in my mother.

"I asked you a question."

"She needs to stay here until the guards can come get her."

Her arms crossed over her chest and her chin lowered into battle position. "I see. So you're taking it on yourself to imprison her."

"No, the hospital is, as they should. Her release order was a mistake and you know it. She's an escaped convict, Gran. If they don't take her back to the island she'll wind up in jail here again. The last time almost killed her. She has to go back."

Her lips pressed together in a tight line. She didn't argue with me on that. She couldn't. So she changed the subject. "What is this Lana tells me about you taking Ivy from her? Your sister's ghost is all your mother has left of her. You've no right . . ."

My eyes rolled automatically. I couldn't seem to help it and it didn't improve Gran's mood. "I didn't take Ivy's ghost away. I couldn't if I wanted to. Ivy has her own mind and does what she wants. But I'm not going to let Mom steal another woman's child by having Ivy overshadow her."

Gran puffed up like a blowfish, her face getting red. "Overshadow a living child? That's . . . *evil.* My Lana would never!"

The truth hurt, but I wasn't going to let the charade go on anymore. "Your Lana damned well did. And as for evil, well, that's my mom."

Her hand struck out in a blur. Not a fist, but a good, hard slap to my face. I was so shocked I didn't even try to avoid the blow. I just stood there, mouth hanging open, as the grandmother I adored turned her back on me and walked away.

20

left another message for John from my car, becoming increasingly worried about him. I might not have intuition like Rizzoli believed, but my instincts told me I wasn't going to like the final result. But what else could I do? I simply didn't know him well enough to call friends and search his known hideouts. I didn't know any of them.

That was bugging me more and more.

I called Andrew and Gillian again, but did nothing but worry them further. Gillian promised she'd call the L.A. police when the full forty-eight hours had passed. At least it was something. Then I called Molly Murphy. She'd heard about the zombie, so she was fine with my going home. "Besides, there's nothing you can do. Nothing any of us can do." Mick had finally arrived from the airport with his mother. Mick and Molly stood vigil over Julie while his mother went to the house with Beverly.

The bacteria had necropsied Julie's whole arm and part of her chest and she was on oxygen. I told Molly I'd be right down, but she said no. They'd moved Julie into the ICU and she couldn't have any visitors, not even family. The same was true with Willow. All we could do was hope.

Hope. I had to have hope. Hope that Julie and Willow would make it; hope that my gran would get past our argument.

But what if she didn't? Gran loved Mom. She was willfully blind to my mother's faults, enabling her at every turn. If she had to choose, I'd lose her. I'd already lost Mom. Not going and standing vigil the way Molly and Mick were for Julie hadn't even been a conscious decision. I just hadn't. I suppose I should feel bad about that and, in a way, I did. I will always love my mom, but her words and actions in the bar had finally finished it for me. *You're a devil child.* I'd believed for so long that if she just had a chance to dry out, we would be happy again. But she'd said it herself. She didn't want to. Didn't want *me*.

If that was true, and I believed her, then she was never going to change. She'd never be the person I'd loved, who'd loved me. We'd reached the end of the road. She made her choice. She loved the bottle more. I couldn't live with her choices . . . no, *wouldn't* live with her this way. It was over. But, oh God, how it hurt. She's my *mom*. I wanted her to be my mom.

But she didn't want to be.

I sat in my car and cried until there were no more tears left. I felt . . . beaten. And I stank. The fight with the zombie had been ugly and messy. I wanted a shower. I needed food. Since the office was closer than the house, that's where I went.

Traffic thinned out the farther I got from the hospital. I'd bet if I was in a helicopter flying above the city, it would look like either a multistar benefit concert was happening at the hospital or a tsunami had hit the coast.

I was within a few blocks of the office when a black sedan cut in front of me with a screech of tires and blue, rubber-scented smoke, startling me enough to make me jump and jerk the wheel, curbing the car. Damned if they hadn't tried to run me right into a tree. Palm trees don't look like much, but they're a hell of a lot bigger than my Miata. I probably would have wound up right back at the hospital.

My foot slammed down on the brake pedal until the air was filled with the scent of burning brakes. I gave in to the desire to blast the horn and flip off the driver. What I found interesting is that when I got back onto the road and sped up to write down the license number, the rear plate was missing. That turned it from careless to intentional, which ticked me off.

The next interesting thing was that the car pulled into my office's parking lot at a speed that caused the muffler to scrape on the concrete when it hit the entrance—hard enough to raise sparks. Another screech of the tires made me fight to look around the palms, and when I saw the rear door open and a large object get thrown out, I put my foot to the floor and pulled in behind the sedan, hoping to keep them in the lot. But the driver was good—very good. He skittered past my sliding Miata by putting his car into a glide that might have looked like ballet to a passerby or at least a "professional driver on a closed course." I couldn't pursue the black car without running over the inert form lying on the pavement.

It was a body and it wasn't moving. There was a smear of red across the concrete where the body had rolled. I threw the car into park and forced my sore feet into a run as I glimpsed the gold Rolex on the man's wrist and the honey color of his hair under the crusted blood.

When I cautiously rolled the man onto his back I let out a noise from the back of my throat and my hand went to my mouth. "Oh God, John." Creede's face was a mess of bruises and cuts that had taken some time to bestow, including a gash over one eye that would need stitches and a split, purpled lip. I couldn't feel any magic from him at all and that worried me most. Who the hell could do this to him?

He was breathing, thank God. When I tentatively touched his stubbled chin on the way to check the pulse in his neck, he stirred and his eyes fluttered open. I kept my voice soft and confident. But there was fear threaded among the words. Were the bruises only the beginning of the beating or, worse, were they not from a beating at all? What lay below the surface? "Just lie still. I'm going to call nine-one-one and get you to the hospital."

I felt a surprisingly firm hand on my arm. "No."

His eyes might not have their usual flames in the back, but there was fire there. Still, he couldn't be serious. "You need a hospital, John. You could have internal injuries and—" No. I wasn't going to tell him about *M. necrose.* All I had to do was get him to the hospital and they'd fix him. They had to fix him.

He started to pull himself up, using my arm like a rope climb. "Just get me upstairs. I'll be fine." He coughed shallow and then deep and then spat thick blood onto the sidewalk, not just red-tinged spit. Crap.

"Oh, for God's sake. Just quit the tough-guy thing and admit you need a doctor. I'm calling an ambulance." Now I was getting angry. A beating like this could kill him if he was bleeding internally. I shook him off and started around the car to get my cell phone.

"Celia." The tone in his voice stopped me. I couldn't describe it, exactly. But I turned and looked at the pain in his face. "The press would crucify me and my company. We're already in trouble because of Miller's death. We employ thousands of people around the world. *Thousands.* Just help me upstairs. Please."

The press? I thought about it for a long moment while I stared at the hideous damage to his body. I knew his partner's death had hit him hard personally, but it had never occurred to me how it would affect the company. Miller & Creede was the best of the best. But to have one owner die while trafficking with demons and the other . . . shit. It was one thing to protect your client and get beat up. That happened to all of us. It was another thing altogether for a bodyguard, not to mention a defensive mage, to be snatched, beat up like a mugging victim, and dumped. He was right. I hated it, but he was right. I let out a harsh growl. "I've got some medical charms in my office. We can at least get that cut near your eye fixed. It's bleeding pretty bad."

He shrugged as best he could and I got the feeling he'd had worse in the past . . . another thing he should have told me about. "It's a head wound. They bleed." I helped him to his feet and got an arm around his broad back. At the first step he put his full weight on my shoulder before pulling in a hiss of air. "Hope one of them mends bones. I think my leg is broken."

A frustrated sigh slipped out of me. "Yeah. If it's not fractured too bad. Can you put any weight on it at all, or do I need to carry you up?"

He turned his head enough to look at me as if I'd lost my mind . . . even though he probably knew I *could* carry him up two flights of stairs. His voice was dry and firm. "I'll manage."

My eyes rolled automatically.

Men.

21

t took nearly half an hour to reach the third floor. Thankfully, the cat had realized now wasn't a time to be affectionate and weave between our legs. She'd taken one look at us and gone back to her favorite perch on the windowsill. I was just glad we hadn't tumbled down the stairs. The treads are narrow and it wasn't easy to keep our balance while he hobbled and hopped.

We paused by my office door for John to catch his breath. That's when I found a note taped on the paneled wood.

Tenant Meeting on Tuesday at 10:00. Be there.
Ron

I yanked it off the door and crumpled it in one hand before throwing it on the floor. Yeah, I'd be at the tenants' meeting all right. I couldn't wait to see the look on Ron's snotty face when he found out I was the new building owner. Maybe I'd kick his ass to the curb.

John was pale and sweating from the stress of the climb up the stairs, but he wasn't making a sound. I had to give him credit. "Okay, it's only a few more feet to your office." John's office was right next to mine. He'd rented it a few months before during the blowup with Miller. I wasn't quite sure why he'd kept the lease after Miller's death. "Hang in there for just a few more seconds and you can lie down."

"There's nowhere to lay down in there. All I have is a desk and a safe."

Okay. Change of plans. I pulled out my keys and opened the door to my own office. In a few minutes, I had John settled on my couch. When I put one of the pillows under his head, he grunted. "It's comfortable."

I had to let out a small chuckle. "Glad it suits you. I bought it after the last time I wound up sleeping on the office floor. It's good to sleep on after long nights. Hang on while I get the med kit out of the safe." He turned his head so he could watch me open it. He's mentioned more than once he finds the whole process fascinating. He should. The safe is top-of-the-line and takes a good part of my income to maintain. The day we'd first met, John had planned to stay outside the building and watch the perimeter while guarding his movie star client, but the sheer power of the safe's magical wards had intrigued him enough to come inside and check it out. He could still feel the energy from the look in his eyes. I shifted position so he wouldn't see me enter the combination, looking at him over my shoulder.

At my move, a glimmer of humor returned to his face, which was nice to see. "Always the professional. I wouldn't expect any less. Besides, I don't mind the view." He looked me up and down once, slow. "Nice outfit."

He was being sarcastic, of course. I looked down. The splatters of zombie goo were now accented by splotches of John's blood. Oh shit, zombie goo, in open wounds. What the hell had I been thinking?

"John, you're going to *have* to go to the hospital. I'm sorry. Really. I didn't think. But I fought a zombie—a guy who'd been infected with *M. necrose*. . . .

To my surprise, he only shrugged, then winced. "I've been vaccinated."

I looked at him with disbelief. "Don't bullshit me, John. Nobody gets vaccinated for a weird disease like that."

He chuckled. "You do when you're guarding a group of doctors from Physicians Médecins Sans Frontières in Papua, New Guinea. Especially when *M. necrose* is what they're going there to treat." Maybe my disbelief continued to show, because he shrugged. "It's on the list of immunizations in my passport in the safe in my office. When I can walk I'll show you."

My knees went weak with relief, and I had to steady myself for a second. The thought that I could've infected him . . .

"I'm glad it matters so much to you, but could you get a move on? The leg really hurts."

No doubt. I pulled myself together and hurried over to the safe that takes up most of the wall behind my desk. The charms, like most of the really valuable stuff I keep on site, were locked inside.

My safe is both magically and scientifically biometric. After I entered a code onto the keypad, a palm plate popped out to test my DNA and fingerprints. The display reminded me that I was nearly at my "due date." When I was turned, the safe didn't recognize me anymore. My software guru suggested I use the pregnancy override to account for my changed body. It worked, but when the nine months were up, the safe might not open. I was going to have to remember to clean it out completely before my "due date." It's a *big* safe, so that will be a pain in the butt.

Once the lights all turned green the locks disengaged with heavy thunks and the door cracked open. It's easier to open now that I've got the extra strength, but I'm still glad the door is well balanced. The med kit held all the new stuff I'd bought at Levy's. I hadn't planned to use the charms quite this fast. "Okay, let's see what we have here." I dumped everything on the coffee table. The one I wanted landed on top. "Here we go. *Leg Set*." I read from the back: "'For relief of simple breaks of toes and legs. Not for use on ankle or knee joints or when bones protrude from skin. Severe breaks should be treated by a physician or licensed healer." I looked at his left leg. "I don't think you could have walked at all if the bone was protruding. You probably would have passed out. But we should probably check. Upper or lower?"

He raised his leg slightly and turned his foot toward me. "Lower. Feels like it's just above my ankle."

At least he was wearing sneakers, so I didn't have to worry about getting a boot off. I carefully pulled up his pant leg and took a look at the leg. He had really nice calves. He must swim or run. The whole front of the leg was definitely swollen and red, but there was no lump that might indicate that the bone was separated. "You'll need to get an X-ray even with the charm to make sure there aren't any chips in there."

284 * CAT ADAMS

He raised his brows. "Of course. But let's get it to where I can walk on it."

I opened the package and wrapped the hook and eye fastener around the area and then squeezed the plastic vial inside the covering until I heard it crack. A glow enveloped John's leg and he sucked in a sharp breath. "You didn't mention the stinging."

A quick glance at the warnings revealed the answer. "Ah. 'May cause swelling, itching, or burning sensation for first thirty minutes. Reaction is generally mild to moderate. Leg should not bear weight for thirty minutes and patient should not run or attempt strenuous activity for twenty-four hours. If pain continues for more than sixty minutes, a spiral fracture may be indicated and professional treatment should be sought.' So, I guess we'll see, huh?"

He nodded. "Actually, it's starting to fade already. Or at least it's not as bad as when you first put it on."

"Your lip's bleeding again. Try not to drip on the rug." He shot me a sarcastic glance and opened his mouth to say something, but I didn't give him the chance. "How about we just fix it?"

He shook his head. "Eye first. It's swelling enough it's getting hard to see."

That was easy, but, "Well, that should take your mind off the leg." I smiled, but he didn't. Oh, well. It was the truth, because I was going to have to sit down on the couch next to him and hold the cut together while I poured on the skin-mend powder. Nothing like squeezing an open wound for sheer, raw pain.

Worse, it was a long cut and tricky to hold. I finally wound up positioning John's fingers on one half. He blistered the air with swearing as I poured, but he didn't move. Soon enough he had a thin, angry red line over his eyebrow instead of the once-nasty cut.

"Okay, then. So—" Next was his mouth. "Any loose teeth?"

He nodded. "I probably took one or two kicks. One molar and an upper canine are loose. But at least they're all there."

It was time to bring it up, while I pulled another package from the stack on the table. "So, what happened? Who messed you up?" He was silent for a long moment while I read the instructions for the charm. I decided to break the silence. "Oh, this is the 'new and improved' version. I need water. Hang on while I get a cup." I paused before I left the room. "You can decide what you want to say, but I think I've earned an answer."

He let out a harsh breath as I walked to the bathroom down the hall for a paper cup and some water.

John was in a sitting position on the couch when I returned. That was probably better for swallowing. The intensity and anger in his eyes was hard to watch, but I was pretty sure it wasn't directed at me, so I sat down on the couch next to him and handed him the cup before reading through the instructions. "Okay, it looks like I pour in the potion and you hold it in your mouth for thirty seconds, swishing it around." I did it and watched as it bubbled and frothed. "Save a little and I'll hold it to your lip from the outside."

He held the cup for a long moment and looked at me. "I have no idea who jumped me or what they wanted. They hit me from behind, blindfolded me, and took me somewhere in spelled cuffs. They somehow stole my magic before I could even react. I couldn't cast a single spell. Not even break the emergency spell ball. After that, I don't remember a damned thing until I came to in the parking lot."

Ouch. That's gotta be hard on a mage's pride. "Pour, swish, and swallow. But save some."

He poured nearly the entire contents of the cup into his mouth and closed his lips. I tilted the cup against his mouth and let the remaining liquid rest against the damaged skin. I started to stare at my watch to count off the thirty seconds required. But my gaze was pulled back to John's face when I heard odd noises coming from his throat. His lips were still closed, but I could tell he was close to gagging. His expression was one I'd seen in movies, when a kid took a big spoonful of castor oil. John started to turn to spit it out, but I held his head steady. He raised his hands up to push mine away, but I wouldn't have any of it. "Hang in there, tough guy. Don't spit. You need to swallow it in ten . . . nine—" I kept counting until I reached "zero" and pulled away the cup.

He swallowed, but it was a hard effort. Then he did start gagging and turned on the couch in case he wound up throwing up. It took a few deep breaths before he finally sat up again. "Jesus. That stuff tastes like rotten eggs. What brand is that so I never use it again?"

I showed him the package and he shuddered.

"How are the teeth? Your lip looks great." It did. The bruising and cut on his lower lip were completely gone and the skin was smooth and new.

He used his tongue to feel around. His face registered wary surprise when he picked up the box again. "The teeth are solid again. Damn it. I hate it when something that crappy tasting actually works."

I noticed another bolded bit of text on the front. "And apparently it leaves your breath minty fresh. Better than the taste of old blood, I guess. Does your mouth feel *minty*?" I said it with teasing in my voice and he let out a small chuckle.

"You tell me." He blew out air softly toward my face.

I had to lean down to catch the scent and closed my eyes to identify it. "Actually, it does. Peppermint." I opened my eyes to find I'd leaned startlingly close to his face. His hazel eyes stared deep into mine. He didn't say a word. Just stared, and before I even realized I'd done it, I pressed my mouth against his so-soft healed lips. Firm, full, and . . . damn. He let me, relaxed his jaw so that my mouth partially fell into his. His peppermint-flavored tongue touched mine, toyed with me, passed along the potion's tingle to my mouth, and sped my pulse. Slow, so slow and sweet. His hand rose and touched the braid tight against my head, stroking the twists until he reached my bare neck. My own hands were busy exploring his neck and shoulders. I'd heard his shallow breathing and didn't want to put any pressure on his chest. Well, actually, I *did*. Wanted to put pressure in a number of places. But I didn't.

He didn't have any supernatural energy to rush over my skin, but I shivered nonetheless as his fingers drew patterns on my neck. I pulled back from the kiss with a nearly violent shudder that raised all the hair on my body. "How do you do that?" My words were breathless, nearly panicked.

"Do what?" he whispered.

"Make me tingle like this without any magic."

He didn't answer right away . . . only offered a quirk of a smile while running his thumb along the line of my jaw. "You tell me."

I pulled back from him, trying to find my focus again. "I should help you up so you can get that passport to show the doctor."

He was amused now and continued to tease. "Y'know, not *all* of my body parts were injured." He wiggled his eyebrows at me while still stroking a finger down my cheek. I wasn't sure if he was joking but decided to treat it that way.

"Keep it up, buddy. I can fix that." Now he did laugh and it sounded good. Relaxed. But there was still a haunted look at the back of his eyes. It sucked not remembering. "I've been there . . . the not remembering part. It's hard."

He nodded. "I think I need to find out somehow. It'll bug me forever otherwise."

"Okay, then how about focusing on something else. What did you find out about the spell on me? I got your messages but then . . . well, you know. Why does my head hurt so much?"

He sighed and leaned back into the pillow. "They were right. It's a memory-wipe spell. It's trying to rewrite your past, like it changed the memories of the others so they forgot about the bomb. But the vampire healing has been fighting the spell. That's where the headaches come from. And I bet you've been having more trouble with the vamp side of your nature as well. The reason it was so hard to work with is that someone went to a *lot* of trouble to make it untraceable and difficult to unwind. I managed to get to the bottom of it before . . . well, before. Now that I know what it is, it will be a simple matter to remove. I can do it when my power is back, or you can go to Jean-Baptiste."

"Oh, thank God." I didn't bother to hide my relief. "I was afraid . . ." I stopped before I could finish admitting that I was terrified I was actually becoming a vampire. The very first thing the magic that creates a vampire does is erase all memories of the bat's human life and personality.

"It's okay to be afraid, Celia."

I frowned because of the way he sounded. "What's wrong?"

I could tell he didn't want to answer, but he finally sighed. "I can't feel my magic. It's like your foot going to sleep. It's just . . . numb. I'm hoping it's temporary."

Crap. I didn't know what to say about that. I touched his cheek and couldn't fix what was in his eyes. "John, I—"

Another male voice sounded from downstairs. "Celia? You up there?"

It was Bruno. "Up here!" He started to bound up the stairs and I realized at the last second how it would look. Sitting next to John, my hands on his face and his fingers stroking my shoulder. I stood up and John's face took on a flat, emotionless expression.

Damn it. I couldn't win.

Bruno started talking before he reached the entry. "Are you okay? The front door was wide open. Your purse is still in the car and there's blood on the sidewal—" His heavy footsteps came to a stuttering stop when he could see inside the room. His eyes flicked from me to John to the open med kit and the charm on John's bare leg. He fixed his fellow mage with a steady stare. "You look like shit. What happened?"

John shrugged. "I'm fine."

"Oh, for God's sake," I whispered, and started to clean up the empty boxes scattered on the floor. Putting them in the trash can, I could only shake my head at the rising level of testosterone in the room. It was better if I stayed out of the line of fire.

"Mm-hmm." Bruno's voice was understandably skeptical as he tossed my purse on the desk and turned one of the wing chairs around with his free hand and sat down. He didn't take his eyes off John. A long pause was filled with tension before Bruno asked again, "So. What happened?"

"Fell down a flight of stairs." I raised an eyebrow but didn't say anything. Maybe this was what it would take to get him to talk.

"Really." Bruno kept a straight face and leaned back into the cushions before raising his coffee cup to his lips to take a sip. Once it was down, he remarked drily, "That's a damned long flight of stairs. How'd you make it around the corners?"

I snorted while John glared at him. I couldn't help it. "Just tell him, John. He might be able to help."

John looked my way. "Celia, could you go get my passport from my office?"

"I thought it was in your safe. And besides, I don't have a key."

"There's one in Dawna's desk and I just remembered the passport is in my center desk drawer. Bad of me to forget to put it in the safe, but there you go." He gave me a serious look. "If you don't mind."

Ah. Guy talk. The best part was that I could probably hear it if I listened close.

But by the time I reached the front desk I hadn't heard anything new. Bruno asked a couple of good questions about sounds or smells John remembered before he blacked out, but the memory was just gone. John's voice was frustration personified. "It's starting to drive me nuts."

I really did know how he felt and that made me realize there might be a solution to his problem—the same solution I'd used. I wouldn't call her today, but Dottie might be able to help. We'd met when a friendly cop had asked her to help restore my missing memories.

When I reached the third floor again, they stopped talking until I passed by. "Got the key. Be right back."

As I opened the door to John's office, I realized I wasn't sure what to expect. When I flipped on the light I was taken aback at the massive casting circle that practically filled the space. It was set up on the equivalent of a portable dance floor. All there was room for outside of the circle was a desk and a single armchair that matched the ones in Bubba's room. Heck, maybe it was one of those *from* Bubba's office.

The safe in the corner wasn't as big as mine, but it was equally well protected by magic wards if the energy surge that hit me when I got too close was any indication. The power crawled along my skin like biting ants and I was forced to hop to the side before the sensation dug any farther down inside my arm.

The desk wasn't what I expected. I'd always imagined John as a clean-line, *Architectural Digest* kind of guy who would have a glass and chrome look. But this desk was hand-carved of heavy, knotty wood and had a . . . *country* feel that screamed "home on the range."

Interesting.

I opened the middle desk drawer and right on top was his passport. It was well used and about to expire. His photo inside was nearly a decade old and a seal identified him as a licensed mage at level 8.5. The intense, dangerously competent look he gave to the camera in his photo made me shiver. I flipped through the pages. He really had been all over the world. Stamps and stickers from countries I'd barely heard of filled nearly every sheet and he wasn't kidding that the back page listed a host of weird vaccinations—one of which was for *M. necrose*. Who'da thunk?

The built-in bookcases along the wall were identical to mine and he'd filled them with a variety of leather-bound texts–magical volumes, given the crawling sensation on my arm when I passed by. I had just cleared the books when I noticed the line of framed photos on the shelf next to his desk. I couldn't resist and back-tracked to look.

One shelf was a tribute to the wine he'd helped develop. Witches' Brew was the world's first magical wine. It tasted exactly like the best wine you ever had. If you like cherries, it tastes like cherries. I'd been to the wine's debut party and had a very good time. Right up until the rift tried to destroy the world.

On the next shelf, was a photo of John and George Miller in younger days—standing in front of the dilapidated building that would become the home of their business and one of the most recognizable addresses in L.A.

There was another photo of John in a family setting, like a studio shot, showing him along with three women and a man who had an older version of John's strong features. I was betting one of the women was Gillian, but I had no idea which. And I had no idea who the other, younger woman might be.

But it was the last photo, shaded partially in darkness, that made me gasp and stare as the passport fluttered to the carpeting from my suddenly limp hand.

Fuck a duck.

A familiar face smiled out at me from the silver frame and it made my blood run cold.

John Creede had a framed photo of the woman who'd bombed six grade schools and had tried to kill me twice . . . that I knew of.

What the hell?

22

picked up the frame, half-expecting it to burn my hand. But the silver frame was cool to the touch and the figure in the picture didn't move or reach out to grab my throat. I retrieved the passport from the floor and carried both items down to my office.

I threw the frame down on John's lap hard enough to make him wince. "How in the hell do you know Linda Jamisyn?"

He picked up the frame and stared at the woman's face. Then he looked up at me with confusion and a healthy dose of wariness. "Who? And why do you care if I know Glinda?"

I stood there with my mouth suddenly open because it occurred to me that he thought I was flying into a jealous rage. Bruno's expression was ... odd and it made me blush furiously. "No! That's not what I ... oh for the love of heaven." I took two steps and poked my finger at the picture. "This is *her*. This is the witch who's been trying to kill me and bombed those schools. Wait. Why did you call her Glinda?"

The expressions of both men suddenly changed. Bruno leapt to his feet to come closer to the couch and

John handed the photo to him with a weary sigh. "Because that's her name. Glinda Miller. She's George's daughter and she isn't a bomber. Far from it. But I stand by what I said on the phone. She's a scapegoat. There's no other explanation." He met my eyes, trying to convince me of her innocence by sheer force of will.

What he said on the phone to *who*? He never mentioned that name. I interrupted before he could go any further. George Miller's daughter? Great. The whole family was evil. "Look, John. I saw her yesterday— she attacked me with powerful magic in a bar. Tried to kill me with billiard balls and wooden pool cues through the heart. I got a good look at her from five feet away."

He shook his head "Not possible. Glinda lives on the East Coast. If she was in town, she'd have called me. She's like family, Celia. I've known her for more than ten years. Besides, she's only a level four. She wouldn't have the oomph to pull off an attack with multiple objects."

"I'm not the one who's confused, John. She's freaking powerful, and she's *nuts*. She slammed me with a spell that had everything in the bar trying to kill me. I also didn't imagine the blast of power that picked me up off a pool table and threw me into the wall a dozen feet away. No, this is her."

He hadn't liked my tone, or the fact I'd called her crazy. His eyes were narrowed down to slits. His voice was low, and carefully controlled when he warned me, "Be very careful what you say, Celia. Remember, she's George's daughter."

Fine. If we were going to escalate, let's remind him of some facts. "Let's also remember that George was trafficking with demons, John. Siren influence or no,

296 of CAT ADAMS

who knows what bargains he . . . or his family made with them. Have you seen her since his funeral?"

Bruno interrupted before Creede and I could go any further with our argument. He was shaking his head. "I don't recognize her, Celia, and I know most of the upper-level witches."

John raised his hand, slowly, carefully, and stared from me to Bruno. "*Exactly.* She's a four. She works as a secretary for a boring company in a boring town, and not even in a magical capacity. She doesn't have alias names or hang out in bars. Maybe you saw someone who looks like her. I know this woman. Trust me. And while there were traces of her magical signature in the spell used to attack your memories, I'd swear there were traces from me and at least twelve others who couldn't possibly have been involved."

He seemed so confident that it made me wonder if he was right. Could it be a different woman? I mean, they always say everyone has a double somewhere in the world, and there are plenty of lesser demons—who can shape-shift—that were trapped on earth after the rift closed. I let out a slow breath. "I really think it's her. But I'll give you the benefit of the doubt. *You.* Not her."

Creede dipped his head, acknowledging my effort. "I was trying to reach her before I was attacked. When she calls back I'll find out if she's been visiting here. But I doubt it. Since George died, she hasn't had much to do with me or the company. She wanted to work for one of our companies a few years ago, but George and I both knew she couldn't command the loyalty of the employees, so he said no. She took it gracefully, took the money he gave her, and went back home. Of course, when he died, she inherited his money, but he left the company to me. She said she was fine with that and I believe her. It's a demanding business and she doesn't like working long hours."

Would losing the company make her bitter? I could see the possibility, but for most people, money heals a lot of wounds. "You've talked to her recently?"

He nodded. "A month or so ago. She was fine. Happy and living it up on George's money."

Bruno shrugged. "I have to agree. A level four isn't a powerhouse of talent. And unless she made a demonic pact, I just don't see it. Plus, from everything I've read, most pacts were severed when the rift closed. I'm not saying it's not *possible,* but it's very unlikely. I think we're dealing with a look-alike, or maybe a spawn. They're half human, so closing the rift didn't get rid of them, and some of them can look like anything."

I still believed it was her, but there was no point in arguing with both of them. So I changed the subject. "How's the leg feeling? Ready to go to the hospital?"

John let out an exasperated sound. "We already discussed this. I'm not going to the hospital. There's no need."

I crossed my arms over my chest and stood as tall as I could. "You haven't moved more than a few millimeters since we've been talking and your breathing is wheezy and shallow. Remember, I've got sensitive hearing. At the very least, you cracked some ribs. At worst, you've punctured a lung. I'm betting if I took off your shirt, I'd find bruises and mysterious lumps over some of your major organs." I stared at him and he stared back defiantly. "Care to prove me wrong? Take a good deep breath. Or just stand up and walk across the room. If you can without throwing up blood like you did outside, that is."

The staring match continued until his eyes shifted. Uh-huh.

Bruno let out a little chuckle that was three parts amused and one part worried. "You won't win this one, Creede. You can't *imagine* how stubborn she is on stuff that matters to her. If you want, I'll drive you and we can go through one of the back entrances. I'll even introduce you to Dr. Gaetano. He'll keep it quiet. Plus, you really do want to get tested for the disease. This is a mutated variety. Won't hurt to get a bump on your vaccine." He shrugged, then added the thing that sealed the deal. "If they ask, we can say we ran into a group of vampires and took them out. No witnesses, no proof, and no stigma in the press."

Stuff that matters to her. I didn't focus on much past that part. He was right. I'd done the same thing to Bruno more than once. Because it mattered . . . *he* mattered. Crap.

"I've been inoculated." He gestured to the passport. "And bodyguards don't get the shit kicked out of them." It was a lame excuse from John and wasn't even true.

I let out a rude noise that was close to a raspberry. "Bullcrap. We most certainly do. It's part of the job. Maybe you lofty mages don't, but the rest of us regularly get punched and kicked around. We just tend to give as good as we get. This time you didn't get to." I smiled and there was a dark edge to it. "But there's always next time and you can bring friends to the party."

Bruno likewise smiled dangerously, at my expression and probably at memories of when we'd done just that in the past. Was I willing to kick some tail in retribution for a friend? Sure.

"I suppose it won't hurt to have the leg X-rayed. There's still a little stinging going on. Could be a faulty charm."

I forced myself not to roll my eyes. Stinging was normal until after an hour, which it hadn't been. But fine. Whatever justification he needed. "Great. You guys take off and I'll meet you there. I want to change out of these clothes and get some food in me."

Bruno helped John up and I watched carefully to see if the leg would hold his weight. It did, but I could tell it would be slow going down the stairs. John took a few tentative steps, testing his mobility. I looked at Bruno. "Make sure he hangs on to the rail going down. And go *slow.*"

He gave me one of his inscrutable looks and then sighed before moving his chair out of John's way. "We'll be fine." He stepped into the hallway with John close on his heels. "C'mon. I'm parked out front."

That's when I noticed the small blue book still in my hand. "Wait! Passport." John took it, but not before giving my fingers a light squeeze.

"Thanks." He didn't smile, but his eyes did and I knew that the sentiment was for more than just the papers. "See you soon."

"Yep."

I listened to their slow descent while I got out of my bloody clothing in the bathroom. I was going to have to burn the clothes. Nobody'd told me to, but it just made sense, and they were ruined anyway. It hadn't escaped my notice that Bruno was wearing borrowed scrubs. My braid was still hanging in there with the exception of a few strands. Still, it felt weird, so I took out the band and bobby pins and brushed it out. Soft waves framed my face and actually looked pretty good. Different, but good.

I stripped down, showered, and shampooed. I didn't take long, but I was thorough—very thorough. Just thinking about the zombie made me shudder. I had to scrub every inch of me down twice before I really felt clean. It wasn't until I climbed out and shut off the water that I heard a familiar female voice talking to John and Bruno downstairs. I hastily yanked on my clothes and hurried to the railing over the stairs to confirm what I heard. "Dottie? Is that you? What are you doing here on a Sunday?"

"I saw myself giving a reading today and it seems the others in the vision are here as well. Please come down, dear. You'll want to see this."

I grabbed my hairbrush, using it to comb through my wet hair as I went to join them in the non-damaged portion of the reception area. John was already in a chair, looking a little too pale for my taste. It made him look older than Dottie. Dottie is a little ball of fire, despite her age. With her bright eyes, warm smile, and vivid blue warm-up suit, she looked ready for anything. Dottie's walker, complete with carry basket and the requisite chopped tennis balls on the front feet, was next to the couch and her silver and crystal viewing bowl was on the table, along with a bottle of holy water. Bruno was pulling two more chairs around for us to sit on the other side of the table.

She looked at John. "Have you ever had a reading of a past event, young man?"

He shook his head. I got the feeling he wasn't trusting himself to talk for fear he'd start coughing. He looked at me with penetrating eyes and spoke directly into my mind. *You're too perceptive some days.*

I keep forgetting he's a telepath and while I try to believe he's ethical about it, I wondered just how much of what had been flitting around in my mind upstairs had been "overheard." He didn't say a word, just quirked one corner of his mouth in a smile and returned his attention to Dottie.

Damn it.

"Are you really sure this is the best time, Dottie? John really needs to get to the hospital." *Where they would hopefully poke and prod him until he screamed.*

Yeah, he heard that all right and turned his eyes to me with an amused expression.

She nodded, her eyes bird bright, already in "seer" mode. "Yes, dear. Now is the perfect time." She poured holy water until the bowl was half full and then looked at John with one hand extended. "I'll need something you were wearing during the event. Metal works best."

He shook his head, finally trusting himself to talk. But there was a hoarse edge to his voice that worried me. "I don't have anything like that."

It made me frown. "What about your watch? That's metal."

He shot me a horrified look. "It's a *Rolex*! You don't put quality watches underwater."

I sighed and shook my head wearily. Looking at Bruno didn't help. He had unconsciously put a hand over his own *quality watch* and wouldn't look at me. "It's metal, John, and I'm sure that a Rolex is water resistant. She has to have something you had on at the time." Which made me wonder *why* he still had his watch. I mean, it *was* a Rolex. A gold one, and they'd left it. "Doesn't it strike you as odd you still have that watch?"

That did it. He looked at the timepiece suspiciously and undid the clasp. Dottie closed her eyes and put her hands on either side of the bowl. Her chant was a common meditative exercise that I occasionally used when I was doing yoga.

With a sad sigh, John let the Rolex slide into the bowl. For a long moment it lay there quietly. Then a bubble rose to the surface, causing him to wince.

"Sheesh. Boys and their toys."

Bruno snorted. "Says the woman who screamed when I had to cut off her *designer* pant leg." Hey, that wasn't the same at all! I glared at him until he smiled. Okay, fine. Point to the men.

Concentric circles of water abruptly raced from the bubble toward the edge of the bowl, pulling our attention back to the reading. When the waves hit the glass, flames erupted, racing around the silver rim. Both Bruno and John were taken aback. But then, they'd never seen it before. It was pretty cool. Smoke gathered above the water's surface to form a black-and-white image.

John was getting into his Ferrari when a blast of power hit him in the back. He slumped forward, unconscious. Two men grabbed his arms while a third tied on a blindfold and gag and tied something around his neck that I couldn't make out. Whatever it was made him bow his back and let out a scream before collapsing again. Then they pulled him backward toward the black sedan I'd seen return him here.

"Wait," John said quietly. "How can this be showing things I couldn't see?"

I whispered the answer. "The object is tied to the event, not your memories. It'll show things you couldn't see and hear as long as they happened in the watch's presence."

He let out a pained sound as one of the goons stroked a hand down the paint job of the Ferrari and then got behind the wheel to follow the black sedan.

Bummer. That was probably the last John would ever see of that car.

One of Dottie's best abilities was the way she could skip passages of time that had no meaning, like the car trip. Soon John was being dragged into a building and down a flight of stairs. I couldn't swear it, but the stairwell looked familiar. No matter how hard I tried to pinpoint the memory, it eluded me. John was looking at me expectantly, yet all I could do was shake my head. "Sorry, it's not coming to me where I've seen this place. I'll think about it while we watch."

He nodded and Bruno just looked confused. I shrugged. "Telepath, remember? I thought I remembered seeing this place somewhere and he picked up on it."

Bruno swore under his breath, apparently also just now remembering John's mental abilities. It's easy to forget because we all like to believe we're alone inside our own minds.

"Where do you want him?" The taller of the goons was speaking to a person not yet revealed.

When I heard Glinda Miller-Thompson-Jamisyn's voice (or whoever the hell she was) I turned to see John's reaction. He'd paled further, and was giving little shakes of his head no, like he didn't want to believe what he was seeing and hearing. He looked so . . . pained. I didn't even want to say *I told you so.*

A flicker of motion over Dottie's bowl drew my attention back to the seeing. "Put him over there, in the spelled cuffs. They're strong enough to secure him. And please do be rough."

John swore under his breath as he watched—his eyes fixed firmly on the vision of a woman staring at him with hate in her eyes. "Glinda. I . . . what the hell are you doing?"

The men chuckled and I winced at the image in the bowl as John's unconscious form was chained to the wall to hang by his arms and then used as a punching bag by three men until the blonde finally held up her hand. "Okay, that's enough. We don't want to kill him." Her smile sent the same chills down my spine as it had in the bar. "Yet."

The shortest of the three guys moved back and rubbed his knuckles, which were already swollen and red. "So what'd he do to ya?"

She shrugged and walked toward him, swaying her hips with angry sexuality that the three men couldn't help but notice and lick their lips at. "He was born more powerful than me. He seemed to think that made me *less* than him and his handpicked cadre of *professionals*. But who's more powerful now, John Creede?" She reached up and removed the item around his neck. It was some sort of jewelry—gold with gemstones— and it glowed with energy. She put it around her own neck and likewise arched her back. But it wasn't pain that made her spine bow. It was ecstasy. "Oh, my. That's nice. I like this sort of power. In fact, I think I'll keep it. *All* of it." Her arm shot forward in a powerful, magically enhanced punch to John's face that was the cause of the cut over his eye. His head snapped sideways and hit the wall, giving him the black eye he still bore. "A few more times and he'll be less than I ever was and I'll be more than he could dream of being. Then we'll see who the employees respect."

Ouch. I looked at John. His eyes were glittering with anger, his hands clenched into fists.

But it was Bruno who grabbed my attention when he whispered, "Dear God. That's supposed to only be a *legend*. Where the hell did she get it?"

"Get what? Do you recognize that necklace?"

"It's the Isis Collar," John said coldly. "George had always hinted he'd found something ancient and dangerous in a private collection and was guarding it to keep it from getting into the hands of someone with evil intent. But I had no idea Glinda had found it . . . or would actually *use* it."

"The Isis Collar?" Okay, color me clueless. Apparently this was a big deal, though.

Bruno whispered to me while staring at the image in the bowl. "It was supposedly a gift from the goddess Isis to the fifth Egyptian pharaoh. Most of the pharaohs were mages, but they didn't start to get powerful until later in the First Dynasty. There's a little-known legend that the Isis Collar could steal magic from any mage or witch so the pharaoh was always the most powerful one in the room. Isis is supposed to protect anyone wearing her collar." I was happy to turn to listen to Bruno, to turn away from watching the three goons punch, kick, and slam John's body with everything from crowbars to lead shot–filled saps. Damn. Yeah, he was going to the hospital. I was amazed he was still upright. Even he was paling at the image. But I think worst for him was watching the smile on the face of a woman he'd considered *family* as he was beaten.

"The thing is, magic is part of the user; it's . . . tuned to the individual."

"But mages can share magic. I saw you guys do it with the others at the rift."

"Yes," John agreed. "But that was willingly, and it was a real effort to make it work. Taking it by force, raw and unfiltered . . ."

"Could drive someone insane?" I suggested.

His eyes were haunted. "Oh, yes."

Dottie wasn't listening; her whole attention was focused on the images playing out in the bowl. She was in control, but it was taking everything she had. I'd seen her do this before. She could do it, but she'd be tired for days after.

The image skipped then until what was apparently the next morning . . . *this* morning. Glinda was removing the collar from John's neck one more time as he moaned in pain. "That should be enough. Kill him."

The three guards, who were having coffee and donuts at a table in the corner, raised their brows. "You didn't pay us to kill him. That's fifty grand extra. You got that kinda money?"

Glinda shrugged and put the collar back around her neck with a small smile and wiggle of her hips. "Not at the moment. The amount I had to put out to get rid of the half siren bitch was simply ridiculous!" She pouted. "Fine, I'll wait to kill him. I have to get ready to ship the rest of the antibiotic out of the country so nobody can say I was hoarding it. And the group who bought the rest of the bombs will be at the docks tonight to collect them. Then I'll have all the money I need and the best part is that it'll be loony religious zealots who take the blame for the whole mess. Then I'll just buy Miller and Creede at auction after he's been dead for a few years."

Fuck a duck. The prisoner at the FBI had been right. There would be more bombs. Worse, she was shipping the drugs away. Who knows how many would die?

The small goon in the image got a worried look on his face. "But we get the shots now, right? Before they're gone?"

She waved her hand dismissively. "Of course. Of course. Go to the lab. Tell them I sent you. There's still a few hundred doses I haven't moved to the warehouse. But be careful not to get spotted by anyone on the first floor. One woman's unusually nosy. Maybe she needs to be the first person with a full-blown case." She smiled again. "In fact, why don't you collect her? I think she needs to be late tomorrow. And then I'll need to start looking for a replacement."

Wow. Wasn't she a sweetheart?

"That'll cost you extra," said the big guy.

She let out an exasperated sigh. "I've only got a few thousand left and I've got to live on that until the wire hits the Swiss account." She looked at John's limp form and sighed. "Fine. Take him back, but not to his house. Dump him at that crappy office he leased here in the city. I'll give you the address. He won't remember anything anyway, so we can always pick him off later. And if the siren is still hanging around there, see if you can put her in the hospital."

As they moved through the swinging doors, I got another chill to my blood. "Oh, and once I get the money, there's another mage I want to you find. . . ."

Dottie came to with a start. She shook her head and took a deep breath. "My. That was draining. I believe some tea is in order. Celia, would you mind?"

She's really good at breaking the tension in a room with grace and poise. And I had to admit I was happy to escape.

By the time I got back with the tea, John and Bruno had gone. I was surprised I didn't hear them go, but I was sort of preoccupied. "Did they go to the hospital?"

"I believe so, dear." She patted the couch next to her. "Come sit down so we can talk."

I set down a cup of tea in front of her but really had no time to talk. I had a ton of things to do, the first of which was to call Rizzoli. He needed to find some way to locate the remaining bombs and find and arrest Glinda. Glinda the *wicked* witch. "No time, I'm afraid. But thanks for this. And for the call yesterday."

"Yesterday?" She blinked, her eyes still a little glazed. "Did I call you?"

Yeah, I wondered if that might be the case. "You called me during a trance to give me information I needed. It helped and everybody got out safe."

"Oh my goodness! That must be when I found myself in the kitchen holding the phone. But there was a dial tone, so I'd presumed I hadn't made a call. I'm so glad it helped. It's important to be a good prophet if I'm going to be one at all."

Prophet? I looked at her warily. One of the things the siren queen, Lopaka, told me was that true sirens have spirits who attend them and prophets to guide their future, that ghosts and seers seek them out to offer their aid. I'd always considered it coincidence that Vicki was a clairvoyant and Ivy haunted me. And Dottie was just a nice old lady who needed a job. "Why do you say that?"

She tipped her head. "Because I am, of course. Before she died, the queen's prophet, Pili, called me and explained how it worked." She smiled at me and I frowned in return. "Don't be so fearful, dear. It doesn't change anything. I merely allow myself to be . . . *recep-*

tive to your life. Just like I used to with dear Karl. It helped him do his job and made me feel useful. I do like to feel useful."

Karl Gibson had been the cop who'd introduced me to her. He'd died in the line of fire when a demon attacked at the World Series. "I don't want to be a burden to you." I was serious and it probably showed on my face. "I don't need a prophet, or a clairvoyant. I do okay on my own."

She nodded patiently but gave the mark from the death curse on my palm a pointed look. "If you say so."

23

I called Rizzoli on my way to see Dr. Jean-Baptiste. I wanted to know how Mikey was doing, and Julie, and all the other kids who had been infected. I thought of all those doses of medicine hidden somewhere while Glinda waited for the *price* to go up and I wanted to hurt somebody—preferably a certain platinum blonde.

Rizzoli didn't pick up the line, but he called me back as I turned into the doctor's parking lot. I could hear exhaustion and strain in his voice the minute he said hello.

"How's Mikey?"

"Better. They aren't making any promises, but he's improving. Julie's still hanging in there, too. But . . ." He paused, and I steeled myself for bad news. "Willow Harris didn't make it. The hospital crematorium's getting quite a workout today."

I couldn't help but remember that feisty little girl with the big brown eyes. Tears blurred my vision and I slammed my fist against the steering wheel. Damn it!

"The drug company says they're running out of the

antibiotic, and that they'll have to scramble for the immunizations as well."

One death is bad enough, but I was seething that they were willing to let others die, too. "They're lying. I was calling to tell you about a vision a powerful psychic I know had. Glinda and the drugs are hiding in the same place. But the worst part is, she's getting ready to ship them out of the country. I swear I've been to that warehouse before, but I just can't remember where or when. I'm walking into the doctor's office right now to get the memory corruption spell removed. I'll call you the second I know."

There was a long silence. When he finally spoke it was very quietly, his voice intense, but controlled. "We need those drugs, now. You do whatever it takes to make that happen. *Whatever* it takes. And when you find the bitch responsible for this . . ."

"Hey, why tell me? I'm turning the whole mess over to you guys, Rizzoli. I don't plan on running into her at all."

"Yeah? We'll see about that. Let's call it a *hunch* you see her before I do."

He hung up without saying another word. Just as well. My mouth was a desert and my mind, well . . . my mind was reeling. I'd had too many shocks today. It didn't seem possible it was the same *week* when I'd been working out with Dawna, let alone sunset of the same day.

Sunset . . . the realization hit me at the same instant my inner vampire washed through me in a wave of power, hunger, and need. I hadn't eaten, hadn't even thought about eating. I froze with my hand on the door handle. My chest started to heave like I'd run a mile.

I should go back to the car, check and see if there were any shakes or baby food in the trunk. I should. But I didn't want to. I wanted to go through those doors and find the nearest source of fresh blood. I wanted to stalk my prey until the adrenaline filled their system and take them down. I could feel them inside, feel their tiny lives that could be mine.

My hand pulled so I could explore and a burst of chilled air hit my face. I shuddered, swallowed convulsively, and wiped a long line of drool from my chin before it dripped down my shirt.

Slowly, carefully, I made myself let go of the door handle. I forced myself back to the car. I could do this. I *would* do this. But it was so hard. Part of the problem was physical. The food in the trunk would take care of that. The other part was mental and emotional. I felt such rage at what Glinda had done to innocent children, to John. The vampire part of my nature drew power from negative emotions, and it was harder to control **right now** than it had been since the very first night after the bite. I kept my eyes closed as I guzzled three nutrition shakes in a row and then liquid vitamins, shuddering at the taste—not because it was bad, but because it wasn't what I wanted, needed. I rested my palms on the trunk lid and lowered my head, trying to get control as the liquid hit my stomach. If I just stayed very still, concentrated on feeling the shake slide down . . .

A male voice behind me made my breath catch. Fingers turned to claws, convulsing with lightning speed. I struggled to keep them in place on the shiny paint. "Ms. Graves, are you coming in for your appointment or not? I have plans later this evening." Dr. Jean-Baptiste tapped his watch with one finger.

His voice pounded my temples and I struggled to stay calm. "I need to grab a bite to eat."

He scowled. "Couldn't it wait?"

"No. It couldn't." I turned red eyes toward him. They had to be red and glowy because I could see him only as bands of color. "Not if you like your staff and don't want to be sued by the families of your deceased patients." I opened the last thing in my arsenal, a cherry-flavored sports drink. I chugged half while continuing to stare at him. His pulse was speeding up, but fortunately, my stomach was now full of liquid. I'd mostly stopped feeling vampirey. Of course I'd have to pee something fierce in about a half hour, but there you go.

I twisted the cap back on the bottle and stuck it in the trunk of the car. Slamming the lid shut, I followed him through the front doors and empty corridors and into his office. "Where's Simone?" I was surprised she wasn't here. It was late, but not nearly as late as my first appointment. In fact, the whole place was deserted. I was surprised only because the office was open on the weekend and closed on Monday and Tuesday. I got the impression that it was a religious thing.

"You needn't have worried. I let the staff off early." He held open the door to the back hall. "Go all the way back. I'm going to want to use the big summoning circle. John Creede explained the situation fully."

I did what he asked, but I was puzzled. John had made it sound like this would be no big deal. But I wasn't the doctor, or a mage. I was just a patient. A very impatient patient, so I didn't ask what would normally be really obvious questions.

I can be so freaking stupid.

I didn't even hear the sound of the Taser charging

until it was too late and I lay twitching on the cold, hard linoleum. At first, I wasn't too worried. I've been tased before and heal from it pretty fast. But I hadn't expected that he would push the button over and over before my muscles could recover, sending charges of electricity through me until I was screaming. I'd heard you could stop a heart with enough jolts, but he didn't stop until I was totally helpless, nearly unconscious. I couldn't stop him from taking my cell phone and keys away, then dragging me by my feet into the casting circle set into the floor to join a wide-eyed Simone, who was gagged and bound with layers of silver duct tape— her arms fastened behind her and her legs strapped so tight her ankles were already swelling. I only noticed because they were right next to my nose.

Soon I looked just like her, shiny with silver tape, except for my mouth. Damn it.

Jean-Baptiste took a step away from the circle. With will and a word he powered up the magic, creating a barrier that would be impassible from the inside. Any living creature could break it just by crossing from the outside to in. But there was no one in the building to do it. I was just as much his prisoner as Simone.

He strolled over to the phone on the wall next to the chicken roosts. With nimble fingers he pulled a slip of paper from his pocket and dialed a number. Someone must have answered, because he said, "Tell Glinda I've got the siren. I'll turn her over tomorrow at midnight in exchange for a hundred thousand dollars."

Son of a bitch.

He frowned at whatever the person on the other end said. "No, that's not negotiable. Tell her to have the full amount ready. I'll call with a location." He shook his head in wry amusement as he hung up the phone and addressed us like we were pals in the process or something. "Really, can you believe the gall? Trying to dicker? Please. If I were actually doing this for the money I'd be furious."

I was still lying on the floor unable to move. I couldn't really even think clearly yet. I knew I *needed* to, vaguely and distantly. But the surge of electricity through my body seemed to have affected my ability to feel as well as think clearly or act.

My captor walked calmly up to the very edge of the circle, but was careful not to cross it. He peered at me for a long moment, lips pursed. Apparently he didn't like what he was seeing, because he went and put on a headdress. When he returned he started muttering: first a spell, then profanities.

"You, Ms. Graves, are extremely annoying. The spell I put on the front door was not a weak one. You should have been overwhelmed with uncontrollable bloodlust that would send you hunting the nearest humans. You should have torn into Simone like a ravenous beast."

I still wasn't capable of movement, but my mind was starting to clear, enough that I could hear Simone trying to curse him through the duct tape. She strained against the bonds, the sinews in her neck stretching taut with rage and terror. And I didn't feel a thing.

He tapped his lip thoughtfully with one finger. "Perhaps I should have used a lower setting. You're not a large woman. But I couldn't take the risk, particularly after you fought off my spell."

He was talking to himself more than to me. I'd seen it in a couple of other doctors in all my medical visits of the past few days. It was almost as if I wasn't real to them as a person, but bedside manner requires they at least act like they care. So they'd talk, but they really didn't want or expect a response. Good thing in this case. Strength and clarity were seeping back into me, but it was a slow seep . . . a trickle of water through the solid stone of frozen muscles.

He stripped off the headdress and turned away. Setting it on the counter next to the monkey staff I remembered so well, he said, "You'll have to excuse me. I need to e-mail my wife that I'm going to be late. I'll be back in a few minutes to check in on you and see how things are progressing." He left, closing the door behind him. The instant he was gone Simone began working her arms back and forth, trying to loosen the duct tape and free her arms.

Good luck with that, I thought. *I've been bound like that before. Duct tape is a lot sturdier than most people realize from casual use.*

If you have a better suggestion, I'd love to hear it.

Her voice in my head was acerbic. I blinked. *You're a telepath.*

Yes, which means I have absolutely no excuse for him getting the better of me. Fool that I am I trusted him. By the way, what is wrong with your voice? It's really garbled and rough, like fingernails on chalkboard. I can only understand about every third word. It hurts my head.

Apparently I sound like a gull. Or so say the other sirens. The pain in her mental voice was scalding. "Sorry." I tried to say the word out loud. It came out sounding like I'd just come from the dentist, but the fact my mouth actually was working at all was good news. In a few minutes I might actually start feeling like a human being again. I was looking forward to it.

I'll do what I can to pull the words out of your head, so you don't have to send them. It'll give me a migraine in the morning, but at least we might have a morning if I do. Can you function at all? He won't be gone long.

The way she said that "he." Ouch. They'd been lovers and it had ended badly. I could just sense it. So there was no chance she was going to survive this. I had even less chance. Could I function? I sure as hell was *going* to function, whether or not I could. I tried moving. I was still a little uncoordinated, but I managed to get my arms and legs to work enough to start dragging myself across the floor. Movement was helping. The energy and will I'd lost were coming back more rapidly now and I knew that in a few minutes I'd actually be more like myself again.

Simone moved with a combination of rolling and an awkward caterpillar crawl until she was lying next to me, her back turned so that I had a clear view of her bound wrists. He'd done a fine job of it. I really needed a knife to cut her loose. I could tear the tape if I could get both hands in position, but the force it would take would probably snap her wrist.

I worked myself awkwardly into a sitting position and tried to work at the tape with my fingers, back-to-back. But it was too tight. Lack of circulation was making her arms swell up, the sticky fabric digging painfully into the skin.

Use your teeth.

I shook my head. *Bad idea. The way your skin's swollen up I'd be bound to nick your skin.* I didn't want to think about what would happen next. Yes, I was full. But the same adrenaline that was bringing me back to my senses was bringing the inner beast to the forefront. Tasting blood would be really, really bad.

Well, we have to do something! He wants to turn you completely. He's not just a mage. He has necromantic magic as well. I saw it all in his head just now. He wants to use you to get close to Glinda, then kill her. Then he'll take the collar for himself.

Wow. That was unexpected and yet totally logical. *How does he even know about the collar? It was supposed to be a myth.*

She let out a harsh breath through her nose, obviously still annoyed with herself she was in this predicament. *He had it years ago, but George Miller stole it from him. Or so he claimed. Obviously, I'm starting to doubt anything he told me. But I do know when he saw the memory spells affecting you, he knew the collar was being used. It wasn't rocket science to figure out by whom. Who else would it be but a pretender to the throne? After all, Miller had power. John Creede has power. He would just keep it locked away the way Miller had. So it had to be someone new to the game. He did a tracking spell and there she was.*

So maybe the way to Glinda was through the doctor. Backward, but it could work. *Does he know where she is?*

I don't think so. But he doesn't need to. She wants you dead. He believes she'll come to him.

How did he know she wants me dead?

I don't know. But he does. Are you making any progress?

I'd been pulling at the edge of the tape with my fingernails and had managed to get an end loose, but he'd gone around her wrists enough times that it wasn't exactly *progress.* We needed a better plan. As I pulled at the tape binding her I looked around the room.

Just use your damned teeth!

No. Damn it, you just listen with your mind and let me know if you can sense him coming. . . .

Her head turned almost backward. Her amber eyes were flashing with frustration and fear. Thankfully, my nose wasn't working worth a damn, so it didn't make my stomach rumble. *I can't! The circle blocks my talent. Otherwise I would just have used my ability to call for help. He did it specifically to guarantee you wouldn't be able to use your siren talents on him. He's heard rumors you killed someone that way.* She paused and held very still. *Did you?*

I worked really hard to hide that answer in the depths of my mind. Apparently it worked, because eventually I felt the tickle of her mind back away from mine. Instead, I got back on point. *Could you at least use your* ears? *I have an idea.*

Once before, I'd been able to use my affinity with gulls to save my butt from a lesser demon. But as I tried to direct my thoughts at them . . . I hit the smooth, solid wall of the casting circle.

Crap.

Fine. Help would have to come from outside. At least he hadn't put tape over my mouth. I whispered quietly at first and tried to send out panic from my pores.

It wasn't hard.

"Ivy? Can you hear me?" I called my sister's ghost, hoping she'd come, worried she wouldn't. She'd wanted to stay in her borrowed body as much as Mom had wanted her there. She could be angry with me.

She didn't come.

But someone did.

The temperature in the room dropped at least ten degrees in as many seconds.

What's happening? Simone's mental voice wasn't panicked, but she was definitely nervous. Couldn't say as I blamed her.

It's a ghost, or spirit of some sort. I'm not really sure what it is.

And this helps us how?

"Oh, ye of little faith." The voice was amused, male, and audible. "What did you have in mind, Celia?"

"If you throw one of the chickens over the edge of the circle it should break the casting."

"And why would I want to do that?"

"Please?"

A pause and then an almost eager confidence that made my stomach roil. "You'll owe me a favor."

Simone was nodding vigorously. I could hear her mental voice ordering me to do *it. Do it now!* Do it!

I swallowed hard and tried not to overthink this. I have control issues and always try to make decisions that won't wind up coming back to bite me. "Tell me who you are first."

"You know who I am."

Did I? I thought it was Jones. Maybe. Or possibly a demon. I didn't buy the theory of the angelic. I could never be that lucky. "No. Actually, I really don't."

A low chuckle raised the hair on my arms and the back of my neck. It was distinctly male but not at all familiar. Damn it. Or perhaps . . . damn me. "Then you'll have to take your chances. Do we have a deal? Yes, or no?"

It was hard to tell over the sound of the waterfall, but I thought I heard hurried footsteps coming down the hall. We were running out of time. I took a deep breath and closed my eyes, resigning myself to whatever future would get me out of the present. "Do it."

Things happened fast after that. There was an indignant squawk and a big red hen came flying across the room at me. It skidded the last few feet on the ground, trying desperately to keep its balance on the stone floor with clipped claws. But it worked. Wings flailing, it broke the chalk circle with a flare of power that lashed against my senses like a bullwhip. I leapt to my feet as Jean-Baptiste burst into the room. I dived out of the circle at the same instant he released his will to power it back up. Magic seared whatever hair was still inside the circle when it rose, assaulting my nose with the sizzling strands. Not exactly how I'd planned to get a haircut.

He chased me around the room with careful blasts of power that erupted from the mouth of the monkey on the end of his casting staff. I managed to stay just one step ahead of him. There was nowhere to go unless I abandoned Simone, and I wasn't willing to do that. At least by chasing me, Jean-Baptiste was wearing himself down, and not sacrificing the woman in the circle.

I was afraid my freedom would be short-lived, but the entity went above and beyond the call. I felt my arms burst apart from each other, the tape separating, dissolving like a spiderweb before flame.

I might be the vampire, but it was Jean-Baptiste who hissed in fury. I saw a flare of colors as he threw a spell at the entity, banishing it in a flash of sulfur-scented smoke.

But somehow I didn't think he'd actually performed a banishing. I got the feeling the entity simply decided to leave. Maybe it would be back, maybe not.

I had no doubt we'd meet again in the future. I tried not to think about that.

With practiced ease Jean-Baptiste grabbed one of the ceremonial knives used to kill sacrifices and began circling toward me. His movements were smooth, coordinated, but not skilled. He wasn't used to actual infighting and he wasn't a professional.

I am.

I'd rather he have the dagger than the casting staff, so I actually rushed him, surprising him so much he didn't have time to stab at me. I grabbed the monkey staff before he could blast me again, and turned quickly away. He used that the second I was turned to move in, as I'd known he would. I twisted, using my leg to scythe his legs from under him. And in a single, smooth motion I swung the club with all my strength, burying the wood deep in his temple.

I felt the impact in my shoulder as the wood connected with the thickness of his skull and then the abrupt give and soft finish as it shattered—spraying me with blood and other, thicker things.

Dr. Jean-Baptiste fell to the floor and didn't move again.

24

There was a body on the ground, a victim to console, and a villain to catch.

Such is my life.

The cops don't like me for this very reason. So I didn't call them. I called the Feds. Rizzoli picked up on the first ring. I told him what had happened. He said he was already on his way. Why wasn't I surprised?

It had been one of the longest and hardest days of my life. Even with Rizzoli keeping most of the heat off, I knew there would be statements to give, questions to answer, and favors to repay. At that moment, I wasn't sure which I was dreading more.

I realized when I hung up I hadn't mentioned the entity, and I wasn't entirely sure why. Maybe dwelling on a nebulous future would be too taxing. At the very least, it would be distracting, and I'd need to be at my best.

It took some talking to convince Simone to wait for the Feds. I had to guarantee she wouldn't see any jail time for her part in getting to this point. I didn't want her to go, so I made the promise. But it wasn't my promise to make, so all I could do was hope she hadn't done anything irretrievable in Rizzoli's eyes.

While I waited for the cavalry to come and deal with Jean-Baptiste I did the two most sensible things I could think of: washed the blood off my face and hands, and curled up to sleep on the first examining table I found.

Rizzoli showed up some time later with Gail Jones in tow. I was interested to see her move around the room, sensing the energies. I think she realized something bigger than just a demented witch doctor had been here, but she didn't mention it to Rizzoli.

Interesting.

But the best part is she knew what to do to remove the memory spell once she talked to John on the phone. There was clear fangirling on her part while talking to John.

She was also looking forward to meeting Bruno. Her bright, clear eyes when she said "Mage DeLuca" practically screamed *hero worship*. I haven't felt that way about anyone in a long time. Not since El Jefe.

I really wanted to remember the moment I was able to . . . well, *remember,* but the whole spell was a blur. Maybe it was painful. I was certainly stiff and sore when I came to. Normally I don't pass out during spells, but this time I did. Probably best not to know what happened. All I know is when Dom and Gail arrived, it was pitch-black, the darkest part of the night. When I came to, it was afternoon. Never a good sign.

Rizzoli looked at me oddly for a long time when I was drinking down a chocolate nutrition shake, so definitely best not to know.

Still, it's amazing what some sleep and the lifting of a memory corruption curse can do for a gal. I felt good, better than I'd felt in weeks. I felt even better when I figured out a way for someone to bring me my best weapons and some fresh clothes.

There's only one person on earth other than me who has access to my safe—the designer, Justin. I'd thought I'd have to pay an outrageous fee to have him meet Rizzoli, Bruno, and John at the office for me. I was willing to, but he refused to take any money. He told John to tell me, "Anything you're into that is this hairy, you need your stuff," and, "I prefer live and paying customers."

The boys all came into Dr. Jean-Baptiste's exam room together. Bruno was carrying the duffel I keep in my safe. I was so happy to see it, and him, that it took me a second to realize who else had tagged along.

"Kevin?" He gave me a nervous half smile, no doubt worrying I was still angry with him. Yeah, I was, and I wasn't sure why he thought I'd trust him. "You can't imagine I'll work with you. Can you?"

He remained very still but met my eyes without flinching. "Emma sent me. She called and told me where to be. Apparently, you're going to need me tonight."

Crap. Emma's not a terribly powerful clairvoyant, but when she gets a vision, it's good as gold. She's come through in the clutch before, so she was probably right. And while I was still hurt and angry with Kevin, he was one of the best of the best black ops guys, even with PTSD.

"You sure you're up to this?" Rizzoli asked him.

He let out a snort. "No. But I don't think I have a choice. If anything happened to Celia when I could have done . . . whatever it is I do to save her, I wouldn't last a week. Even her enemies would come after me.

Let's not talk about what her *friends* would do. They'd make me beg to die, just to end the pain."

Hard to argue with that logic. Looking at Bruno and John, I had the feeling he was right.

"Celia?" Rizzoli inquired.

I could only shrug. "It's your party. You've got the badges. You could make any of them sit this out and I couldn't do a thing about it."

"Glad to see *somebody* realizes that." He glared at the other men, but not like he meant it.

"You need us. Glinda's going to be using magic that's the equal of mine, plus whoever else she's robbed. Every mage you have is on duty at the hospitals on zombie watch," Creede said calmly. "But you're in charge. I get that." It drew my attention to him. He looked better than he had. Not good, but better. His physical injuries were less obvious, and he held himself with more of his usual confidence, and I could sense magic in him. That surprised me.

He heard my thoughts, and answered them, even though he still had eyes locked with Rizzoli. *DeLuca helped me. We worked closely on the rift. He knows my signature. So he gave me a . . . transfusion. If he hadn't, my magic would be gone for good. I'm not myself, and there are some control issues. But, I'll eventually heal up.*

That was . . . awesome. There are plenty of people who wouldn't have been willing to share their powers like that, even if they could. But that was Bruno. He has his faults, but he's one hell of a guy.

Yeah, he is.

"Glad you realize that." Rizzoli gestured for us to gather around. He spread the blueprints he'd been carrying out on the examining table. Plopping a box of latex gloves on one end to hold it flat, he pointed out specific features of the building where they thought she was.

"We traced the number Jean-Baptiste called to a prepaid cell phone that is currently at this address. It's on the border of the warehouse and red-light districts."

I didn't smack myself on the head, but I wanted to. I remembered now. I'd seen that staircase the night I was bitten and half-turned. I'd been guarding a demon spawn posing as a prince who'd taken us on a tour of the seediest, bottom-of-the-barrel strip clubs in the area. This one had been in a converted warehouse. The main bar and club were in an open area spanning all three floors, with the storerooms and dressing rooms on the north wall of the first floor. The "lap dance" rooms had been on the second floor. There were catwalks leading to the lighting fixtures attached to the ceiling beams. Clubs like that come and go pretty quickly. I wasn't surprised she'd been able to buy the place. Probably for a song.

"Celia?" Bruno's voice brought me back to the present with a start.

"Sorry. Just remembering. I just realized I've been here."

Male brows raised all around.

Jeez. "Get your minds out of the gutter. It was on a job. The night I was attacked. But she may have done some remodeling since then."

Kevin got closer. "You're right. That's the alley where I found you. I know a back way to get there . . . where they won't see us coming. I never made it inside, but I can get the second group there without a soul seeing."

Rizzoli nodded. "I'll take any advantage we can get. And here's another advantage." He opened his hand to reveal tiny dots about the size of BBs. "We'll be using technology and magic to get intel on the layout. All we know so far is the place has some major shielding."

Magic and technology that can get through shielding. I immediately thought of a gadget John had invented that could turn the tide in our favor.

But he was already shaking his head sadly. "Can't. The fly is gone. They stole it along with my car. All that was left of the Ferrari by the time the cops closed in on the chop shop was the section of the frame with the tracer on it."

Aw man. That car had been his baby. I remember flying down the interstate with him, wind in my hair at speeds that were well past illegal . . . except during a magical crisis, which made even cops change lanes to give way. And the fly, a prototype of a magical device he'd invented himself. Both gone.

It reminded me I wasn't the only one who'd been having a crappy time of it lately.

I touched his forearm to find it tense. "I'm sorry. That sucks."

"Yeah." Man, he really was choked up by the way the sound crawled out of his throat.

"Ahem." Rizzoli looked from John to me. "Focus, people. Celia, since you've actually been here, and fairly recently, walk us through the layout."

It didn't take long. Other than the rooms on the one wall, the place was mostly a big open box. Which would make it seriously hard to do anything sneaky. Glinda was definitely going to have the advantage when it came to terrain.

I suggested I go in alone, as though I'd been enthralled by Dr. Jean-Baptiste. I could play dumb pretty well. People sort of expect it from a natural blonde, so I practice. It's good to keep people off-balance by living down to their expectations. The others could follow while I kept her distracted and we could overwhelm her with sheer numbers.

Not unexpectedly, Bruno, John, and Kevin didn't like that idea. Not at all. They explained in the finest detail and strongest wording why it was unworkable, illogical, and . . . well, that pretty well said it all.

Only Rizzoli nodded. "There are six entrances on the ground floor, one fire escape attached to the office areas on the second floor, and skylights on the roof. It could work. Yeah, she's got shielding and there are lookouts and guards, but really—our best option is to go through with Celia's plan." The boys turned as one and looked horrified, which was flattering. "At least partially," Rizzoli amended. "I think I can go one better, though, so I've brought in a very special agent from Dallas."

On cue the woman who had been waiting in the hallway walked in. Tall, slender, she was like a carving of a goddess done in ebony. She could've walked any fashion runway and made a fortune, and I wondered why she'd chosen a career with the Feds.

The boys' reaction was less favorable. Bruno was fine. But Creede took a step back, his eyes narrowing, and Kevin gave a barely audible growl.

"Can it, Fido," she warned impatiently. "I'm on your side."

"What's up?" Bruno asked. He didn't seem to know what was bothering them any more than I did, but he was alert, and I could feel him gathering his power.

Rizzoli sighed. "Special Agent Matumbo's mother was human, a witch. Her father was a demon."

She was a spawn, with *magic*? Oh, *crap*. There were spawn working for the Feds? That was disturbing on so many levels.

"She is a trusted field agent"—he glared at each of us in turn—"and has the ability to shape-shift convincingly and produce powerful shields. Her magic is primarily defensive. She will be going in with Celia in the guise of Jean-Baptiste. You"—he pointed to Bruno—"and I are going to be his hired thugs. That will get us in the front door so we can find and disable the source of the shield."

Bruno nodded. "It has to be an artifact. A shield as powerful as you say is hard to maintain for any length of time. It takes constant attention for things as stupid as mice and bats—the outdoor kind that eat bugs. They really mess up a building shield. A single person would spend all their time sensing problems in the shield and correcting them, so it only makes sense to give the task over to an object that handles the dirty work. If it's an artifact, I can find it. It's what I do for a living."

Creede started to protest that he should go in with us, too, but Rizzoli silenced him with a gesture. "The rest of you will be waiting outside the perimeter. We have to have a second mage in case the first wave is killed. Once we're in, we might not have communication. It'll be Celia and Matumbo's job to keep Glinda distracted. You"—he pointed to Bruno—"have one job. Get that barrier down. Don't worry about me or Celia. This witch can't be allowed to keep that collar. What the demons and the rift couldn't accomplish in destroying the city, she just might."

"What will you be doing?" Matumbo asked.

"I'm the floater. My gift will put me in the right place to do whatever needs doing." He was very matter-of-fact about it. I had a feeling he had reason to be. "Creede, you're a registered telepath, Celia, you're a siren, so I'm assuming you can do the telepathy thing as well."

"Um . . ." I hated to disagree, but now was not the time to have lofty expectations. "I'm not very good at it. I can speak with other telepaths, but generally they initiate the conversation and drag words out of me. I can't guarantee I'll be any help."

Rizzoli shrugged. "My gut says you'll do fine. It'll help with communications between the group inside and our reinforcements. But because the rest of us mere mortals can't do any head talking at all, we're all going to be wearing some very high-end technology. Stuff that doesn't appear on the radar with anyone, so nobody can track it or spot it. But I don't have enough for everyone, so Celia, do your damnedest." He passed out the tiny headsets, not much bigger than a swollen-up tick, which attached to the inside of the ear about the same way. Press a button and tiny jaws clamped down right on the skin, making everyone flinch. It looked a little like a mole. But definitely not like a microphone. He tapped on his ear and Bruno jumped. Even I could hear the sound. "Try to stay silent, people. We don't know what kind of magic and tech she has going on and we don't want to give anything away."

Made sense to me. The part I really didn't like was agreeing to meet her on her own turf. But she'd insisted on it when she called back Jean-Baptiste's phone. Rizzoli had made some convincing grunts and growls when the phone rang earlier, before Bruno and crew had arrived, and she'd bought he was the deceased doctor.

But we were going in early, hoping to throw her off-balance. It wasn't a perfect plan, but it was the best we could do. We needed to act fast. Children were dying.

"We leave in a half hour. Be ready and at the front door. Landingham, come with me. There's something we need to go over with you." Rizzoli rolled up the blueprints and left, with Matumbo and Kevin right behind him.

I grabbed the duffel, pulled out one of my daggers, and checked the edge. It really could use some sharpening. I'd been taking them to the gun range to practice throwing them. They weren't really intended to be throwing daggers. But the last few times I'd used them, throwing was what ended up happening.

Bruno was watching me work with the daggers, but his brow furrowed when I took out the second dagger, the black one. "What the hell? What happened to that knife, Celie?"

I flinched. I didn't have any reason to feel guilty. But I did. "I threw it through Lilith's heart. The ancient vampire who attacked Matty? Might have been a spawn that got turned, or worse. It's been black ever since. It still works, though." He reached for it and I handed it to him. His hand began to glow when he passed it over the flat blade.

John looked interested. "Can I see the other one?"

I looked at Bruno. He shrugged, so I handed it over.

John let out a low whistle as he handled, flipped, and glided fingers over the blade. "Man! Sweet piece of work, DeLuca. What was the production time?"

"Five years."

I thought John was going to spit up blood again the way he was coughing. "Five *years*?! Actual working, bleeding yourself, or just manipulation?"

Bruno dipped his head with pride and fire in his eyes. "Actual working. I did it to keep Celia alive. She wouldn't be standing here today if not for these. That's what Vicki Cooper predicted back in college and it was worth every cut, every drop of blood, every *minute* to see Celie here today. Fangs and all. She's alive, has her soul."

Awww— I smiled at him and he smiled back. John took a serious look at the interaction and suddenly wasn't so sure of himself, and his effect on me. There was a bond between Bruno and me that even the pain of his actions lately couldn't completely erase.

John handed the knife back, hilt first, and I slid it into the sheath. Bruno did the same. The forearm sheaths were nearly part of me. There were even permanent dents in my skin where the leather braces crossed, like a dent in a finger where a ring has remained for years without removal.

"I hope you all brought me some fresh clothes." I stank. Seriously. I'd been tazed, fought, and had slept in these clothes. "And a toothbrush."

"Toothbrush, yes. Change of clothes, no," Creede answered. "You're supposed to have been Jean-Baptiste's captive. But I did bring beef broth." He handed me a still-warm Styrofoam container.

I accepted the meal gratefully, but it sucked about no change of clothes. I could pull down my sleeves over the sheaths, but the outfit I was in really didn't have anywhere for me to hide much in the way of spell disks or other weaponry. Definitely sucked. Big pond scum–covered rocks.

"You always look good to me," Bruno said.

Creede rolled his eyes. "Yeah, right. Whatever. Go brush your teeth and get ready for the party."

25

We strode boldly up to the building. Well, Matumbo/Jean-Baptiste and the "guards" strode up. I was supposed to be a captive and injured, so they were pretty much dragging me. It was harder than it should have been for me to remain passive. My vampire nature was rising as the sun lowered, and adrenaline was pounding through my system. I managed it by reminding my inner beastie that we would get a chance to fight; we were just waiting for the right target.

Despite the fact that we'd arrived at sunset rather than midnight, the barrier I'd felt burning against my skin for almost a mile lowered when we approached.

The door swung open of its own accord—not like automatic doors at the grocery, but the slow, ponderous grating of squealing metal as the two-story delivery doors opened inward. It was meant to be creepy, and succeeded admirably. Even creepier, the witch was using magic to create invisible walls forming a hallway leading to the very center of the room. Those walls were all that shielded us from dozens of *M. necrose* victims who shambled and scraped across the floor toward the living, moving beings they could sense but not see.

If I'd thought Principal Sanchez and the guy in the hospital were the worst things I'd ever seen, I simply had nothing to compare them to. Now I did, and the principal and her security guard were positively red-carpet material by comparison to the creatures pressing in against the magic. Skin hung in shards from nearly liquified muscles and bones that glowed with an eerie green-white. The sounds they made as they shuffled and scraped were . . . wet and made me want to claw away from Matumbo and run out in panic.

Where was aggression when I really needed it?

Glinda's voice came from above and to our left. "You came early. How rude! I haven't even had the chance to finish my preparations." She was standing on the second-floor balcony, staring down at us like a Roman empress looking down on the Circus Maximus.

Those who are about to die, and all that. But I didn't plan to.

"I brought the siren bitch." Matumbo was flawless in her portrayal of Jean-Baptiste. There was contempt in the voice as she dropped me heavily to the floor.

Wish she'd given me warning she was going to do that. Ow. I pretended to rouse slightly, as though I wasn't in my right mind.

"So I see." Glinda looked me up and down critically. "Hmph. *This* is what my husband betrayed me for? By the way, did you enjoy fighting him, Siren? It seemed perfect retribution to send him to the hospital to kill you after what he did. I really thought that would have done it. But really, he died to protect *that*?"

That was Jamisyn? Yeah, he deserved it, but I felt sort of bad about snapping his back now. Oh, and the incinerator, too, I suppose.

"I want my money!" The fake Jean-Baptiste was doing a bang-up job keeping Glinda distracted.

Until she wasn't anymore.

"Oh, I don't think so." And she dropped the walls.

The smell assaulted me first and my stomach threatened to bring up the beef broth. I kept it down, but it was a struggle.

I'd really hoped to keep up the charade of the trance until I was closer to her. But I didn't know if Agent Matumbo could be killed by *M. necrose*. I didn't dare take the risk. Instead, I took the initiative and leapt forward, kicking the first zombie off her feet. My foot sank into what appeared to be a solid calf and squished. Eww. Sheer instinct made me pull it back before I normally would have and scrape off the gook on the floor so I didn't slip later.

Oh, I was so throwing away everything I was wearing tonight if I made it home alive. I didn't want to look at their faces closely. I was afraid I'd recognize someone from the school. Matumbo raised a shield that stopped them cold, and Bruno reached around it to throw a fireball at the nearest zombie and slammed the fallen zombie with multiple spells that froze her in place. Apparently, they'd discussed a strategy that I didn't know about. Rizzoli had drawn his firearm, and began carefully putting a bullet between each zombie's eyes. The creatures burst into flickering blue-green flame. The effect was eerie as hell, but effective. *What in the hell?*

He turned to catch my eye. "Experimental rounds." He put down two more zombies in rapid succession. Between all of us, we were nearly through them. "The director commissioned them for use on vampires, but this works, too."

I have got to get me some of those.

"We get through this and I'll make sure you get a box."

The key, of course, was getting through this. Because losing a few zombies wasn't going to stop Glinda. There were plenty more coming, crawling over the bodies of the fallen. Plus, she still had all her stolen magic, and who knew what else in reserve. Since the troops hadn't come in, the barrier had to be back up, and its magic made it impossible for me to speak mind-to-mind to John.

The action didn't stop while I was thinking this. In fact, it had intensified. Glinda threw a blast of power our way that narrowly missed hitting me in the leg. I threw myself sideways and skidded across linoleum slick with vile fluids. Bruno and Matumbo sent nearly simultaneous attacks at her from opposite sides of the room, but she stopped them effortlessly.

I noticed, when the guys attacked, that the glow from the collar diminished a bit. Maybe she hadn't taken enough power to keep it regenerating. I had to tell the others but couldn't let her know what I noticed. It was time for me to, as Rizzoli put it, do my damnedest. I pressed fingers to my temples and shouted in my head for all I was worth, praying that Matumbo would keep the zombies from sinking fangs and claws into me.

Aim for the collar. Make her defend it. Can you take down the barrier, or is she the one powering it?

I felt a tentative brush of words against my head. It hurt to listen for it, as though it was on the other side of a powerful waterfall. *No, it's not her. I've been trying to feel for the power source, but that damned neck-*

lace is putting out too much interference. If you can keep her off-balance, I'll see what I can do.

For the most part, she was ignoring me as being beneath her notice. They needed a distraction, and I was the only one available to give them one. I could jump straight up twenty feet if I tried, but she'd simply blast me out of the air. But if I moved from perch to perch, she'd have to focus on me to hit me. That could give the mages the time they needed. If I was really lucky, I might even get within striking distance.

I moved to where she couldn't see me very well and crouched, ready to pounce to my first spot. That's when the cavalry arrived in the form of a dozen FBI agents, a glowing John Creede, and one tall gray wolf. They all aimed weapons for the balcony and apparently Rizzoli wasn't the only one with the special shells.

Glinda took one look at John Creede, his eyes filled with fire and fury etched on his face, and panicked. She pulled a small ceramic disk from her pocket and hurled it onto the floor between Bruno and Matumbo. It shattered, as Glinda had meant it to, and I felt a sickening, and all-too-familiar lurch.

She'd summoned a demon.

Oh, crap.

We'd closed the rift, so demons could no longer pass through at will. But their dimension still existed. A human stupid enough, with enough power, could still summon one. And Glinda had summoned a doozie. I wondered immediately if it was the demon disk Eirene once lost in the desert. People had searched for hours but came up empty. She had the money to pay for it if someone found it and decided to profit from the sale.

The demon screeched with a lipless mouth, showing row after row of serrated teeth that dripped venom. His bellow of fury was loud enough to make my ears bleed, and I found myself as deafened as if I'd been standing next to an explosion.

He stood three stories tall, his hide like that of a rhinoceros—if the rhino came in black with oil-slick-colored highlights. He had only one pair of legs, but sported six tentacled arms. Each one of them had a weapon and they all moved independently of the others.

Fuck a duck.

A mace ball the size of a chair descended on us and Matumbo barely managed to get a shield up in time. It deflected the blow but sent us to our knees. She looked at us like we'd lost our minds. "So what are you waiting for? Attack it!"

Bruno returned the shocked look. "You'd have to lower the shield. You're nuts!"

Apparently to prove a point, John raised a hand and flung a fireball at the creature, right through the shield, causing a new screech. "Most of my ability is offensive magic. It's why George and I made a good team. He was a defensive guy. You just keep the shield moving with us. I'll fight right through it. It's my best thing."

Bruno was suitably impressed, as was I. We attacked. Not that it did a lot of good. The thing was huge, and fast enough that it was nearly impossible to see the blows that were raining down on us. On the bright side, they were raining down fast enough that it would be hard to miss. Drawing my knives, I struck blindly, and felt the blow hit home down my arm to my shoulder.

I was knocked off my feet and skidded across the floor. Another tentacle came down that I fully expected was going to lop off my head and there wasn't a thing

I could do about it. But the blow never reached. Instead, I saw teeth and claws and fur fly past my face and the demon screamed again from the werewolf attack.

Way to go, Emma. I owe you one.

The beast appeared to shriek again if the open mouth was any indication, as Kevin attacked again. Gook abruptly splashed on my skin, burning like hot oil mixed with acid. I was actually glad I couldn't hear anymore, because both Matumbo and Bruno flinched in pain at the sound.

Celia, you need to do that again. I need a distraction to make my way over to that door. Bruno pointed. *The power for the perimeter is coming from there.*

I could see his lips move, but I was hearing him with my siren gift. Matumbo nodded grimly and blocked another blow with a shield of magic. I couldn't hear her in my mind but could read her lips. "We'll keep it busy." She shook her head, trying to keep her balance.

Apparently I wasn't the only one whose ears were shot. I yelled in my head, hoping she'd hear. I really needed to start to train the telepathy. "*Get ready. On three.*"

On three I threw myself forward and the shield moved with me. I sliced the nearest arm twice. My knives cut in deep and true and the arm fell off the body in a flood of eerie green blood. But this time I didn't wind up with any demon blood scorching my skin. Let's hear it for shields.

The beast turned, swinging a mace in a heavy blow, not at me but at Matumbo. He was smart enough to know that breaching her shields would leave us all vulnerable.

The shield fell abruptly and I had to duck a lightning flash of magic. Matumbo was knocked unconscious. I had to get her out of there or she'd wind up zombie food.

We definitely had to take out Glinda.

I wasn't the only one to think it. I caught a bare glimpse of Rizzoli standing at the top of the stairs, firing methodically into the witch's shield. It was a good move so long as he had ammo. Because unlike the spawn, Glinda couldn't maintain her shield and attack us at the same time.

Movement was all around me, men and women in navy jackets with block white lettering reading *FBI* who were shooting at everything. Zombies were falling but had stopped burning. Maybe they became immune? I hadn't a clue, but the bullets didn't have the same oomph as when Rizzoli fired the first shot.

None of the FBI were mages but Matumbo. But she was out of commission for now. John and Bruno joined forces, doing their best to shield everyone but the demon. Unfortunately, it couldn't last long, and on the second floor Glinda had used magic to mow down three officers who'd come in from the fire escape. I could hear the screams of the wounded. My ears had finally healed, at least until the demon's next scream.

Glinda was holding Rizzoli off as she inched her way backward.

Don't let her escape, Rizzoli!

I'm trying, damn it! But I'm almost out of ammo.

The demon's attention was on the Feds, who were finally starting to make some headway. It gave me the opening I needed. I sheathed my knives and pulled Matumbo into the most sheltered spot I could find, then dashed to the floor beneath the balcony on the end opposite from Rizzoli. Leaping with every ounce of my strength, I was able to grab onto the balcony railing and pull myself upward—in time to be greeted with a blast of power from Glinda that hit close enough to singe my hair and melt the clothing to my skin on my left side. I howled in agony, stumbling to one knee. I could see Rizzoli pull the trigger, aiming to take her with her shield down. But his gun clicked empty. She whirled to face him. With a triumphant shout she let loose a bolt of energy that hit him full in the chest, sending him into the wall behind with a sickening wet thud.

I guess intuition isn't always infallible. Like clairvoyance.

Pulling my knives, I pounced. I hit her before she could shield, driving both knives deep into her chest. I knew when one of them found her heart, because her eyes dimmed, and the fire of magic that had flickered and glowed around her died.

The witch was dead.

I had to get back to the fight. But I wasn't about to leave the collar on her neck. God knew who was liable to pick it up. When my hand touched the clasp I felt a surge of power unlike anything I'd ever encountered. Sudden, blinding light that seemed to scorch through my retinas. My eyes watered and I couldn't breathe.

"You summoned me?" The voice was alto, tinged with a hint of an accent, and came from inside the light . . . no, it *was* the light. I looked away, blinking away the tears, and realized that everything else had stopped. The creature's arm, raised in a blow meant to crush the huge wolf that was Kevin, was still and suspended in the air.

The light had stopped time.

Oh, crap.

That just wasn't possible. Except maybe for God.

The voice took on a melody of humor. "Or a goddess."

"There's only one God." I believed that. Even now, facing . . . this, I believed. Maybe my gran's lessons had sunk in after all.

When I turned back a woman had appeared before me. She was Egyptian, beautiful beyond measure. "You are a true believer. And yet I am still Isis." She wasn't happy. But she didn't seem angry, either. More curious, and amused. "Goddess of magic, the home, and children. You touched the collar that was my gift. More, you have done me a great service, taking my tool from a hand that wielded it against all I hold most dear. What do you seek? Wisdom? Power?"

"Take it back."

The voice turned in an instant. No longer amused. Now angry. "Excuse me?"

Okay, that had been blunt, almost rude. I wouldn't get away with talking like that to Queen Lopaka or King Dahlmar and they were *mortals*. "Please, Isis, the gift of the collar was meant for the pharaohs. But they are no more. Take it back, away from those who don't understand it, and don't respect it."

"You could take the collar as your own, or ask for power, make yourself desirable to all men, whatever you wished. And yet you choose to throw it away?"

I sighed. I so didn't want it. But I didn't want to insult her, either. Still, as I looked down at Bruno and Creede, frozen back-to-back, moments from death . . . we were all moments from death, even without Glinda to add to the storm, there was no question in my mind. "I mean no offense. But I already have more power and men than I'm comfortable with. Sure, I'd love to get rid of the demon, cure everyone here afflicted with this disease, make sure Rizzoli's all right. But mostly, I want this—" I deleted the expletive that came to my lips as I looked at the bejeweled golden artifact, and simply extended it toward her. "I want the collar gone."

She smiled, and it was as if the sun rose. "Very well. I will take the collar from this plane. And I offer you a piece of wisdom. All power, including the collar, is no more than a tool: like the knives you wear, or the *guns* so favored in this time. In the hands of an ethical person with training and skill they serve a noble and useful purpose. They protect the innocent, keep the world safe. It is in the hands of the untrained and unskilled, or morally corrupt, that power becomes dangerous."

She wasn't talking about the collar now. "My siren abilities."

"And your vampire nature. Use them with skill or risk corruption." And with that she vanished, in a literal puff of smoke.

So did the demon. Just like that, with nary a tentacle left behind, leaving everyone in the room looking around at each other in confusion. But they were all healthy and literally glowing with power.

Even the zombies who hadn't yet burned up.

Shit.

26

I slept for an entire day, then began to address cards because I was too restless, but the city was nearly shut down by the pandemic. Highways had been turned into inflows to hospitals. It was impossible to get around the city, according to the news, so I didn't try.

The pandemic was increasing, with no end in sight. I'd either been too specific with my wish to Isis, or it had been beyond her ability. The whole city was going to change and there wasn't anything I could do about it.

I wrote condolence cards mostly. Reality bites sometimes, but as Gran always said, "It's the little niceties that hold humanity together." One for Officer Harris, another for the school, then get-well cards for those who were improving. I decided Julie and Mikey should get balloon bouquets once they were out of ICU. At least they *would* come out. They were healing slowly, and while there would be therapy required, at least for today I could breathe a temporary sigh of relief.

The only call I took was from Rizzoli's wife, Karen. I'd thought it was Rizzoli because that's how it came up on caller ID. "Ms. Graves? This is Karen Rizzoli, Dominic's wife."

I'd never talked to her, but the voice matched the photo. Soft, sweet, loving. He was a lucky man. "How is he? I haven't seen him since the EMTs took him away in the ambulance."

"He's improved a lot since last night. It's so strange to watch bruises disappear as I watch."

I was still struggling with the appearance of a goddess, or whatever she was. But there was no denying her power. People who were doomed and dead came back. "It does take some getting used to. So his prognosis is good?"

"He died." Her voice sounded odd. "He told me so. He . . . saw things. I think he'll need to talk to someone about it. But the Bureau's really good about that sort of thing. He'll get the help he needs."

Oh. Near-death experience. Yeah, I'd had more than one of those. I'm pretty good at repressing them, but eventually I know I'll have to deal with them myself someday. "Well, give him my best. I'm sure he'll need some time to—"

"Actually," she interrupted. "That's not why I'm calling. He asked me to tell you they found your book. He said it was a very rare volume and he wanted you to have it. Dom said maybe it would give you answers, or clues, about other things."

Oh! The book Dr. Sloan gave me. "That's awesome! Who do I need to talk to to get it back?"

"He said he'd get in contact with you soon. He also wanted to thank you for saving Indira—Agent Matumbo. She was able to impersonate the witch you caught at the docks later and a whole bunch of extremists are behind bars." Yay! What great news.

"Confidentially," she added in a quiet voice, "I think he's embarrassed he pushed you into this."

What? "He didn't. Not a bit. Going after the witch was my choice. I had people involved that she'd intentionally hurt. It was my fight."

Karen sighed. "I don't think Dom feels that way. He worries when he sends people into dangerous situations. I'm glad you weren't hurt for purely selfish reasons. He'd never forgive himself." She then went on to add that the Feds had found Glinda's stockpile of drugs, and the interim president of the drug company was working with the government to get them distributed to the victims. Of course, everyone there swears Glinda was acting alone.

I don't know if I believe it. It's awful ambitious for one person, collar or not.

I rang off with Karen, suddenly grateful for so many things. But I was still too weary for excitement. And I was still sad that Gran wouldn't return my calls. There'd been a message on my machine to say Mom was back on the island and had a new personal guard . . . Baker.

But no Gran and no Ivy. That hurt. A lot.

Bruno and John both came to my house near dusk, for different reasons.

Bruno arrived first and wrapped me in a hug when I opened the door that left me warm but breathless. Then the kiss he bestowed turned what was left of my muscles into Jell-O. "How you doin'?"

I let out a slow sigh and allowed myself to rest against his muscled chest. "Better. The Feds used some magic on me. Apparently, my vampire healing doesn't work on magical burns, just natural ones. I could still use a little more rest. You?"

He nodded and lowered his mouth to mine once more. I could feel his warm breath on my face as his mouth ate at mine gently. God, those lips. I'd missed them. He smoothed his hands down my back, knowing just where to touch to make me moan. I pulled away after a few moments, shaky but pleased. "Mmm. Much better now. Actually, I'm headed back to New Jersey. Just stopped by on the way to the airport."

It startled me and I pulled away farther. "Why?"

He shrugged and smiled just a bit. "Gotta pack up my apartment to move here. I don't want anyone handling my magic stuff. Not even family. Besides, I promised Mom I'd be there for her Ascension."

"Ascension?"

"Yeah, they're making her Grand Hag of the East Coast."

I knew Bruno had gotten his power honestly. His mother was a witch. His father a mage. But . . . Grand *Hag*? I bit my tongue. Hard.

Because I didn't disagree with the title for his mother.

"Don't," he warned. "Not one word. It's a big honor and a huge responsibility."

I tried to say something nice; it *almost* worked. "I'm sure she'll do a fine job." Of course he knew what I was thinking. Not because of any mind-reading ability. He just knows me that well.

I backed away just a bit and he noticed my outfit. "Wow. You look stunning. What's the occasion?"

"Dinner with me." John's voice. I hadn't heard him drive up. Bruno's shoulders dropped as John climbed the stairs, and he let out a sigh.

I shrugged. "He asked first. I'm trying to play fair."

John slid to my side and touched my cheek with his lips but added a flick of his tongue that Bruno didn't notice and that gave me shivers. "Sounds like I have a couple of weeks to work my magic, too. Feel free to keep taking these trips, DeLuca. They're doing me a world of good." Their eyes met and I could see genuine respect in both men. Demon fighting seems to be a guy-bonding activity. "I dropped the directions for the body-binding charm on your car seat on the way up. Seemed only right after you gave me the energy boost."

Bruno smiled and he really did seem amused, rather than hurt or angry. There's nothing he loves more than new spells to try and that one really was amazing. "Just keep your calendar free in two weeks, Celia. I'm going to take you somewhere that will knock your socks off."

I smiled at him as he climbed down the stairs, while on the arm of the other man in my life. Yeah. He was and I didn't have a clue what to do about it. "Looking forward to it."

Once his taillights were on the road toward the gate, I turned to John, who looked amazing in a sport coat and open-necked cream silk shirt. He was wearing the cologne that made my knees weak and made me want to nuzzle his ear. He smiled at me. "Ready?"

"Where are we headed?"

"Dinner. Then maybe dancing if you're up to it."

I hadn't been dancing in . . . wow. I still hurt, but not too bad. Maybe I could manage one song. "Actually, dinner sounds good, but I need to ask you something first." Something that could completely ruin the date. And where better than right on my doorstep?

He frowned just a bit when he saw that in my mind, and backed up until he was in the shadow, where I couldn't see his face well. "What's up?"

"Why haven't you told me anything about you?" I started the list. "I didn't know you had a sister, or that you met her every Saturday. I didn't know about your food poisoning or the casinos in Monte Carlo or how many places you've traveled for jobs. Hell, I don't even know what you do to keep your calves looking that good."

His face was calm and unreadable. "You've never asked."

That was no answer. "I've told you a ton of stuff about me."

He nodded once. "Because I asked." When I opened my mouth, he raised a hand. "Celia, I'm a mage and I'm in security. I don't tell just anyone my life history. Knowledge is power and in magic it's deadly. But you feel the same, whether or not you realize it. It's taken verbal crowbars to get you to reveal *anything* about your past. There are a dozen questions I've asked that you still won't answer. So why in the world would I volunteer information when you've obviously had no interest?"

I stood there openmouthed for a long moment, "But I *do* want to know."

He shrugged. "Then ask. I can't promise I'm an open book. Not yet. But eventually, when we both trust each other a little more, we'll see. But the simple stuff— likes, dislikes, family, beliefs—sure. I'd love to tell you."

I decided to use a line from one of my favorite novels to open the conversation. "So, tell me of your home-world, Usal." John smiled and stepped forward into the light. Apparently he'd read the book, too. He held out his hand and I took it. When he started to turn to walk down the stairs with me, I noticed something.

Not a new thing, but a *missing* thing. "John? Where's your siren charm?"

He let out a small sound that I couldn't decipher. "I don't know. I think they stripped me of all my magical items when I got jumped. But I didn't see that in the bowl reading. I'll make another one, though. It'll only take a few days."

"You said knowledge was power. What does a missing piece of . . . *me* mean?"

He put an arm around me and pulled me close to him. "I don't know. I'm hoping it's in Glinda's effects. I'm trying to get a court order to let me look at the other items in George's safe, too. It'll turn up."

"What if it doesn't? What if it wound up in the demon dimension? Things were flying thick and fast in there."

He tried not to let me see the shudder that overtook him. "We won't think that way. Because that would be bad, Celia. That would be very, very bad."

TOR

Award-winning authors
Compelling stories

Please join us at the website
below for more information
about this author and other great
Tor selections, and to sign up for
our monthly newsletter!